HEART IN A BOX

ALLY SKY

CW01496995

Dreams,
xoxo Ally

Translated from Hebrew: Ayelet Svatitzky

Editor: Shannon Eversoll

Cover design: Vixen Designs

ISBN: 9781973285328

To Mom

*C*olin Young was the love of my life. From the moment my eyes met his in our high school's cafeteria, I knew I was doomed. Especially when his chattering groupies appeared and smothered him rather pathetically. Yes, Colin Young was the guy everybody wanted. Whether you were an enthusiastic fan of the football team, for which he played as captain, or you were just an average girl who spent hours at the library hoping to get into college, like myself. We all had a common dream—to meet Colin's supple lips up close and personal, the same lips that had smiled at me that Monday and smashed my heart to bits.

I could have sworn he hadn't noticed me, that he was smiling at someone else. I was nothing short of shocked when he later approached me in the hallway, leaned nonchalantly on my locker and asked quietly if I wouldn't mind meeting that afternoon and helping him with his math homework. I'm pretty sure he said math, though it could have been literature, or history. At that point my brain turned into mush. I nodded without saying a word. He laughed and said he would come by my house at around five. I nodded again and he turned his back on me and disappeared.

I came back to my senses after an hour or so.

The main question I faced was: what to wear. The cold truth is I resented myself. I'd always been scornful of the girls who lost their heads over boys and spent all their time fiddling with their wardrobe instead of hitting the books and scoring another A+.

How on earth had I become one of them in thirty seconds?!

I blamed my seventeen-year-old hormones (biology seemed like a logical explanation for my embarrassing situation), chose a white T-shirt and skinny jeans (there was a limit to how nerdy I allowed myself to look), and swore I would not stammer when Colin appeared.

I almost succeeded. When the doorbell rang, I leapt off the couch, tried to calm my pulse, which insisted on racing like mad, thanked God for the long hours my parents spent at work and were absent from home, opened the door with a smile—and froze. My mouth actually did open in an attempt to release a word or two. 'Hello' would have been a suitable one. Even 'Hey' and maybe 'What's up?' Instead I stood there, mute, in front of blue eyes, blond hair and the smell of a guy who had just come out of the shower (after training, if I had to guess).

Colin laughed. Again.

"Are you going to invite me in?" was what he chose to say. I nodded like an idiot and wondered if he regretted asking for help from the stupid girl in front of him. I led him to my room and left the door open, as if something could happen between me and . . . well, this hot guy who seated himself on my bed and stared at me.

"So," I mumbled like a fool, "you said . . ."

"I just want to make something clear." His intense voice caused uncontrollable constriction of all sorts in my internal organs.

"Yes?" I muttered again and cursed myself for the thousandth time.

"I'm not enthusiastic about this," he shifted uncomfortably. I wasn't enthusiastic, either. "So if you're thinking of going 'round telling everyone . . ."

"Telling everyone what?" What did he think was going to happen here?

"You know, that I . . ." He raised his hand and pulled back his damp hair. I folded my hands on my chest in the hope of stabilizing my stance. I didn't want him to see my knees shaking.

"That you . . ."

"Don't understand."

At that moment I didn't quite understand myself. "What don't you understand?"

"You know . . ."

"No," I frowned, "I don't know."

"All this school shit." He tried to sound casual, but I got what he was saying and I got that his indifference was completely fake.

"So you need help."

"I guess." He leaned back on his hands and his shirt rose just above the line of his pants, revealing a line of hair leading straight to the elastic waist of his boxers. At that point, all I could do was swallow my saliva and try to stop imagining what was hiding under the boxers.

I had a pretty good idea, in theory. I saw pictures of guys who didn't really wear anything, and I occasionally heard other girls talk in the locker rooms after sports, but I *never* sat in my room with a guy who let his shirt rise like that. Okay, to be honest, I never sat in my room with any guy, period.

"Hello?" Colin's voice brought me back rather sharply from the land of fantasies I had sailed into. "Do you hear what I'm telling you?"

"Sure, sure, you need help." I needed help at the same time. Of a psychiatrist.

"So what are the chances you and I will have some kind of arrangement?"

"Arrangement?"

"You know, you'll help me with my homework, and I'll help you with . . ." He tilted his head to one side and gave me a smile that looked utterly malicious. "What is it you need help with?"

My thoughts blurred and my cheeks turned red in a second and a half. I felt as if my face was on fire. "Why do you think you can help me with anything?"

"Just a wild guess." He winked. "Everyone needs help with something."

"Not me," I replied at once, tightening my hands.

"Really?" He smiled widely and exposed his white teeth as I struggled to breathe regularly.

"Really," I tried not to pant out loud, "no help needed, got it all covered, thank you."

"I can't pay you." He sat up and his shirt once again covered what he had just revealed.

"You don't need to."

"So, I guess we're done here." He rose slowly, making me step back.

"We're... what?" I stared at him towering over me.

"I was hoping we'd come to some sort of arrangement." He pulled back his hair, sounding frustrated.

"Why do we need an arrangement?"

"What do you mean?" He stared at me with his blue eyes.

"You said you needed help."

"I have nothing to give you in return." His grave gaze drilled into me.

"I don't need anything."

"I don't need your favors."

"No," I sounded a little more confident than I actually was, "you need help."

"Why on earth would you help me?"

"Because you asked me to."

"You'd help me just 'cause I asked?"

"Umm... yeah?"

"Are you for real?" He tilted his head again, examining me as if I had grown three heads.

"Insults are not the way to get my help," I muttered.

"Sorry! I'm just not used to girls like you."

"You mean girls who don't drool all over you and lose their shirt before you even ask?" I was stunned by my own words.

"Yeah, exactly what you said." He laughed, and his laughter sounded magical. I may not lose my shirt, I thought to myself, but I certainly might drool.

"I didn't mean to offend you."

"You didn't, I know exactly what you're talking about." He put his hands in his pale jeans pockets. "So, you think, maybe you could . . ."

"I could," I finished his sentence. I had already gotten the feeling he didn't enjoy pleading. "But do me one favor..."

"Sure." He shrugged his broad shoulders.

"If I invest my time, make an effort to show up and don't bail on me. You don't have to pretend you know me when we're at school. I'm sure you're not too happy explaining how you know the 'Library Geek', but my time is valuable, please make sure it is valuable to you, too." I looked at Colin with embarrassment. Where I got the courage to dictate my terms, I don't know. But I did, and Colin agreed immediately.

"Your time is valuable," he nodded, "and you're not the 'Library Geek.'" His lips curved into a charming smile.

"I have no problem being the 'Library Geek' if it gets me to college," I confessed quietly.

"I'm sure you'll have no problem." At that I blushed.

"On a scholarship," I emphasized the point. The only way I could get to the college I wanted was if *they* paid for it.

"I understand."

"Where do you wanna begin?"

"Math." He pulled one hand out of his pocket and scratched his head. "The exam on Friday is going to kill me."

Friday's exam was a walk in the park, but I shut my mouth.

"Let's start," I motioned to the heavy desk in the corner. The thought of sitting close to Colin made my heart skip a beat.

Shit! I forgot something.

"I'll get another chair from the kitchen." I smiled in embarrassment.

"Sounds like a good idea," Colin teased me and sat down on the wooden chair in my room. I went out into the hallway and took a deep breath.

Colin Young, in my room, and I was acting like a child.

He just wants you to help him, stupid. My inner voice brought me back to reality. I closed my eyes, but only for a moment. I really hope I didn't make a mistake. I really, really hope this isn't going to backfire on me, that this isn't some joke at my expense.

CHAPTER ONE

"*V*ivian Heart!" My scream echoes through the tiny apartment, "We're going to be late!"

It's Monday morning, my shift is about to start, and if I don't get there on time . . . I'll be there on time. If I could only get my four-and-a-half-year-old, who insists on changing her shoes for the third time this morning, out of the house. Okay, she changes her shoes every morning, but today we woke up late.

"Sorry Mama." She comes panting, carrying her small backpack. Her blond hair is pulled up to a tight ponytail and her blue eyes are fixed on me. "I'm ready."

She doesn't look like me. Objectively, I can testify that she didn't inherit my dark red hair nor my green eyes. At least I can take comfort in the fact that she has inherited her sharp mind from the right person.

"Hurry." I open the front door and turn to lock the house before rushing the bouncing creature toward the battered, silver Toyota also known as my car. After buckling Vivian up in her seat, I jump behind the wheel, say a prayer and turn the key. Thank God.

I swing into reverse and exit the driveway. In seven minutes

I'll drop Viv at her daycare, in twelve minutes I'll start my shift and, with a little luck, no one will notice. I can't afford to lose this job.

Although, I am just a saleswoman at *Blant Furniture* store, it's the one place that has agreed to give me only the morning shifts, and the tight salary pays the bills. Barely. Not that I complain, I have no right to. I've made my choices. I use my family's help much more than I would like, but that's how it goes. Vivian is worth it. All the sacrifices, all the losses.

"Mama, the light is green," Viv calls from the backseat.

"Sorry, sweetie." I accelerate and cross the intersection. Morning traffic can be brutal. If it was up to me, we'd live in a quieter part of town, but this is all I can afford—the same small house I've been living in since I was eighteen. Not far from the city-center, it's within driving distance of everything.

Our town is a strange place to live in. It seems that it hasn't yet decided whether it is a small town, where everyone meddles in each other's lives, or a modern city, where people maintain a safe distance and privacy. Just an hour's drive from Dallas, it has an excellent high school, convenient public transportation and parks. In recent years, tall buildings have begun rising at a rapid pace, changing the landscape beyond recognition, but I suppose it's like that everywhere. The high-tech offices and the new cultural centers are the city's way of attracting new residents.

"You're dreaming." Vivian laughs loudly. Yes, she got his laughter, too. That bastard, couldn't he leave me one thing?

"We all dream," I answer her, smiling in the rearview mirror. "What are you dreaming of?"

"An Elsa dress." Her answer is expected.

"For your birthday," I reply, as usual. I don't have one cent to spare. Luckily the dress isn't that expensive.

"And I want an Elsa cake and a trampoline for the back yard," she adds.

"We'll see about that." I force my laughter. She would have to

8

make do with the dress. She knows I can't buy her a trampoline for the yard.

"We're here," my beauty calls out. I park in the designated place, unbuckle my seatbelt, get out of the car, pull Viv out of her car seat and rush inside. Mrs. Robbins greets us as she helps Vivian with her goodbye.

"Have a wonderful day," I kiss her golden hair.

"You, too, Mama." She sends me a kiss in the air, I pretend to catch it and stick it to my cheek, then I run out the door, and into my car.

Time to go to work.

Sixteen minutes later, I lock my Toyota in the parking lot of the shopping center, curse the traffic jams that have caused me a longer than usual delay, and hasten my steps to the shop, making an effort to ignore the sign hanging on the door.

For Rent.

Mr. Blunt hung it twenty-eight days ago and from that moment we all got nervous. Does this mean now I'll have to look for a new job?

Henry, who has been working with me for two years, wasted no time opening the paper and circling every position he found that fit. We both know this won't be easy. Knowing each other since middle school, Henry is pretty much the only friend I have these days. After all, we were both the "Library Geeks" who had big dreams… and never fulfilled them.

You gave up everything for that bastard and see what you got in return?

I open the store's door and find Henry is staring at me disapprovingly from behind the cash register. I hand him my bag and he pushes it under the dark wooden counter.

"You know," I'm afraid he's going to start with another mathematical explanation like he likes to do, "you're late an average ten days a month. You're losing about five hundred and twenty-two dollars every year."

"About?" The calculated accuracy makes me smile. "Couldn't you round it to five hundred?"

"You know what I mean." He doesn't seem to like my mocking tone.

"How many cups of coffee could I buy for that sum?" I lower my head with a grin.

"Starbucks?" He frowns as he calculates, but I hasten to stop him.

"It was a joke."

"Oh." He shrugs.

"Did you find a job?" I change the subject, to both of our relief.

"No. You?"

"Nah."

"Have you even been looking?" He knows me too well.

"Didn't have the time," I lie, knowing he won't say anything.

"Oh."

"We need to expand your vocabulary, dear." I fix my red mane to a tight ponytail and push my locks behind my ears.

"Mr. Blunt will be in at ten," Henry updates me. "Do you want to mop the floor or dust?"

Indeed, such a difficult choice. Mr. Blunt, our boss, is in his sixties and, if it weren't for his back problems, which prevent him from cleaning the store and moving heavy furniture around, I might not have a job.

"Dust," I reply without thinking too much about it.

"Okay." Henry straightens his white button shirt, which rests carelessly on his body. His brown hair is as messy as it is on every other morning. Come to think of it, Henry isn't a lean, awkward guy, as you'd expect him to be given his mannerisms. He's tall, his eyes are brown, and when he smiles his eyes smile, too, which make him look good.

Not my taste, but I'm sure he's someone's taste. "You have to get a haircut," I throw him a glance as I make my way to the storeroom.

"In three days," he mumbles from behind me, as we get ready for another day of perfect boredom.

How long have we got left here? Neither of us has a clue.

"I DIDN'T HIT HIM BACK!" Vivian stands in front of me in the middle of our living room, an angry look on her face, her hands folded and tears of insult running down her cheeks. So she did inherit something from me after all. Great.

"Mrs. Robbins said," I answer quietly.

"She's lying!"

"Vivian, Mrs. Robbins doesn't lie," I try not to raise my voice. It would be easiest to send her to her room—

To our room, I remind myself instantly. The lousy house has one bedroom, in which I managed to cram a bed for my child. Colin and I rented the place, in what seems to be another life. We were only eighteen and had plans to move after I gave birth. Plans I had shelved for lack of choice. At least we have a back yard and parking, I try to cheer myself up.

"He started it," Vivian's weeping interrupts my memories.

"You know it doesn't matter who started it, we don't hit."

"He deserved it." She wipes the tears with her little palm.

"Next time, I want you to go to Mrs. Robbins and ask for her help."

"Okay."

"Okay." I spread my arms in a gesture of reconciliation. She hastens to cling to me resting her head on my stomach, reminding me, in one embrace, why everything was worth it.

"I love you, sweetie," I whisper to her. "Let's make dinner."

"I want pizza." She sniffs.

"We can definitely make pizza." I never spend money on take-out. Not with my kitchen skills.

"I wanna watch TV."

"Sure, hon." I release her from my embrace, pick up the remote control, and turn on the old television that is doing me a huge favor and not dying on me. Viv climbs onto the sofa that is covered with a burgundy cloth blanket, the sole purpose of which is to conceal the stubborn stains I couldn't remove. I've owned it for six years and will own it for another six, if it's up to me.

"Frozen," she commands me with a smile. I turn on the DVD and the movie begins.

"I'm in the kitchen," I say, as if she could miss me. The kitchen is right behind her.

"Shh!" She puts a finger to her mouth as the movie plays. I kiss her, go into the kitchen, take a bowl out of the cupboard, and get ready to make the pizza. Thank God for Anna and Elsa and small favors.

HOURS LATER, I close the cramped bedroom door, crash on the sofa and stare at the ceiling. Nine o'clock in the evening, the kitchen is clean, the house is tidy and my child is asleep.

Just another day, like all the previous days and all those that will follow. This isn't how I imagined it would be. In spite of the effort to push those thoughts back to where they came from, they are getting the best of me tonight. I pray not to cry. Vivian might suddenly wake up and panic. She never sees me crying.

When she was younger, I would run to the bathroom and sob, my face buried in a towel. Now that she's older, I can't hide from her. She sees my red eyes and always demands explanations. I learned to stifle the lump in my throat and wait for the hours when she slept. The hours when I drop down on the couch exhausted, wondering how I got here.

At twenty-six this is my life. No college degree, no savings, no husband.

If only Vivian looked more like me, everything would be

easier. If only she looked less like him. Sometimes I allow myself to wonder what would have happened if he hadn't approached me that day. If he hadn't appeared at my door that afternoon. What if it had all been a joke at my expense, that the captain of the football team had decided to play a little game with the "Library Geek" and made me sit at home waiting for him in vain?

But he didn't play, not even for a minute, and he didn't pretend I was air, as I expected him to, and the glances he threw my direction changed every day, and my breath accelerated every time he appeared. Each time he sat next to me in my bedroom and his thigh touched my thigh. He didn't understand the material, and yet he never gave up. He insisted and tried harder. I couldn't help but admire him even more. I couldn't help falling in love with him.

I never thought Colin Young would be my first kiss.

Never thought he would be the one who took my virginity.

The one for whom I would give up everything.

Life played a cruel game on me, devouring the cards, leaving me at the age of twenty-six crying quietly on the sofa for what I still can't understand.

CHAPTER TWO

*T*he furniture store is empty of customers. I finish mopping the floor and join Henry, whose standing behind the cash register leaning against the dark, wooden counter.

Most days, that's how we spend our time. The shopping center where the store is located is usually crowded, but the recession combined with the furniture's prices stop the flow of buyers.

I can't blame them. I myself wouldn't pay what Mr. Blunt is asking for a sofa or a dining table, no matter how "high-end" it is. Our customers aren't stupid. They know as well as I do these days everything is manufactured in China or some other third world country, and I can't fool them. All Henry and I can to do is stand idly by and look out the window at the people passing by the store, not bothering to peek inside.

"If I'm left with no choice, I'll clean up apartments," I sigh loudly as Henry and I desperately evaluate our professional future. I have to support my daughter, and if cleaning apartments will put money into my bank account, that's what I'll do.

"I was thinking of applying to college again," he reveals to me for the first time.

"Really?" I find that I'm the only one despaired by the situation. My friend, I realize, has plans.

"I think the time is right." He shrugs. Henry would have no problem getting accepted, he's the brightest guy I know. How many people read two books a day and remember every word? If it hadn't been for the car accident his mother had when we were in our senior year of high school, he would have finished a few degrees by now and gotten a doctorate.

"I think you should apply," I cheer him up. He'd enjoy his studies.

"Maybe we'll apply together?" He is quick to offer, breaking my heart again.

"You know I can't."

"Because of Vivian?"

"Because of Viv, and 'cause I don't have the money, and I'm sick of asking my parents for help all the time." This, unfortunately, isn't going to change. I'll continue to lean on their help and money.

"Shame." He doesn't read the disappointment on my face. "You're really smart."

"She always was," the low voice coming from the door sends a shiver down my entire body. My pulse accelerates to a frightening speed and, as if in slow motion, I look up and pray that it will all be a mistake.

My eyes travel up the long legs hidden behind gray trousers to the muscular thighs. Then, to the solid abs protruding from a tight, black polo shirt. His chest is huge, and so are his arms— enormous and covered with tattoos that weren't there before.

"Elizabeth," he calls my name coldly. My eyes rise to his clenched jaw, his familiar lips, his blue eyes. The way he looks at me sends a wave of chills through me, as if someone is washing my bloodstream with ice water.

I stare at him with hate. Hate that has been burning threw me for five long years, hate I didn't know existed until he did what he did.

I can't make a sound. My words refuse to come together to one coherent sentence. I stay silent, struggling to breathe. He doesn't look like the guy who left.

The jeans and t-shirts he used to wear have been replaced by these clothes, which make him look a hell of a lot more serious. His body was always muscular but now he has grown to a monstrous size.

Everything about him is different—from the blank stare he gives me to the neat haircut.

"Hello, Henry," he addresses my friend with the same remoteness he did me. Henry looks almost as stunned as I am and doesn't say a word. I'm sure he, who's heard me say a thing or two about the maniac in the past five years, doesn't like him, to say the least.

"You have some nerve," I squint at him as I manage to overcome the gap between my brain and mouth.

"Maybe we can go outside." Did he really just suggest that we move our drama to the huge parking lot, where everyone can see?

"I'm going nowhere." I don't take my eyes off the bastard who stands before me, all puffed up. "You can leave."

"We need to talk."

"'Excuse me?" I burst at him from behind the counter, making Henry jump. "We what?"

"You're surprised."

"Surprised?" I snort. "Nothing you do now will surprise me. I was surprised when you didn't show up for our wedding or for your daughter's birth or for any other event in the last five years."

"I think I'll leave you two alone," Henry stammers and turns his back on me, slipping into the storage, allowing me more privacy to explode on the scum that has appeared out of nowhere. I didn't think Henry would stay, he isn't the kind of guy who copes well with confrontation.

"You're expecting explanations." Colin doesn't take his eyes off mine and all I can see in them is distance. There is no trace of his caressing voice or the love he once gave me.

"What explanation could you give me? Was the gym more important than your daughter? Because, apparently, that's where you spent your time!" I give his huge arms another look. Yep, without a doubt caused by weights, a balanced diet, protein shakes and a whole lot of money, that I should have gotten for our daughter.

"You're busy." He pulls out a wallet from his back pocket and hands me a business card. "This is my number."

I crumple it between my fingers and throw it at him without thinking.

"You can shove your number." He takes a deep breath, puts the wallet back in his pocket, glares at me hard, and out come the words that crush my frail world into a thousand pieces.

"I want to see her."

"Forget it," I whisper as I try to breathe. My heart has trouble pumping blood all over my body, which makes me pale. "You won't see her, you lost the right."

"She's my daughter."

"Really?" I thank God for my anger, which prevents my tears from breaking out. "If she's your daughter, please tell me, where were you when my water broke in the middle of the night and my mother had to take me to the hospital while I was terrified to the bone?"

His steady posture doesn't change, his body doesn't move an inch, even as my words beat him mercilessly. "Where were you, when the monitor showed she was in trouble and I was rushed for a C-section? When I got out of bed, sore, stitches on my belly and went to see her in an incubator 'cause she couldn't breathe?"

"I deserve that," he answers in a steady voice, free of apology.

17

"Where were you when she was two years old and vomited so much she suffered from dehydration and I had to hold her when they stuck a needle in her vein? When I held her hand and there was no one there to hold mine, where were you, Colin?" My voice cracks as I shout, "Where the hell have you been?"

I want to hear his answer, but the ringing of an unfamiliar phone interrupts my racing thoughts. He reaches into his trouser pocket, pulls out his cell phone, and without looking away from me, answers confidently.

"Colin Young."

I have to figure out a way to make him disappear. To make him crawl back into the hole he came out of. If he thinks he can just show up here with delusional demands, he is wrong.

He wants to meet her . . . She doesn't even know who he is!

"Don't make me laugh, not more than a dollar. I'll handle it the minute I'm in front of my computer." His voice is steady and authoritative. "I know it's urgent, I'll get back to you as soon as I can." He hangs up and puts the phone back in his pocket.

"Let me guess, something came up." I cross my arms over my chest.

"Work."

"You have a job?" I mock him. "How nice."

"I have a business. Elizabeth, we need—"

"I don't know what you thought would happen when you came here, but you're wrong if you think I'll just let you show up in Vivian's life, just to disappear—"

"I'm not going to disappear," this time he interrupts me. "I'm staying in town, I'm back, and I'm not leaving again."

"You can't meet her," I insist.

"We need to come up with a solution."

"No solution, take me to court."

"I really would rather not." His answer makes my knees shake.

"You won't do that to me."

"You need time."

18

"No time in the world will convince me to change my mind," I sneer at him. "No time in the world will change the fact that all you left behind was a note."

"I don't expect you to understand."

"I understand just fine," I raise my hand in front of his face, "you pretended to love me for four long years just to have a roof over your head and food on the table. When I think of all the things I did, everything I gave you . . . I should have listened to my father."

His jaw tightens in a second. I see his face darken and something passes through his gaze when I mention the man who raised me.

"Your father hated me from day one," he says, trying to hide the loathing in his voice. I know he's right but still, he has no right to talk badly about my father, who has saved me time and again over the last few years.

"My father loves me," I remind him. "He tried to warn me about you, tried to save me from the fate that awaited me, but you . . . crawled into my heart like a snake."

"The fuck I did," his words destabilize me. He never spoke to me this way. "You know it had nothing to do with me."

"You're all the same," I repeat the sentence he's heard more than once. My father told him to his face again and again. I should have to listen to him.

A football player?

You know why they can get away with it.

You know who they really are.

"I have to go." Colin realizes he won't get what he came for.

"Of course you have to go," I reply scornfully.

"Think about when I can meet her."

"There's nothing to think about," I shake my head. "You have to disappear."

"That's not going to happen. I don't expect you to forgive me, but we have a child, and I want to know her."

"Not in this life." I've got to get him out of here before the tears overcome me.

"I'll be in touch." He gives me a last icy look. "Goodbye, Elizabeth."

He turns his back on me and walks confidently out the door, and the dam brakes.

OH GOD. Oh God. Where did he come from?

Breathe!

He thought he would just show up here and . . . and . . . and ask to meet my daughter?

My daughter! He isn't anything more than a sperm donor who broke my heart. I gave him four years of my life just to stand at the alter at twenty-one with a five-month belly in front of all our guests.

Screw him!

I wipe the endless tears.

I don't know him. I used to think I did, but I was wrong. I don't know what else he is capable of. As far as I'm concerned he might . . .

Oh God!

My heart is threatening to collapse, I grab my bag from under the counter. Henry emerges from the storage and stares at me with sympathy.

"I have to go . . . I. . ."

"Are you sure it would be wise to drive in your condition?"

I'm not sure of anything. It took me five years to get my life into some kind of order, and the bastard has just pulled the rug from under my feet again. I have to get to Vivian.

"I'm sorry, I . . ."

"Go, do what you need to, I'll back you up." Henry gestures toward the door. I run out of the store, get into my car and pray I'm not too late.

.   .   .

I CURSE every driver who moves too slow, every car that stops, every red light that refuses to change and makes me wait patiently. I have no patience, and I have no time, because if the bastard decides to pull a number on me . . .

I haven't heard from him in five years, and from nowhere he appears at the door and asks to see her. With what right?

I can't trust him. I mustn't believe a word he says, I have to protect Vivian.

With a screech of brakes, I stop the car in front of the daycare and burst in, panting in front of Mrs. Robbins' stunned face, staring at me in confusion.

"Elizabeth, is everything all right?"

No. Nothing's all right and it won't be all right until I take my daughter from here, home.

"I have to get Vivian." My eyes are searching for my child, who is nowhere to be seen.

"Okay . . ." She hesitates. "Maybe you want some water first?"

What good will some water do me now?

"Mrs. Robbins, I know I look…" Hysterical. "I just need to get Viv, there's an emergency in the family." I blurt the perfect excuse I had prepared in advance to explain my situation.

"Oh, of course. I hope it's nothing serious."

"Nothing serious, no need to worry," I reassure her.

"She's in the backyard, I'll go and get her."

"Thank you." I take a deep breath. She was in the back yard, he hasn't reached her.

Mrs. Robbins turns, walks out the side door and comes back after two minutes, which I passed trying to arrange my red hair so that looks less terrible.

"Mama!" Vivian comes running and jumps to my arms.

"Sweetheart," I crush her into my chest, "I've come to pick you up early."

Real early, considering it's eleven in the morning.

"Where are we going?" She wrinkles her sweet face.

"Home." Straight home, without stopping.

What if he knows I've never moved? What if he appeared there?

Okay, I have to calm down, this paranoia doesn't help one bit.

I look up at Mrs. Robbins, who still seems unsure of entrusting Vivian with me, in my state.

"I'll be in touch." I give Viv a hand and walk her to the door.

"I'll wait to hear from you," Mrs. Robbins calls, as I step out the door and rush my girl into the car and fasten her seatbelt.

We've got to get out of here.

PLEASE WAKE UP. Wake up and find out it was just a bad dream.

The solemn prayers I carry in my heart as I press the accelerator never come true. In the backseat Vivian plays on my phone, while my eyes jump to the mirror to see if anyone is following us.

I breathe slowly, begging God not to cry again. I can't even run away. I don't have the privilege of disappearing, throwing a suitcase into the car and never looking back. In order to run away, you need money, the kind I don't have. To escape, you need a plan, and I have a child. I can't tear her out of her life.

Why did he come back? Why couldn't he stay away, why was he so selfish and so inconsiderate? I am beating myself up again.

The man I loved never existed. He was just a creation of my wild imagination. The outcome of a calculated blindness. I wanted to believe that someone like him could love me and was left with a child who doesn't know her father, a minuscule salary and an apartment to keep. He will pay for what he did. He'll pay big time.

"WHAT DO YOU MEAN, he just showed up?" My mother yells so

loud on the phone that my ragged nerves are about to surrender again to tears. I stand outside my house so that my four-and-a-half-year-old won't hear a thing. I turned on the TV, turned up the volume, and snuck out, hoping that maybe my mother would have something smart to say.

"You can't tell Dad," I plead. "He'll go look for him, and we don't know how it will end."

We know exactly how it will end. At the police station. My father has already stated more than once that if he ever sees Colin's face, it will end badly. He may be willing to forgive a lot of things, but not my crushed pride.

"You shouldn't have taken Viv out." My mother is breathing deeply.

"What was I supposed to do, leave her there in hopes that he wouldn't decide to go tell her Daddy's back?" The thought makes me sick.

"Shit, that's not good," she murmurs tensely.

"You think?" I yell.

"And he didn't explain himself, didn't say where he was all these years?" She continues her investigation.

"At the gym," I grumble in disgust.

"What?"

"Nothing, he didn't explain, I didn't give him the chance."

"What are you going to do?"

"I don't know." I sit down with my back to the front door, fold my knees to my chest and drop my head. "I don't know what to do."

This little confession makes a tear trickle down my cheek. How could I love him? What a fool I was.

"How does he look?"

"What?" Why does my mother care what he looks like?

"You know, does he look like he's on drugs?"

"Drugs?" I'm stunned by her question, "No, he looks . . ."

For the first time since this morning I allow myself to think of

23

what Colin looks like. I think of the clothes he wore, sitting on his enormous body perfectly, as if tailored to his size. I see in my mind his safe stance, remembering the confidant tone of his voice. He is no longer the boy who sat on my bed and let his shirt rise. Come to think of it, in the end, whatever was waiting under the waistband of his boxers is what got me in trouble.

And I think about that now?

"Lizzie, are you there?"

"Sorry," I hasten to apologize and reprimand myself. "He looks healthy."

He looked really good, not that it matters, not for a moment.

"And he didn't say anything?"

"He said he's back in town and has a business. I didn't ask questions." Maybe I should have gotten more details out of him. Find out what I'm dealing with. "I have to go, we'll talk tomorrow, and shut your mouth around Dad."

"Elizabeth . . ."

I know what she's going to say. She doesn't want secrets kept between her and her husband, but it's my decision when to tell him. My parents have a perfect relationship, the kind one hardly ever sees. Not an easy thing considering what they've been through. As if I'm not short of trouble, their anniversary is approaching, and they're going to celebrate like they do every year, a constant reminder of what I don't have.

"Give me time," I ask of my mom.

"All right," she sighs from the other side.

"Thanks." I hang up the call, put the phone on the floor beside me and lean my head on my lap. This is not happening to me.

THE WHITE LACE trail of my dress is gathered into a pile on the floor of the car. On my knee lays the veil I chose, the one that had not been used. I'm sitting in the back, my hands on my growing belly, bowing my head to avoid my mother's looks, who sits behind the wheel in silence.

Every once in a while she glances at her cell phone, as if it'll ring any second. She steers the car through the streets. My father is gone, I'm afraid to think where.

"Are you sure?" My mother asks quietly for the thousandth time. I look up and gaze at her with a stare that immediately silences her. I'm not sure of anything, I just want to get home.

Twenty minutes ago I stood in front of everyone I know and in a trembling voice sent them on their way. My groom never showed up. No one had seen him, heard from him. The worry consumes me like fire spreading in a field of thistles.

Where are you, Colin?

The car pulls up in front of the house. I open the door and, without waiting, pick up the hem of my dress and start running, my mother following me. The key to the house rustles in my hand as I push it into the keyhole, push the door, and burst inside.

Please be here. Just tell me you got cold feet, I can live with that. Panic is something I can forgive.

The dark house doesn't bode well. I turn on the light in the living room and stop at the entrance to our bedroom. My eyes dart from the bed I arranged this morning to the open wardrobe and my heart drops. My dresses still hang where they were this morning, my clothes folded in piles.

And Colin's shelves are empty.

A flood of emotions batter me at once. The worry dissipates into smoke, replaced by confusion and anger of intensities I didn't know could be felt. He left?

I look around, maybe I'll find an explanation. Maybe it's not what I think. I'm pregnant, he wouldn't do this.

On the dresser beside the bed, under the bedside lamp, lies a piece of paper that looks as if someone has ripped it off hastily. With trembling legs I walk into the room, move closer and lift it between my fingers.

The words are written in black, in handwriting that I have learned to recognize as well my own. Words that threaten my breathing and change my world order. Words that ruin my life.

This was all a mistake. I don't love you anymore.

OUR SMALL HOUSE IS QUIET. I finish washing the dishes and peer into the bedroom. I hate this time of day, when the sun gathers into the horizon and everything darkens, and I have no dinner to cook and no girl to shower. When everything is still and the street seems to be preparing itself for the night Vivian sleeps, and I'm left with my thoughts.

She behaved so well throughout the evening. She ate her food, played with her dolls, and I cleaned the house like a madwoman in a psychotic attack. It was as if removing all the dust would also remove my troubles.

I used to wait impatiently for this hour. Colin would come back from work on the scaffolding, dusty and smiling, always tired. He would go into the shower and then sit at the table and, together, we would have dinner and exchange experiences from the day we went through, even though our days were usually dull and sounded just like the day before.

Colin could make everything sound funny and intriguing, like that lady who used to walk under the building every morning and shout obscene words at the workers for no reason. We were both trying to guess what her story was, inventing strange and illogical plots until my stomach ached with laughter.

Then we would lie on the couch in front of the TV and stare at the screen. All I was really interested in was Colin's fingers stroking my forearm and chilling me, as if he were doing it for the first time.

Most nights I would fall asleep with that movement of his fingers on my skin. A feeling forgotten in the countless days that had passed since the last time he stroked me, countless evenings that had led to countless nights. The only thing that broke the solitude was Vivian's breathing. The only thing left of him.

I curse in my heart the boy who pretended to have a life taken out of a Hollywood movie, the boy who revealed the truth only to me. The blond boy with the blue eyes, Captain of the football team, who returned every day to a house no one would want to live in.

The tears run down when I think of what was deprived from Vivian, of what was deprived from both of us: The right to lean on someone, the promise that he will always be there. The father he chose not to be, who abandoned his daughter before she was even born. I didn't imagine he, of all men, would run away, but he did and he left us alone. And now he is back, but the loneliness is not gone. It is still there, in the empty bed he left behind, the dinners he never attended, in the trust he broke, that no man after him could repair.

I look at Vivian sleeping, oblivious to the storm in our lives that is about to sweep us both onto an unfamiliar beach. The man who calls himself her father is back, and I'm the only one standing between them, trying to save her from heartbreak. What if one day she finds out that I was the one who kept her father from returning to her life, and doesn't forgive me?

What if he really is going to stay?

I close my eyes and try to soothe my breath. I have no idea what his plans are, but it's too early to let him get close. What Colin did was unforgivable, and my heart will not forget so quickly how he broke it.

THE SMELL of pancakes fills the house and I take another sip of coffee in hopes it'll wake me up after my sleepless night. The fears I managed to hold back finally came in full force and for most of my questions I have no answers.

What does he want, except to meet Vivian? Does he want to keep in touch with her? Custody, visitation rights?

"Why are we staying home today?" Viv asks, for the third time since she woke up, as she takes the maple syrup out of the fridge.

"I thought we'd spend the day together," I lie to her, putting a plate of pancakes on the table. Last night I called Mr. Blunt and apologized for my expected absence. I'm not sure he took it well.

"What do you want to do?"

"Tea Party!" she climbs to her chair and opens the bottle.

"We can have a tea party."

"And bake cookies!"

"Sure." Baking cookies sounds like something we can do.

"And then we'll go to the playground and rock on the big red swing." She pushes a piece of pancake in her mouth.

"We'll see." I load pancakes on my plate, aware of the fact I have no intention of going to the playground today. "Eat with your mouth closed," I tell her, before she raises any more ideas that I will have to rule out.

We're staying home.

CHAPTER THREE

"Why can't I go to Tania's birthday party?" Viv looks at me disappointedly, tears in her eyes. We spent the last two days at home, baking, cooking, playing cards, trying on dresses, applying nail polish and even make-up. The last, in particular, made my child very happy, as I don't normally agree to that. I left behind the pretense and the attempt to be someone I was not at the age of seventeen, the evening when Colin walked into my room and found me wearing a tight dress.

"Going somewhere?" He mocked me, as he used to do to disguise his insecurity. I forgave him most times.

"I was just trying it on when you arrived," I lied in embarrassment.

"I can see your panties." He raised an eyebrow, and I responded by pulling my dress down so hard my bra showed.

"Um . . . Tits or legs. Tough choice."

"Stop that."

"Stop trying to be someone you're not." He gave me a serious look. From that day on, I stayed in the jeans and a T-shirt.

"Mama!" Vivian's crying makes me jump. The bastard is back and so are the memories. Screw this.

"I'm sorry." I hug her.

"Tania is my best friend."

What am I supposed to do? Let her go and hope her father doesn't show up?

"Okay," I feel the pressure rising in my chest growing, knowing that I'm reacting hysterically to the situation. But how can I not?

"We'll go to the birthday."

"You're not invited," she protests firmly. "All mothers go home."

Dammit!

"Are you sure?" I ask, though I know she must be right. She nods quickly.

"Okay, go get dressed and I'll get Tania's present." I take a deep breath, trying to calm my pulse, if only slightly. Luckily I'm a girl who likes to be prepared so I bought Tania's gift a week ago. Better not to leave things for the last minute. Viv runs into the bedroom and five minutes later appears dressed in a festive pink dress and shiny red shoes.

"Ready?" I brush her long hair with my fingers.

"Ready." She smiles a huge smile. I open the door and hurry her into the car.

THE DOOR of the Margolis family is decorated with balloons and a large, colorful sign, informing everyone they have come to the right place. Vivian knocks on the door and waits impatiently, while my nerves become more ragged every passing second.

Mrs. Margolis opens the door with a wide smile.

"Vivian, you're just on time, come in." She has hardly completed her sentence before my four-and-a-half-year-old ignores any politeness I ever taught her and runs into the living room. Mrs. Margolis laughs loudly, "I understand someone is excited."

"Very," I nod and glance into the house, freezing in front of the scene that I see. Tania's white dress flutters in the air as Mr. Margolis swings her like . . like no father ever did my daughter. My heart collapses into itself.

"Elizabeth?" Mrs. Margolis asks in a low voice.

"I'm sorry" I try to smile, "when should I come to pick her up?"

"In an hour and a half, we're having 'Max the Great.'" a broad smile comes over her lips. Max the Great is the neighborhood children's favorite attraction. He is known for blowing up balloons, magic and asking for a price I could never afford.

"I'll come back later," I say my goodbye, the bitter disappointment growing inside me. Just one more thing I can never give Vivian. The thought of having to host all these children in my house, and the cost all that entails, is tension I don't need.

Don't think about that now, you have other things to deal with. Stay focused!

YOU'RE LOSING IT COMPLETELY, I scold myself as my eyes scan the street outside the Margolis house. Inside, the children are celebrating Tania's fifth birthday, and outside I sit, in the car, watching the house.

I don't know how to act differently. Really. I wish I could be one of those calm mothers who isn't upset about anything. I wish I had a big house with a white fence and a husband to return to at the end of every day. I wish my dreams didn't crash because of a quick, heartless act from someone who claimed to love me.

The black car on the road makes me tense. The driver behind the wheel is unaware of my existence as she drives past.

What car does he drive?

I don't know anything. Not which car he has, nor what he does for a living, not even where he lives. Is that how I'm going to keep him away?

I look up at the mirror, examining the small lines at the sides of my eyes.

My mother claims they're my imagination, that only I can see them, but they are there. Tiny slits, incriminating evidence. I'm not seventeen anymore, not even twenty-one. I am scarred and frightened, and life alone has raised my anxiety to a threshold I didn't know was possible. Vivian is my whole world, and now someone is threatening the little family I've built. I know it's crazy to think he'll get her or something, and yet, here I sit in my Toyota, imagining the worst.

AN HOUR AND A HALF LATER, I ring the bell and pick up my happy child, her face covered with chocolate cake.

"Enjoy yourself?" I pick her up and carry her to the car.

"Yes!" she rejoices. The thought of her missing her best friend's birthday because of me fills me with sadness.

It's not because of you, it's because of him.

"Let's go home," I put her in the seat.

"I want to go to Granny's," she protests against my plan to lock us in again.

"I don't know if she's free."

"Ask her."

I dial my mother and wait. After Vivian was born, my mother, who runs a beauty salon, cut down her hours. She claimed, of course, it had nothing to do with me having a baby. I'm not sure I believe her. She wanted to be there for me.

Maybe if she'd cut her hours when I was in high school and the house wasn't empty, I would have refused Colin and not invited him. God knows, if my father had discovered him there, it would have ended badly.

How many months did we sneak behind their backs?

Colin knew to keep our secret and not show up uninvited.

At one point I had to tell him. I had to explain why the situation was complicated.

We sat on my bed during one of our breaks from studying and talked endlessly, until I stole a glace at the clock and panicked.

Colin laughed and asked if it was my bedtime.

I didn't smile. Not one muscle moved in my face as I tried to find the right words.

They mustn't know you're here. I know we're just studying, it's not about you. But you're a football player. My father will freak out. It's because of Morgan. He was . . .

"ELIZABETH, ARE YOU THERE?" My mother's voice shouts in the speaker. How many times had she called me already?

"Sorry, sorry," I apologize and curse the memories again. "Viv wants to know if you're home and if we can come over."

"I'm home, you can come over."

"We're on our way." I sneak a glance at Viv, who smiles broadly.

"I'll be waiting for you." She ends the call. I start the car and steer my way to the house where I grew up. Where I hid my love until I could no longer.

"ELIZABETH, you can't lock your child at home." My mother sighs when I finish telling her about the semi-psychotic attack I've been having. It's seven-thirty in the evening, Vivian is playing quietly inside while we sit on the front porch on the swing. I look at her and examine her beautifully arranged red hair. Her make-up is meticulous, the amount masking any wrinkles or signs of worry. She is groomed, her nails always painted with nail polish, her lips red and full. And she got me, the girl who doesn't like

ALLY SKY

dresses, who doesn't understand why one should apply face cream every night before bedtime, who prefers comfortable clothes that you can just throw on. I take comfort in the fact that her granddaughter is like her and loves lipstick, too.

"I am not locking her at home," I try with all my might to concentrate on the conversation. "I just have to think."

"You should talk to him."

"Absolutely not," I murmur.

"You need to figure out what he wants and draw him some boundaries."

"What I need is to take him to court and make him pay for what he did."

"That's also an option."

"A good option."

"Call him."

"I don't have his number," I reply immediately, remembering how I crumpled his card and threw it at him furiously.

"I'm sure you'll find a solution."

"Don't you understand that there is no solution?" I resent her suggestion.

"You keep forgetting something," my mother loses her patience. "There's someone else involved in this, and if you want to protect her, you have to plan your moves. Do you think you can prevent him from seeing her forever?"

"Yes."

"You're wrong. If he's serious, he'll find a way, and it won't be your way. Sweetheart, I know it's a lousy situation, but you have to think. Hiding Vivian at home in hopes that this will resolve itself isn't the answer."

"I hate him," I mutter angrily.

"I know, and I truly hope you don't blurt it next to the girl and screw her up."

"I'm not a monster." I never said one bad word about him to her.

34

"Find out what his plans are."

"I'll think about it," I reply as I get up from the swing, signifying the subject is closed. I just need a few more days, that's all. A few days to let him disappear. That's what he knows to do best —to decide that he's changed his mind, to pack his bags and evaporate. So I'll give him the chance to do just that, disappear back to the same place he spent the last five years. There, and only there, I want him to stay.

MY PHONE RINGS the next morning as I finish washing the dishes. I quickly wipe my hands on the small kitchen towel and answer the unfamiliar number.

"Hello?" I glance into the living room where Vivian is playing on the carpet.

"Elizabeth?" The deep, bass voice makes my heart skip a beat. I never changed my number, should I have expected this call?

"You didn't go to work," he says quietly, keeping his cool as if expecting an attack.

"I'm on vacation." I don't bother to explain and turn my back on the girl who isn't aware of what's going on. "Please don't call me again."

"We need to talk."

"I've told you," I open the door and sneak out, "we're not going to talk."

"You can hate me all you want, but she's my daughter, too."

"And you'll keep away from her and me," I say firmly.

"That's not going to happen." His answer makes my heart run wild.

"Why are you doing this to me?" My voice cracks.

"I don't want to do anything to you, I just want to see Vivian, please don't drag us into a war."

Will he really take me to court? Because if he does, I'll lose for sure. They might make him pay what he owes me, but they won't prevent him from seeing his child. No matter how hard I try, in the end, I'll lose to the son of a bitch. The one thing left for me to do is to try and delay the meeting as much as I can.

"I took her out of daycare." The words roll out themselves. "After you came, I took her out of the daycare and stayed with her at home."

"Elizabeth," he sighs, and for a moment the distance in his voice is gone.

"So if you were thinking of looking for her there, you can forget about it."

"Do you really think I would do that?" He sounds hurt.

"Since when do I know what you plan on doing?"

"I guess you're right." His voice changes again without warning and the coolness returns. "Take her back, she needs her routine."

"Now you know what she needs?" I snort.

"Children need their routines."

"Are you talking from experience?" I don't know where this question comes from.

"Am I what?"

"Do you have other children?" The thought that somewhere in this world he has another child he was raising shrinks my heart in a painful way.

"I have no other children than Vivian." His answer loosens the pressure that has accumulated in my chest.

"I don't want you to approach her." I can't steady my voice and I hate the thought that my confidence is gone. Five years without him forced me to be as strong as I have ever been, and now that strength isn't there.

"I won't approach her, I give you my word."

"Your word is worth nothing, Colin," I clarify. "I need time, don't ask me how much, don't ask me when your meeting will take place and don't approach her."

"Take her back."

"You will fulfill your duties to us before you have any rights." This could be an excellent test. Maybe this will make him disappear again. Maybe he will run away, and all will be solved.

"Just say what you need from me." He remains calm.

"The Child Support I never got for a start," I murmur angrily. The struggle of the past years hasn't been easy and has taken its toll on all of us.

"How much?" His question takes me out of balance for a moment.

"What?"

"How much money?" His voice remains steady.

"Since when do you have money?" Even before he left, it wasn't easy. His high school grades were not enough to get a scholarship, and there was no way in hell he could pay for his studies at college. Instead, he moved from one job to another, never resting. He always hoped something better would come. We lived in our tiny house and saved every cent for the birth and dreamed of the day we could move.

"I told you I had a business." He takes me back to the conversation.

"You owe me alimony for the last five years." I want to make sure he understands what I'm talking about.

"How much money, Elizabeth?" He doesn't fold. I wonder if he's lying and whether I want his money at all. Only God knows where he got it.

"I don't know how much."

"So sit down, think, and give me a number. I'll make sure it goes into your account."

"It doesn't work that way," I grumble. "I don't know what your income is or what extra expenses you have."

"It shouldn't interest you."

"Maybe we'll let a judge rule."

"If that's what you want, though the courts work slowly and I'd rather you just tell me how much you need."

"What are you doing?"

"What do you mean?" He sounds confused.

"Your business, is it legal?"

"Yes, I'm a liquidator."

"What's that?" Did he invent an occupation?

"I buy stuff for cheap and sell it at a profit." So the guy found something to do with his life without a college degree. Amazing.

"Well, I suppose that could be profitable. Thinking about it, you didn't have big expenses like kids, for example."

"I don't blame you, you have every right to be mad with me."

"I'm not mad at you, Colin, I hate you. Do you know how many nights I cried myself to sleep? How many times I have cursed you?"

"I can imagine." He doesn't apologize for what he did.

"I have to go check on my daughter."

He doesn't correct me, doesn't insist on noting that, after all, she is his daughter, too. "Call me when you have the numbers."

"It'll take some time, I'll have to consult someone."

"Okay," he says, "just call me if there's anything you need."

"I need a time machine, do you have a time machine Colin?" My voice is but a whisper, "Because I'd be really glad to go back to the moment you stood in our bedroom and kissed me. The moment after we made love and you promised to see me in a few hours. I would be so very happy to look you in the eye and see where I was wrong."

I hang up the call, leaving him hanging in the air. Let him taste some of his own dish. God knows I've been choking on it for the last five years.

AT NINE IN the evening a knock on the door makes me jump off the couch. I open it and stand silent in front of my father's anger.

His hair is graying, his face is wrinkled, tired. He isn't young, and the long hours at work come with a heavy price. He knows it. And we all know why he does it. He pushes himself so as not to think, to overcome the pain that never leaves him.

"Hello, Elizabeth, how nice of you to call and inform me on all that's been going on!" Damn my mother and her big mouth.

"Don't shout. Vivian is sleeping." And she isn't aware of the drama, and that's how I want to keep it.

"Tell me you're not seriously considering letting him see her."

"At the moment, the only thing I'm considering is how many zeros to add to the number I'm going to give him," I mumble, as an annoying headache begins to bother me.

"What number?"

"Come in," I gesture toward the living room. "You wanna beer?"

"What do you think?" He walks into the house, closes the door, and sits down on the sofa. I head to the fridge thinking of how I'm going to tell him my life has changed directions in no time.

Fifteen minutes later I pat myself on the back, mentally. I managed not to cry, an impressive achievement by all accounts. My father, on the other hand, looks like someone is going to die.

"You listen to me," he takes a sip of the second beer I've served him. The first he finished in five minutes. "You are not to talk to him, he is not to come anywhere near you."

"I can't really stop him."

"You need a lawyer," he states decisively. "That boy is a lot of trouble."

"He isn't a boy anymore." When thinking about it, Colin really isn't a boy. He's a muscular, tattooed man, and if his arms look like they do, God only knows what his abs or thighs look like . . .

These thoughts have to stop! What does it matter what his abs look like?

"I don't want you to talk to him. I know how he'll crawl straight back into your life. You never could resist him."

"It's not that simple."

"It will be simple if you don't complicate it. He has to leave, he's dangerous."

"Colin isn't dangerous." I don't know why I insist on defending him. An old habit I guess. I've always defended him, always stood by him, especially in regards to my father.

"You're blind," Dad reprimands me. "You had a bright future before you met him. We told you to stay away from the football team."

"Colin wasn't 'the football team.' He was just the captain, he never abused anybody." No matter how many times I said it in the past, my father refused to listen and he is refusing to listen now.

"If you'd kept away from him, maybe you would've achieved what you wanted."

"You never gave him a chance."

"I saw him for who he really was, forgive me for trying to protect you!"

"You saw *those* boys and what *they* did." I almost regret my words, but I can't ignore the fact that I'm right.

"You don't know what you're talking about," he tries to stop me in vain. He knows where I'm going.

"I know all too well. It shouldn't have happened, but there was nothing you could have done, Dad. Morgan didn't tell you."

There is a tense silence as that name is mentioned. Morgan is no secret, he's just someone who isn't talked about, and I just brushed the dust of those memories, knowing how much pain I'm inflicting and how delicately I should approach the subject.

"I'm warning you, Elizabeth." Dad clenches his teeth and his jaw tightens.

"Dad, you couldn't do anything."

I put a comforting hand on his knee, but I can't really help. He is the father who walked into the garage one afternoon and found his son, only fourteen years old, hanged. The father who put together the pieces of information that were revealed in the weeks after Morgan's death. The father who heard what the football team had done for months, day after day, hour after hour, until Morgan's only solution was to kill himself. No matter how many years have passed since, it doesn't matter that we relocated when I was only four years old. The pain is there, burning and destroying.

"I was supposed to look after him and I failed," the fury echoes in his voice. "There's no way in hell I'll let something happen to you. All the time you spent in school went down the drain when that boy come into the picture and destroyed your future."

"He will pay for what he did to me, but I won't blame him for what other boys did, in another city, when I was a child."

"You don't know who he is."

"And you do?" I sigh and lean back in preparation for a lecture I've heard a thousand times or more.

"They are all the same. Thugs, violent, ticking bombs waiting to explode, we lost one child, we are not going to lose you, you chose—"

"You're right," I interrupt. "I chose him despite your warnings, I fell in love with him, got pregnant, but you blame him for something that has nothing to do with him."

"Colin and his ilk are people who see only themselves. They don't think about the future or about those who might be hurt by their actions."

"You can't protect me anymore, you've done that my whole life."

When I was young, I often asked myself whether my role in the world was to be a compensation for a loss, a role I played with great success. I was protected and safe, barely allowed to move. I was the good girl my parents wanted. I believed they had suffered enough and I didn't want to add more.

"We don't choose who to fall in love with" Colin whispered on the phone one night, after I'd cried endlessly. I knew I was going to hurt them. Colin wanted to console me and failed miserably. I didn't choose to fall in love with him and I was not willing to give him up and, for the first time, I wasn't their good girl anymore. I was being me.

"If that boy comes anywhere near you, I won't be responsible for my actions." My father's voice brings me back to my tangled present.

"I'm asking you not to do anything. I don't need any more problems." I don't want people to start talking again, especially now that Vivian might hear. I don't want to run away from the looks of anyone who knows us.

They whispered as my belly grew, and when Viv was born, and when I pushed her stroller down the street. I didn't want that for her. I didn't want her to grow up being the girl who's father ran away.

"You need a lawyer, I have a friend who owes me a favor."

"You're not helping me," I sigh. "You all seem to know exactly what to do. Mom wants me to find a solution, you want to kill him and I just want to make ends meet."

"Who do you want to kill, Grandpa?" Viv's sleepy voice alarms us both. Great, just great.

"Mom was joking, Grandpa doesn't want to kill anyone." I get up slowly, ready to put her back in bed.

"That's why you cried?" She surprises me.

"When did I cry?"

"A few days ago." She yawns.

"It's nothing, sweetie." I pick her up, walk into the bedroom and put her in her bed. Leaning over, I cover her with a blanket and kiss her.

"Go to sleep."

"Please don't cry," she mumbles as she slips into her sleep. If only I could assure her that it would be so. When I go out to the living room, my father is gone. On the dining table is a note with the phone number of his lawyer friend. I fold it up and put it in my purse, turn off the lights and lock the house. Everything will wait for tomorrow.

CHAPTER FOUR

"*I'm seeing someone.*" *My hand begins to tremble, and I pull it off the table and hide it, hoping my voice will remain steady enough not to betray my panic.*

"*You have a boyfriend?*" *My mother is quick to show interest.*

"*Something like that,*" *I deliberately diminish the relationship Colin and I have been engaged in for months.*

Yes, I'm going out with someone.

Yes, he's my boyfriend.

No, I don't think it will go smoothly.

"*What's his name?*" *My father asks between one bite and another.*

"*Colin Young.*" *I don't think his name will tell my father anything, and I really don't think the investigation is over.*

"*And what does Colin Young do in his life?*" *My father proves me right.*

"*He's studying with me,*" *I move uneasily in the chair,* "*we study together.*"

"*When will we meet him?*" *My father looks up over the plate.*

"*He's very busy,*" *I evade for another second and let him enjoy his final moments of peace.*

"*Busy with school?*"

"Among other things," I take a deep breath and prepare for the storm that is about to break out. "With school and trainings."

My father freezes. His fork stays in his hand, hanging in the air, a piece of steak stuck on it and refusing to enter his mouth.

"Training?" My mother's voice is much calmer than the look on Father's face.

"He's . . . the captain . . . of the...football team."

My father's fork drops. He shoves his chair back and when he rises, the chair crashes to the floor.

He glares at me.

He doesn't say a word.

He leaves the house slamming the door and shaking the windows, my heart and my fragile world.

My mother is silent.

I have nothing to say, either.

I hope he can see that Colin is different, that Colin loves me and I love him, that he's not like them.

He really isn't like them.

He's sensitive, goodhearted and funny, and if my father could only see it, beyond the intense hatred that strikes him, we have a chance.

A WEEK HAS PASSED since my phone call with Colin, since my father gave me the lawyer's phone number who asked me dozens of questions that I didn't know how to answer. Couldn't he just throw me a number?

The silence on Colin's part drives me crazy. Not that I want him to call, but not knowing where he is or what he is doing bothers me. I wonder if he is giving me some much needed breathing space or leaving again.

He said he was staying.

But he has said many things, and I stopped believing them at all.

My phone rings at five in the afternoon, I answer while

Vivian sits in the plastic little tub I set on the shower floor, playing with soap and water.

"Hello?" I put the phone to my ear, careful not to take my eyes off my child.

"Tell your father and his friends they failed their mission." The indignation in Colin's voice makes my heart start beating wildly.

"What are you talking about?"

"If they think some bruises and a shiner will scare me out of town, they underestimate me and my seriousness."

"They what?" I shout, and the phone falls from my shoulder to the floor. I hurry to pick it up with trembling hands. "Colin, I swear, I didn't have anything to do with that, I'll kill him."

"Mama, you said you were joking." Vivian stops playing and looks at me. God, give me a break!

"I'm still joking, sweetie, go back to your game."

"Was that her?" Colin's voice joins in, sounding as if a lump has been lodged in his throat.

"Don't change the subject."

"Elizabeth, please," he clears his throat.

For the first time since his return, I realize that he isn't calling me any of the nicknames he used to in the past. I'm not Lizzie or Liz and certainly not *his love*. I'm Elizabeth, and this formality no longer evades me.

"Would you mind letting me hear her?"

"Yes." I lean against the doorpost, looking at the blond girl, who looks exactly like the guy on the phone.

"Please, talk to her."

"No," I quietly refuse again. "Just wait until I get my hands on my father."

"You won't have any trouble recognizing him, he's the guy with the broken nose."

"You broke my father's nose?" I whisper in horror.

"There were three of them, waiting for me outside the gym. Not really fair play, if you ask me."

"I'm sorry, I swear I had no idea." I close my eyes. This is getting ugly.

"Give me a number, Elizabeth. I know you need the money, let me take care—" He cuts off midsentence.

"I'm working on it." I really need to sit on it and finish.

"I can deposit something in the meantime."

I'm about to refuse him. I don't want him to think I'm buying into this good guy pretense.

"Mama, I want out," Viv calls.

"I have to finish."

"I know." He knows his time is over. I hang up, put the phone on the floor and pull the towel from the hook to wrap my daughter, the little one that was mine and mine only, and now a stranger wants to become a part of her life.

"Mama," Vivian looks up at me over her dinner plate, a rebellious lock of hair falling over her forehead.

"Yes, Viv?" I bite into the roast chicken.

"Do you think my daddy's in heaven?"

I cough loudly as the chicken gets stuck in my throat. There have only been a few times that Vivian has asked me about her father, I suppose because she grew up without him and didn't know anything else. I have a feeling she's been hearing things this past week, even if she doesn't quite understand what.

"Your father isn't in heaven, Viv." I try to remain indifferent in the face of the storm gathering momentum inside me.

"Daryl said anyone who dies goes to heaven."

"Is that what Daryl said?"

"Yes, like his granddad. Daryl draws him." She fills her mouth with potatoes.

"What do you think?" I cast about.

"About people who die?" she asks, her mouth full. "I think they're going to heaven. Is that where my dad is?"

47

Another loud cough attacks me. I always knew that the moment would come, and with it the difficult questions. If only I could put this off a little.

"Your father isn't in heaven." I take a sip of water.

"Is he in hell?"

I wish.

"Your father isn't dead."

In fact he's not too far from here, and I keep him from seeing you. Maybe I shouldn't say that.

"So where is he?" She stops her chewing in anticipation of an answer.

"He left."

"When will he be back?"

Damn you, Colin!

"I don't know, darling, not all fathers come back."

"Louisa's father came back."

"Louisa's father went to New York on a business trip." Yes, we all heard about Louisa's father's trip, the one that became longer and longer because of a certain blond woman with impressive cleavage, or so I've heard. Louisa's father returned after six months and Louisa's mother was a sucker who took him back.

"Can I paint him a painting?"

"Louisa's dad?" I twist my face.

"My dad," she answers innocently. My heart is crushed, literally, crushed and burned.

"You can draw for him. Now finish eating your chicken." I look down at the plate and load my fork with potatoes. If only the subject won't open again.

"WHAT THE HELL WERE YOU THINKING?" I shout into the phone, standing on the porch at nine in the evening, after I've put Viv to sleep, letting my father understand exactly what I think of his behavior.

"I just told him to stay away." He doesn't get excited.

"From what I heard you got yourself a broken nose."

"A small price to pay. You're my daughter, and if you thought I would sit still . . ."

"I'm trying to solve this!" If my family doesn't stop interfering, someone will pay. "I told you, don't interfere."

"Don't you think you're confused?" He laughs out loud, "I'm not your child."

"It's not your problem." I try to sound firm.

"I told you a thousand times, he is dangerous."

"Stop interfering."

"He needs to leave." He hangs up the call without letting me comment.

I swear loudly, go into the house and sit down on the couch, picking up Vivian's painting to a father she doesn't know. Blue sky, green grass and three figures holding hands. That's how it was supposed to be. Two people in love who brought a child into the world, and together they can whether the storm. I get up slowly, open the cupboard under the TV and hesitate for just a moment before reaching deep in and taking out the old photo album hidden inside. I sit down on the rug, put it on my lap and open it, looking at the eighteen-year-old girl whose hand is around the broad waist of the blond boy beside her. We were photographed at the summer fair, just before the school year was over. Just before I made the fatal decision that would change everything.

The girl I used to be smiles innocently from the photo. In her eyes, I see she believes everything can be mended. The world hasn't spoiled her and she is swept off her feet by a blonde boy who sells her illusions. Did he ever really love me?

The question occupied me for so many long nights while I laid in bed, my hands on my stomach and the baby in my womb kicking. How can one leave without giving an opportunity to understand?

He just… stopped loving me.

Perhaps one of us got sensible in time. Maybe I wanted to believe the illusion, and Colin couldn't pretend anymore. Either way, life went on, and my baby grew up to be a beautiful girl, full of confidence and smiles.

The boy in the picture disappeared only to return and raise those unanswered questions. To open the box where I locked my heart and stab it, one last time that would kill me forever.

CHAPTER FIVE

Standing in front of the ATM, I stare at the my bank account's balance and roll my eyes.

Twenty-five thousand dollars. More than I've ever had, but if someone thinks he'll buy his way back into our lives, he's in for a painful awakening.

I planned on spending my lunch break sitting on the bench in the car park eating the sandwich I'd brought from home, but I lost my appetite. I take out my cell phone, dial and wait.

Breathe. Breathe, and don't lose your cool.

The mantra I memorize doesn't help. My phone is pressed to my ear, I'm waiting nervously for my ex to answer and get a good one from me.

"Elizabeth," he answers in a steady voice. He has no idea what is coming his way, because the girl he left behind and the girl I am today are not the same.

"Do you think I'm a whore?" I fire with disgust.

"What the . . ."

"I asked, do you think I'm a whore?" I repeat the words just to shock him more.

"Since when did you start talking like that?" His tone tenses.

"Since I had to raise my child alone!" I imagine my words hitting him hard. "What made you think you could come here with your money and buy us?"

"That's not what I did."

"That's exactly what you did. We got along fine before you returned. No one needs your favors or you!"

"That's not your decision." He manages not to raise his voice.

"You won't come here and wave your dollars in expectation that I'll follow them blindly."

"I've known you long enough to know nothing will blind you."

"You don't know me. You don't know what I went through because of you." The words rolls from my tongue in anger. "Because of your lies, the girl I was is dead. You killed her, Colin. You stole my future and you're hallucinating if you think giving me mone . . ."

"It's not your money, it's Vivian's money." His semantics don't work on me.

"I'm not one of those dumb cheerleaders who followed you 'round school. Maybe you should have married one of them and not ruined my life."

"I didn't expect you to welcome me with open arms, but she is my daughter, and I will do as I see fit, when I see fit." He takes a deep breath, "And next time you call yourself a whore . . ."

"Don't make me feel like one." I struggle not to stammer.

"I'm not doing you favors," he says in a cold tone. "I'm fulfilling my duties."

"Until when? The next time you decide you don't love her anymore?"

"You're still not listening," he says nervously, "I'm not leaving."

"I listened to you for four long years and see where I ended up?"

"I see quite well," he sounds impatient. "It seems the only one who doesn't see is you."

"Please don't hurt her," I plead.

"Hurt her?"

"She's just a girl, she doesn't know anything, don't get into her life if there's any chance you'll get out of it."

"I've told you and I'll tell you again, I won't approach her without your permission, but I ask that you allow us to meet. Not today, not tomorrow, but sometime in the near future, let me meet her."

"Show me you're trustworthy," I answer without hesitation.

"That's exactly what I intend to do."

"Are you sure your business is legit?" Because I wouldn't be surprised if I found out that he was involved in the mafia, or some other organized crime, or any crime when you think about it.

"The business is legit. Are you sure you haven't heard our advertisement on the radio?"

"I don't know," I reply in an insulting tone, "let me think about it, since I don't really listen to the radio, and all my time is devoted to my daughter."

"I understand," he answers quietly. That just shut his mouth.

"That's the problem, Colin, I don't think you do understand. I don't think you know what it's like to hate someone so much you'll pay any amount of money to make them go away."

"You forget where I came from." He is serious.

"I never forgot where you came from, just as I never forgot your promise to never hurt me like," I cut my sentence at once. I hate him, really, and still, the girl I used to be prevents me from pressing that point. To mention the life he had. For a few moments there's silence between us.

"Are you there?" I ask.

"Just wondering if there are any more skeletons you want to get out of my dusty closet."

I deserve it. In spite of what he did, there are things he doesn't deserve to have slammed in his face.

"I'm sorry."

"Call me when you have the numbers." The call ends.

I went too far, and now I hate myself. The secrets he shared only with me shocked me to my bone. I swore never to compare, never to mention the past, and I didn't keep my word.

I know everything between us is diminished by what he did, and that his abandonment was the worst thing he could do, and yet I know his scars, I know where each and every one is placed, and he didn't need a reminder.

I take a deep breath. How easy it is to come back out of nowhere, crash into other people's lives and come up with demands. Did he stop for a moment and think about me? During those years, did he ask himself how I was doing? How Vivian was? Because the way it looks from here, he hung out and made money, and let us struggle. Now he wants to come back? I don't think so, mister. I don't think so.

HENRY REALIZES that something is wrong when I return to the store with a sagging face. He glances at me over his shoulder and mumbles something to the impressive customer who takes interest in the round coffee table that has been standing in the corner of the store for months. I approach both of them, ready to help Henry and perhaps justify the salary I receive mainly for keeping the place clean. The tall woman makes him agitated. I see him shifting his weight from one leg to the other and biting his lip. I also know that if Henry's parents had not been Mr. Blunt's childhood friends, he would probably have been fired long ago

"Good afternoon," I greet her, trying not to stare at her shiny blond hair. She looks like someone who has the money to buy the table. Hell, she looks like a thirty-year-old who has the money to buy a sofa, a dining set, and a few pictures and mirrors. All I can hope is that I am not mistaken and that our client is potentially furnishing her house.

"Hello," she reaches her hand in a gesture that confuses me. "I'm Danielle."

Why does she think I should know her name? And why is her black dress sitting on her illegally well?

"Elizabeth," I shake her cold hand, fighting instinctively to pull my hand back in recoil. "Can I help you?"

"This nice guy just helped me understand."

"Henry," I correct her.

"Yes, Henry." She smiles and reveals her straight teeth. "Like I said, Henry helped me figure out some things."

"Maybe I can help, too," I insist.

"You're expensive." She doesn't beat around the bush.

"Quality costs, Danielle." I'm not taken aback by her statement. I hear that claim from every customer who enters.

"Very expensive, Elizabeth." She tilts her head sideways teasingly. Okay, I don't like her. As far as I'm concerned, she doesn't need to buy anything. She can just get out empty-handed and sleep on the floor in her unfurnished house.

"Are you working on fees?" Her question undermines the little confidence I have.

"No," I answer in a steady voice, barely.

"No wonder," she mumbles to herself, her eyes quickly examining the variety of furniture that has been standing in the same place for months.

"How can I help you?" I don't think she's going to buy anything. She must have just been bored and came into the store to spend an hour of her life harassing Henry and me for fun. Another former high school cheerleader who teased others for sport.

"Henry has already answered all my questions." She smiles at Henry, and her smile makes him chew his lip even more.

"Maybe I can show you something else. What exactly are you looking for?" I make one last effort to sell her a piece of furniture she probably doesn't need.

"I don't think so." She shakes her head and her blond hair moves from side to side elegantly. My mother would love her, her makeup and her upright posture. Of that, I have no doubt.

"Maybe another time." I hold out my hand to shake hers in order to end the encounter.

"Maybe." She squeezes my hand tightly, her eyes on Henry. "Thank you for the help, young man."

Young man? I hold back a laugh. She doesn't look much older than us. Who does she think she is?

"You're welcome." Henry manages not to stammer, and she reaches forward, waiting for him to shake her hand next. He stares at her hand, her long fingernails painted in shiny red nail polish.

"Will I wait long?" She laughs and wakes him from his coma.

"Excuse me," he grabs her hand clumsily and squeezes it, "nice to meet you."

Oh Henry . . .

"Very nice." She laughs again. "Have a good day."

She releases his hand, smiles at me for the last time and walks away confidently, her high heels knocking on the parquet floor, until she reaches the door, opens it and walks out.

I let out air demonstratively, a long, desperate breath.

"What was that?" I ask Henry without expecting a real answer.

"Customer," he murmurs, "a scary one."

"Was she? Scary?" I twist my face.

"She asked a bunch of questions, tried to confuse me, maybe she was a little successful."

"Confuse you?" I laugh out loud, "Henry, you know every nail in the wall."

"Did you see her?" He stares at me with a look I have not seen on his face for a very long time.

"Henry?" I raise an eyebrow mischievously.

"She's beautiful." He manages not to stammer again. "Very beautiful."

"Very beautiful," I repeat his words.

"She's smart, too, her questions were good. She wanted to know how big the store is, how many people come in every day, what our average sales are."

"Jesus Christ." My brain works quickly and processes the data that Henry seems to have missed because the girl is beautiful. "She's not a customer, Henry, she's renting the store!"

His hand leaps to his mouth and his eyes open in horror.

"You think?" he filters the words through his fingers.

"Yes." My heart is accelerating. "She's going to fire us, for sure."

"Crap," he doesn't take his eyes off me. "I should have lied to her."

"No." He couldn't have lied to her, even if he wanted to. "It was bound to happen sooner or later, even though I would have preferred someone else to rent the place, and not . . . her."

"Because she's beautiful?" Henry doesn't take his hand from his mouth.

"Because she's vain, self-confident and very unpleasant," I sharpen my point.

"She was actually nice."

"She called you a young man." I stare at him reproachfully.

"Oh, that." He finally lets go of his mouth.

"Yes, Henry, that, and the tone in which she spoke." I'm sure he missed that, too.

"I guess it's time to enroll in college." He shrugs his shoulders in disappointment.

"The sooner the better." I sigh loudly, my insides making an impressive somersault.

I'm going to be fired. I know that.

Cleaning apartments here I come.

WHO THE HELL calls me at eleven o'clock? I pull my phone out sleepily, glancing at the screen.

Colin? He must be angry at our last conversation. Angry at me and the promise I broke.

My heart drops as I get out of bed, walk out of the bedroom into the hallway and answer quietly.

"Hello?"

"I want to see her," he fires without waiting.

"You can't."

"I don't care how you organize it or under what conditions, I—"

"Is it because of what I said this afternoon?" I sit down with my back against the wall. "That's why you woke me up?"

"No." He's lying, I know that. "I didn't mean to wake you up."

"You woke me up because of what I said."

"Don't look for reasons, I want to see her because she's my daughter," he replies firmly.

"I'm sorry if I touched a sensitive nerve," I hasten to apologize again.

"You didn't touch anything, what's in the past stayed there."

"We both know that's not true." What happened will never be locked in the past.

"I want to see her," he continues to insist.

"I don't trust you."

"You'll have to learn."

"Colin," my voice shakes, "she's four and a half, she doesn't know you."

"She's almost five, and she'll get to know me."

"I need more time," I almost beg.

"More time for what? To convince yourself that I'm a no-good who left? You've had five years, I'm pretty sure you're convinced." His voice doesn't resemble the guy full of confidence he's trying to be. The guy on the other side of the phone sounds desperate.

"What do you want from me? You don't know what I went through."

"Do you really think I can't guess for myself?" He raises his voice. "I left you behind on our wedding day, pregnant. I left you to deal with everything, do you really think I don't know?"

"How much did you drink?" The question comes out of my mouth unexpectedly.

"I don't drink, Elizabeth," he says scornfully.

"You see, I don't know anything about you."

"I want to see her and I'm still waiting for the final amount. I'm losing my patience here."

"*You* are losing *your* patience?" I shout in shock. "That's rich."

"What will you do? Send your father and his friends to deal with me again?"

"You know I didn't send them."

"I don't know anything! I don't know what happened to the life we were supposed to have." He stops abruptly and I can hear my heart pounding wildly in my chest.

"You left a note, made it clear that you didn't love me, that it was all a mistake." The tear barrier is breached. I pinch my nose and sob into the phone without shame. "This . . ." I can't stop crying. "This is what you left behind, and now you want to come back. Do you have any idea how scared I am? I'm a single mother, Vivian is all I have, I'm the only parent she knows, and you are losing your patience?"

"She's all I've have, too," he whispers.

"What about your business, what about all the money? You seem to have built a good life, while I stopped everything." I shut up before I say something I shouldn't. Colin isn't the only one who has secrets. There are things he shouldn't know.

"All I did was with the intention of coming back and being someone Vivian can be proud of."

"She didn't want to be proud of anyone, she wanted a father," I sob quietly.

"She has a father."

"Until when? 'Til the next time you leave?"

"I'm not going anywhere, Elizabeth. Take it in, let it sink in.

I'm staying. You're not supposed to believe me, but I'll prove it to you in time. Let me see my child."

"Let me sleep on it, give me time," I plead again.

"The clock is ticking." He hangs up the call again, leaving me on the hallway floor with my phone in my hand for another sleepless night.

Were the signs always there? Was I blind, naive to think that we could overcome everything? How could I fool myself that my love alone would suffice?

We never had a future together. I was his escape, the only comfort he knew. The one who accepted him unconditionally, the one who gave up on the future he didn't even know was within her reach. I was the rock on which he shattered, until he no longer needed me. He had to stay away from me to survive. I was unnecessary baggage, a weight that dragged him down. So he cut the rope, swam to shore and left me to drown.

CHAPTER SIX

J've never been a popular girl in high heels (I tried to wear them once and the experience ended with a sprained ankle. I learned my lesson.) I never tried to appeal to people I didn't have anything in common with. I didn't feel like playing the social game, which everyone seemed to have drifted into in high school. I found my corner in the library or under a tree in the park. I preferred my loneliness, which was not terrible at all. It was easier than standing in front of the mirror every morning for an hour wondering what to wear (I was satisfied with jeans, a t-shirt, and sneakers).

From my place at the bottom of the social ladder, Colin Young looked like a Roman emperor who could sentence you to life or death with a flip of his thumb. Everyone wanted to be his friend. All the girls wanted to get a party invitation from him and agreed to settle on a few minutes in his bed, if that's all they could get. Colin had a kingdom to rule and I was the last of the maids. Or so I thought. Sometimes reality is simply not what we believe it to be.

When I discovered the truth, it was so ugly I vomited that night. Colin swore me to silence. Okay, he threatened me, and I believed his threat. The panic on his face was raw when I appeared at his door and found him holding an ice bag to his nose. An hour earlier he'd forgotten his history book in my room. The test was the next day, and I assumed he would like to study at night and I just didn't think. I didn't think of anything when I jumped on a bus and went to his house without notice.

"What on earth are you doing here?" He barked at me, and I cringed at once.

"You forgot the book," I mumbled in confusion. "And I thought . . ."

"Get out of here, Elizabeth." He gritted his teeth and closed his eyes, out of what looked like pure pain.

"What happened to you?"

"That's not your business!" Blood ran down the corner of his mouth and made my stomach sick.

"You should see a doctor."

"And who's going to pay for it, huh?" He opened his eyes and gave me a murderous look.

"Do you want me to look at it?" I suggested, although there wasn't much I could do.

"Now you're a doctor?" He mocked me. The truth was that was exactly what I had hoped to become one day. A noise from inside the house made me look over Colin's shoulder and my eyes caught on the huge figure swinging in the living room, a bottle of beer in his hand. The terrifying man kicked the little coffee table and tossed it to the edge of the room effortlessly.

"You piece of shit, where did you hide the remote control?"

I didn't have to be a rocket scientist to add one and one and understand what had happened to the guy who stood in front of me terrified.

"Elizabeth, get lost, now!"

"He hit you?" I whispered in shock.

"What don't you understand? Go back to your perfect home and your perfect life and forget you saw anything."

As if I could forget even if I wanted to, and I didn't want to. I didn't want to go and leave him there with the bully who looked drunk and dangerous. "Colin," my voice quivered.

"If you don't come here now and find the fucking remote, you'll regret it." The drunken man roared.

"If you tell anyone about this, you're finished, do you hear me, you'll regret the day we met." Colin's eyes burned into me.

"You need help."

"You and your fucking help!" He lost his patience. "A stupid little girl who doesn't listen to what she's being told. Get out of here, Elizabeth, get the fuck out, and never come back!" He slammed the door in my face, leaving me standing with his history book in my hand, my legs threatening to collapse. The perfect life of Colin Young was light years away from his fake pretence, and I was the only one to discover that the king was naked.

MY PARENT'S front yard is decorated. Their house isn't very fancy and not too big, but it has always been enough for all of us. It is located in one of the nicest areas of town, a quarter of an hour from my little home. My parents worked hard to buy it and taught me to work hard, especially after my plans went down the drain with my dreams.

Vivian leaps out of the car and runs toward her grandfather, who stands on the front lawn among the many guests who came early. A wide smile comes over his face as he sees her. I stay behind the wheel for another moment and watch them. My father reaches for her and picks her up without effort, though he seems to be careful not to hurt his nose, which still looks purple under the bandage. Her dress flaps in the wind, like the white tablecloths on the tables laden with refreshments. My mother is dressed solemnly in a red dress, displaying her thin legs and smiling at my father. I know she isn't pretending. The look on her face is real and full of love and appreciation.

My parents have had a good marriage for more than three decades, and I left the church alone, no ring on my finger.

I open the car door, thank the warm weather that greets me, remember to take the gift I bought them—a sophisticated coffee machine—lock the car, and examine the new dress I bought especially for the occasion.

It's black, with thin spaghetti shoulder straps, the material clinging to my chest with a bow tied beneath my boobs. There, it spills down to my ankles, hiding my black flats.

I stood in front of the long mirror in my bedroom for twenty minutes and wondered if I should give it up and throw something else on. Even my make-up didn't make me feel better. I applied some rouge, eye shadow, heroically survived painting on eyeliner, pulled my eyelashes with mascara and my lips with gloss. Finally, I scattered my red mane of hair and prayed it would get a decent shape, any shape, just so that my mother wouldn't raise an eyebrow and cluck her tongue.

My body has changed. If Colin grew muscle, I just grew fat. First during my pregnancy, and then over the years. I'm no longer the thin-ish girl he knew. Now I'm curvy and I'm sure he noticed. Mr. 'Health-N'-Fit' came back to find I was no longer the geek from the library, just an average, neglected single mom.

With hesitant steps, I join the crowd on the grass. Everyone I've ever known is here or about to arrive, and the country music playing in the background is sometimes swallowed up by a laugh from one of the guests.

No one misses my parents' parties. The drink flows like water, the food is fine and the only celebration that competes with this event is the Fourth of July party they are planning.

If I know my mother, she is already thinking about how she will top last year's production.

"Elizabeth!" My mom reaches out to hug me, but stops when

she sees the big package I'm carrying. "You shouldn't have bought us anything."

"Happy anniversary," I ignore what she said. I wouldn't have come empty-handed. Besides, whether I liked it or not, the fact that someone has put money in my bank account sure helps me a lot. More than I would like to admit.

"Your daughter grew up," Mrs. Errlis, my parents' neighbor for decades who is currently standing beside my mother nods. "Does your granddaughter bring you much pleasure, Darlene?"

"Of course she does," my mother replies with a smile, "so smart, and so beautiful."

"We all know who she looks like," Mrs. Errlis mentions.

"She's takes after my daughter." My mother isn't flustered. I don't know how she manages to keep her cool. "She is as intelligent and she listens to what she is told."

"I heard he came back." Mrs. Errlis' words send a wave of chill down my back.

"Kirsten," my mother loses some of her color, "you don't have to believe whatever nonsense you hear."

"He was seen at the gym," Mrs. Errlis doesn't know when to keep quiet, "and shopping at Walmart, and I think Mrs. Haines saw him running in the park." She looks up at me as if waiting for an answer. Gossipy and prying!

"Perhaps you should mind you own business and not mine?" I explode before my brain can stop me. Mrs. Errlis turns white in the face of my inappropriate reaction, but she deserves to hear the truth. Someone has to shut her mouth.

"Elizabeth," my mother scolds me, trying to silence me before I insult her guest any further.

"You know I'm right." I strengthen my grip on the huge package in my hands so as not to fall from the shudder that overcomes me. "You know it's no one's business." I aim the last words at Mrs. Errlis, who has not yet recovered from my first reaction.

"I didn't mean," she says innocently.

"You meant it, Kirsten." Her name rolls off my lips contemptuously. "You sure meant it."

"Darlene," she sighs to my mother, "your daughter has forgotten the most basic etiquette."

"Her daughter is twenty-six," I snort, before my mother can answer. "What do you think she'll do, send me to my room?" I don't think my mother has ever sent me to my room. I never gave her a reason, but now I give her a good enough reason to stare at me with a look intimating I had better not add more fuel to the fire.

"No wonder he left. With that mouth of yours?"

Mrs. Errlis' venomous words permeate my veins. She's about to get some, no matter the consequences.

"You must be right," I sneer. "He left 'cause of my mouth."

"He left 'cause of something," she sips her wine, not lowering her evil stare. "Who can blame him?"

So that's what they think? That he left because of me?

"At least I don't pretend to have a good marriage while my husband comes back in the morning, three times a week," I let Kirsten Errlis know I'm not a sucker. "Remind me who it is this time, the young bartender or the saleswoman in the deli? Or do you still believe him when he says he fell asleep in the car?"

Her face, which was white, starts turning more and more red by the second.

"Yes, ma'am, I'm seeing things, too."

"The nerve you have," she says, staring at my mom with a look that could kill.

"Sorry to disappoint you, Kirsten, I'm no longer the little girl who hid in the house with her baby so ya'll wouldn't talk."

"No one talked," she tries to defend herself, but I interrupt her sharply.

"You all talked, bunch of gossips!" That's what they are. Bored bunch with nothing to do but mess with other people's lives.

"Elizabeth!" My mother is blazing.

"I knew it was a mistake to come." I hand the package over to my mother aggressively with the clear aim of running back home.

"Put it in the kitchen." She doesn't cooperate, nodding toward the house.

"Mom," I grumble loudly.

"In the kitchen," she doesn't retreat from her position. With unmistakable frustration, I walk away from them, through the open door of the house, through the spacious living room and the impressive dining area. My father built the massive wooden table and the eight chairs years ago. He has good hands, which he obviously didn't leave me. I joked about it, but it never made my father laugh, only reminded him of the son he lost, who might have inherited the work shed in the back yard. He never said that, but I'm sure the thought crossed his mind more than once. I'm sure he wondered what could have happened if Morgan had grown up to be a man and had not stayed fourteen forever.

I put the package down and lean against the counter, my head dropping between my shoulders.

Maybe I'm not so different from my parents. Their house doesn't have pictures of Morgan that will keep reminding them who they lost, just like Colin's albums that I hide in the cabinet in my living room.

As if I could hide his existence.

It worked for five years, and now everything is crumbling.

He was seen at the gym, shopping, running in the park. He's having a good time, while I have to deal with the rumors, the criticism, the endless gossip.

He didn't leave because of me, I know that. Nothing will convince me that I'm to blame. If he wanted to break up, he just had to say something, not leave a note and disappear.

"Elizabeth." My mother's voice makes me startle and I turn to her with a miserable look.

"Why did he have to come back?"

67

"Stop worrying about why he has come back." She shakes her head. "You don't want Viv to hear it from anyone else, it's only a matter of time before . . ."

Before someone says the wrong thing next to my girl or even asks her if she met her Daddy. Her friends' parents might talk, and we all know that Daryl's mother can't be trusted to shut her mouth around him.

"What am I supposed to tell her?"

"You have to meet him, hear what he has to say and set out rules for him," she replies firmly. "And you have to do it quickly. If Kirsten Errlis knows, soon everyone will know."

"It's too soon." My thoughts are running.

"Lizzie!" she loses her patience. "I know you're frightened, but you have to take over the situation, and you can't explain to Vivian where her father was if you don't know yourself!"

"I don't care where he was!" I burst out, "He should have been here, he should have . . ." stayed.

"You can't change what happened, but you have to understand, if he takes you to court, you'll lose. You don't want anyone else telling you when he can see his daughter."

"She's my daughter!" I turn a warning finger at her. "Don't forget that!"

"She is his daughter, too, in the eyes of the law," she insists. "And he will have no problem proving it if you don't refuse to let go of the past and move on."

"Don't talk nonsense," I wave dismissively. "Go back to your party, I'm sure your guests are waiting to see the constant love display you put on every year."

I pause in embarrassment. Where did those words come from? Where does this anger come from, and why do I turn it against my mother? She isn't to blame for anything.

"Elizabeth." She lowers her voice in sympathy.

"I'm sorry, it's just . . ." Too much. Year after year, these festivities are like a knife in my heart. I didn't have the privilege of celebrating even one anniversary. My mother asked that the food from our reception be transferred to the nearest shelter and the gifts she gave back, making it a little easier for me.

If I'd had to deal with it, I would have gone mad. Months of planning went down the drain. It was supposed to be the wedding of my dreams and what I got was a nightmare that refuses to end.

"You can have it all, too," my mother sighs quietly. "If only you tried, if you didn't insist on being alone."

"You know very well why I don't have," I cut midsentence, leaving my words hanging in the air. I won't get into that today, I can't deal with anything else, with more pain.

"Colin isn't the only man in the world."

"I know that," I snort.

"So stop acting like he is," she says emphatically. "Now let's go outside and save your father from his granddaughter, and keep your mouth shut."

She stares at me for the last time, straightens her dress, examines herself once more and walks out of the kitchen without a word. Colin isn't the only man in the world, he's just the one who took my heart and smashed it with one sharp blow.

I fail to convince myself to join the celebrants outside and climb up the stairs to the second floor, into my old room. My parents left it as it was, for Vivian's use.

When she's here she sleeps in the bed that was mine, in the room where I fell in love with her father. I open the door, turn on the light, and sit down on the edge of the bed. In the corner is the desk I was using and the same chair stands next to it. Even the smell has not changed. Everything froze when I left at eighteen, as my father protested. He claimed I was too young, throwing my future into the trash, that I would discover my mistake when it was too late. He was right about everything.

The certificates on the wall are a reminder of my failure. I shift my gaze from one to the other. The outstanding student finished her career as a saleswoman in the furniture store. Not impressive at all. I shake my head in frustration. How did I let it happen? I lay back and take a deep breath and look up at the ceiling. My life was planned, my future paved for years, until the captain of the football team crept into my heart just to break it. Who does that? Maybe he hasn't changed. Maybe he was always the indifferent guy he is now and I only saw the mask he was wearing. Maybe it was all a show, and the lead actor decided to quit. Decided not to get stuck at twenty-one with a woman and a child, while all his friends graduated from college and built careers. That's what he did, after all, built himself a successful business and an over sized bank account.

With the fatigue that has been with me for days, I get up from bed, leave my memories behind, turn off the light and go down the stairs. It's time to return to the present, as painful and frustrating as it is.

FOR THE NEXT HOUR, I make a supreme effort to avoid any conversation that might spill over into subjects I don't want to talk about, ignoring the glances and whispers directed at me. Mrs. Errlis must have told all her friends how Darlene's daughter spoke to her, and now they have something more to gossip about. Vivian plays with the neighbors' dog, who didn't bother to tie him up at home, instead letting him run around everyone's legs.

My daughter looks happy, unaware of the fact that her life is going to change beyond recognition. She pulls the leash around the dog's neck, ignores her white dress and rolls with him on the grass. I don't say anything even when it fills up with green stains that can't be removed.

The dress is lost, almost as I am.

"So you're taking him to court?" My father's voice surprises me from behind and destroys my plans not to talk about my ex.

"I'm not sure yet," I mumble without looking at him, not taking my eyes off Vivian.

"What are you waiting for?" He comes to stand beside me.

"I'm not waiting, he gave me something for the time being."

"Something?" My father tenses.

"Twenty-five thousand dollars." One hell of a 'something', not that I think my father is impressed. My parents may not be the richest in the country, but I am pretty sure that here and there they have a savings plan or two. After all, they help me, and quite a lot.

"Where did he get the money from?" I'm faced with another question I have no answer to. I don't seem to have a good answer to anything.

"I don't know, he's got a business, I didn't get into it," I reply coldly.

"Are you thinking about finding out?"

"I'd rather not think about it now." Or talk about it or deal with it, until I have no choice.

"Did you talk to the lawyer?"

"Yes, and I'm telling you again, I don't want to talk about it now." The last thing I need is for my father to make a fuss just because I can't answer him.

"Twenty-five thousand dollars," he says nervously.

I turn my head slowly, the look on my face dead serious. "You're not listening to what I'm saying. I don't want you to interfere, you're not part of the equation. Not you and not Mom, so stop pressuring me and let me solve the problem!"

"Frank," my mother comes out of nowhere, her sharp senses telling her that the conversation is escalating. "We ran out of beer, do you mind bringing another box from the fridge in the garage?"

"Yes, Frank," I imitate her, "do you mind bringing the beer and minding your own business?"

"Watch your mouth," my father says angrily. "You knew well

enough where to find me any time you got a call from your bank manager. If your ex-boyfriend thinks he'll show up here and take my granddaughter . . ."

"Frank," my mother doesn't let him finish, "no one is taking Vivian anywhere!"

"Who's taking me?" A small, squeaky voice makes us all look down at the girl in the stained dress, who stands before us with large curious eyes and waits for an answer.

"Grandpa thought of taking you for ice cream tomorrow." My mother saves the day.

"Yes!" Viv jumps up and claps, "I love you, Gramps."

She crashes in to him with a hug, her arms around his thighs. He leans and lifts her to him, presses her against his chest and kisses her head.

"He's just worried," my mother mouths without a sound.

"I know," I whisper back. I worry, too.

My father puts Vivian back on the grass. She doesn't linger and runs back to the dog just as I spot a black jeep parked across the street. My pulse accelerates to a frightening speed when I recognize the man sitting behind the wheel looking at me and my daughter.

Our daughter.

What is he doing here? He's insane. He promised he would keep his distance. If my father sees him, all hell will break loose. I steal a quick glance at my father, who makes his way to the garage with his back to us. When my gaze returns to the jeep, our eyes lock.

Please, go.

Colin's hands are on the steering wheel. My chest goes up and down and I feel suffocated in the damned dress. I look like a clown with this make-up, my hair is a disaster, and I don't want to care about what he thinks. So why do these thoughts creep up and bring tears to my eyes? My lip begins to tremble and in a second everyone will see. He has to get out of here, now. He has to stay away from the girl who doesn't know who he is. I wonder whether to go over when the monstrous car begins to move, sliding down the street, then accelerating. The pressure in my chest refuses to release.

If he decides to make a move, I won't have any control over it. If he decides to surprise Vivian and me, I can't do anything. I really need a plan, and a good one. A plan that will restore the control of the situation to my own hands and won't let him manage me as he did in the past.

CHAPTER SEVEN

I can't take my eyes off the girl with the perfect blonde hair who has been wandering around the store alongside Mr. Blunt for the last ten minutes, examining every crack in the floor. Henry stands beside me with a humiliated look, occasionally glancing at her. She catches his glances even when she is turned away, as if she has eyes in the back of her head, turning to smile and making him blush. Why is she doing this? Why does she embarrass him, when it's obvious she has no interest in him?

"Do you think she'll fire us?" Henry whispers, after receiving another look and, if I'm not mistaken, even a wink from the blonde.

"How should I know?" I grumble nervously.

"I hope she fires me." He leaves me stunned by his statement.

"What are you talking about?"

"It's probably better than her smiles," he murmurs in frustration.

"You'll get into college and it'll be really good," I try to cheer him up.

"It'll be really good, Liz? Like it was really good in high school?" The pain in his voice strikes me like a knife.

"We're not in high school anymore."

"I'll go to college and I'll be the oldest one there."

"And the smartest. They'll beg for your help."

"Like Colin begged for your help?"

"He stood by you more than once," I remind him. Not that I think he has forgotten. Colin defended Henry, and when he did, I just fell in love with him even more.

"He was a really good guy, you know, before he . . ."

"Left," I complete the sentence for him. "He was a really good guy, before he left me pregnant."

"I would never do that," he looks down again, "if someone was crazy enough to want to . . ."

"Stop it." I ache at his pain. "One day someone will show interest and you'll have smart, beautiful children, and you won't leave her."

"You know as well as I do that won't happen." He chews his lip again.

"She'll come, you'll see, one day you'll come across her, and she'll be perfect."

"Danielle is perfect," he gestures awkwardly at the girl who today wears a white flapping dress that exposes a lot of thin legs.

"She's a monster," I laugh quietly.

"God, I hope she'll fire me. I hope you won't let me stay and make a fool of myself."

"You're not making a fool of yourself."

"You're nice," he whispers, "but I am making a fool of myself."

"Someone like her should wish for you to want her."

"She must be eating men for breakfast." He laughs quietly.

"Spreads them like butter on toast," I happily agree.

"I'd love to be spread—" his hand leaps to his mouth as he open his eyes.

"Henry?" I don't know how to react to his burst of enthusiasm.

"I'm twenty-six, Liz, we both know I've never—"

"You don't want to be spread with Danielle," I insist.

"Easy for you to say. Colin and you must have been spreading everywhere. I remember how you used to look at him."

"And look where it got me," I point out.

"I'm willing to let her throw me away when we're finished." He laughs quietly again.

"No you're not." I shut up as the blonde and Mr. Blunt approach us.

"Elizabeth," Mr. Blunt turns to me, making my body tense. "Henry, I believe you've met Mrs. Cole."

"Yes," I reply coldly.

"Elizabeth." She hands me her hand again. Reluctantly, I shake it quickly.

"Mrs. Cole," I emphasize her name formally.

"Danielle," she corrects me. "Hello, Henry."

"Hello." He blushes beside me.

"Mrs. Cole and I are just summarizing the final details." Mr. Blunt takes the trouble to let us know.

"I promise we'll update you as soon as we can." She smiles at the two of us, her phone ringing. "If you'll excuse me."

"Of course," Mr. Blunt puts on the widest smile I have ever seen. Danielle takes the phone out of her bag and sends Henry another look, the only purpose of which is to make him blush. I stop myself from rolling my eyes as she walks to the door, the phone at her ear.

"Danielle Cole," I can hear her say, closing the door behind her.

"I assume the deal will close in the next few days," Mr. Blunt returns to the main issue.

"What about us?" I ask hesitantly. "She's going to fire us, right?"

"I'm sorry," he sounds sincere, "I don't know what the plans are."

"Wonderful," I sigh.

"I'll be in my office." Mr. Blunt leaves Henry and me standing in the empty shop like two fools who don't know what to do.

"She's so out of my league." Henry finds it difficult to take his eyes off the door. As though if he looks at it long enough, Danielle Cole will come back inside.

"She would be lucky to be in your league."

"We have to go out."

"Danielle and you?" I'm horrified by the thought.

"You and I," he laughs, "go out for dinner and pretend we're not the poor ones nobody wants."

And so, without warning, he sticks another knife in my heart. The poor one nobody wants. When was the last time someone asked me out? Probably a year ago. There was that guy, Jonathan. We went out to dinner, after my mother insisted and took Vivian over to her house. He was nice and polite, the kind who opens doors and pays for everything. The kind that laughs even when you're not really funny. But he had nothing interesting to say. We talked about my work and then about his. He was thirty-eight, his parents had died years ago, and for a moment I felt old. I felt like that was what I deserved, a guy in a suit who kissed me every morning, walked out the door with his leather briefcase, but never stirred my heart. The same heart that had trembled before. At that moment, I remembered how it felt. How those butterflies floated in my stomach every night before I fell asleep. I remembered how another man's hand held me to his chest just after he was inside me, I remembered his kisses. And I hated him at that moment, hated him for not being forgotten, for disappearing and leaving behind a memory that my scarred body remembers. I hated my love and his lies and his breath on my skin, and I couldn't let a man whom I'll never love like that take his place. I left my broken heart locked in a box, protected from harm, faithful to the boy I loved and hated and thought I'd lost. And now the boy is back, but the lock has rusted and the key I threw away. The boy is back, and I am terrified he'll break my daughter's heart.

. . .

THE DOOR to the store opens and my mother stands in the doorway, panting and with disheveled hair, as if she's been running from the car.

"Where's your phone?" she manages to ask. "Get in the car!"

"What happened?" Pure panic overwhelms me.

"Viv fell, she's in the ambulance." I can't breathe. I quickly bend under the counter and pull my bag hysterically, throwing glances at Henry.

"Go!" he hurries me. I run after my mom to the car, fasten my seatbelt and open my bag in search of my phone.

"It was on mute?" I mutter, confused. "It's never . . ." How could I be so irresponsible?

"It doesn't matter now, Mrs. Robbins is with Viv."

"What happened?"

"She fell. That's all I know."

I stare out the window and try not to think the worst. If something happens to her . . . no, she has to be all right. She must be fine, because if she isn't, what would I do? The loneliness of the thought overwhelms me. Again I'm dealing with everything by myself, like the day she was born and all the days since then. She is my world, morning and night and everything in between. The best thing that has ever happened to me, and now something has happened to her, and I'm not by her side. She must be frightened and crying, and I'm not there to hug her. She needs me, and if my mother doesn't press the gas, I'll go crazy.

The ride doesn't take more than ten minutes. My nausea increases, my hands tremble. I focus on my breathing. In. Out. In. The car screeches in front of the emergency room and I burst through the doors, running to the front desk.

"Vivian Hart," I pant in front of the receptionist. "I'm her mother."

"The doctor is with her now. The nurse will take you to see them."

She gestures to a nurse in a white uniform and asks her to accompany me to the examination room. Inside, I find Vivian sitting on Mrs. Robbins' knee, crying. Her teacher holds a bandage on her forehead, from which a bloodstain emerges.

"Mama," she holds out her arms to me and I gather her up and hug her tightly. The bandage stays in Mrs. Robbins' hand, and now I can see the cut, right at her hair line.

"Oh, God, what happened?" I hurry to take the gauze and hold it tight against the cut.

"She fell and hit the corner of the table." Mrs. Robbins looks shaken.

"Are you in pain?" I put some pressure on the wound that is still bleeding.

"Yes," Vivian sobs.

"I know. You're so brave." I kiss her head gently.

"Mrs. Heart?" A young doctor appears in the doorway, a stethoscope hanging around his neck. His face is much calmer than mine, I can safely say.

"Yes," I reply. He walks in, and Mrs. Robbins vacates her chair, gesturing for me to take a seat.

"I have to go back to work," she apologizes. "I'll call you."

"I'll keep you posted," I promise. She closes the door behind her and leaves me with the doctor and the four-and-a-half-year-old girl who is relaxing in my arms.

"I'm Dr. Diaz. Please, have a seat," he gestures to the empty chair. I don't hesitate and sit down opposite him. His doctor's robe looks especially white against the background of his olive skin. "I checked Vivian." He smiles at her warmly, his dark eyes shining as he speaks in a calm, confident voice. "She was a true heroine, but I'm afraid she will need stitches. We will numb the area first so she won't feel a thing.."

He wants to stitch her? I must be paling because the young

doctor is quick to reassure me by putting his hand on my knee.

"Vivian is in good hands. Is there anyone you want to call?"

"No," I answer automatically. My heart drops, and I hurry to regain my composure. "My mother is here."

"We'll give Vivian something that will numb her a bit and we'll go from there."

I nod without being able to speak.

"Are you sure you're all right?" He pushes back a strand of brown hair that falls on his forehead. I nod again.

"My head hurts . . ." Viv mumbles into my shoulder.

"I know, I know, sweetheart, the doctor will take care of you," I promise and kiss her hair. She's all I've got, and when she's hurting, I feel like I'm hurting, too. I'm not even sure there's room for anyone else, not at all sure that a stranger will understand the connection between us. Maybe that's why I chose to stay alone?

Our doctor leaves the room and my arms wrap my child into a hug. If only I could protect her better. If only I could lock her out of the world that is about to change forever...

VIVIAN SLEEPS. Her body looks tiny on the hospital bed. I stroke her hair, four stitches on her forehead. I allow myself to cry silently, allowing tears to flow. My mother went to fetch coffee, and the tension of the last hour finds his way out in the quiet room. I pull my phone out of my bag and dial.

"Elizabeth?" Colin sounds surprised.

"That's why I hate you," I whimper. "That's what I've been through in the past five years, when you were gone."

"What happened?" His voice sounds panicked.

"Vivian's in the hospital. Do you feel your heart accelerating?" It must be the meanest thing I could say to him.

"What happened to her?"

"Do you feel helpless, Colin?"

"What happened to her?" he shouts.

"She fell and they stitched her forehead." He can shout all he wants.

"Why didn't you call me?"

"Because you're not her father, you're nobody to her." I look at the girl lying on the bed. "You were supposed to be the one who protects her, but you couldn't even comfort her, you wouldn't know how."

"Then let me change that," he bursts out, but he can't penetrate my armor. I hear him, but push him away.

"What for? So you'll hurt her like you hurt me?"

"Elizabeth, please."

"I was sitting in the examination room and the doctor asked if I wanted to call someone and without thinking I said no. We got used to being alone, only me and her. My mother brought me here and we didn't miss you." I turn the knife in his heart.

"Don't do that," he whispers.

"I hate you!" I cry loudly. "And I'm hurting. I've been hurting for years. I'm tired, I'm twenty-six, and I'm tired, it's not fair."

"Let me in, let me be in her life. Don't take it away from her, she needs a father."

"I needed a husband," I whisper.

"Elizabeth . . ." He seemed about to say something, but cut himself off. My eyes burn and I wipe the tears with my palm as Vivian moves in the bed, sighing quietly.

"I have to go. Good bye, Colin." I hang up without letting him add a word, put the phone back in my bag and lay my head on the bed beside Viv. Please don't let her hurt her when she wakes. I'll solve the rest, one way or another.

"ELIZABETH!" The scream coming from the hallway makes my body hysterical and I glance at Vivian who is still asleep. "Elizabeth Heart!"

My mother, sitting on the chair next to me, tries to stop me, but I shake her off and jump to the door.

"Elizabeth!" Colin roars, and I hear the commotion growing around him.

"What are you doing here?" I glare at the puffed-up guy standing, panting in a tailored white button-down shirt and black trousers, giving him a threatening look. The two nurses standing behind him seem helpless against his size, especially with his sleeves folded in a way that exposes his tattooed, enormous arms.

"Are you kidding me?" he fires back. "Did you really think I'd sit at home with my daughter in the hospital?"

"Lower your voice," I strain between clenched teeth, staring at him with a look that could kill. "She doesn't know about you."

"And if you want it to stay that way, over the next few minutes you'll update me on her condition. Starting now." He dares to throw an unspoken threat into the air.

"Do you think that's what I need right now, to deal with you?" I turn my hand to him with contempt. My mother comes out of the room and puts her hand on my shoulder, but I shake her off again. He thinks I'll let him get close to Vivian? I glance over my shoulder at my mother, who is staring wide-eyed at the new Colin standing in front of her.

Yes, Mom, he's changed.

"Don't mind him," I respond scornfully to her catatonic state, "he has time to spend in the gym. Money, too, don't you, Colin?"

"Elizabeth," Colin's jaw locks, his nostrils flaring. "Start talking."

"Remind me who you are?" I clasp my arms over my chest. Now I'll give him a taste, the power is mine.

"Mrs. Heart," Dr. Diaz comes out of the room next to ours, quickly realizing that he has a problem in the middle of the emergency room. He glances between Colin and me.

"Don't interfere." Colin stands his ground.

"And who are you?" Our doctor doesn't retreat, he doesn't seem alarmed by the size of my ex.

"He's nobody," I shoot an arrow straight into Colin's gut, which must be turning over now.

"I'm Vivian's father."

"And where exactly is that written?" I don't stop myself. He is about to find out there's a heavy price for his disappearance.

"Elizabeth," his voice sounds more and more threatening.

"I'm sorry, were you going to say something?" Our eyes lock, and his blue eyes are burning.

"Excuse me, Mr . . ." Dr. Diaz steps in my direction and stands beside me in a protective posture.

"Young." The doctor's movement in my direction seemed to raise Colin's nerve threshold to a new level.

"Mr. Young, are you the legal guardian of Vivian?" The wonderful Dr. Diaz isn't stupid, and he knows his work, thank God.

"He's not," I reply confidently.

"You're playing with fire." Colin gives me a warning finger.

"I don't think so," I shrug. "Are you leaving alone or should we call for security?"

"Lizzie!" my mother cries out. I guess the beefed up guy has more influence on her than me. She doesn't want to find out what will happen if he decides to use his muscles. I, on the other hand, am not afraid at all.

"Don't interfere!" I don't take my gaze off Colin.

"Maybe you should listen to your mother," Colin makes another futile attempt to get something from me.

"The days when you tell me what to do are gone," I sneer at him. "Are you leaving or should the good doctor call for someone to escort you out?"

"Mr. Young," Dr. Diaz interjects again, "I suggest you two solve this later. I have patients to take care of. Vivian is one of them and I'm sure you want her to get my full attention."

"This is far from over." Colin turns his finger again.

"Whatever," I wave him off. He gives me one last look, turns his massive back on us and walks agitatedly down the hall, slamming the wall hard on his way out.

Suddenly I can't breathe. The adrenaline evaporates at once. I fall to my knees, my strength gone. Dr. Diaz quickly puts his hand on my shoulder, presses his fingers on it, while I'm struggling for the next breath. What will Colin do now?

LATER, in the house, I leave the bedroom door open a little so I can hear Vivian and sit down at the dining table in front of the cup of coffee Mom made me. Completely shaken by everything that happened, I sip and confess. "I called him when she was out."

"That's how he knew where you were."

"Yes," I lower my head. "And I hate who I've become. I called him to hurt him."

"You were upset."

"Don't make excuses for me." I know I was upset, and still I loathe what's been coming out of me in recent weeks. It's not me, that's not how I was raised and not who I want to be. What happened today, the way I responded and the terrible phone call I made, reveal aspects of me I don't like.

My daughter has a father. I can hate him 'till tomorrow, and that fact won't change. I have to start internalizing it, before I become a bitter monster and lose whoever I am in this storm.

"Elizabeth," my mother puts her hand on my forearm. "What do you want?"

"I have no idea," I shake my head.

"To punish him?"

"Sometimes. Does it make me a terrible person that I want to punish him for what he did to me?"

"Even if Viv will be the one to pay the price?" she challenges me.

"I want the life he promised me," my voice cracks."

"You can't have it. What you can have is a chance, a chance

that your child will have a father, a chance that he will stay, a chance that he will be a good dad."

"A risk," I correct her.

"Take it. You won't forgive yourself if you chase him away."

"If he hurts her he's dead," I counter. "He won't hurt you unless you let him."

"I was talking about Viv." I raise my head and stare at my mom.

"And I was talking about you." She doesn't fold in front of my penetrating gaze. "I may be old, but I'm not stupid. I'm your mother, and I know you. You're afraid to let him get close."

"Don't be ridiculous," I snort. "I hate him."

"There's a thin line . . . your history haunts you."

"Bullshit." She won't sell me that cliché about the thin line between love and hate. I know what I feel.

"Give me the name of one guy who took his place in the last four years, and I'll leave the subject." She insists on proving her stupid point.

I raise my hand in a dismissive gesture, "Who had time? I wasn't free to have a relationship, and you know it."

"I was talking about your bed."

"I have a four year old in my bedroom." What does she think I can do there?

"Ever heard of a babysitter?" she rolls her eyes. "You had one man. One. Deep down you waited for him."

"You should see a doctor," I dismiss her. I didn't wait for anyone. At first, maybe. In the months after Vivian was born, sure. I thought he'd come back, but it was a long time ago, and I've learned not to wait any longer and live my life. If I had no one else, it's because...

"When you stop lying to yourself, you can let him come closer." My mother stands up and then leans over and kisses my head. "Call if you need me."

I put my hands on the table and lower my head on them,

closing my eyes. It's so much easier to look in from the outside and judge. Easier to give advice when it's not your life that's about to change.

COLIN YOUNG: I hope you have a good lawyer.

AN INCOMING MESSAGE beeps at ten-thirty, as I sit next to Vivian and watch her sleep. I walk quietly out of the bedroom, pour myself a glass of wine and fiddle with the phone between my fingers.

I didn't really believe I'd startled him, but now I'm about to find out the price of the war. I sit down on the couch and dial in an attempt to soothe my heartbeat.

"Colin?" I ask, when I think he answers the call without saying a word.

"How can I help you?" His voice is cold and distant.

"Listen—"

"You listen now," he says angrily. "You can be as angry as you want, but once you say she ain't my daughter—"

"That's not what I said," I defend myself without success.

"That's exactly what you said!" he raises his voice in a roar.

"You surprised me, from the moment you came back, all you do is surprise me. You sat in your car, in front of my parent's house... do you know what would have happened if my dad had seen you?"

"I don't give a shit about your father," he replies angrily.

"I do. He's Vivian's grandfather, you can't just show up everywhere."

"If you'd meet me, I wouldn't have to *show up*," he emphasizes the words.

"Colin, please," I sigh in frustration.

"Do you want to give me your lawyer's phone number or

make the effort and meet me?"

His request makes my heart drop and find a place somewhere at my feet. Can I even sit down and talk to him? How terrible would it be? How painful? Sitting in front of the guy who abandoned me and didn't even bother to apologize?

"Are you there?"

"I'm here," I whisper.

"How's Vivian doing?" His voice loses some of the toughness he shows me. I can tell him, it's probably better than a letter from his lawyer. If we get into a legal battle, all the money he gave me will be lost. Viv's future will go to hell, and I want to keep the money. God only knows when I'll need it. "She slept for most of the afternoon," I update him quietly. "I guess she'll be okay tomorrow."

"What did the doctor say?"

"The usual instructions, not to wet the seams in the first twenty-four hours, to keep her from going wild. That's not a problem."

"She's four and a half." He doubts my words.

"She's not too naughty, she's a good girl." And if you'd stayed, you'd know that. You would know how wonderful she is, smart, stubborn, and how loved she is.

"She's your daughter." He knows the stories about my childhood. I was a geek from the day I was born.

"She looks like you. A small, accurate copy of you." He already knows that. He discovered it alone when he sat in the car and watched us. What if that wasn't the first time? What if he's been following us for weeks, months? Maybe he's even been photographing me, collecting information for the law-suit he's going to bring down on me. If he tries to portray me as an incompetent mother, I'll kill him.

"Does that make you angry?" Colin's hesitant voice forces me to put aside for a moment the growing anxiety in my heart. "When you look at her?"

"No. She's not at fault." It's just hard on things, that's all.

"Do you think you can send me a picture of her?" His request makes me miss another beat.

If he's serious, he'll find a way, and that won't be your way. My mother's words echo in my head. If he wants to see her picture, he will find the way to get one. At least this way I'll have some control over the matter.

"Hold on," I move the phone from my ear, go into the pictures gallery and choose one: Vivian playing in the sandbox, looking at the camera and smiling broadly. Her hair shines in the sun and her blue eyes fill the screen. I send the picture and return to the conversation.

"Colin?" I ask after a few seconds of silence.

"I'm here," he answers. I think he put the conversation on speaker, probably staring at the picture.

"She's stunning, isn't she?"

"Yes," he mumbles hoarsely.

"You killed me, Colin. Piece by piece. If I had not been pregnant, I wouldn't have survived it."

"I am asking again, meet me." Again his voice stabilizes, increasing the distance between us.

"I need to stay with Vivian at home tomorrow. I can meet you Thursday at four. I can ask my mother to pick up Viv so we'll have time."

"Where?" he asks immediately.

"There's a place, not far from my work, a small café. We can sit there quietly."

"I'll be there, send me the address."

"I need to check on Vivian."

"I'll see you on Thursday."

"Good night, Colin."

"Good night, Elizabeth." He hangs up the call, I lean back and sip my wine. Did I just make the biggest mistake of my life?

CHAPTER EIGHT

"*Don't touch me!*" *Colin stands in my bedroom, his eyes darting, shirt torn and sweaty. "And don't look at me with your pitying looks!"*

My legs tremble and my heart goes wild. I stand helpless facing something that feels overwhelming, way too big for me to handle.

"Let me help you."

"You can't help me!" he bursts out.

"You can sleep here tonight," I suggest without thinking, not sure the idea will be welcomed by my parents.

"That's the best solution you could come up with?" The scorn in his voice is jarring.

"If you want to unleash your anger on me, go ahead!" I shoot back. "But I'm not the one who beats you, not the one who did this to you, I'm the one who loves you!"

I freeze, taking in what I said. I've been hiding it from him for six months, pretending that I'm only interested in helping him with school, that I'm excited to see him succeed. For six months I have been silent, and now the truth stands between us.

"No one can love me." He stares at me with contempt. "I know what

you really think—poor Colin, it's not enough that he's stupid, he's letting his father beat the crap out of him, too."

"I don't think you're stupid," I murmur awkwardly.

"No, you're stupid, if you think you love me."

"I'm smarter than you'll ever be, and I'm sorry if you think my love makes me stupid." The choking in my throat grows. If you know what's good for you, you won't cry in front of him.

"What do you know about love?"

"Enough," I whisper. "Enough for both of us."

"You're embarrassing yourself," he mumbles.

"I am willing to embarrass myself if it means not hiding anymore. You can accept my suggestion to sleep here or go. Your choice."

"You don't love me." He doesn't take his eyes off me.

"Think what you want."

"You don't love me."

"Colin . . ." I whisper in embarrassment. Why doesn't he believe me?

"You don't love me!"

"I do!" I shout at him with all my might, and before I understand what is happening, he clings to me, his hands in my hair, his mouth covering my mouth and his tongue meeting mine. I can't breathe, and I'm willing to never breathe again, if it means he won't stop. I don't want him to stop kissing me. Ever.

I can do this.

Wiping the dust off one of the store shelves, I'm convincing myself everything will be all right. I'll sit in the cafe opposite the man who was supposed to be my husband and act like a grown woman.

After all, if the only reason I'm meeting him is to throw more accusations his way, what's the point? I could just as well cancel now. No, I have to see him and decide whether to let him get close to my daughter or fight him with everything I have.

. . .

YOU HAVE NOTHING.

IT'S JUST another thing I hate about him—this insecurity, which never leaves. All that happened in the four years we were together was a show. The friends who surrounded us were never my friends. They were his party and disappeared on the day Colin disappeared. What do football players and the "Library Geek" have in common, right? It must have not surprised them that he left. They must have asked themselves behind our backs, when will it end and what does he do with her?

Hell, why am I thinking about it now? I have to relax and meet him, and get it over with. That's all.

AT THE ENTRANCE to the little cafe I've chosen, I take a deep breath and glare at my clothes. How appropriate. I'm still the girl in jeans, t-shirt and sneakers.

I OPEN the door and go inside, the wonderful smell of fresh coffee engulfs the place. Looking around, my heart skips a beat when I recognize the pair of familiar blue eyes fixed on me. Colin, dressed in a black polo shirt that's tight on his huge arms, doesn't take his eyes off me. I manage to make my legs move toward the table. His enormous body rises, and then freezes.

Yes, Colin, I'm not really in the mood for a hug.

"Elizabeth," he mumbles with a touch of discomfort.

"Hello, Colin," I reply coldly, sitting down on the creaking metal chair. Lifting the menu like a barrier between us, I prevent myself from looking at him for a few seconds, at least until I gather my thoughts.

He's huge. Seriously, I don't want to think about it, but every muscle in his body looks sculpted. It's the last thing I needed. If only he had come back with a massive beer belly and balding hair. No, he had to look like this, like a guy no woman refuses.

"Do you have a girlfriend?" I'm experiencing a total failure between my brain and mouth, placing the menu on the table and staring hard at the blond who looks stunned.

"No," he replies immediately. "Not right now."

"Not right now," I reply contemptuously and cross my armsover my chest defensively. What kind of answer is that? Do you have a girlfriend or don't you? What do you mean, *not right now*? Are you looking for one?

"Is that what you wanted to know?" he asks indifferently.

"Just curious, not that it's any of my business," I shrug.

Excellent, keep that cool and you'll be fine.

"And you?" He gives me a question of his own.

"Boyfriend?" I snort. "Who has time?"

"I'm sure you could find the time," he replies defiantly.

"I suffer from a slight trust issue when it comes to men." I hit one under his belt. Well, so much for keeping cool.

Our waitress comes up behind me and asks what we'll drink. I order tea and Colin asks for a short espresso. She disappears as quickly as she came and leaves us to continue the battle.

"So, what's the story with the gym?" I take another look at his arms.

"It started as something that helped me release stress and gradually became serious."

"Very serious."

"Yes, very serious," He nods.

"And the clothes?" I insist on understanding where the dramatic change has come from.

"You came to talk about my wardrobe?" He shifts, looking restless.

"What happened to the jeans and t-shirts you always liked?"

"I still like 'em," It seems that he doesn't like the topic of conversation. "This is what I wear to work."

"I didn't know I fall into the 'work' category," I mutter.

"I didn't have time to change. I'll throw something comfortable on when I get home."

"Are you not comfortable in that?" I interrupt his sentence unintentionally.

"I'm comfortable with these clothes, and I'm also comfortable with the sweatpants I wear to the gym, and I'm fine with jeans and a t-shirt, too. I don't understand why we're discussing this."

"I'm just trying to figure out who you are," I reply without getting confused.

"Do you think my clothes will give you the answer?" his tone is borderline mocking.

"At least one thing hasn't changed," I reply. "You still like to laugh at me."

"I apologize if I offended you." His words, and the tone in which they are spoken, don't convince me. He doesn't care if I'm hurt or not.

"Is that the only thing you'll apologize for?" I drop the bomb without preparation and my body tenses.

"What am I supposed to apologize for?" His penetrating gaze turns my guts.

"Are you serious?" I open my eyes wide.

"What apology are you waiting for?" He doesn't fold, his indifference taking me out of my mind.

"You left me on our wedding day, you were not there when I had our child or when she celebrated her birthdays, or every time she was ill and I had to be absent from work, because you're a coward, irresponsible and selfish. You can choose what to apologize for, the list is long."

"Will it make you feel better about yourself?" His answer leaves me stunned.

"You're really not going to ask for my forgiveness?"

"Will it make you feel better?" He repeats his question, "Will it change the situation?"

"No." I shake my head without taking my eyes off him, "I'll still hate you every minute I'm awake."

"Exactly what I thought," he replies directly.

"Why did you come back?" I give up trying to look for something else to talk about. We should get to the core of it or we'll sit here all night.

"You know why." He leans back and runs a hand through his hair.

"Why now?" I make it difficult.

"The time was right," he answers vaguely.

"The time was right?" I snort.

"Elizabeth," he loses patience, "you asked a question and got an answer, the time was right. We can sit here till midnight or talk about our daughter, who I want to meet."

"She doesn't know who you are."

"I want to change that."

"It's not that simple."

"I didn't say it was." His phone rings. Colin picks it up, glances at the screen and hurries to silence it, something in his face tenses. Something in his eyes turns somber and makes me shudder.

"You can answer," I motion my head at the phone vibrating between us.

"No," he answers in a cold, distant tone. "I'm here to talk about Vivian."

"I can't invite you to the house and tell her Daddy's back, not without preparation." I sniff nervously. "Not to mention the fact that my father wants to kill you."

"Your father never liked me," his tone is full of resentment. "I've never been good enough for you."

"You know something," my voice shakes with pain, "I was the only one that mattered, and I thought you were the best thing that ever happened to me. How could you do that to me?"

"It's complicated," he answers with another response that explains nothing.

"You are not serious," I laugh at him. "Complicated, Colin? Do you really think I'm an idiot? Your evading instead of answering the tough questions."

"I can't give you better answers!" he bursts out, and for a moment his blanket of indifference unravels and gives me a glimpse into his eyes, burning in frustration. That look I know, it hasn't changed.

"Where did you go? Where did you disappear to as if the earth swallowed you?"

"To Afghanistan," he mutters quietly. The words that come out of his mouth freeze my blood, and my face pales.

"You went *where*?" I whisper in shock. "What did you do in—"

"I enlisted." His gaze doesn't waver from me, as if waiting for my reaction. But it doesn't come. I sit opposite him in shock.

"Please say something," he whispers after the seconds pass silently over us.

"You enlisted," I manage to answer.

"Yes, I didn't have anywhere to sleep or anything to eat, I barely had money. It looked like a good solution."

"So you enlisted." I repeat the words again. He was a soldier, in Afghanistan. The pressure in my chest increases. Our waitress returns with our drinks, placing them on the table. I don't touch my tea and Colin doesn't touch his coffee.

"Elizabeth," he doesn't take his eyes off me.

"I don't know what to say." I swallow to overcome the lump in my throat. "I don't know what to think, I feel like I don't know anything about you."

"You know all that matters. I'm here, and we have a daughter, and I love her."

"You don't know anything about love," I raise my hand in front of him, "people who love don't disappear to Afghanistan."

"Elizabeth . . ."

"I can't do this." I push my chair, which grinds loudly. "I can't."

"We didn't talk about Vivian," he tries to stop me.

"You can't cram five years into one conversation."

"How long do you need?"

"As long as it will take." I grab my bag, and leave the cafe. My footsteps pound the concrete and I fill my lungs with air as soon as I reach the corner of the street. Breathe. Slowly. You know what to do. Breathe.

MY EYES ARE RUNNING and I struggle to remember where I parked the car. I stumble over the street, my thoughts running through my head. Afghanistan. I can barely imagine it, Colin in uniform, dusty, lying on a field bed in a desert tent. What happened to him there?

I manage to calm my pulse only slightly, reach my Toyota, open the door with trembling hands and step into it, clutching the steering wheel. He was so desperate that he thought the only solution was to go to war? How could I not see it? Blind. Just as I didn't see that he didn't love me.

The tears run down my cheeks, I drop my head to the wheel and let them come. He didn't say a word. Not when he got down on one knee that afternoon in the park, blushing like he never blushed before and said I was his everything. Not when I lay beside him in bed and I raised the pregnancy test in front of him, and in response he covered my face with kisses. Not when he pulled me into his chest on the morning of our wedding day, in our little bedroom, and whispered in my ear the last words I would hear from him for five years. *If only I could make you as happy as you do me.*

I hate him, the shattered dream, the lies and everything he took from me. I weep for the life that was stolen from me and the man I trusted, who enlisted and didn't look back. I've never loved anyone like I loved him, and I've never hated anyone more.

. . .

MY PHONE RINGS at nine thirty in the evening, lying on the sofa in front of the TV. I picked Vivian up from my mother's house late, after taking the time to relax and suppress the signs of crying from my face. I didn't say a word about the meeting with Colin. My mother thought I had to stay at work late. Well, that's what I told her.

"Colin," I reply anxiously, what else will he tell me? Where else has he spent the last five years?

"I'm sorry I dropped it on you like that."

"It's not important." I stare at the ceiling.

"It's very important, I was not going to hurt you."

"You didn't hurt me . . ."

"We both know it's not true," he interrupts me, before I go on.

"How many years did you serve?"

In the last few hours I tried not to think about it, about him in the desert. How terrible was that? How dangerous and lonely?

"Three, and after that I lived in LA, first with a friend from the army and then alone."

"Have you dated anyone?" The dumb question still preoccupies me, as if that's what is important.

"No one serious," he answers evenly. "I always knew that the moment would come when I would leave everything and come back here, and I didn't want to leave anyone behind."

"Except me," I say in frustration.

"I was afraid you'd met someone," he confesses, and my heart misses a beat.

"Why?" He's the one who left, so what does he care who I go out with?

"Because I'm selfish. I didn't want Vivian to have another father." He moans, "God, I'm a shit person."

"You're not," I reply out of habit. That's how it was when we were young.

You're not stupid, Colin.

You are not impervious.

I love you . . .

Damn those memories!

"Where do you live?" I continue to investigate.

"I have a house, not far from Richmond Park." I don't want to think of Richmond Park, where he proposed to me.

"Great area." I wish I could afford to live there. The area is quiet and well maintained, and the playgrounds are wonderful. But all the neighborhoods there are terribly expensive, at least by my miserable standards.

"I like the location. Did you know they cleared the lake of the swans?"

"I had no idea," I reply quietly. "I don't really go there."

"Dormont Park is closer to you."

"Listen . . ." I panic at once. He knows I didn't move and knows the address and the house.

"I'm not going to show up uninvited."

"That's not what I meant," I lie.

"It is, and I can understand."

"Sorry," I hasten to apologize.

"You've changed," he mutters quietly.

I keep silent and try not to think how much I have changed. I went up two sizes in my clothes and got some scars, the ones you see and the ones that you don't. You should have married one of your cheerleaders, Colin.

"Elizabeth?" he asks quietly in a confused voice.

"You didn't really think I'd stay twenty-one forever, did you?" I mutter through my own screen of pain.

"You scare easily."

"Ever since she was born," I confess. I don't know if it's the fatigue of the day I've been through or the last few weeks, but tonight I don't have the strength to fight anymore. I don't have the strength to lie and pretend.

"Because you were alone?" He continues on the same line.

"I don't know, it could be. I might have become scared, even if you were here."

"Maybe," he mumbles again.

"She's not like me, you know?"

"No?"

"She's fearless."

"She's four and a half."

"It bothered me for a long time that I inherited these anxieties."

"No one judges you."

"You're so wrong." I take a deep breath. "Everyone judges me, my motherhood, my choices, my decisions." Sometimes it seems to me that the whole world stands by and gives me a score. Why didn't I go back to my parents' house? Why did I choose to live alone? Why did he leave me?

"No one has the right to judge your motherhood," he whispers.

"It was not supposed to be this way." I struggle with the suffocation in my throat.

"I know. Elizabeth, please let me see her," he asks again. "I don't want to go to court, I just want to know my daughter."

"You can come tomorrow at five. Stay for dinner." In a moment of weakness and fatigue, I surrender to him, to the guy who broke my heart and fled to the desert. "I'll tell Viv you're a friend of mine, that's all I can offer right now."

"Thank you." His answer comes immediately.

"I'll see you tomorrow, at five." I close my eyes.

"I'll be there," he promises, and I pray that he won't disappoint me again or disappear.

CHAPTER NINE

*T*he sweaty boy standing, panting on our doorstep, makes my breath disappear. An apologetic smile is smeared on his face, as if he's embarrassed.

"Colin," I manage to stammer.

"Sorry, practice went on and on. You said your time is valuable, and I didn't want to be late." He wipes the sweat off his forehead. I think he ran all the way from school.

All this just to be on time?

"I'm sorry, I shouldn't have turned up like this, I can go . . ." He doesn't even complete the sentence before I interrupt him sharply.

"No." My cheeks redden, "Come in, it's fine." It's not really fine. His smell is the last thing I need right now. Really, how am I supposed to concentrate?

"Are you sure?" he frowns.

"Yes. My parents aren't home, do you want to shower?"

My question makes his eyebrow rise mischievously, which makes me force my legs together. A pleasant feeling spreads between my thighs, and I swallow thinking that at this rate, not only my panties will get wet. How embarrassing would that be?

"I didn't mean that . . ." I falter, suspecting that this is exactly what *he wants to happen. "Not you and I together . . . just . . . you know . . . if you want . . ." What I want is to stop acting like someone whose brain is fried!*

"Sure?" he asks arrogantly as he walks past me and rubs his shoulder with mine. If he forgets his shirt in my room, I'll smell it all night. Don't think about that now!

"School work, Colin, that's why you're here, don't get ideas into your head." I manage to raise some confidence.

"You're the one who offered." He laughs, pulls his shirt over his head and throws it at me. I catch it awkwardly.

"I didn't . . ." I'm not going to survive this evening.

"Relax," he sneaks a glance at me, "I don't mess with virgins."

My heart falls, and I think even Colin heard the crash.

"And I don't . . . mess with . . ." The words refuse to come.

"With?" He teases me, again. It's become an obscene habit.

"With male whores." My hand leaps to my mouth before I say anything else.

He freezes, then turns slowly with a look that scares me for a moment.

"Is that what I am?" he asks in a low, low voice.

"I'm sorry," I say through the barrier made by my fingers.

"Don't be sorry." He winks. "That's exactly what I am, and you don't get any. Now where's the shower?"

He turns his back again, and with arrogant steps, goes up the stairs to the second floor.

I can't believe I said that, and I can't believe he's the guy I'm in love with.

THE SIGN on the furniture store door is gone.

My heart drops as I take in the meaning behind it's disappearance.

I'm going to be unemployed.

Henry is leaning against the counter, his eyes betraying his worry. He doesn't like change and we are both facing a rather large one.

"We're history." I toss the bag at his side and take out the shopping list I've started to do. I have no intention of letting Colin come into my house and think my cabinets and refrigerator are empty. Not that they are empty, not at all, but I don't want to take the risk.

"Cooking?" Henry glances at the ever-growing list.

"I'm hosting," I concede.

"A battalion of the army?" he mumbles, but his remark shrinks my chest. Not a battalion, just one soldier. It's going to kill me. Thank God for the twenty-five thousand dollars that went into my account.

"I'm making dinner and not sure what to cook." So I'm going to buy everything I can think of.

"You invited him, didn't you?" Henry exposes me quite easily.

"Yes." I feel the lump forming in my throat. "Who else can I invite over?"

"Anyone would be lucky if you were to host them," he tries to cheer me up. "You're smart and beautiful."

"You forgot single-mom living in a two-room bungalow," I grumble. So I'm smart, wow, like it did me any good. I'm not pretty, and I have an ugly scar on my stomach that would probably scare any guy who sees it, let alone my other complicated issues.

"Elizabeth, Henry." Mr. Blunt's voice surprises us both. Where did he sneak up from?

"Mr. Blunt," I answer with concern.

"I wanted to let you know that the new owner will be moving in in the next few weeks."

Great. Just what I needed today, when my ex is coming to dinner.

"We'll have to pack the furniture, I hope I can count on you."

He stares at me disapprovingly. I've been missing a lot of

work this month, and I know that if I miss anymore, Mr. Blunt won't accept it with understanding.

"You can count on us," I answer firmly.

"Happy to hear, you can start on Monday. Whatever you need is in the storage."

I am not eager to hear that we are about to spend the next week wrapping all the pictures, mirrors and scribbles that fill the place.

"Everything will be ready for when the trucks arrive." I don't think Mr. Blunt will be taking the furniture in his car.

"I'll let you know as soon as I know." He glances around his beloved store, which is about to close, turns his back on us and walks away to the office.

"Do you still think Danielle Cole is the girl you want to be with?" I grumble to Henry, who seems desperate about the situation.

"Not so much," he mumbles.

"I bet not." I go back to my shopping list. To hell with Danielle Cole, and to hell with this dinner that is going to drive me crazy.

I DRUM my fingers nervously on the steering wheel. In the backseat, Vivian is listening to music on my cellphone, giving me a few minutes of silence to gather my thoughts. The stitches on her forehead are healing nicely, and now she is about to meet . . . Maybe I should cancel, maybe it was a bad idea from the start. What was I thinking when I invited him to come, and what am I supposed to say to my daughter?

Nothing. I shouldn't tell her anything. Yet.

I'm going to be out of work if I don't find something fast. But I am so limited in my hours, not many places hire single moms. How many days have I missed in the last few weeks? Four? Fuck, it'll take revenge on my salary.

You don't depend on that now, you have money, and Colin will pay.

I scold myself immediately. I'm not going to depend on him, and the money he gave me has to go to a savings account for Vivian's college. At least she will make something of herself, if she doesn't make the mistakes I made myself.

I park the car in front of the house, turn off the engine and release my seatbelt.

"We're here," I turn to look at Viv.

"Who's that?" She scrunches her eyebrows, her gaze toward the house.

"Who's who?" I turn my head and freeze. Why was he early?

"Ah, this is Mom's friend, I invited him to dinner." My heart starts beating faster. Colin stands in front of us, his hands in his jeans pockets, the sleeves of his t-shirt clinging to his muscular arms."He's huge!" Vivian laughs.

"Do you think?" I don't take my eyes off him.

"You never invite your friends."

That's because I have no friends. Except for Henry, and he doesn't really count.

"Well now I have. I thought it would be nice." I stare at the guy who smiles at us from the porch, shifting uncomfortably.

"Will you behave?" I turn back to Vivian and try hard to hide the panic attack I'm about to get. What was I thinking? What the hell was I thinking?

"I need to pee!" Viv releases her belt, takes out the earphones, leaves the phone on the backseat and opens the door.

Oh my God. It's really happening. He is really going to meet her.

She leaps out of the car and runs toward the house.

"Viv!" I call as I pull out the keys, rush to open the car door and run after her. "The house is locked!"

"I need to pee!" she jumps in place. I run to the door, open it, and let her inside. Slowly, I turn to Colin, who stands stunned.

"You're early," I mutter, his eyes still looking into the house. "Colin?"

"That's . . ." He can't speak.

"Vivian."

"She's beautiful." He seems hypnotized. She looks like him, and he's not ugly. He's as far from ugly as possible, and if I used to think he looked good, now he's plain hot. God, what is with me? And why did he have to have those tattoos that look perfect on his arms?

"I have to take the groceries out of the car." I clear my head of my thoughts, walk past Colin, open the trunk, and begin to take out the bags.

"Let me help you." He emerges from behind me and his proximity makes me jump. His smell is different and, as for his size, I've always felt tiny beside him, but now it's ridiculous.

"I've got this." I try to breathe and hope he'll move away.

"I'm sure." He ignores me and leans into the trunk next to me, grabbing the bags. "To the kitchen?"

"Yes, please." I nod, he straightens up above me, turns his back and walks to the house. I pick up my cellphone, lock the car, and join him in the kitchen. He places the bags on the small marble counter and starts to inspect the place.

"I want to play in the yard." Vivian returns from the bathroom, and Colin doesn't take his eyes off her. Here it comes.

"Do you want to say hello to Colin?" My voice is shaking like a leaf.

"Hey," she smiles at him. I see his body tensing, shifting his weight from foot to foot.

"Hey," he answers softly. "I'm Colin."

"I'm Vivian. My father's name is Colin, too."

In one second I feel like a complete idiot. I should have thought about it, or come up with some other name for Colin, or have just activated my dead brain cells in some way!

My heart is racing. Thank God she had not seen any pictures

of him. Thank God they are hidden well. I hated myself when I lied to her and said we had no picture of him, I didn't want her to look at them again and again. I hated myself then, but I'm relieved now.

"I have stitches." She gently pulls her hair back and shows him her forehead.

"I see. Why did you need stitches?" he pretends not to know.

"I fell, and the doctor gave me juice and made me sleepy. He was nice."

"Yes?" Colin's voice fails for a moment.

"Very nice, wasn't he, Mom?" She turns her head to me quickly.

"Very nice." How did she notice? Dr. Diaz was professional and sensitive and cared not only for Vivian. He also took care of my wellbeing, which earned him a few more points.

"Nice, huh?" Colin asks intently. I guess he's not a big fan of the doctor after their encounter.

"Very professional," I wave off his inappropriate question.

"He looks like Flynn," Vivian rejoices. "Can I go out now?"

"Yes, I'll open the door for you." I walk over to the glass door in the living room wall and send the little monster out. What now?

"Do you want to listen to music?" I ask trying to change the subject.

"No." His eyes remain on me.

Dinner won't prepare itself, you know?

"So, who is Flynn?" Colin is intrigued.

"Flynn?" I rummage through my memory. "Oh, a character from one of the movies she loves."

"What movie?" He scrunches his eyebrows.

"Tangled," I reply.

"Is that her favorite movie?" he continues to investigate. His daughter is four and a half, and he has no idea what movies she likes.

"It was. At the moment, it's Frozen." If Disney doesn't release something new soon that my daughter will love, I'll go crazy. How many times can one hear the same songs?

"Does she like to play outside?"

"Yes," I manage to free my legs from their momentary paralysis and go arrange the groceries in the cupboards. "She also likes to play with her dolls, watch TV and bake with me."

"And she's okay outside, alone?" He looks at the glass door.

"I fenced the yard, there's nowhere she can go." I open the refrigerator and put in the groceries. "Would you like something to drink?"

"Coffee, thank you." He goes back to inspecting the house. I wonder if he is filled with memories, if his head throws him into those days, when this place was his home.

"Listen, Colin . . ." I put the kettle on and turn to him.

"Do you want to move?"

"Move where?" His question confuses me.

"To a bigger house."

"Okay," I take a deep breath. "Let's set some rules, so we can get through the evening safely."

I lean back against the marble counter and cross my arms on my chest.

"Like old times," he mumbles.

"Don't go there, Colin. I'm not looking for a walk down memory lane." I've been walking there for weeks, and it isn't nice, believe me. "And as for the rules, you're not here to fix anything, you're here to meet Vivian and get to know her. I didn't invite you over so that you'd take one look at the place and think it was uninhabitable."

He frowns. "That's not what—"

"That's what your question implied. So I'll spare you the trouble. Vivian sleeps with me in the one bedroom, the shower's dripping, the television breaks down, the kitchen sink sometimes gets clogged, and my car lives on borrowed time. And you know something, it's really okay, so don't come in here with your money, which God only knows where you got it from, and try to bribe me."

"I wasn't bribing you," his voice turns serious. "And I didn't say that the house was not habitable. I asked if you wanted to move to a bigger house, because that was our plan, and I can afford it."

"And you want to help," I finish his sentence scornfully.

"I'm taking responsibility."

"Too late for that, Colin." I hug myself harder.

"I hope not." He runs his hand through his hair and pulls it back. Hell, every move he makes seems familiar. I know how tense he could be, how he moved and how his eyes would follow me. In perfect timing, Vivian comes running and saves us from the embarrassing silence.

"Do you want to tell me how your day was?" I take a deep breath as she climbs onto a chair and sits down at the table. I turn my back on her and make chocolate milk for her and coffee for Colin and me—God knows I need it.

"Mrs. Robbins reminded me to be careful," she says in her squeaky voice. "And not to go on the slide, and watch it when I wash my face."

"I'm happy to hear that."

"And Daryl said my brain will pour out," she grumbles.

"I think I should have a talk with Daryl's mother," I mumble quietly.

"Who's Daryl?" Colin's bass voice is inquiring.

"He's my best friend," she chirps. "He knows everything."

"Really?" I hear a creaking chair. Glancing back, my body tenses as Colin sits down beside his perfect duplication.

"He's really smart and he's going to be an astromount," she miss-pronounses the word as she always does. The smile on Colin's face makes them both shine. I swallow, when a forgotten sensation makes it's way to parts of my body that have been in a coma for years.

You're not serious!

"Daryl will be lucky if he graduates from high school," I mutter to myself again, taking the milk out of the fridge.

"And this astromount is your friend?" Colin follows suit with the word.

"Yes, I'm going to marry him."

"We'll see about that." I put the coffee on the table. We do not mention weddings in this house, certainly not now.

"I understand we like Daryl," Colin raises an eyebrow and gives me an amused look.

"Don't encourage her," I say, turning to Viv. "What do you want to do next?"

"Rosie has a birthday, and I want to bake her a cake."

"That's very nice of you," Colin is impressed.

"Rosie is her doll." I lower my head.

"I understand."

"I have to make dinner."

"But I have to celebrate her!" Vivian insists.

"You can take cookies from the jar," I suggest.

"I want four."

"Two," I hold up two fingers.

"Four!" She doesn't give up.

"Two or nothing."

"You're no fun!" she protests firmly.

"How about we go celebrate Rosie's birthday and let your mother prepare dinner?" Colin suggests. I blink my eyes several times just to make sure I'm not dreaming. "What?" he laughs in response to my face.

"You don't know what you've gotten yourself into," I shake my head.

"I'm sure I'll survive," he shrugs. "Where are the cookies?" he winks at me. I should have guessed. The guy was always hooked on cookies—with coffee, without coffee, a cookie on the way, a cookie before bed.

"Trickster," I mumble. "Top shelf, she'll show you."

Before I know what's happening, Colin gets up and picks Vivian up by her waist.

"Lead the way, Captain!" My heart crashes in my chest. That's exactly how it was supposed to be. That's what I imagined, that's what I dreamed of, and that's what he stole from us.

"Higher!" Vivian cries out, and Colin lifts her up without effort. I want to kill him for the ease with which he captures her heart, the smile he puts on her face, which should have always been there.

"Mom, look, I'm an astromount!" she laughs.

"I have to make dinner." I turn my back to them as the choking in my throat increases. Viv takes the cookies out of the jar, puts two on a plate, and all the while she doesn't come down from Colin's hands. They move into the living room and sit on the carpet. I manage to breathe and occupy myself in the kitchen between the glances I sneak their way. It's so easy to come for a few hours and play with the girl and be the good guy.

"How old is Rosie?" Colin is leaned back against the couch.

"Twenty-ten," Viv answers with utter seriousness.

"Wow."

"I know!" she rejoices. "She says you're welcome."

"Thank you."

"You have to wear this." She goes over to the little wooden box and opens it. Now, this is going to be fun. Pulling out a golden crown she places it on Colin's head. "Perfect!"

"So," Colin straightens the crown, "what are we doing at this party?"

"Visiting the beauty salon!" Vivian jumps up. "Mama, can you get your nail-polish, please?"

"Sure, honey." I smile nastily at Colin, who seems to have lost some of his ample confidence. "Use the red, Colin will look great in it."

"I love red," Colin smiles back at me.

"I'm sure," I grumble to him. How's your porridge now, huh?

AN HOUR LATER, Vivian gets up from the dining table and leaves me alone with her father, whom I hate more and more with every passing moment. I made pasta with tomato sauce and pretended I'd forgotten he hates tomatoes. He ate anyway and tried to look brave. He must be sick now.

He spent twenty-five minutes on the carpet with Viv and asked her so many questions, I had trouble keeping up.

Who her friends were, what color she liked best, even what she'd asked for for her birthday. She, of course, mentioned the dress and the trampoline I was not going to buy.

You don't really think you can cram four years into an hour, do you?

"The nail polish suits you," I smile. His fingernails and substantial parts of his fingers are painted bright red, and he doesn't seem to care, which is even more annoying.

Damn him and the lightness he my girl inherited from him!

"Acetone, you know," he raises his hands and pretends to be impressed by his nails. "What I wouldn't give to see you go into the pharmacy and buy the bottle."

"You're jealous because I was invited to Rosie's birthday, and you were not."

"She's twenty ten, who do you think celebrated her twenty ninth birthday?" We sound like two stupid sixteen-year-olds. Very mature, Liz. "We both know that for another cookie you would sell a kidney."

"You're probably right," he shrugs again. I know I'm right, and he has to go.

"I have to shower Viv and put her to bed." I get up from the table and start to clear it.

"I'll wash the dishes," he volunteers immediately and gets up behind me, his phone is ringing again. How much work does he have that people are calling him at all hours of the day?

"YOU DON'T HAVE to do the dishes," I stop him, as he glances at his phone before shoving it back in his pocket. "You must be busy."

I don't want him to stay. The evening was challenging enough and should end now.

"I was hoping we could talk," he answers quietly.

"I'm tired, I'll probably fall asleep next to her." I really don't want to talk.

"Maybe next time," he sounds disappointed.

"Maybe." Life is hard, Colin, and the times when you got everything you wanted are long gone.

"Elizabeth . . ."

"Vivian!" I call, "Say bye to Colin, he's leaving!"

"Bye, Colin." She waves to him from the living room and he smiles at her warmly.

"Bye, Vivian, thanks for the party."

"Tomorrow I'm celebrating Theresa's birthday," she informs him. I almost lose it. He is not going to come every day!

"I'm afraid I can't make it, but give her my love." I breathe a sigh of relief. Thank God, he has a little decency. Like, a drop of it. He turns to me and the smile disappears from his face. "Good night, Elizabeth."

"Bye," I answer in the most indifferent voice I can muster. You came, you met the girl, you can go. He turns his back on me, opens the door, goes out and closes it behind him. Leaving a deceptive silence, and my body tense as a spring. I lean on the sink and try to breathe regularly.

CHAPTER TEN

"**W**e don't have to do that." Colin strokes my red hair, which is spread over the pillow. Lying in my bed, his other hand resting on my stomach.

"Why do I feel like you don't want me?" I sigh in frustration. We've been going out for two months, I'm eighteen, and we haven't done it yet. Maybe he isn't attracted to me? God knows he has been with the hottest girls in school, and possibly some in college.

"Are you telling yourself stories again?" he raises an eyebrow.

"I'm sorry if my insecurity doesn't appeal to you." I sit up and pull my shirt down.

"Baby, we don't have to hurry." He pulls my hand but I shake off his grip.

"Do you have anyone else?" I stare at him angrily. "Is that it? Do you have someone else you fuck after you get out of here with blue balls that need release?"

Wow. Where did that come from? And why the hell won't he sleep with me?

"Do you think I'm cheating on you?" He leaps out of bed, closes the button on his jeans and pulls his T-shirt from the back of the chair.

"I'm looking for an explanation, Colin." My voice is small. "You say you love me, and you had no trouble sleeping with all the other girls, so why not with me?"

"Because I love you!" he glares at me. "It was easy with the others!"

"And it's hard with me?" I ask indignantly.

"You're a virgin," he tugs at his hair.

"Really? I had no idea."

"I don't want to hurt you," he says, closing his eyes, his shoulders drooping, his stance losing it's familiar arrogance.

"Colin," I mutter. "Someone will have to be my first, don't you want to be that someone?"

"What if you bleed?" He shakes his head as if the thought alone shocks him.

"Then I'll know I'm normal." I try to suppress the thought that I'll bleed.

"What if it won't feel good to you?"

"It will be good." I'm not sure who I'm convincing, him or myself.

"How do you know?" He opens his blue eyes, doesn't take them off me. "How do you know it will be good with me?"

"Because I love you and I trust you, and I don't intend to let someone else be the first."

"You're so sure . . ." he mumbles in what seems like insecurity. I think I'm the only one who knows this side of him.

"Make love to me." My eyes shine and my heart thumps wildly. "I'm ready."

He looks at me for another moment, in hesitation, then reaches back and pulls his shirt and throws it to the floor. I lie down and watch him taking off his jeans, then climbing into the bed in his underwear. His lips find mine immediately, and he kisses me and takes my breath away.

I LIE in bed staring at the ceiling. Midnight. Vivian has been asleep for some time now and I'm turning from side to side and finding no rest. What happens now? Where do we go from here? And why of all things am I thinking about our first time?

I have to think about our last morning and the promise he broke. I have to think about the day when he didn't answer my calls, and I made up all those explanations: he must have forgotten it at home, probably forgot to charge it. I have to think about the white dress I tore from myself and the note he left, the hours and days when I thought he would appear and apologize and plead for my forgiveness and explain himself.

But the weeks passed and he had disappeared as if the earth had swallowed him, and my belly continued to grow and grow until I stopped counting the days and stopped waiting.

I reach to my belly, my fingers brushing over the scar. How could you not be there, Colin? How could you let me go through it alone? I close my eyes and try to silence the thoughts that insist on invading my mind and chasing away my sleep.

MY MOTHER FREEZES, her coffee cup midair, as we sit in her kitchen at five in the afternoon. She seems to be making an effort not to let her slumped jaw drop even further. Vivian is at a friend's house and I'm going to pick her up in an hour.

"So... that's pretty much everything we've been through," I finish updating her on all the events that took place last night. Today was probably one of the worst days I've had. I walked around restless, trying to fend off all the fears that have arisen in me since Colin left my house.

"And how was seeing him again?" My mother gets over the shock.

Of all the questions, that's the one that interests her the most?

"I leaped into his arms and showered him with kisses, and I told him I always knew he'd come back," I reply sarcastically.

"Elizabeth!"

"How do you think it was?" I roll my eyes. "You should have

seen him sitting on the rug with Viv, playing with dolls, as if he'd done it all her life."

"Maybe he won't be a terrible father, after all," she mumbles.

"Come on, he could be on a plane on his way to the other end of the world, and I wouldn't have a clue."

"You'll have to go one day at a time," she uses one of her clichés. "Did you two talk about what happened? What happens next?"

"Barely," I shake my head. I didn't tell her about the meeting at the cafe or the phone call that followed.

"You know he won't make do with this one visit." My mother puts her hand on my shoulder, "It was just the beginning. It sounds like he wants to build a relationship with Vivian."

"We'll see," I shrug.

"Liz, stop fooling yourself, you have to have plans."

"What plans, Mom? How many days a week he can see her?"

"For a start."

"You're not serious, he came back three minutes ago, and you take his side?"

"I'll never take his side, I'm thinking about your daughter," she answers quietly.

"Thank god you remember she's my daughter," I continue. "What are you going to say next, that he's her father, that he has rights?"

"I'm not saying anything, you're jumping to conclusions, and if I were you I'd think good and hard how to tell your daughter her father is back."

"Don't you think you're getting ahead of yourself?"

"How long will you pretend? A month, two months, a year?"

"Until he leaves again?"

"Is that what you really want?" She glares at me hard. "Would you rather he leave and Vivian not have a father?"

"I don't trust him!"

"Of course you don't, and no one blames you, but you have to put your child as your number one priority and not let your fierce hatred blind you!"

"Why do you love him so much?" I stand up angrily, pushing my chair back. "Dad hates him, he warned me, and you . . ." I wave at her.

"I what?" She doesn't get riled "I should have hated him because he played football in high school?"

"It worked for Dad," I remind her, not that she's forgotten.

"And that would have brought Morgan back?" The words spill out of her in pain. "Would turn the wheel back, if I hated Colin so you weren't with him? So you could have suffered in the name of Morgan's memory?"

"Dad expected me to punish myself for something I don't even remember," I almost whisper. "I can barely remember what he looked like."

"Your father didn't want pictures of him anywhere, and I respected his wish."

"He didn't want to talk about him, he didn't want us to mention him, and in the end, I had a brother I hardly knew. I don't remember any other life. From the age of four I was an only child, and I fell in love with the wrong guy."

"Do you think Colin was the wrong guy?"

"I think Dad was right."

"Your father was the one who found Morgan," her voice shudders. "He just wanted to protect you, he never stopped blaming himself for what happened."

"I don't want to upset you," I try to interrupt the conversation.

"You don't upset me," she dismisses my attempt with a wave of her hand. "I live with it every day, every hour, but Colin isn't guilty, you have to talk to him."

"Why are you pressing and pressing and not respecting the fact that I need time?"

"Are you planning on staying alone?"

"What?" I cross my hands, still standing in the middle of the kitchen, unable to move or sit. Is that what matters to her now? That I find someone?

"Alone, for the rest of your life?" She stares at me sternly.

"Of course not," I snort.

"Than what are you waiting for?"

"You know why I'm single." I shrug my shoulders with false indifference.

"You don't trust anyone, and you don't trust yourself to cope with it," she says.

"I think I've proved my coping skills, thank you very much," I defend myself.

"You're twenty six years old, you have no friends, and your life revolves around a four-year-old girl, and working in a furniture store." She hits more than one sensitive point.

"That's what there is." I can't tell her that even the work in the store is about to be history.

"That's what you choose, and the moment will come when it blows up in your face. You'll be resentful and take it out on someone. I'm guessing it'll be on the child."

"What?" I shout in shock.

"If you keep telling yourself that you are putting your life on hold because of her, you'll believe it in the end. Let him be a father, that's all he wants." Her gaze seems to ask wordlessly if any of the things that were said are getting through to me.

"You know what, I don't need this." I grab my bag from the back of the chair and hurry my steps to the door. Damn you, Colin!

"WHAT DO YOU WANT FOR DINNER?" I ask Vivian as I park the car in front of our door. I turn off the engine and release the seat belt. For the past ten minutes, she has not stopped telling me about her afternoon experiences with Tania.

"Pancakes!"

"All right," I open the car door and walk out, wait until Viv comes out of the back and lock the car as she runs forward.

"Mama, look," she pauses at the door, waving a package wrapped in colorful paper. "A gift!"

I approach her, take the gift, and my blood begins to bubble as I read the attached note.

To Theresa, hope you love the new company. Happy Birthday.

He didn't sign. How nice of him, as if I don't know who it's from. He's such a manipulator. Oh, he'll hear from me! About this and about the conversation with my mother and about . . . everything else he deserves to hear about!

"What does it say? What did they write?" Viv jumps around. I read the greeting to her with a false smile.

"Who sent it?"

"Santa?" I try to get away with it.

"Mama!" she laughs. "It's from Colin. He has to come over," she announces in her squeaky voice.

"He's busy." I open the door of the house and Viv runs past me, throws the wrapping paper to the floor and sits down on the carpet, staring at her gift.

"It's . . ." she falters. "It's a singing Elsa, like Tania's!" Her eyes widen in amazement at the doll.

"Is it?" I approach her, pick up the box and curse my ex for the thousandth time. He bought her the Elsa doll whose dress glows, and she sings and talks. If he thinks he can come here and wave his money . . .

"Get her out, Mom!" Viv commands me. I take the box to the kitchen and look for a pair of scissors with which I can . . . stab Colin!

We're going to have a serious conversation about this!

"IT WAS REALLY DIRTY OF YOU," I shout into the phone five minutes after Vivian falls asleep. I spent the afternoon with ragged nerves, having to listen to Elsa singing again and again. I could barely separate her from Vivian for shower time, and she barely touched dinner.

"I'm sorry, it was impulsive. I saw the doll and . . ."

"And you thought you could buy Vivian's heart for thirty-four dollars?" I can't control my anger.

"You know how much it cost," he mumbles.

"Of course I know, I know how much everything she wants costs!" Tears choke my throat.

"It's only thirty-four dollars."

"That's what you think. The doll is just the tip of the iceberg, and if I agree to anything she wants, there's no end to it. Thirty-four dollars here, ten dollars there, you know how much a trampoline costs these days?"

"I have no idea," he whispers.

"I've been refusing her for weeks, making her promises, and you've just come out of nowhere and . . ."

"Fuck," he curses loudly. "I didn't think."

"No, Colin, you didn't think!" I can't stop the crying. "You left me a note, you just stopped loving me!"

"I never thought you'd stay with me!" he fires back. "I waited for the moment when you'd realize who I was! I was sure it would end when you got your scholarship. You'd leave me!"

"I got the damn scholarship, you piece of shit!" The words stream out before I can stop them.

"What are you talking about?" His voice becomes stiff and cold.

"UT Southwestern Medical School." My heart breaks when I think of my foolish concession.

"Elizabeth, do not tell me . . ." he threatens.

"I was accepted. Full scholarship, as I wanted," I murmur the words in tears.

"You got the scholarship?" he asks hoarsely.

"Yes."

"And you didn't think of telling me?" I hear the accusation in his voice.

"I made my decision."

"To hell with that, Elizabeth! What were you thinking?" He falters in despair. "I'm so pissed at you right now, that was your future!"

"Silly me," I reply sarcastically, "I thought my future was with you."

"Fuck that!"

"It was my decision!" I yell back. "I was the one who chose to stay with you. I loved you more than I knew I could, so excuse me if I was eighteen and I didn't want to lose you!"

Without warning, the conversation ends. He hung up. I lean against the wall and let my hand fall. Defeated and exhausted by the emotional jolts of the past few weeks, I can't stop the overwhelming weeping that threatens to drown me.

My fingers fumble with the white page I hold, as if my brain refuses to accept its authenticity. Sitting on my bed, my heart beats rhythmically. This is what I wanted. This is what I've dreamed of, all that I've been working for for years. A full scholarship...and now these doubts won't leave.

Am I really considering giving up all this?

I'm not normal. No one should give up such a golden opportunity. This is my future, but what about my future with Colin?

God, the pain in my chest.

I know it's not that far, but how will we survive it? The distance, the brutal hours, followed by my residency. My future wants to take me in a new direction, one in which Colin has no place.

What did I think would happen?

My life no longer revolves around grades and hours in the library.

My life is no longer a regular route from home to school and back. Someone got into it, someone I can't imagine my life without.

No one should know.

They'll say I'm wrong. They won't understand. They can't understand that I won't leave Colin behind. It has to remain my secret. Forever.

CHAPTER ELEVEN

"*E*lizabeth," Mr. Blunt calls my name just as I finish wrapping one of the mirrors I've removed from the wall. I really hope he has no more serious tasks for me, because I'm exhausted after not sleeping all night. I woke up late, rushed with Vivian to the clinic so that she could finally get her stitches removed, dropped her off at daycare and from the moment I got to the store, I've worked myself to the bone, trying not to think.

I look up and freeze in front of my boss. Beside him stands the wicked Mrs. Danielle Cole and . . . my ex. His hands are tucked into the side pockets of his gray canvas trousers, a white button shirt clutches against his chest, the top button open, and his smooth skin sticks out from under the shirt's neck.

What the hell is he doing here?

Lately I've been seeing Colin dressed so differently than he used to and, even I have to admit it's a crime. The button shirt, the canvas pants, and the dark brown shoes make him look like a serious businessman. Only the look in his eyes is somber, and I shrink in front of him like a little girl.

"Elizabeth," Mr. Blunt wakes me up from my daze. "The trucks will be arriving this weekend and I want to make sure everything is packed and ready."

Danielle tilts her head sideways with a fake smile and examines me from head to toe. What are you looking at?

"Everything will be packed," I manage not to stammer, to my delight.

"Everything will be cleared by Monday, Mr. Young." Mr. Blunt smiles at Colin, who doesn't move a muscle in his face.

"Did you hear that, Danielle?" Colin asks without looking at her. His eyes are focused on me, and only me.

"I heard very well, Colin. We'll bring in the goods on Tuesday."

"Excellent," he answers sharply.

"Excuse me," I manage to get a word out of my mouth.

"Yes, Ms. Heart?" Colin decides to be formal and remote.

"I thought you . . ." I turn to Danielle in confusion.

"I'm not," she raises an eyebrow. Pointing to Colin, "He, however, is."

He is the new owner? He is the reason I'm losing my job?

"You said you were a liquidator," I remember, "buying cheap stuff and selling it for profit or something. Why do you need the store?"

"I need a display area to reach private customers." He refuses to thaw, the cold coming from his direction driving me crazy. "I have items that are closed up in warehouses, I'll be happy to get them out of there."

"And the only place you could find is the store where I work?" I question in growing fury.

"This is the only place that was big enough and it's in the best location. If I had not rented it, someone else would have."

"I understand."

"I'm sure we can use your skills as a saleswoman when the store re-opens." The words come out of Danielle's mouth in a tone I don't like.

"Over my dead body!" I shout without thinking.

"Elizabeth," Colin's voice warns.

"You think I will come work for you?" I laugh contemptuously. "Rely on your kindness?"

"It's too bad you don't have a college degree, don't you think?" He takes his hands out of his pockets to cross his arms over his chest.

"If I had a husband who shared my livelihood, I'd have no problem, don't *you* think?" I sting, regardless of the audience we have. "Enjoy the new store!"

"I'm not firing you, if that's what you think," he says between clenched teeth.

"You never hired me, Mr. Young," I retract to the formality he opened. "Therefore, I'm not working for you."

"I'm sure we can talk about this next week," Danielle tries to calm the situation, and Mr. Blunt looks confused.

"There's nothing to talk about." I throw the tape in my hand on the nearest couch. "I'm done."

Without waiting for an answer, I flippantly turn my back on them and hasten my steps to the door. He really came back to town to make my life miserable. To leave me destitute, dependent on the money he deposited in my account. Is that how he plans to force me to introduce him to Vivian?

"Elizabeth." A strong hand grabs me from behind. I fail to shake Colin off me, untamed tears rising in the corner of my eyes.

"Leave me alone." I'm suffocating.

"Why did you do it?" He drops his hand from my arm, his voice full of resentment. "Why the hell didn't you go to UT?"

"Because I loved you." I can't stop the silent crying. "I couldn't imagine my life without you, I didn't want to live without you, but you forced that reality upon me."

"You were accepted to medical school, it was your dream, and it was within your grasp."

"Which only proves what an idiot I was," I sob.

"Because of me." His jaw tightens.

"For you," I correct him, "and especially for me."

How much I loved him. I'm not at all sure that one can over-come such love, that one can let someone else fill the void. What if my mother is right? What if our history will haunt me until my last day? How can I sell another man the illusion that I'm not flawed, that my heart and my body are intact?

Colin's damn phone rings and he's rushes to silence it.

"God, how do you run a business if you never answer?" I stare at him with teary eyes.

"Danielle takes care of it," he answers in a matter-of-fact, cold tone.

"Danielle takes care of it," I imitate him, as jealousy lifts its head and attacks me from nowhere. "Is she taking care of other things?" Now I envy other women in his company. Where does this come from, what do I care who takes care of him?

You'll always care. Don't lie to yourself.

"Don't cross that line," Colin warns, "your problems are with me, not with her."

"I should have gone to UT," I whisper in pain. "I should have left you behind, become a doctor, made something of myself and not be . . ."

"Vivian's mother," he reminds me deliberately of what I would have lost if I had given him up. If I had left him, my child would not have been born, and I wouldn't give her up, despite everything I've been through, despite everything he did. I couldn't imagine my life without him then, and I can't imagine it without Vivian now. Colin knows that, she's here because of him.

"Do you enjoy this?" I pull my nose and wipe the tears from my cheek.

"Not for a second," his voice cracks.

"Then stop it," I beg in a trembling voice. "Stop breaking me. I can't do this anymore."

"I just want to be her father." He is horrified at the idea of me coming between them.

"And you will be, once you prove that you are trustworthy." I open the shop door and run away. If only for one hour, I could escape from myself.

"WHY DON'T you invite Colin again?" Vivian asks innocently at dinner, making me choke on a piece of chicken.

"He's busy, honey," I hurry to busy myself with my glass of water.

"Is he always busy?"

"I don't know."

"Why don't you ask him?" She makes it difficult. "Don't you have his phone number?"

"I do," I nod and put another forkful in my mouth.

"Can I call him?" she stares at me pleadingly.

"What? No!" I almost choke again.

"Why not?"

"Because he is my friend, not yours." I take a deep breath.

"Theresa wants to thank him for the gift." Ah, the little snake.

"She can draw him a painting."

"Like I did for Dad?" God, save me, please.

"Yes, like that."

"No. I want to call him," she insists.

"You can't." I manage to remain calm.

"You're not nice!" she gets mad. "You never invite friends!"

The thought pinches my heart. What am I teaching Vivian, to be alone? Children imitate their parents, is that what I want for her?

I just want to be her father . . .

"Okay," I surrender. "You can call him and thank him for the gift."

"Now." She crosses her hands.

So stubborn! I take my phone out of my pocket and dial Colin as my heart begins to pound.

"Elizabeth?" He probably didn't expect me to call.

"Hello, Colin, I'm putting you on speaker," I hasten to make it clear that our conversation at the store isn't going to continue. "Someone wants to talk to you, if it's a good time."

Breathe. That's what matters right now.

"It's a good time. I wonder who it might be," his voice softens in a second. Viv reaches for the phone and I stand up to clear the dishes as I listen.

"Hey, Colin."

"Hello." He sounds happy. I can't imagine what's it like not to see your child for so many years, not to talk to her, and then to live so close to her, and still be forced to stay away.

"Theresa loves her doll," she informs him.

"She does?" he laughs.

"Very much, but Mom said she was annoying."

"I didn't say that," I defend myself.

"She did, I heard her standing in the kitchen. It's because Elsa is singing."

"Does she sing beautifully?" he cooperates lightly.

"Yes, and her dress glows, and Mom wouldn't let me take her to daycare today."

"Your mother's probably right." Ha, he's smart enough to back me up.

"Daryl said I was lying, that nobody bought me the doll."

"Did he say that?" Colin's voice becomes firm and protective.

"Yes, he said no one ever buys me anything." The glass in my hand slides and shatters in the sink with a loud noise. I stare at the broken fragments beneath my fingers.

"What happened?" Colin's voice panics from the commotion.

"Mom broke a glass," the little snitch tattles.

"Elizabeth?" he calls my name anxiously.

"I'm fine, it's nothing," I grumble. That Daryl boy. If he doesn't stop bothering my girl, he'll be dealing with me!

"Mommy's clumsy," Viv laughs at me.

"I don't think that's true, I've known your mother for many years."

Yes, Colin, we know how many years you've known me, you don't have to mention it.

"Daryl's mother bought him a spaceship," Viv continues. "He let me play with it so we can fly to the moon. Daryl wants to live there."

"Oh, that sounds like a good idea," I can't resist.

"I want to live there with him. You can come with us, Colin."

My loud coughing must have been heard on the other side of the phone.

"I'd be happy to come." The bastard can't stop himself.

"Hey, Judas," I remind him of who's side he's supposed to be on.

"I think your mother will miss you terribly if you go to the moon."

"She can come with us."

"I'm staying here, thank you." I finish picking up the broken pieces of glass from the sink and throw them in the trash.

"Because you're no fun. My mommy isn't fun," Viv protests in her pouty voice.

"I'm not supposed to be fun, I'm supposed to be your mother," I defend myself immediately.

"She's supposed to be your mother," Colin answers in a serious tone, though for a moment he sounds like he's teasing me.

"Thanks."

"You know I don't have a dad?" Vivian's words cause silence to occur at once. My eyes are fixed on the phone from which a response is due. "Mom says he left, she doesn't know if he's coming back."

"She doesn't?" Colin mutters in a disturbing tone. It's time to end the conversation between these two.

"Colin," I warn.

"Do you want him to come back?"

"Colin!" I raise my voice.

"All children have a dad. I drew him a painting. Mom, where is Dad's painting?"

"Yes, Elizabeth, where's the painting?" Colin sounds as if he's accusing me of a crime against humanity.

Fuck.

"It's in the living room."

"What did you paint?" He tries to develop the conversation with her. Enough.

"I think it's time for your shower, Vivian." I wipe my hands on the kitchen towel. "Say goodbye to Colin."

"Bye, Colin!"

"Bye, Vivian, thank you for calling," he says, before I snatch the phone from her hand and hang up immediately. That was close. Way too close. How long can I go on with this?

COLIN YOUNG: I want my painting.

My cell beeps at ten past nine. I mute it, lying on the bed, watching Vivian sleep.

Elizabeth Heart: If you give me your address, I'd be happy to send it.

Colin Young: I can come pick it up.

Elizabeth Heart: I don't think so.

Colin Young: You want to meet for coffee?

Elizabeth Heart: No.

Colin Young: We need to talk.

Elizabeth Heart: About what?

Colin Young: Vivian, of course.

Elizabeth Heart: Talk.

Colin Young: I want to see her again. I want her to know who I am.

Elizabeth Heart: Not yet.

Colin Young: When?

Elizabeth Heart: I don't know.

Colin Young: You can't hide it from her forever.

Elizabeth Heart: Are you sure?

Colin Young: Elizabeth, she should know, and I need to see her. Let me take you out for dinner.

Elizabeth Heart: Why?

Colin Young: Why not? What does she like to eat?

Elizabeth Heart: There's this place . . .

My fingers come to a halt a second too late. The message has been sent. There's this place, and of all places, it's my daughter's favorite.

Colin Young: What place?

Shit.

Colin Young:?

Elizabeth Heart: Maples.

Here it comes.

Colin Young: She loves Maples.

Elizabeth Heart: I know.

That was our place. That's where we'd go, when we wanted time for ourselves or when we were looking for a quiet corner. We knew exactly when to go, when it wasn't busy.

Colin Young: Tomorrow?

I should refuse him, but perhaps, this way, I can let him see how much work it takes to raise a child. Yes, that would scare him away. That would make him pack his bag and disappear.

Elizabeth Heart: At six.

Colin Young: Good.

We're meeting at Maples, out of all the places in the world. It brings back memories that should have been forgotten, buried to never emerge.

CHAPTER TWELVE

*A*t six sharp I open the restaurant's door and Vivian rushes to find her new friend.

"Colin!" she rejoices when she recognizes him in one of the corner booths, sitting on the red leather couch. His body fills the small space between the couch and the table.

"Hello, Viv." He stands up to her and she hugs him tightly. For a moment his enormous body seems to freeze, with her tiny body curling up on him.

"Hey." He manages to sneak a smile at me and Viv releases him from her grip and sits down quickly on the sofa opposite him.

"You look nice," he compliments her as she arranges her hair behind her ears. I sit down beside her, tense.

"You're a giant," she giggles. "Right, Mama? Isn't he huge?"

"Huge." I let go of a single word and give Colin a look that makes it clear his appearance may work on her, but not on me.

"I brought you something." He takes out a flat, paper-wrapped package that must be from the bookshop.

"What is it?" Her hands hurry to open the wrapper, which she throws aside, her eyes darting.

"If you want to be an astromount, it's never too early to prepare." He seems pleased with himself.

"It's not for her age," I caution. "She can't read."

"She can look at the pictures, can't she?" He turns his face to me.

"I suppose," I reply coldly, keeping my distance.

"Maybe she'll go to NASA, if she doesn't make stupid mistakes," he mumbles the last as if I won't hear.

"Maybe," I reply defiantly, looking directly into his eyes. "If I can keep her away from the wrong crowd."

"Daryl is gunna die!" The little one interrupts our momentary sparring.

"Yes?" Colin smiles broadly.

"Look, Mama!" She enthusiastically points to a picture of a spaceship.

"That's the Challenger," I explain. I have no intention of telling her how that story ends, and with one look at Colin, I make it clear to him to keep his mouth shut, too.

"So . . ." he understands, thank God, "let me guess, a hamburger with no onions and pickles, extra fries and a diet coke."

"Big deal," I roll my eyes. As if I don't know what he's going to order: medium size cheeseburger with onion rings and a coke.

"What will you have, Viv?" he turns to the girl who is busy with her book, occasionally mumbling words like 'super-cool' and lots of 'wow'.

"Waffle!" her eyes pop at me pleadingly.

"Real food first, please," I make it clear.

"Mama!" she protests immediately.

"You know the rules."

"There are rules?" Colin sounds confused.

"Yes, Colin," I breathe air demonstratively. "There are rules. They help us keep order and sanity, when the ground seems to fall from under our feet."

"And what happens if we break the rules?" He insists on not accepting my explanation.

"You don't want to know."

"I'm dying to know." He tilts his head sideways teasingly.

He thinks he will side with her and dictate new rules while making a mess of the good order it took me god knows how long to impose in the process?

"Vivian," I pull my bag from the table, "we're leaving."

"No," she whines in alarm, "I didn't eat waffle!"

"Let her have it," Colin tries to intervene, but I interrupt him with a withering look.

"You don't get to decide."

"Elizabeth," he puts his hand on mine, his touch tingling up my forearm. Goddammit. I look down at where his hand touches me, and forgotten currents make my mind cloud for a moment to when I was seventeen and his thigh rubbed against my thigh.

"It's just a waffle," Colin's voice is soft as he raises his hand and leaves a strange sensation behind. Stimulating.

Don't be stupid. You hate him, and he doesn't love you. Get a grip!

"It's not just a waffle, it's . . ." I breathe deeply, "the boundaries that begin to blur, and before you know it . . ." my voice crackles. The waitress comes and saves the day and Colin stares at me as he orders my food.

"A children's meal with chicken tenders and an orange juice," I insist, "and she'll have a waffle for dessert."

"And I'll take a double cheeseburger, double fries, and the biggest strawberry milkshake you've got," he surprises me. "Oh, and I'll have a waffle for dessert, too."

The waitress nods and walks away from the table.

"What happened to onion rings and coke?" I wonder aloud.

"Don't know," he shrugs, "I guess I got used to eating more."

"A lot more." Double burger with double fries and a huge milkshake? He eats for three people.

"My calorie burn is high, I'm hungrier than before." He keeps his cool. "I treat myself from time to time, it's not something I usually eat."

"I bet not." If he ate this dish every day, he would not look . . . like that.

"I'm more into cooking," he replies, making me cough.

"I'm sorry?" Since when did he cook? As far as I can remember, the guy was a disaster in the kitchen. If I had not cooked myself, we would have eaten macaroni and cheese from a box or lived on cereal. So, he learned to cook, what else did he learn to do in his spare time?

"It's healthier and more economical than eating out," Colin explains, as if I don't know myself.

"So you cooked those muscles?" I point my head towards his arms.

"I'm taking supplements."

"Of course you are," I reply. "How much does that cost you?"

"Quite a lot." He doesn't take his eyes off me, blue and stormy.

"I'm sure." I try not to remember all the times I looked at them and deluded myself that this was what love looked like.

"I can afford it, my business is profitable."

Ah. Colin's mysterious business. I wonder what he'll tell me about it now.

"I still can't believe it's legit," I blurt.

"Why?"

"You have too much money," I answer straight away. "I don't know many people who can spend twenty five thousand dollars without thinking."

"Who said I wasn't thinking?" He isn't impressed with my accusation.

"You know what I mean," I don't cave in.

"I know exactly," he says bitterly, "you meant that I was the last person you expected to have an impressive bank account and a comfortable cash flow, and you are trying to figure out how the guy who worked in construction might be driving a jeep like mine."

"That's not what I said."

"That's what you said."

"You're twisting my words," I say quietly. "I'm just saying I don't understand how it works."

"I told you, I buy goods and sell them for a profit, how complicated do you think it is?"

"Is that the whole story?"

"Elizabeth, how complicated can it be?" He rolls his eyes. "You just have to know the right people, make the right deals and gain experience and reputation."

"You haven't lived here for years, since when do you know the right people?" When did he make connections in the city?

"Danielle knows them," he mentions the blonde, and my blood starts to bubble up at once. Colin's voice interrupts my inappropriate thoughts of Danielle. "I planned the transition for months, and my business is based on working relationships, it wasn't complicated to move it here."

"When did you manage to build it?" I wonder aloud, hoping he won't insist that I work for him again.

"Once I had enough money."

"From the army?"

"You were in the army?" Nothing dodges my daughter. Her gaze leaps from the book and she stares at Colin.

"Yes, Vivian, I was in the army."

"Fighting the bad guys?"

"Sometimes."

"You won?" she enthuses innocently.

"Okay," I try to interrupt the conversation without success.

"You have a picture?" She leaps to her feet and jumps onto the leather couch.

"Vivian Heart!" I scold her and out of the corner of my eyes I see Colin's face fall.

"Heart," he mumbles, and even I, with all my fierce hatred, can hear the pain in front of me.

"Yes." I swallow the lump stuck in my throat and thank God, and our waitress who comes back with our order just in time. Another quick look at Colin reveals to me that the matter has not been closed.

He doesn't take his eyes off me, but there is no blame. Perhaps only towards himself.

"Sit down," I gently pull Viv's hand and sit her down, praying that the rest of the meal will pass quietly and we can run back home.

"AND THEN ELSA melts all the ice, and they chase Hans away, and Anna and Kristoff can get married!" Vivian rejoices, again, when she finishes telling Colin the whole plot of her favorite film, from start to finish, after we've finished eating.

"And all Anna needs is to pray Christoph won't change his mind." I can't keep my mouth shut.

"Mama," her scolding tone is accompanied by a smile, "he loves her!"

Colin keeps his mouth shut and doesn't interfere.

"Can I go play?" she pleads in a sweet voice, looking with eager eyes outside the window and at the play castle.

"I'll come with you." I stand up immediately, open my bag and pull out my wallet.

"Don't insult me." Colin's cold voice makes me freeze.

"I . . ." The words get stuck. I wasn't even thinking. It's just habit.

"Go outside, I'll join you after I pay." He shakes his head in frustration.

"Colin," I feel an urge to explain, but Vivian slips under the table and I have to run after her.

Damn.

137

. . .

My hands are clasping my bag to my chest while I try to breathe and fight my tears. Colin and I sit on a bench in the shade and watch Viv jump all over the castle. Yes, he stole that from us, too, the normality of a man and a woman sitting and looking at their daughter. Together.

"I wasn't trying to offend you," I manage to say through the choke. "I didn't think, it was . . ."

"Automatic," he completes the sentence.

"Yes, automatic, like a lot of other things. Like making sure three times that she buckled herself up, and that the door is locked, and that no check has bounced."

"Your checks bounce?" his voice becomes hoarse.

"Not usually no, but the fear is always there. It was a struggle, Colin, it still is. Every day."

"You can't live in fear," he says quietly.

"Shall I remind you what brought me to this state?" I formulate my words carefully so as not to quarrel with him again. "Do you think I thought my life would look like this?"

"I can't change what happened." He doesn't take his eyes off Vivian, and for a moment I think he apologizes to her, even if he refuses to regret what he did.

"Would you change the decision you made, now that you know your daughter, that you understand what you've lost?"

"I told you it was complicated."

"You took everything from us—your security, your love."

"I couldn't stay, Elizabeth." I'm not at all sure I want to hear his explanation, how in one day he just stopped loving me.

"You couldn't stay," I repeat his words. Maybe if I do so enough times, I'll catch up. I'll understand why he disappeared.

"I don't want to hurt you any more than I already have." He looks at me for a moment and then back at Vivian.

"In the end, this is the point we got to, huh. You hurt me, and I hate you."

"Do you really hate me?" his voice is almost a whisper.

"You broke my heart, you left me alone, what do you think?"

"Did you tell her?"

"What?" I frown as I look at him.

"Vivian." He tilts his head in her direction, "That you hate me, that I'm a piece of shit."

"I have never spoken a bad word about you to her. Do you know how hard it is, explaining to a little girl where Daddy is when you have no idea?"

"Did she ask?"

"She rarely asked why you weren't with us. She just wanted to know if you didn't love her. I didn't know how to answer that."

"What did you tell her?"

"That you had to go, and I didn't think you were coming back. I didn't want her to have false hope."

"You still think I'll leave again."

"Yes." My eyes go back to Viv. It's easier not to look at Colin when I tell him the truth. "I think anyone who ran away once, will run away again."

"I'm not that boy anymore," he mutters.

"That's what you say."

"Do I look like him?" Colin turns his face to me. He seems to be on a mission of convincing me I'm wrong.

"Your muscles are trying to hide the truth, but it's there," I insist. "In your stare, in your eyes, when I look at them, I see you, and you're still that boy."

"Who you loved." The three words that come out of his mouth take me off balance for a moment.

"You are still the one who appeared at my door with a bleeding lip. The one I hugged, who made promises and abandoned me."

"Elizabeth." He doesn't seem to like what I have to say.

"You didn't find anyone better, so you came back."

"You know that's not true," his voice, though quiet, booms. I turn my head to him and stare at him with my pain.

"How many girls have you been with, Colin?" my voice cracks. "Do you have any idea?"

"Not many."

"Not many . . ." I don't want to imagine him with others. Whether there were few or many, the thought of him with someone else . . . "I had no one."

"Say that again?" He pauses, his eyes searching my face, trying to identify if there is truth in my gaze. He knows I'm not lying.

"Someone had to raise your child," I grumble. "I didn't have time to play games."

"You've had no one?" He looks shocked. "Just me?"

"Ages ago."

"Only me," he repeats the words. How hard is it to understand? He knows me, he knows who I am.

"Are you going to repeat that many more times, stroke your ego a little more?" Unlike me, I'm sure he likes the answer he got, but I can erase the smile off his face before it even appears. "It just goes to show you how much you've hurt me, how much my trust is shattered, that I haven't wanted to be with anyone."

"If it comforts you, I didn't love—" I rush in before he can go on.

"Comfort me?" I snort, "What do I care who you loved? As far as I'm concerned, you don't know what love is."

"You're wrong."

"Am I really? Because I'm pretty sure I'm not. You've had plenty of opportunities to come back, but you chose to stay away from us for all these years, from me and your own daughter, who needed you." I breathe. "I think the conversation is over, we're going home."

"When can I see her again?" He looks up at Viv, who keeps on jumping.

"I don't know. I'll let you know." I stand up and straighten my t-shirt.

"Call if you need something, anything." He stands beside me, and I feel myself diminished by his enormous body.

"Vivian!" I call aloud and wave my hand at her. She continues to jump in complete disregard of my existence.

"Viv!" I wait another moment and try again, and get the exact same response. She doesn't hear me, or chooses not to listen, and I begin to lose patience.

"Vivian," Colin's voice booms over me, "your mother wants to go, let's see how fast you run!"

She hears this, and her competitiveness, which she inherited from him, makes her leap out of the castle and reach us at top speed.

So you listen to Colin?

"Thank you," I grunt, holding out my hand to Viv, who grabs it.

"It's nothing," he answers quietly. "Good bye, Vivian."

"Bye, Colin, thanks for the book," she remembers to thank him.

"My pleasure." His smile widens. "I hope Daryl loves it, too."

"He'll die for it. Can I take it to daycare, Mama?"

"You can," I agree immediately. We'll see if Daryl ever says again that no one buys my daughter anything. "Let's go home."

"Bye, Colin!" she calls back at him once again as we walk toward the parking lot.

"Bye, Viv!" He remains standing there. "Good bye, Elizabeth."

I nod quickly and wait for the moment we get into the car and drive away.

"I NEED TO PEE!" Vivian whines from the back seat of the Toyota that decided today, of all days, not to start.

"Just another second," I sigh and turn the key for the umpteenth time.

"Pee! Urgent!" she cries miserably.

"Just another second, Viv!"

"It's coming out!" She waves her legs in the air. "Why can't Colin drive us home, doesn't he have a car?"

"I don't know!" I raise my voice and give up trying to get the car to move. Colin has a car, all right. The maniac drives a terrifying jeep while I'm stuck with this shit. "Let's go back to the restaurant, you can go to the bathroom."

She unfastens her seat belt and opens the door quickly.

"Wait for me!" I call after her and hurry out of the car. We'll just go into the restaurant, use the toilet, and call my mother and ask for help, again. How wonderful.

"ELIZABETH," my mother sighs as we sit at my dining table drinking coffee, after she came to the rescue and called the towing company. Vivian fell asleep only a few minutes ago, and we're waiting for my father to bring me his car so I can get to work tomorrow. "We need to talk to your father."

"Do you really want to tell him I took Viv for dinner with the guy who broke his nose?" I defy.

"I want to know you're making plans and not letting things just happen."

"We're talking about Colin, remember?" I snort, "What's the point in making plans if he disappears again?"

"The way it looks from here, you're trying to scare him away."

"And that's so terrible?" I roll my eyes.

"I can understand why you want him to suffer, and he earned it honestly, but you're destroying yourself, don't you see?"

I know she is right, but this desire for vengeance refuses to be released. After all these years I'm finally the one with the power in her hands, and it's up to me now.

"Why couldn't he stay away?"

"Is that what you really want?" Her gaze penetrates. "Think of Viv."

"What about me?" I burst out. "What about what I feel, when will I think of me? All I did was for her."

"You're her mother." She doesn't really have to remind me.

"I'm twenty six, look at my life." I sigh in silence.

"You're upset." She puts her hand on mine and presses her fingers into mine. Of course I'm upset. I'm going to be unemployed, dependent on the money I don't want to make use of and the man I can't trust, and worst of all, Vivian is dependent on me, which means now she is dependent on him, too.

"What kind of a mother am I," I wonder aloud, "that I want to care about myself first with this?"

"Human." She isn't moved by my real distress. "You're a good mother, you've made her your top priority. You're allowed to think about yourself, you deserve to be loved."

"You won't let it go, will you?" I grumble.

"I don't want you to grow old alone because you're scared. Colin hurt you, but it's been years, he's not the only man out there."

"No one will want me." The words roll from my mouth, echoing in the air and dissipating in front of the unhappy look on my mother's face.

"Don't talk nonsense."

"I'm faulty. You know it, I know it, and it's not something I can hide."

"You should stop using that word and trust the right guy to come and accept the situation as it is." She insists that someone will want me. How wrong she is.

"I have a new word for you," I defy her, "barren."

My attempt to push back the pain fails. First I lost Colin, then I was bleeding on the operating table just to wake up from the anesthesia and discover that I'd lost my womb and, along with it, the ability and perhaps the desire to meet someone who would want to start a family with me.

"Elizabeth," her pain comes through in her voice.

"The right guy will come," I continue, "and accept that I can't have children?"

"There are other solutions," she tries to cheer me up, not for the first time.

"The only thing I have is a scar on my stomach that reminds me every day that I'll never be pregnant again. Excuse me if I think I'm defective, if I don't jump into bed with anyone," I mumble as I recall Colin's reply to my question.

How many girls have you been with?

Not many.

I don't know if I believe him or why it even matters. He was with others, while I stopped my life.

"Why do you believe every man you meet will leave when he finds out that you . . ." She refrains from saying the word.

"Why should he stay?"

"Because you are smart, beautiful and loving, and you have other things to give."

"Except for children," I insist.

"If Colin couldn't have children, would you leave him?" Her question lands on me like a ton of bricks. Nothing would have made me leave Colin. Not getting into UT, not the constant struggle for the next paycheck, and certainly not the inability to have children. Nothing would scare me away.

What if my mother is right? I deserve someone to lean on, someone to be there for me. Vivian deserves someone like that who will be part of her life, and her father I have already learned not to trust.

I sip my coffee quietly and meditate over the last few years. The last weeks. I think of the lost boy who returned from the desert, a man I don't know.

CHAPTER THIRTEEN

*M*y ragged nerves refuse to settle as I walk around the shop forced to spend the day with Henry, Danielle and my ex. If I thought it would be bad, I had no idea just how bad it could be.

His smell stayed the same, and every time he walks by, a wave of memories shatters upon me without warning. I don't know if Colin is aware of it or just doesn't care, because he seems to be near me all the time. Occasionally his hand rubs against mine and sends a shiver that makes my skin stand on end.

I'm tortured by every passing minute. Glancing at the clock again and again, I pray the workday is over so I can run away from him and his blue eyes, that are sneaking me glances I cannot decipher.

What does he want from me?

I really don't know, because if he has something to say, he is keeping it to himself. Danielle, on the other hand, doesn't hide anything. She goes on giggling with Henry, making him blush. She seems to derive great pleasure from it.

"Elizabeth," Colin calls out to me in his rough voice from the far end of the store, "do you know anything about jeans?"

His question is met with silence. I stare at him confused, standing with the phone to his ear and waiting for an answer.

"I don't understand what you're asking," I admit nervously. I know American literature, biology, even in math I'm not bad at all, but fashion? I'm not the right person to answer his question, and he knows it.

"How much?" he frowns.

"I still don't understand what you're asking. Maybe if you care to explain yourself instead of being vague, we'll all be smarter."

Yes, Mr. Young, if you explain yourself and we all find out why you left, maybe we won't feel like complete fools.

"Danielle?" Colin raises his voice to the blonde, who stops the mock giggle she is throwing at Henry.

"Not more than a dollar, and call Elijah," she answers without asking what it's all about.

Does he do it on purpose? Show me I don't know anything?

"Good idea." He nods at her and returns to the conversation.

"Thanks a lot," I mutter in frustration.

"You're welcome," Danielle replies sarcastically, tossing her hair from side to side.

"If that's how you're trying to get me to stay, you're dumber than I thought." I strain again and seal the large cardboard lying on the floor at my feet with tape.

"Dumber?" Colin comes up behind me, making me face his intoxicating smell for the thousandth time.

"What do you want from me?" I sulk as he sits down on the couch in front of me, crossing his long legs and folding his hands.

"Do you want to try to close the deal?" He looks at me closely.

"How many times do I have to say it?" I let out air demonstratively. "I'm not working for you."

"It's a pretty simple deal," he deliberately ignores my disapproval. "You buy the jeans for a dollar and sell them for three."

"Wow!" I answer with exaggerated enthusiasm. "You just

earned two dollars. Well, Colin, no wonder you can afford the jeep you're driving if these are the deals you do."

"Ten thousand dollars." He shrugs his shoulders with an arrogant smile and hands me the phone. "Are you sure you won't try?"

"No one will buy your jeans for ten thousand dollars." I emphasize the contempt in my voice.

"Maybe not, but Elijah would be happy to buy five thousand jeans for three dollars a piece, if you call him."

"Five thousand?" I crinkle my forehead.

"Tell him they're packed in cartons and the shipping is on him. He will try to lower the price. Don't let him. Give him the shipping but leave the price at three dollars a pair."

"I'm not working for you!" I raise my voice to match Danielle's laughter, who seems amused by the situation as she approaches us in the tight purple dress she wears, her high heels knocking on the floor.

"Give me the phone." She snatches the phone from Colin's hand with a smile. "Elijah won't refuse me. He'll pay for the shipment and, if I have to guess, he will also invite me to dinner the next time I'm in Chicago." She turns quickly to the shy boy standing stunned by the incident. "How far is it to Chicago?"

"One thousand sixteen miles, the trip will take about fourteen hours and thirty eight minutes, do you want to know how much it will cost?"

I look to Colin, who raises an eyebrow at the knowledge my friend pulls out effortlessly.

"That won't be necessary," Danielle laughs, "Elijah will pay anyway. And you," she turns and points the phone at me without intending to hand it, "you lost your commission."

"Don't say I didn't offer it to you first." Colin raises his hands submissively.

"Keep your games to yourself," I clench my teeth, "and don't involve me in your dubious deals."

"You're missing out, Elizabeth." He smiles smugly again.

"The only thing I'm loosing is time with my child." I take a deep breath trying to soothe my muscles that start to tighten. "I'm going to pick her up now, enjoy your jeans."

Without waiting for a response, I turn my back on them, grab my bag from behind the cash register and leave the store angrily. The nerve he has, trying to drag me into his business with his smiles, the confidence he radiates and the arrogant behavior. That doesn't work on me. And Danielle . . . throwing at me the commission I lost. Let me tell you something, lady, I've been raising my child on my own for years. I've lost a lot more than his miserable commission!

How much did he want to pay me anyway?

"MOM, LOOK, IT'S DR. DIAZ!" Vivian hops enthusiastically around the shelves laden with bread and pastries at our nearest Walmart branch. Our car finally came back from the shop and it cost me a fortune. I shift my gaze to the end of the aisle and examine the man smiling at us.

It really is Dr. Diaz. Wearing dark jeans and a black button shirt, he's tall, but not as muscular as Colin.

You don't think of Colin that way!

I smile back at him as he approaches us and holds out his hand.

"Hello, Vivian and Vivian's mother. Please, call me Luis." He reveals perfect white teeth.

"Elizabeth." I shake his hand quickly.

"Hello, Elizabeth." He bends down and leans in front of Viv's bright face. "How's my patient?"

"I'm fine," she chirps.

"I'm glad to hear that. Are you taking care of yourself?"

"Yes, I'm careful." She glances at me for approval, and I nod in agreement. She does a pretty good job.

"I see they took your stitches out." He examines her hair line.

"It hurt," she tells him in a much less happy tone. "The nurse wasn't nice."

The nurse was impatient. Vivian was crying, and I just wanted to finish and run. What a nightmare.

"I had to hold her," I share the story with the kind doctor, who straightens back to standing. "It wasn't fun."

"I'm sure." He reaches out and rubs the back of his neck. "I'm sorry you had to go through that, it's never easy."

"It was our first time, and hopefully our last one." I stare quickly at Vivian.

"Mom's watching over me," Viv updates Dr. Diaz.

"I'm sure." He smiles at me. "Next time you need a doctor, come to me, I can remove stitches."

"Forgive me if I keep hoping that we won't need your services." I laugh, and the smile on Luis' face grows.

"I certainly forgive and hope we won't meet again at the hospital," he nods, "but maybe we can meet somewhere else?"

"Meet where?" I scrunch my brow.

"I hope I'm not crossing the line," he lowers his voice, "but would you like to go out for coffee?"

"Coffee?" It takes me a moment to realize what he wants. Idiot, he's asking me on a date!

"No, I'm sorry . . . I'm not . . ." I falter in confusion and tighten my grip on the shopping cart.

"Ah, well, I thought I had nothing to lose in asking," he quickly apologizes with a smile, but my mother's words scream in my head. *The right guy will come and accept the situation as it is. You are smart, beautiful and loving, and you have other things to give.*

Colin had no problem sleeping with others, while I waited and waited and convinced myself no one would want me. And now Dr. Luis Diaz is asking me out. He knows I have a child, he met my ex in the hospital, a meeting that was not particularly happy, and he wants to go out with me. Maybe he won't run away when he finds out.

I-D-I-O-T, tell him yes. Go out with the nice doctor for a silly date, just to remember how it's done. Do you want to be alone? Colin isn't the only man on the planet!

"Maybe," a moment of madness grabs me, "maybe we can have coffee after all."

"Yes?" He seems surprised at the dramatic change in my mind.

"Sure." I nod like a sixteen-year-old who doesn't know what she's doing.

You really don't know what you're doing.

"Here's my number." He pulls his wallet out of his pocket and hands me a business card. "Call me."

"Okay." I examine the little paper in my hand. I'm going on a date with Dr. Luis Diaz, who is going to find out what a flawed loser I am. Amazing.

"Good bye, Elizabeth." His voice makes me look up from the card and smile at him. "Bye, Vivian."

"Bye, Dr. Diaz." She waves good bye to him. He steps away from us lightly, and I remember to breathe.

"Mama," Vivian calls to me from the back seat as we make our way home. "Why don't you go out for coffee with Colin?"

The car in front of us stops abruptly. I curse loudly, press the brake and turn my head back to check on Viv, who doesn't seem particularly upset.

"Are you okay?" I regulate my breath from the unexpected stop.

"Why don't you go out with Colin?" She doesn't take her blue eyes off me.

"He's just a friend." I look straight and continue driving.

"He's nice," she says firmly.

"Dr. Diaz is nice, too."

"Colin is funny. Daryl wants to meet him, he loved the book."

I know that Daryl loved the book, I listened to her for a whole afternoon telling me again and again how they were both planning to fly to the moon.

"Colin is just a friend," I make it clear again. "I've known him for many years, and Dr. Diaz can be funny, too."

"How do you know?"

"He has good eyes, and he took care of you with devotion."

"What's devotion?" She makes it difficult.

"It means he treated you very nicely, and that means a lot." I try to explain in words she understands.

"Colin has beautiful eyes." She doesn't let the subject go. "They're blue, like mine." The suffocation in my throat makes me tighten my hands on the wheel. Just like yours, Vivian, and they've gotten me in trouble more than once.

"What do you want for dinner?" I pull myself together. We've talked enough about the new boys in our lives.

"I want ice cream. Grandpa promised to take me, and you said that if you promise, you have to keep the promise," she tells me.

My father did say he would take her, and then she fell and was hurt and the plan was forgotten. Apparently someone remembered, after all.

"I'll call him and see if he's available, but I want you to eat something real before that."

"Grandpa will buy me something real." She runs the matter with a high hand. I dial from the speakerphone and wait to hear if my father wants to take his granddaughter for a joint outing.

"Lizzie," he answers after three rings.

"Grandpa!" Viv calls out to him.

"Sweetheart," he sounds eager to hear her, "how are you?"

"You promised me ice cream!"

"And I didn't take you? That's wrong of me. " He laughs. "Where are you?"

"On the way home," I reply.

"Your mom isn't far away, she can pick up Vivian. Do you want to join?"

"Mama's going out with Dr. Diaz," the little snitch shouts into the car.

"I'm sorry?" My father makes sure he hears right.

"I'm not going out with him," I grumble. "He invited me for coffee."

"I see," he whispers quietly.

"We'll be home in a minute, tell Mom to meet us there and don't bring Vivian back too late!" I warn. My father has a tendency to ignore my daughter's bedtime, which makes me angry again and again.

"I'll bring her back when we're done." He doesn't promise to follow my rules.

"I'll talk to Mom." I can trust her. "Bye, Dad." I hang up the conversation and steer the car down the street all the way to our driveway.

"I HEARD YOU HAVE A DATE." My mother is standing in the door waiting for Vivian to join her when she finishes in the bathroom.

"Jesus Christ," I grumble to her, "you bunch of gossips, that's what you have to say? How about 'Hello, Elizabeth, nice to see you?'"

"Hello, Elizabeth," she teases me. "When are you going out with him?"

"I'm not going out with him!" I'm losing my patience. "What is it with you people?"

"I'll bring Viv back by eight and put her to bed, just in case you get delayed. Call him." She raises an eyebrow.

"I'm not calling anyone."

"Because you're waiting for Colin." She irritates me more.

"In your dreams," I snarl angrily.

"So go out with the doctor," she continues.

"Okay!" I give up dramatically. "I'll go out with the doctor, happy?"

"Why is Mom angry?" Vivian emerges from behind me.

"She's not angry." My mother picks her up. "She's busy, and we're going to see Grandpa."

"And eat ice cream," the little one recalls, in case anyone had forgotten.

"Definitely." My mother kisses her head. "Elizabeth, you have a phone call to make."

"Put her to sleep on time," I insist.

"Good bye, my dear." She smiles broadly. I close the door behind them and take Dr. Diaz's business card out of my bag. I'm not waiting for Colin, and if my mother thinks I am, I'll prove her wrong.

WHAT WAS I THINKING?

I stand in front of the mirror, staring at the figure reflected in a dark blue dress and high heels. Dr. Diaz, or Luis, as he insisted I call him, was overly excited by my call and he agreed to meet.

Having chosen one of my old dresses, high-heeled shoes that survived the years they lay in the closet, I now stare at my cleavage and curse. My breasts grew when I gained weight, and they're threatening to burst out of the dress and shame me.

Colin would laugh at you.

Colin has lost the right to say something, anything, and he doesn't get to decide what I wear. I grab my bag and go out of the bedroom quickly before I change my mind and switch into jeans. I'm going on a date, I'm allowed to dress up and I'm allowed to wave my boobs, no matter how big they are.

AT THE ENTRANCE to the cafe, where we have arranged to meet, I notice Luis and feel more foolish than ever. He's dressed in pale jeans, a white t-shirt and sneakers, and I'm suffocated in this silly dress, trying to look like someone I'm not. As I approach him he smiles broadly and, to his credit, his eyes remain on my face and don't wander to my chest making its debut.

"Elizabeth," he tilts his head slightly and opens the door politely. His strange smell hits me and my guts make another unimaginable roll. I try to put a more confident look on my face, in order to disguise the growing tension in my body, walk in and greet the silence of the empty cafe. Apart from us, there is only a single couple at one of the tables, so I choose one in the far corner and place my bag on my knees.

Luis sits down opposite me, relaxed and confident, I think. The waiter comes over to us and takes our order, tea for me and coffee for my date.

"Do you want something to eat?" Luis makes sure, before the waiter moves away.

"No thanks." I have no appetite and, to be honest, I'm mostly nervous about it all.

The waiter smiles and goes to handle our drinks and Luis sits back in his chair.

"So . . ." He smiles, again.

"So . . ." I almost have to force my jaw muscles to create a semblance of a smile.

"How's Vivian?" He chooses to talk about my child. Is that supposed to tell me something?

"She's okay."

"Spending the evening at her dad's?" He steals a curious glance at me. That's where he's going. I get it.

"She's with my parents." I choose my words carefully. "Her father came back recently, and she still doesn't know who he is. He left before she was born." If I begin to explain, we won't leave here until nine. We won't leave until morning, if I tell him the whole story.

"Complicated." He purses his brow.

"Yes, we're not together."

"I think I figured that out myself at the hospital." He tilts his head slightly.

"Right." The conversation is making me quite uncomfortable, so I decide to direct it to him. "And you, an eligible bachelor?"

"Divorced." I don't know why his answer surprises me. I didn't think anyone would divorce the successful, smiley doctor. Maybe he divorced her. Maybe he's a terrible man and only pretends to be a nice guy. I repress my anxious thought in favor of the conversation.

"Do you have children?" I'm carefully inquiring. Maybe he has children and he doesn't want any more? That could be perfect.

"No." He smiles, his answer isn't what I had hoped for. "Not yet."

"Do you like your job?" I try to calm my wildly beating heart.

We're just having coffee and I'm already thinking about kids, but how can I not?

"I love my work." Our quick waiter comes back with our order. I pick up my cup of tea and blow on the hot drink to cool it.

"That was my dream once," I share, "to become a doctor."

"Yeah?" He sips his coffee carefully.

"I was accepted to UT."

Colin is the only one who knows about it. I can only guess what my father's reaction will be if he finds out one day.

"What happened to your dream?" Luis returns my thoughts to the present.

"I gave it up, so I wouldn't have to leave . . ."

"Vivian's father," he completes my sentence.

"Yeah," I nod.

"He was your high school sweetheart."

"He was."

"You sacrificed your future for him, and he left?" He finds it difficult to understand the sequence of events.

"He didn't know I was accepted." Not that I think it would have changed anything.

"How old are you?" he puts his coffee down on the table, seemingly trying to guess the answer to his question.

"Twenty six," I reply, "and you?"

"Thirty one. And where do you work?"

Painful subject number three or maybe four, I've lost count. My life is sliding down a slippery slope and I can't stop it. What a loser.

"I work in a furniture store," I take a deep breath before continuing, "but it's closing, and I have to find something else."

"What are you thinking of doing?" He asks another difficult question to which the answer is still unclear.

"I'm not choosy," I avoid, "I'm sure I'll find something."

"If you've been accepted to medical school, I'm sure you can find a good job. I'm still paying my student loans." He barely smiles as he takes a sip of his coffee.

"I just want to stay free to take care of Vivian, so my hours are limited."

"Your parents don't help?"

"They do, I just don't like asking for favors."

"She's their granddaughter, I don't think they're doing you a favor." He laughs quietly.

She is their granddaughter, and they do me a lot of favors. They save me when the car gets stuck, pay for daycare when I can't, take Viv when I go on a failed date that leads nowhere . . .

I'm not sure what I thought would happen, but I didn't imagine this conversation. Luis smiles, and he's really nice, but I feel like we're in a job interview. Examining each other, nothing flowing naturally, and it's probably because of me.

"I'm sorry, Luis," I apologize sheepishly, "I'm not good at this dating thing."

"You haven't gone on many, I suppose," he says in an empathetic tone.

"I had a baby at home, and then I just…didn't." What a sorry excuse. Even before Vivian was born, I was not a social type. If not for Colin and his crowd, I would have stayed at home or spent time in the library, as I did before he crashed into my life.

"Maybe you're not ready," Luis guesses quietly.

"I'm ready," I quickly correct him, "really, I just don't know how to do it."

"Do what? Drink coffee?" he laughs. "That's pretty much it Elizabeth, we drink and talk like friends."

"I don't have friends." The sentence escapes my mouth uncontrollably.

"You don't?"

"No friends," I repeat the words that turn my guts. "I've had one friend since junior high, but besides him, I don't really hang out."

"Don't you have a good friend you talk to, pour your heart out to?" The astonishment on his face is obvious.

"I have my mother."

"I don't think that's the same."

"I guess not." I don't argue. It's not the same, but that's how it's always been. "Do you know those girls who read books under trees in the park or carry on their backs a bag full of study materials?" I don't know where the burst of words comes from, but they come, and I can't stop myself. "I had one goal—to be accepted to medical school. Nothing else interested me. I didn't wear dresses or high heels and that hasn't really changed. As for my work, I'm a saleswoman at a furniture shop that is closing soon. I'm going to be unemployed, and I have to find a new job, so I don't have time for friends. I've been a single mom for almost five years, and now Vivian's father is back, and I have to deal with that, too." I finish my speech in a frustrated tone.

"I think you have unresolved issues to deal with."

"I have no unresolved issues." I really don't remember asking for his opinion of my life.

"Are you sure?" His voice grows distant. He leans back, enlarging the distance between us. "Do you still love Vivian's father?"

"What?" I open my eyes. "No, of course not, I don't—"

"Why did you agree to out with me?" he interrupts me.

Because I wanted to prove something to my mother, to myself. Give Colin back to those girls he slept with.

Dumb reasons to go out on a date, no doubt.

"I don't love Vivian's father. He did something unforgivable." Something inside me shrinks when the words are said explicitly. "I'm at a crossroads and I have to decide where to go from here."

"You're not ready," he insists.

"I don't think you know me enough to make that assumption."

"Elizabeth," he says quietly, "don't lie to yourself. We've just finished spending twenty minutes together, trying to figure out what to talk about. I'm pretty sure you're an intelligent woman who could have an interesting conversation if you were into it."

"It's not like that." I refuse to accept his distinction.

"You don't owe me explanations." He raises his hand in a surprising gesture and signals to the waiter to bring the check. I guess he's tired of sitting and hearing what a major loser I am.

"I'm sorry our date didn't go as planned." I pull my bag from my lap.

"Maybe one day, after you take care of your affairs, we can try again." He smiles but, this time, his mouth is drawn into a kind of crooked line, which makes it clear that he doesn't mean it.

"Good bye, Luis." I rise slowly, unable to smile back.

"Take care, Elizabeth," he replies with estranged politeness. I shake my head in a tiny gesture and hurry toward the door. What do I have to do with dates? What do I have to do with good guys? Everyone can see who I am, and the second they pick up on it, they run away. Colin might have taken four years to understand, but eventually, realization came.

. . .

A KNOCK on the door makes me jump off the couch at nine thirty. I go over to open it hesitantly and peer into the peephole to see who is looking for me at this hour. My mother went home after I came back early from my date, which didn't go as expected, and now my daughter is asleep. And beyond the door stands her father, which just makes my anger climb.

"Sorry for the time," he quickly apologizes, as I open and stare at him in anger.

"What are you doing here?" I grunt furiously.

"I was around and I remembered you said your TV breaks sometimes." He frowns and only then do I notice the huge package at his feet. "Is everything okay?"

Is he kidding me? Who does he thinks he is, showing up here at such an hour to distribute gifts no one asked him to give!

"Nothing's okay," I shout, "you've ruined everything!"

"Is Vivian asleep?"

"That's none of your business," I interrupt his inquiry, which comes a few years too late. "Just get out of here, disappear, crawl back into the hole you came out of and let our lives get back on track." I try to close the door, but he grabs it and prevents me from slamming it in his face.

"Elizabeth," he says firmly.

"You come here with your money and think that you deserve rights, that you can buy us."

"That's not what I think. I can take care of the two of you."

"We don't need favors and surely not from you!"

"How long do you plan on having her in your bedroom?" His insolence interferes with my life.

"Who the hell are you to criticize me?"

"I'm Vivian's father!" he thunders in front of my stunned face.

"Mommy?" Vivian's rather alert voice catches us both off guard. We turn our eyes to the girl who is standing in the living room, staring at us in confusion, my pulse accelerating to a frightening speed and the blood running out of my face.

"Are you my dad?" she looks at him and then at me, and the words just disappear from me. She wasn't supposed to hear that, not yet. She didn't have to find out, and it's all his fault. Everything!

"Come to bed," I manage to whisper, leaving the door and moving toward her with my hands outstretched.

"You said he wasn't coming back," she refuses my embrace.

"Colin," I look at him quickly, "please go, please, let me . . ." Let me fix the tremendous damage you've done.

"Good night, Vivian," he says quietly.

"No!" she shouts, "I don't want you to leave!" The invisible cracks in my heart widen a few inches.

"I'm just going to my house," he tries to reassure her. "I'll be back when your mother calls me."

"Why isn't this your house?" Tears come to her eyes and begin to flow down her cheeks. She is frightened and confused and wants answers at nine thirty in the evening. Answers we don't have. "Why don't you live here?"

"Because I had to leave and I hurt your mother very much." At least he knows who is to blame for the situation. I wrap her in my arms and lift her in spite of her resolute resistance.

"Don't go!" She's fighting me. "Mama, tell him!"

"I'm not leaving again," he gasps and sounds almost as frightened as she is, "I promise."

"Don't promise anything!" I shout at him, "Just go!"

"I don't want Luis," Vivian sobs, "I want Colin, I don't want another dad!" God, it can't get any worse.

"Vivian, I'm your dad, and I promise not to leave again." He glares at me as he defies my request.

"I don't want to sleep, I want to stay with Colin!" I carry her crying and shouting into the bedroom, slamming the door with my foot.

"Colin!" Viv cries hysterically. I put her in bed, cover her with a blanket, lie down beside her and stroke her head. "Why can't he stay?"

"He lives in another house." I curl up and hug her.

"Where was he?"

"In all kinds of places. He'll tell you about them." I wipe her tear-stained face.

"Doesn't he love me?" Her question breaks my heart, as if she's closing her tiny fingers on it.

"You're his daughter," I calmly answer, "he loves you very much."

"When will he come again?"

"Tomorrow, okay?" I surrender, only to put her to sleep. "He'll come tomorrow."

"In the morning."

"I don't know if he can."

"Ask him," she doesn't give up.

"After you fall asleep."

"I don't want him to go, I want a dad like everyone else."

I wanted her to have a father like everyone else. I also wanted a husband to be by our side, someone who would be part of the family we were going to *raise* together.

"I know." I kiss her head softly, until she closes her eyes. "I know, go to sleep".

I ANSWER Colin's phone call shortly before eleven, slip into the living room and sit down on the sofa. The television he bought is lying against the living room wall, mocking me. How much money does he have? When did he earn it? I know almost nothing about him. We can't seem to have a single conversation in which I get all the answers. He's dodging, and I let him, not demanding explanations.

"Did she fall asleep?" His voice sounds worried.

"Eventually." My head slumps forward in defeat.

"She shouldn't have heard, it should have been your decision when to tell her, but I'm not sorry she knows." He ends the sentence less apologetically then he started it.

"She wanted to know where you were," I update him on my conversation with Vivian, "and if you love her."

"You know I'll do anything for her."

How easy to say, Colin, and how hard to prove. His words crush my ability to fight my tears and I let go of the brakes now that Vivian is asleep. She knows who her father is and I know what I've been through because of him. How I loved him and how I hate him, and where I ended up because of the mess he caused.

"I'm a failure." I burst into tears and try to silence my cries so as not to wake Viv, biting my trembling lips. "Look at me."

"I admire you," he whispers on the other side, "for everything you did, for everything you've achieved. I know you don't trust me, but I'm here. If you need money, it's yours. It belongs to you and our daughter, and my time belongs to you. If you need help taking her out of daycare or putting her there in the morning, just say."

"I was supposed to be a doctor, I gave on up my dreams."

"Don't you have other dreams?"

"How exactly do I get them, you'll play Santa Claus again?" My voice is full of accusation.

"Start by saying what you need."

"I don't know what I need," I whimper in despair, "I don't know what I want, I didn't stop to think about it."

"So stop now, you're only twenty six."

"I feel like I'm forty," I grumble through tears, "I look forty."

"Elizabeth," he sighed, "you don't."

I do. He didn't see the scar on my stomach, he didn't see how I tried to squeeze into the blue dress tonight and I looked awkward, and he doesn't know about my lost womb.

"She wants to see you." I refuse to talk about my appearance anymore. "She's scared, she needs to see you're staying."

"Just say the word, and I'll be there." His voice is strong.

"She asked if you could come in the morning. I don't know if that's a good idea." Again the unbridled crying takes hold of me, "I don't know anything, Colin."

"Give me the opportunity to help."

"What do I know about opportunities?" I shake my head in frustration. "I went on a date tonight, you know? With the doctor from the ER. I was wearing a dress and high heels and I sat in front of him for twenty minutes and felt like I was nothing. I felt like someone who had a bright future and screwed it up."

"You shouldn't have given up your dreams for me," he falters.

"I gave it up because I thought I'd won something much bigger. I won you, you were my bright future." The tears burn my cheeks, running down my face like rivers rushing in the winter, like there's no end to them. It took me forever to dry them, and now he's back, and the dam has broken, and again my face gets wet at night on the couch, seeping into the pillow.

"You can't leave again," I threaten, "not now that she knows about you."

"I don't think it would be right to talk to her in the morning, I doubt it would be a good time to answer her questions."

"In the afternoon, then." If he doesn't show up, he's dead. I'll kill him with my own hands if he hurts my daughter.

"I'll be there around five."

"Okay." I wipe the tears with my palm.

"Good night, Elizabeth, try to get some sleep."

"Good night, Colin." I hang up the phone, place it on the couch beside me, and cry.

CHAPTER FOURTEEN

*V*ivian doesn't want to go to daycare.

I struggle with her, beg and then glance at the clock for the third time, watching the minutes pass, as she refuses to budge from the sofa, ignoring my pleas.

"He'll come at five," I say again as steady as I can, "he promised."

"Is it because of Dr. Diaz?"

"He's got nothing to do with it, honey, we've got to move, I can't be late."

"You don't want Colin to come because of Dr. Diaz," she accuses me.

"We're leaving now." I refuse to acknowledge her comment.

"No." She crosses her arms on her chest.

"Your birthday present is in danger," I threaten and regret immediately. Only yesterday she found out who her father is, she needs me to reassure her, understand her, put her difficulties before my own. She doesn't need threats.

"Dad will buy me what I want." Her words send a lightning bolt into my guts. Is she already calling him Dad?

"Colin and I will talk about your birthday present. I beg you to get up from the couch and get into the car." I try with all my might to keep my cool, a task that comes to me with great difficulty in this moment.

"I want him to pick me up from daycare." She doesn't move.

"He can't, he'll come at five." How many times do I have to say that?

"You're lying," she throws at me, and I lose my patience.

"Young lady, if you don't get up from the couch now, your actions will have serious consequences!" She opens her big eyes and they begin to shine. Her face turns red and she bursts into tears.

"I'm sorry." I jump toward her, lift her and wrap my arms around her, kissing her head again and again. "I'm sorry, Viv, everything will be all right, I promise, your father will come at five. Shh . . ." She buries her head in my chest and shivers with tears. Her life has turned upside down and I know the feeling. I know what she's going through, and I'm the only one who can protect her and help her through this change.

MY DAY CAN'T GET any worse. I left Vivian at daycare after I updated Mrs. Robbins on everything, and in the last half hour I've been forced to hang out in the store with Danielle Cole, who has smiled at Henry nonstop.

I pack pictures, close them in crates and back again. Above all else, there is the understanding that my time is running out.

"She's not going to fire me," Henry whispers as we bubble wrap one of the coffee tables.

"You think?" I whisper back.

"I know, she told me." I stop abruptly and stare at him. What is she up to?

"Did she tell you?" I follow him back.

"Yes."

"As far as I know, she's not the new owner," I say quietly.

"She said Colin wouldn't fire me," he says, adding, "You're really not staying?"

"To work for him?" I grumble. "No, thanks. When did you talk to her?"

"This morning before you came in, late." He stares at me in disappointment. Does he think his look will change anything?

"I had things to do at home." I don't elaborate.

"She was nice." He continues to describe the morning he spent with Danielle. "She asked a lot of questions."

"What else did she want to know?" They've rented the place, what else can she want?

"She wanted to know how old I was and what I liked to read, ah, and she asked if I had a girlfriend."

My body tenses with motherly defense at the last question. I don't trust her at all. I know girls like her. She flirts with Henry for fun, makes him develop hopes, just to feel better about herself.

"Watch out for her, okay?" I whisper as the door opens. I look up, my eyes fixed on Colin standing at the door. He doesn't move, looks troubled and tired, and doesn't take his eyes off me.

"Liz," Henry tries to attract my attention.

"Sorry." I shake my head and go back to wrapping the table with him, hearing the footsteps coming toward us.

"Elizabeth," Colin's voice rises above our chatter, "can we talk?"

I can't get away from him. He's everywhere.

"You're okay here?" I make sure Henry doesn't need me.

"Yes." He nods and looks up at Colin, who doesn't smile at him. I get up, then accompany Colin to a quiet corner and try to control my breath, which becomes strenuous when I think of Vivian in daycare.

"How was it this morning?" Colin inquires quietly, his eyes dark with worry.

"Difficult." I don't sugarcoat the situation. "She cried a lot. I think I'll pick her up early."

"Maybe I should have come anyway." He pulls his hair back.

"I don't know," I shake my head. "I don't think it would have made a difference, she has a lot to assimilate to."

"You're right, you know her and you know what's best."

"Why did you leave me?" I can't control the rage in my veins.

"I promise to explain." His answer is vague, again.

"Enough with the promises, Colin!" I raise my voice, completely ignoring the fact that we aren't alone. "You've had more than five years to explain why you disappeared and left nothing but a note. I deserved more than that, I deserve so much more!"

"I know."

"So stop dodging," I lash out sharply, "and start providing answers!"

"I told you it was complicated," he bursts back.

"Don't sell me stories!" I raise my hand in front of him. "I want to know why one day you stopped loving me. I need to know how your twisted head works before you run your tricks on my girl."

We both fall silent as the door opens and two men, who look like thugs, appear at the entrance, inspecting the store. Something in my guts signals that they are not here by chance. Something inside me screams that they are looking for trouble. What did Mr. Blunt get into?

"Elizabeth," Colin's voice drops, "take Henry and go to the back office."

I can't move. My feet refuse to cooperate as they step inside, walking past Henry in total disregard of his existence and moving toward me.

"Elizabeth," Colin grits his teeth, "to the back office. Now."

"Young!" Bully number one locks his gaze on Colin, who

stands up, his huge body radiating danger. Are they looking for Colin?

"Not now, not here," Colin answers in a menacing tone, stepping in between me and bully number two.

"Just making sure you remember us." Bully number one cracks his knuckles, making a disembodied sound as he presses them in his palm. I can't breathe, my eyes running from one creature to another, to Henry who's bending behind one of the couches.

"I said not now." Colin manages to keep his cool. "You'll get the money by tonight."

God. What did you do, Colin? My knees are trembling and the nausea is growing in my stomach.

Please god, don't let me vomit.

"By tonight, Young," bully number two threatens and looks over Colin's shoulder, his eyes catching me. "Is this your lady?"

"No." Colin moves his enormous body so that he hides me better.

"What do you say, Craig, do you believe him?" bully number two turns to his silent partner.

"She's his lady, I saw them with the girl. Nice family you have there, Young."

I'm about to collapse. I want to push Colin, jump to the door, and fly to Vivian's daycare.

"Elizabeth, give me your driver's license," Colin says in a cold, sure tone.

"What?" My voice is shaking.

"Your driver's license," he repeats the words without looking at me, his eyes on the thugs.

"It's in my bag, behind the counter."

"Go get it," he instructs me.

"I can't move," I whisper to him in horror, a tear streaming from the edge of my eye.

"Her bag's right there," he turns to Craig, "see for yourself. Her name is Elizabeth Heart. She works here, just a friend."

"Heart?" Craig tries to catch my eye.

"Yes," I nod, "I work here, we're just friends."

I hope they believe me. I hope they just look at the license, see that I'm not married to him and leave.

You owe me so many explanations, Colin! What did you get us involved in? To what complication did you get yourself in?

"Don't screw up." Bully number two gives Colin another threatening look.

"Don't come here again, Jimmy." Colin shows no signs of fear. "And don't threaten me or my friends, or I won't be responsible for what I do."

"Your old man didn't lie," bully number two, or Jimmy, smiles a nasty smile at Colin, who clenches his fists. "The army made a man out of you."

"Get lost, and don't come back." Colin seems as if he's about to leap at them any second regardless of their numerical advantage, the way he must have leaped on my father and his friends waiting outside the gym.

Jimmy points a warning finger at Colin, "The clock is ticking." He turns slowly to the door and Craig follows him kicking in a mirror that stands on one of the armchairs, shattering it. The door opens and they both go outside, leaving behind a tense silence that lasts only for a single second.

"Idiot!" Danielle's voice is carried around the store in full force. "I told you to take care of it, Colin!"

She knows what this is about? Am I the only one who has no idea what the hell happened? I push Colin back with all my strength. He steps forward and turns to me with a shocked look.

"What did you do?" I scream at him hysterically.

"Not now, Elizabeth." He stares at me intently.

"Are you kidding me?" I open my eyes wide. "What's the story, Colin, what did you and your father get into?"

"My father died four months ago," he grumbles.

His father died four months ago? God, Colin, how did you not say anything? With all the hatred I have for the man who raised Colin, my heart breaks. Brakes for the man I loved whose only family he has left is the daughter I'm trying to keep away from him. No wonder he is fighting me.

I want to hate him, to remember how much he hurt me, how he abandoned us both, but I fail in a big way.

My head and my heart are struggling with each other and the strong desire that spreads in my veins to hug him.

"Colin," I whisper in astonishment at the news that has landed on me and the feeling that holds me, as it did in the past, to protect it.

"I can't talk about it now." He takes his phone out of the back pocket of his jeans.

"Your father is dead," I can't keep my thoughts in order.

"Now isn't the time!"

"Now is the time, tell me what you got into and what you got me mixed in!"

"Stop being stubborn!" I see the storm growing in his eyes.

"If you want to see your child, don't evade me!" I shout without any ability to stop. A second later he closes his fingers on my arm and pulls me behind him to the office. My footsteps fail, trying to keep up with him.

"You brought this on yourself," he says as he slams the door behind us, and there's silence in the office. I gasp, my heart going wild, until I can swear Colin hears it.

"Explain to me, please." I cross my hands and keep my burning eyes from him. "And don't waste my precious time."

The past few weeks have turned me into a monster. There is no better way to define this character that has taken over me. A monster that threatens to swallow me in waves of hatred.

"Do you remember our wedding day?" He shifts nervously. "We agreed that I would meet you in the church. You didn't want me to see your wedding dress, you said it was bad luck."

Of course I remember that day, I remember every second of it.

"I spent the day in our house, and right before noon someone knocked on the door. I opened it without thinking twice, and the two morons, who you met a few minutes ago, burst in and caught me off guard."

"What did you do?" I manage to ask almost in a whisper, in terror.

"Nothing," he replies scornfully, "their problem wasn't with me, it was with my father. That didn't stop them from holding me against the wall."

"Your dad?" My legs begin to tremble first, and then the tremor climbs into my stomach and chest, until I think I'll collapse in another second.

"He owed them money, a lot of money, and they came to collect his debt. I asked how was I supposed to come up with the money, and the answer I got was a punch to the face. Jimmy made it clear that he didn't really care where the money came from. That they weren't playing around . . ."

The muscles in my body harden and stretch, my guts begins to turn over in a growing nausea as Colin continues. The loathing in his voice mixes with a note of pain he can't hide.

"All I could think to myself was how lucky my mother was for being dead, for not seeing where I'd ended up."

We didn't use to talk about his mom. The one subject we avoided, that we tiptoed around, was his mother. Colin's father knew and took full advantage of it. Took advantage of the young boy, full of longing, who lost his mother at the age of five and was left with a dad who drank himself to death.

"Why didn't you call me?" I don't know if I could've helped, but I was his girlfriend, his fiancé, hours from becoming his wife. I should have known.

"I wanted to, but your father showed up."

My dad? I give Colin a dismissive look. His story changes

direction unexpectedly, and it's hard not to wonder if he's looking for someone else to blame. What is he up to now?

"You're lying, my father was with me in the bridal salon."

"You forgot your veil, you sent him to fetch it," he reminds me. My father did bring me my veil and then took me and my mother to the church.

"What are you accusing him of?" My father hated Colin, and he's the perfect scapegoat.

"Your father came into our house and found me bleeding and bruised on the living room floor, Jimmy kicking my ribs. You love him, and for the last few years he took care of you and was there when I wasn't . . . I thought I could hide it from you and not break your heart again, but your father isn't the innocent man he's trying to portray."

"Stop lying!" I raise my hand in front of him to shut his mouth.

"He offered to pay the debt if I left!" I can feel the earth trembling, swaying under my feet, and the room spins for a moment and carries with it every bright thought.

You are a liar without limits. Is that what you were taught in the army?

"I don't believe a word that comes out of your mouth," I shoot him a look that could kill.

"You hate me anyway, Daddy's little girl, I was bleeding on the floor, I wanted to call you, but Jimmy wouldn't let me go anywhere without getting his money, and I had no choice. Your dad threatened me that if I ever came back, I'd end up like Thomas Brooke. Do you know who that is?"

"Please . . ." My voice brakes. I cover my ears with my hands.

"Do you know who that is?" He raises his voice, moves a step closer, and holds my hands, pulling them down.

"No." I can't stop the tears.

"He was the guy who hated Morgan more than anyone. He

was the one who tied your brother to the pole and brought the eggs."

"Stop!"

"He's dead!" His voice resounds. "Thomas Brooke died and your father said I'd end up like him!"

"What happened to him?" I whimper uncontrollably.

"Car accident. Your father laughed when he told me that, when he said there was nothing that couldn't be arranged with a little help."

"Are you accusing my father of murder?" I'm going crazy.

"How do I know what he is capable of? He threatened my life, and so did Jimmy."

"He wouldn't do that to me, he was standing beside me in the church waiting for you."

"He told me never to come back and that is the truth. I wanted to take you with me, I wanted us to run away together, but your father said there was no chance in hell he'd let that happen. You were pregnant, what was I supposed to do, marry you and leave you a widow?"

"Why are you back now, and why are they still chasing you?"

"I needed time to make enough money and stand on my own two feet."

"Money?" I bark.

"Money is power! The confidence that no one will mess with us. Do I look like someone you wanna mess with?"

He's a filthy liar, I have to get the truth out of him. If I just ask the right questions, his lies will crumble and the holes in his story will pop up. I can do it, I'll prove to him that I'm not stupid, that I'm not blind.

"They're still looking for you."

"My father's debts piled up again. He went on gambling. Only thing he owned was that shit of a house. I sold it and I needed a few days for the money to come in." He finds another logical explanation.

"How easy it is to blame others," I don't give up.

"Do you think it was easy not being here for so many years?" He fires at me and makes me jump in panic.

"I have no idea." All I can do is mutter in response to the growing rage coming from his direction. "As far as I'm concerned, you invented this story on the way here."

"Ask your father about the money I sent him." He takes his cell phone out of his back pocket and hands it to me defiantly. "Call him now, ask him."

"What money?" I stare at the phone confused.

"The money I sent him every month for you." Colin waves his cell phone, his tone full of disgust. "I guess he never told you."

"There is no limit to your imagination, is there Colin?" I refuse to take the phone from him. Unable to free my hands from my chest, I just hug myself harder.

"I sent him money every month from the time I enlisted, for you and Vivian. He knew where the money came from."

"Not a chance." I laugh in his face through my tears. "I can understand why you're trying to blame my father, you two never hid the resentment between you, but he would never lie to me."

"He would lie if he believed you would look for me, and we both know that's what you would do. You can ask him or continue not to believe me, but my father got in trouble, and his trouble was about to become ours. I couldn't let that happen, I couldn't risk anyone hurting you."

"So you lied to me?" I don't know whether to laugh or cry.

"I wasn't the only one who hid things," he says angrily, "you had your secrets. You wanna tell me you did everything you could to find me? The earth didn't swallow me, Elizabeth, I enlisted."

"You don't know what you're saying." I shake my head.

"Did you file a missing persons report?" He doesn't stop the charge.

"No one wanted to find you!" I glare back. "You left a note, I didn't think anything happened to you, what do you think the cops would have said about it?" My thoughts are running around, spinning in my head in circles. I didn't file a complaint with the police because my father said there was no point. Colin chose to leave, he wasn't missing. My heart is crashing in my chest. I listened to my dad because what he said made sense and, because of my situation, I let him make the decisions.

"You didn't look for me and your father's plan worked, until I came back." He gives up trying to push his cell phone my direction and returns it to his pocket. "Now he can't threaten me anymore, what can he possibly do to me, Elizabeth, kill me?"

"Don't talk like that!"

"I'm already dead!" Pain echoes in every word. "The only thing that kept me alive was the thought that someday you would let me be Vivian's father, and now you want to take her from me. You don't believe a word I say, so what else can I lose?"

"My father loves me." I forcefully push at the thoughts running through my head.

"Your father saw an opportunity to get rid of me and took advantage of it. He took advantage of my need to protect you at all costs."

"No," I refuse to believe him, "you are the one who left."

"That's why you went out with the doctor, to pay me back?" Now he remembers to bring up the subject?

"I went out with the doctor because I'm twenty six," I reply scornfully. "He asked me out and looked like a guy who wouldn't run away, one who doesn't make up miserable lies." I can't stop and the words are just there, on the tip of my tongue and then out, "You promised you would never be like—"

"Like my father." His face turns pale with indignation. "Thank you, Elizabeth, I see I'm not the only one who breaks their promises."

He stares at me one last time, then walks past me, his shoulder rubbing mine, slamming the door behind him. Silence takes over the room. My heart thumps wildly and floods me with guilt again. I took the knife out of the saddle and stuck it deep into Colin's heart, and now we're both wounded, bleeding. We are dragging the ugly past into our frail present and now it's threatening to shatter on us with a deafening crash.

CHAPTER FIFTEEN

The terrible traffic on the road forces me to sit behind the wheel, my thoughts running around, tossed from side to side irrationally, like a tennis ball from one racket to another. My father will put things right, I know that. Colin was so desperate that he decided to invent nasty lies about the man who was there for me, my own father, who saved me time after time when I felt the ground dropping from under my feet. Horrendous lies. He never sent money, because I would have received it. I remember our wedding day, every second of it. My father came back with the veil, and together we all went to the church and waited for Colin. Our eyes were fixed on the door expecting it to open, and my mom glanced at her wristwatch again and again. The minutes passed, and my smile changed into growing anxiety.

I dialed Colin and got his voicemail.

I kept telling myself he must have forgotten to charge it.

I left him a message and kept waiting. My father left first. Without bothering to ask, I assumed he had gone looking for my groom. After all, where else could he have gone?

The traffic light turns green and I hurry up on the road, my leg trembling with the panic attack climbing from my knees to my belly. Lies and more lies, that's what my ex-boyfriend excels at. The masked champion who returned to hurt anyone he could.

I stop with a squeal of brakes in front of the office building, lock the car and walk through the glass doors with quick steps to the elevator that leads me to the seventh floor, straight to *Baringes Export.*

The sign on the door welcomes me. My father has been working here since I was little. How many times did he wait for the promotion that never came? How many times was he passed on, the job given to someone younger than him?

I push away the thought and go in, the receptionist smiling at me from behind the shiny marble counter.

"May I help you?" She doesn't know me, I have not been here for years.

"I'm looking for Frank Heart." I can't smile back at her.

"Is he expecting you?"

"I'm his daughter." I'm sorry I didn't call from the road to tell him I was coming. He would wait and spare me the embarrassment.

The receptionist picks up the phone and dials, waiting quietly for a response from the other side

"Mr. Heart," she says eventually, "your daughter is at the reception desk." After a few more seconds she hangs up and smiles again.

"The last door on the left," she gestures toward the hallway.

"Thank you," I reply, my legs managing to cooperate as I walk down the long hallway and knock on the office door.

"Come in!" My father's voice booms from the other side. I open the door and a sense of shame overwhelms me. Am I really going to ask him after everything he did for me?

"Elizabeth?"

"Can we talk?" I close the door behind me and walk into the little gray office. Behind my father's desk stands a picture of

Vivian smiling broadly, and on the walls hang work boards full of plans.

I have to concentrate on my plan, unveil the lies that Colin told me.

"What's going on?" My father gets up from his chair and moves toward me, worry rising over his wrinkled face.

"I feel like an idiot for even asking," I'm looking for the right words, "an idiot for even considering, but Colin was in the store, and he told me this crazy story."

"Do you want to sit down?" He gestures to the empty chair in front of his desk.

"No," I shake my head, not taking my eyes off him, looking for signs that will reveal the truth. "Just tell me he's lying, that's all I really need, tell me he didn't send you money every month, that you didn't know why he left."

"Elizabeth," he pulls the chair out without answering me, my heart pounding. "You better sit down . . ."

"I don't want to sit!" I step back, my eyes darting between his. "Tell me he's lying and we'll get it over with, okay?"

"It's not that simple." He keeps his cool, doesn't raise his voice even a little.

"Not simple?" I open my eyes wide. "It's very simple, did you meet Colin at our house on my wedding day and make him leave?"

He has to answer this question. He cannot get away from it.

"I was in your house when I picked up something you forgot." He's trying to evade, damn it!

"My veil, what did you tell him?" I curl my fingers so tight I'm afraid I'll cut my own flesh.

"What I did was meant to protect you." He takes a step toward me, but I pull back from him.

"What did you tell him?"

"That he ruined your life the day you met!" he snaps, "And that he'd continue to destroy you and endanger you and your baby, and that I wasn't going to stand by and see my only daughter hurt because of him!"

And just like that, in one moment, the truth is revealed and it shatters the lies, along with everything I believed. My world, as I knew it. The truth is unveiled in all its ugliness, and I'm surrounded by traitors. Everyone lied to me, deceived me, let me believe the false stories.

"Didn't you consider going to the police or telling me what happened? What were you thinking?" I scream, ignoring the possibility that someone will appear at the door and ask me to calm down. "Who gave you the right to play with my life like that, lie to me all these years, let me believe he just didn't love me?"

The realization descends upon me, without my being prepared for it, and floods a thousand new questions—my father forced Colin to write the letter. Colin never meant those words. Has he stopped loving me over the years?

"You would have looked for him," my father continues, refusing to apologize, "and you would have found him easily. What if he came back earlier? What danger would he have put you in?"

"I don't know, you took away my right to choose, you deprived Vivian of her father, we could have solved it."

"You didn't see him," my father raises his hand in the air, "wounded, bleeding, you didn't see the criminals that entered your house. Do you think I would let him stay, let them chase you?"

"Both of you are liars, and I won't be surprised if Mom was also involved."

"Your mom doesn't know anything." My father turns pale in a moment. If my mom doesn't know, she's about to find out, and he'll pay the price.

"You've had more than five years to fix this," I point to my father accusingly, "but you let my heart bleed."

"I had no choice." He seems much less sure of himself now.

"Bullshit!" I shout at him scornfully. "It was your choice to lie to me, to deceive me, to persuade me to move on and find someone else. He was meant to be my husband!"

I can't look at him anymore, am unable to be with him in the same room.

"I'll never trust you again," I take another step back toward the door, "neither you nor him, I don't want to ever see you again."

"Lizzie!"

"How does it feel to lose the only child you have left?" My fingers close on the door handle and when I turn to open it I strain out, "Do you still think you made the right choice?"

"Don't turn your back on me!" he calls out.

"You turned your back on me when you stood in the church and pretended you didn't know where Colin was, when you lied that you were going to look for him." I slam the door behind me, fury in my veins.

Wait till I tell Mom. Wait for her to hear what you did, how you ruined my life.

The descent in the elevator continues for an eternity. The doors open and I burst out of the building, barely managing to get the car keys out of my bag. With trembling fingers, I put them in the door, sit behind the wheel and start the engine.

Colin didn't trust me to deal with the problem. He listened to my father, the man who hated him and waited for him to disappear, instead of coming to me and thinking together what to do. I'd have run away with him. If he had asked, I would have left everything behind just to be with him. The truth is, I will never know what danger I would have put Vivian in or what the consequences might have been. The decision was taken away from me.

I dial my mom and put the phone on speaker, tears streaming down my cheeks and washing my face. If she knew, I don't know what I'll do. If she lied to me, too, I'll be all alone.

"Lizzie?" My mom's sure voice is unaware of the bomb I'm about to throw.

"I know why Colin left." I pull my nose, my voice shivering in tears. "I know everything."

"Everything?"

"Please tell me you had no idea." A miserable sob comes out of my mouth.

"Elizabeth, what are you talking about?"

"About his father debts, that your husband paid and in return forced Colin to leave, and the money he sent dad every month."

"I don't understand a word you're saying." She sounds confused. "What debts? What money?"

"Ask your husband." I wipe my cheek with the back of my hand. "Ask him what happened, ask him how he ruined my life!"

I hang up the phone and sob, my head falling to the wheel with the feeling that the world has come to an end. Where am I going from here? A cruel headache begins to pound in my temples. Ever since Colin came back, it feels like all I do is cry. He broke my heart so many years ago and he keeps breaking it, over and over again. I have to gain back control, but how can I? And how could my father, of all the people in the world, have been able to do that?

I can't move the car from the parking lot in front of the office building, can't move my legs. I ignore the phone that's ringing, and then ringing again.

They're looking for me . . . let them.

If Viv hadn't discovered that Colin is her father, I'd pack our suitcases and get the hell away, but now I can't do that to her. She expects to meet him, and I don't want to think about the moment when I'll have to open the door and bring him back into our lives, her life.

In a few hours she will be back from daycare asking to see him, and I will have to agree.

If you'd just come to me, Colin, and told me back then, we'd have solved the problem somehow. If you had not run away, everything might have looked different.

. . .

My mom wipes a tear from the corner of her eye as she stands behind me in the bridal salon and watches me measure my wedding dress. It's design is so simple, so me. I don't care that my belly is showing and that my chest has grown at least one size. I'd better shut my mouth and not make a mistake remarking how pleased Colin is.

To be honest, I'm pleased, too, especially when my fiancé stares at me at every opportunity and then leaps on me. How fortunate am I? Colin knows how to kiss, and he . . . knows what he's doing, not that I have anything to compare to. Unlike me he came with experience, a thought I repress successfully most of the time.

In the end, no matter how many girls he was with, I'm the one he is marrying. Next week he'll put a ring on my finger, for better or for worse, and I can't wait. I long eagerly for the time we'll go shopping for a baby crib, for the moment we'll hold her in our arms.

Colin will be an amazing father, I know it. He will protect her as only he can.

He will lay the world at our feet, as he promised, but it will be only the icing on the cake, because I already have everything I've dreamed of. Everything I need.

GOD ONLY KNOWS how I managed to get home, how I didn't get in an accident. How I pressed the gas and steered the wheel, how I pulled the brake and parked, shutting off the engine. My autopilot finally kicked into action and got me here, to the couch where I have been crying for an hour and a half. Whoever is knocking on my door can disappear.

"Elizabeth!" My mom's voice reverberates. "Open the door now!"

"Go away," I cry, "I don't want to see you."

"I'm not asking you, I have a key. Open the door or I'll let myself in!"

"What don't you understand?" I scream. "Go away, and take everybody with you!"

I hear the key enter the keyhole, turning and opening the bolt. The knob goes down and the door opens, my mom storming inside.

"Get off the sofa, now!" She walks briskly toward me.

"No." I curl up, bring my knees to my chest and hug them tightly.

"Stop acting like a child and deal with the situation." She stands in front of me with a frown.

"Don't tell me what to do." I turn my back to her.

"You're not a baby, stop acting like one."

"Excuse me?" My body seems to be moving on its own. "I'm a baby?"

"Excellent, you're standing, now you're acting like a grown woman."

"Is that all you wanted, for me to stand up?" I exclaim.

"Elizabeth," she breathes deeply, her eyes burning, "I just got out of your father's office, I'm not in the mood for games."

"What did he have to say?" I roll my eyes in contempt.

"Not much, as you can imagine, and I didn't have the patience to listen to his excuses. Now explain to me from the beginning." She seems to have no intention of settling down, standing in the middle of my little living room and crossing her arms.

"Colin's father got into debt," I repeat Colin's story, only now believing him, or at least a large part of it. "The thugs who wanted to collect the debt came to our house on our wedding day and beat the crap out of Colin, just as Dad came in to fetch my veil. Colin had no money. You know what state we were in. So your husband found a creative solution—he paid the guys so they would not come back to find Colin and me and then he made my fiancé leave."

"What do you mean forced him?" She looks as skeptical as I was when I heard the story just hours ago.

"He threatened to hurt him, that he would end up like Thomas Brooke." The second the name leaves my lips her face turns pale.

"Thomas Brooke died in a car accident," she says with difficulty.

"And Dad told Colin that it was what awaited him if he stayed."

"And he believed him?" She looks stunned, like a mirror that reflects me.

"Colin was laying on the floor bleeding, I think he would have believed anything at that moment," I whisper in pain as pictures begin to crystallize in my head. My mind is doing the worst thing it can, forcing me to imagine the man I loved lying where I'm standing now, wounded and bruised.

"Your father didn't kill Thomas Brooke," she shakes her head. "He might have wanted to, but it was a combination of alcohol and speed."

"How can you be sure?" I mutter.

"Because I know him, he wouldn't. Thomas Brooke was at a party, got into the car and crashed into a tree, and when that happened, I didn't shed a tear."

"It doesn't change the fact that he paid the bullies and made my fiancé disappear." My father may not be a murderer, but he's still another kind of shit.

"No," she stares at me sternly, "it doesn't change that fact. That's why he's packing his things right now and going to find another place to live."

"He's what?" My heart falls in pure panic.

"He needs to think about the consequences and overcome his hatred. What he did to you . . . It's beyond forgiveness."

So now my parents are separating? Now my mom will pay the price?

"I shouldn't have told you." I hold my head in both hands.

"And then what, would you lie to me like he did?"

"He didn't mean to." My father definitely didn't expect for my mom to divorce him. Why the hell am I defending him?

"Your father is an adult and he should have known better. Colin was only twenty-one then and he wanted to protect you. He saw no way out."

"Don't do that," I point a warning finger. "Don't take his side."

"I'm not taking sides, I'm just calling it as I see it."

"Don't tell me why he left, because I know well enough, he chose not to come to me!"

"I won't argue with you about that." She gives up in surrender, when a knock at the door causes both of us to look away together.

"It's your father."

"It's Colin."

We say together in one breath without moving our gazes. The air in the room seems to freeze, and for a moment I forget the summer outside, as waves of chill passes through my body.

"Elizabeth?" The bass voice I feared echoes from the other side.

"I can't talk to him," I whisper.

"You can." My mom ignores me and takes a step toward the door.

"Stop!" I shout at her, "Vivian knows about him, it's not that simple."

My mom turns slowly, her body tense. "When did you tell her?"

"She found out yesterday on accident and she's expecting him to come today. What am I going to do?" I whisper in horror.

"You open the door and listen to him." She throws herself out of her halt and advances with her plan to get my ex in the house.

"Mom, please," I implore her, almost pleading, but she doesn't answer my request and opens the door.

"Mrs. Heart." Colin loses his ample confidence when he stands in front of my mom, who doesn't take away her accusing gaze.

"I'm glad you know who I am." She stands in the doorway and still doesn't let him in.

"I'm sorry." He bothers to apologize to her? Where are all the apologizes he owes me?

"Stupid boy," she says to him. "If my husband had problems, you should have come to me. You knew me well enough to know I could handle him."

"I just wanted to protect Elizabeth." He puts his hands in his pockets.

"You failed, young man." She doesn't approve. "You left her alone. Do you think she was safe, that her heart was protected?"

"Elizabeth," he looks over my mom's shoulder and our eyes lock, confused and helpless.

"If I were you I'd grovel." She opens the door and lets him walk inside. "Call me later, I want to know what the boy has to say."

Colin knows it's best for him to shut up and not resent the nickname my mom chose.

"I'll call," I strain in suspense as she steps out and closes the door behind her, leaving me to face my new reality.

"Elizabeth—" Colin opens his mouth, but I cut him off.

"Why don't you call me Liz?" My eyes are fixed on his surprised face.

"I didn't think . . ." He frowns, as if straining his mind to find a good answer.

"No, Colin, you didn't think."

"I just can't." He remains standing at a safe distance from me by the front door. Not taking any step in my direction.

"Can't what, show some humanity?" I insult him.

"Show you affection." His answer leaves me slack jawed.

"You don't like me?" I mutter through the curtain of shock on my face.

"Is that what you think I said?" He seems astonished by my

conclusion. "I didn't say I don't like you, I said I can't show you affection."

"Just as you can't apologize," I add more fuel to the burning fire that is our lives.

"Yes," he nods.

"You should apologize!" I roar out of nowhere, my patience over. "I deserve an apology, I deserve a thousand apologies and you'll give them to me, you owe them to me!"

"I can't!" He raises his voice back at me, his words hitting me like a fist to my belly, threatening to fold me to the floor.

"When exactly did you stop loving me?"

"Elizabeth," he grits his teeth.

"When did it happen?" The pain cuts through me like a sharp knife. "When you enlisted and didn't look back, or when you slept with the first girl and discovered that you didn't miss me?"

"Watch it," his breathing quickens, his enormous chest rising and falling, pressing against to his white button shirt with every breath.

"Answer me!" I burst out. "When did it happen? With the second girl, the third, the tenth? Or when you ran away on our wedding day and decided to leave me alone, when did you stop loving me?"

"You know the answer!" He gives me a look that makes me shrink. "Don't make me say it!"

"Say it," I whisper stubbornly. "Don't hide anything from me."

"Never." His words are a tornado that threatens to pass my path and take me with it.

"You're lying." I shake my head in total refusal to accept what he said.

"You asked for an answer and you got one." He stabilizes his steadfastness. "You got a lot of answers. Your father forced me to leave, but it was my choice to run away from his threat. I came back because I have nothing to lose anymore, and I've never, ever, stopped loving you."

"You're playing games." I don't know how I still manage to stand, how I manage to breathe. How could it be that he still loves me?

"That's why I don't apologize, Elizabeth." He gestures at me with his hand. "That's why I keep my distance. Because I know that if I get closer, you will reject me. It's easier to stay cold and alienated than to face the fact that you might never love me again."

"You don't know what you're saying."

"Believe me, I've had enough years to think about it, I'm pretty sure of what I'm saying."

"I don't love you anymore." I stick a poisoned arrow in his heart. "And I can't forgive you."

I'm not sure it's true. I'm not sure of anything, but it's better if that's what he thinks. Stop him from getting ideas in his head.

"I didn't think you did." He locks his jaw again, his cheekbones sticking out even more now, "but I still love you, and I'm torn between my heart, that's begging me to woo you twenty-four/seven, and my head, telling me to let you live your life."

"Don't woo me," I falter in alarm.

"Just so we're clear," his voice rattles, "Vivian is not the only one I came back for."

"We're clear." I nod in understanding.

"And tell your mom I'm not a boy."

"She kicked my dad out of the house," my voice breaks. "My family is destroyed."

"The only thing I'm sorry for is that my father didn't die five years ago. I was twenty-one and made bad decisions, but that's no reason for Vivian not to have a dad."

"Your daughter is expecting you at five." I decide to end the conversation.

"I'll come over."

"You can go now." I motion to the door, my headache growing.

"Good bye, Elizabeth." He gives me one final look, then turns his back and walks out of the house that was ours, before foreign forces intervened and changed the rules of the game. I crash on the sofa, my heart pounding wildly.

Never.

He never stopped loving me, and my father is a villain. Colin made the wrong decision, which seemed logical to him at that cursed moment when he lay on the floor bleeding, and from that moment on I had to live with the consequences.

The air is drawn from my lungs, closing on my windpipe.

I don't love you anymore, and I can't forgive you.

And now all I can do is pray to God that he won't make another wrong choice, that he won't harm our daughter who is only starting to know him.

CHAPTER SIXTEEN

*V*ivian and I have spent the time in tense anticipation awaiting the knock on the door, which comes at exactly a quarter to five. She leaps out from the sofa and runs to open it, despite my loud protests.

"Ask who it is!" I raise my voice to her from where I am in the kitchen.

"Who is it?" she shouts at once.

"It's Colin." His bass voice answers from the other side and she opens the door without hesitation.

"Hey, Colin." She stands there smiling broadly at him.

"Hello, Vivian, can I come in?" He sounded confused for a moment. Neither one of us knows what to do next.

"Yeah." She moves and gives him room. He walks slowly and glances at me. I take a deep breath and try to keep my cool for the girl.

"Good afternoon, Elizabeth," he greets me formally.

"You, too," I manage to answer with difficulty.

"Daryl called me a liar again." Vivian informs him and pulls him by his hand toward the living room.

"I'm sorry to hear that." He sits on the sofa, his body tense.

"I don't care." She climbs up beside him and sits on her knees. "He's not always nice."

"That's what I heard. What are you going to do about it?"

"She's isn't even five," I grumble aloud as I wash the rest of the dishes in the sink. "What do you expect her to do?"

"You can choose other friends, Vivian, those who don't call you names." He is blatantly ignoring my question.

"But everyone loves Daryl." She wrinkles her sweet face.

"You don't have to do what everyone else does. You're a big girl and can choose your own friends," he answers in a confident voice.

Yes, Viv. Don't be fooled by guys who everyone loves. That's a good lesson for life.

"Where have you been?" She tackles him with a hard question. I expect more of the same will come later.

"I was in the army," he tries to explain, "in the desert."

"They don't have phones in the desert?" She's not a sucker. Thank God, she's smart.

"Not always," he answers, shifting uneasily.

"And letters?"

"Sometimes." The liar writhes.

"When Louisa's father left, he called every week from New York." She frowns.

"New York is a big city, there are phones everywhere."

"Were you there?" She opens her eyes in amazement.

"Yes, I was in many places."

"Where else?" She gets excited and forgets to make his life hard.

"At the beach," he answers with relief, now that the investigation has changed direction. "Have you ever been to the sea?"

"No." She shakes her head. "Mom said it's dangerous there."

"It's a four hour ride," I defend myself.

"I know." He gives me a look that makes it clear he remembers how long the trip takes. We both remember our vacation.

"What do you want to do with Colin?" I ask Viv so as not to talk about the time we spent on the beach, lighting a bonfire and staying up all night.

"I want to bake cookies." She stares at him pleadingly.

"I'm afraid your mom is the one who knows how to bake," Colin hastens to apologize.

"Can we bake together? Please, Mama?" she chirps.

"I have to finish cleaning and then shower," I evade.

"You took a shower in the morning before I got up." She gives me away. "Your hair was wet."

"I need to shower again."

"But Colin doesn't know how to bake," she protests loudly.

"Then do something else. You can watch TV, he can put a movie on for you." I answer as though they are both five years old and not as if one of them is an adult.

"I'd love to watch a movie with you," Colin picks up the sign without waiting for Viv's answer.

"You'll die for Elsa!" She claps her hands in excitement, "Die."

"I hope to stay alive, if you don't mind, Viv." He laughs loudly at her enthusiastic behavior and turns on the DVD.

"Wait till you see Anna!"

"I see that you haven't yet installed the new television." He stares at the huge box in the corner of the living room.

"I didn't get to it," I grumble. "I had things to do."

"I can handle it when we're done with the movie," he hastens to suggest.

"If you want." I refuse to show enthusiasm.

"Shhh," Vivian scolds me, "you're bothering us!"

Wonderful. He's become a member of her forces, and I'm the enemy.

"I won't disturb you," I murmur to myself as the film begins and they both lean back in sync, as in a scene from Forrest Gump. The blonde girl, who looks exactly like her father, rests her head on his shoulder, unconsciously smashing my heart.

I have to let it happen. I can't stand in her way. Painful as it may be, he returned and he is her dad, and I have to accept reality and not fight it, despite my strong will.

Minutes later, I freeze when something incomprehensible takes place in the living room. With a slowness that goes on forever, I turn and stare at Vivian, who is standing on the sofa, singing with Anna and waving her hands to her father, who is . . . singing with her. Really singing with her, in his bass voice. He answers her exactly in the right line, and . . . Where did he learn the ridiculous words or gestures they both make in the same second?

"What the hell?" I ask too loudly. Colin glances at me over the sofa and shrugs his shoulder nonchalantly. "Have you practiced?"

"Say goodbye . . . To the pain of the past..." He chants and raises an eyebrow at me and . . . No, Colin, it's not funny.

"Love is an open door!" Vivian spreads her arms to the sides and hops.

"Life can be so much more!" he answers her, and I throw the dishcloth on the table furiously, go into the bedroom, and slam the door, shaking the little house. Sitting down on the bed, I let the tears come.

Why is he doing this to me? Why did he tell me he didn't come back just for Vivian but for me, too? Does he have any idea how painful it is? I dismiss the thought as fast as it comes. It doesn't matter. Even if he is hallucinating that he can turn the wheel, we both know it's impossible. We both know that the years have done their part. They have kept us apart, gaped a chasm between us. Now we just have to find a way to build a bridge over it for Vivian's sake. Not for anything else.

"Elizabeth," a voice calls for me from behind the door. I haven't left the room in the last twenty minutes. I just whimpered on the bed in indignation.

"Are you done?" I wipe my wet cheeks.

"I think Viv is hungry, can you come out?"

"What happened, don't you know how to make food?" I shoot without thinking. "You don't know what she likes? Why don't you ask her, why don't you get interested and get to know her?"

"I can order pizza, if you're okay with it."

I'm okay with nothing.

"Do what you want." I refuse to open the door.

"Do you want something?" He doesn't wade into the battle.

I want you to disappear. Can you do that? Can you evaporate and give me back my life?

"I'm not hungry," I sniff.

"Okay," he sighs softly. I can't hide here all evening. I'll have to go out and face his presence in my house, in our world, sometime.

But Viv shouldn't see me crying, it will only cause more trouble.

"Mama, we left you three slices in the fridge." Vivian runs toward me with her arms stretched when I finally leave the room.

"Thank you, sweetheart. Is the movie over?" I pick her up in my arms.

"Yes," Colin replies, rising from the chair, "Vivian helped me connect the new TV. I think I'll go now."

"When will you come again?" Viv turns her head to him.

"I'll talk to your mom about it." He clears the two plates from the table and takes them to the sink.

"Leave them," I say immediately, before he finds another reason to stay. "I'll wash them later."

"Why can't you come tomorrow?" Viv insists on getting answers.

"I'm busy," he says in an uncertain tone that makes me think he's lying.

"Day after tomorrow," she continues her attempts.

"When I talk to your mom," He smiles forcedly.

"You have to get in the shower," I change the subject.

"Bye, Colin," she chirps at him.

"Bye, Vivian," he answers quietly. "Elizabeth . . ."

"Good night," I address him coldly.

"Good night." He pauses for a second and then exits the house, leaving us alone to deal with the new situation he has created.

COLIN YOUNG: We need to reach an agreement.

Elizabeth Heart: Not tonight.

Colin Young: When can I see her again?

Elizabeth Heart: Not tonight, Colin!

Colin Young: There's a fair all weekend, I'd like to take her.

He ignores my request to leave it for one miserable evening.

Elizabeth Heart: Fine.

Colin Young: Sunday. I'll come around four.

Elizabeth Heart: She'll be ready.

Colin Young: Thank you.

Elizabeth Heart: Good night.

I throw the phone on the couch and close my eyes. And so it begins.

CHAPTER SEVENTEEN

*V*ivian stands in front of the mirror and studies the new floral dress I bought her. There is no chance I would send her to him with a worn outfit and give him the chance to say something about it. I go to open the door for Colin, who reappears just in time. Her birthday is approaching and with it my growing anxiety, when I think of what to do.

"Hey." He stands in the doorway and glances over my shoulder.

"She's coming," I inform him. "Don't buy her popcorn."

I have no idea what he knows, so I'd better keep him up to date with what little time I have.

"No popcorn," he repeats.

"If you're having hot dogs, you have to slice them vertically. She doesn't like mayonnaise, and don't forget to fasten her seat belt," my head works overtime. "Do you even have a car seat?"

"I have a car seat," he tries to calm me down, "and I'll never forget to buckle her. I'll do fine. Are you sure you don't want to join us?"

"No," I dismiss his idea outright, "just keep her safe and return by seven."

"We'll be back by seven."

Viv's vigorous voice interrupts our conversation.

"Dad!" she cries aloud and naturally extends her hands to him with the clear purpose of leaping on him.

"Hello sweetie." He swings her in the air. "Are you ready?"

"Yes!" Her eyes shining, "I want to ride a pony and go on the Ferris Wheel!"

"Colin . . ." My anxiety lifts it's head.

"I'll look after her."

He promised to look after me, too, the liar.

"Have fun." I fake a smile as they walk out the door toward the huge jeep parked on the driveway. At least his car is safe . . . and expensive, really expensive when I think about it. How much did it cost? I watch Colin put Viv into her car seat. She waves enthusiastically. He closes the door and glances at the house, but doesn't smile at me. I close the door, lean my back against it and fight my tears. I fIght them with all my strength. He's her father, and he loves her. I do it for her, for the chance that she'll have him in her life and that he'll protect her. I have to try and trust him and hope that he won't break our hearts. I have no choice.

"You're tickling me!" I squirm under Colin's fingers. He's been stroking my stomach for an hour. "Calm down!"

"I can't wait for it to grow up." He leans over and kisses my belly, though it's still flat.

"It's a girl, you know that, right?" We don't really know, but I feel it in my bones, in all parts of my body. I just know it's a girl.

"I know." He kisses my ilium bone. "And I'm going to buy her a million lace dresses and teach her to ride a bicycle."

"You're a bit ahead of yourself." I burst with laughter.

"I'm going to lay the world at her feet," he says, looking up at me, "at your feet."

"I know," I whisper.

"It's a miracle, Lizzie," his voice cracks, "you and I. We're a miracle."

"It was written in the stars," I reply.

"God sent you to save me."

"Since when do you believe in God?" I twist my face.

"Since now." He puts his hand on my stomach. "He exists, Lizzie, and you are proof of that."

I STAND in the living room, the silence in the house seeming to burn my soul. Vivian's absence is noticeable every minute that passes. I try not to imagine what they are doing together, because the pain becomes unbearable.

He's making her laugh.

He was always funny, and so strong that sometimes he would crush me in his embrace. I don't know what I missed the most after he left. Everything was significant. Every word he said to me, every kiss and every message. His love was huge, like him, like his fears.

Am I capable of forgiving?

I lie down on the sofa and close my eyes, the pictures running through my head. Me, standing in a white dress and waiting for him to appear as he was packing his bag and scribbling a few words on the page.

I never stopped loving you.

I try to remove the image of Colin lying on the floor bleeding, my father threatening him and forcing him to leave. Why didn't you come to me? My cheeks get wet. Ever since he came back, I haven't stopped crying and thinking what would have happened if he hadn't left. If he had stayed and raised our family and taught Viv to ride a bike as he wanted. What would have happened if he built her the wooden house he had dreamed of and put her to sleep every night? Maybe I should have looked for him, looked for answers, and not wallowed in my pain, not believed my father, who never liked him. Maybe I should have fought for him.

Maybe he would have stayed, as he had promised. Maybe he really . . . still loves me?

THE PHONE MAKES me jump and I gasp, trying to soothe my heartbeat.

"Hello!"

"Mama, I was riding the brown pony!" Vivian sounds happy. Thank God nothing happened.

"I'm glad."

"I ate a sugar cloud," she continues enthusiastically.

"A sugar cloud?" I frown. "Oh, cotton candy."

"Daddy said it was a cloud."

"That's what he said?" I mutter. "Can I talk to him?"

After a few seconds Colin's voice comes through the phone.

"Elizabeth?"

Something awakens deep inside me, like a monster rising from its winter slumber. "You're having fun." I bite my lips.

"Of course." I can imagine his face shining, "We'll be back in time. You should have joined us."

"Maybe next time," I reply quietly.

"I have to go, we're going on the Ferris Wheel."

"Good," I wipe my eyes from the last tears, "Bye."

He hangs up. Thank God I didn't go with them. Thank God I didn't give in to illusion. I know how I would feel, how tempting it might have been. Drops of normality in a reality where nothing is logical—virtual reality. A dad, a mom and a child, make believe family. An elusive happiness that would disappear within hours and leave behind emptiness. Remnants of love.

"DID YOU ENJOY YOURSELVES?" I ask Colin, who carried Vivian in his arms, after she fell asleep on the way home, so I could put her in bed. I left the bedroom to find that her father was still standing at the door.

"We had a great time, thank you." He moves around and peers at his watch.

"Hurrying somewhere?"

"I have a date," he blurts out to my surprise.

"Date?" I make sure I heard right, "Like, date date?"

"Date." I think he's trying to get back at me for the going out with Dr. Diaz. Actually, I'm sure of it.

"Do I know her?" I cross my arms. If he's thinking of introducing his dates to my girl, he'd better think again.

"Lauren."

"Go to hell," I swear, without attempting to stop it.

"Elizabeth," he says in a calm tone, "we are not a couple. You've made it very clear that isn't going to change. You may be happy alone, but I'm not. I want more from my life. I want . . ."

"You want more?" I snort, "With Lauren?"

"We've gone out twice, I'm not planning a wedding or anything like that." He puts his hands in his pockets.

"Why plan a wedding if you're not going to show up anyway?"

"Will this go on for long?" He locks his jaw.

"As long as I feel like," I say sharply, "Lauren . . ."

"Yes!" he bursts out, "I'm going out with Lauren. At least she doesn't treat me like a total failure."

"Sure, she is not the one you left pregnant!"

"Jesus Christ, Elizabeth, I'm not that boy." He gasps, his chest rising and falling with each breath.

"I don't know who you are." I shake my head.

"You're making no effort to find out! I don't want Lauren, I want you!"

"No."He can't just say that. Can't just throw out words he doesn't mean.

"I can't stop wanting you," he says quietly in a defeated voice, "but I lost the opportunity I had."

I hold the door tightly and worry that, if I leave it, I'll crash. If I let go, he will enter, not only Vivian's life but mine, too.

"You should go," I stammer pathetically.

"If that's all you have to say," he doesn't take his blue eyes off me, "don't blame me for going out with other people."

"Typical man," I sneer, "can't survive a few months without . . ."

"Sex?" he fires the word at me. "Do you think it's about sex?"

"It's sure as hell not because of Lauren's brilliant brain. She, as we both know, is not the sharpest tool in the shed."

Lauren, who was captain of the cheerleading team, is a beautiful blonde and was the object of every high school boy's fantasy. I wouldn't be surprised if she and Colin were sleeping together before we met. After all, Lauren was a perfect match for him.

"She may not be as bright as you are," Colin's voice reverberates in my ears through the screen of the past, "but she's good to me, she appreciates me, she takes interest in how my day was, what I love and what makes me happy. So no, Elizabeth, it's not about sex."

"I'm sure that can't hurt." I can't let go of the subject.

"I have no idea."

"You haven't slept with her?" My mouth opens wide of its own accord.

"No, not that it's any of your business," he states resentfully.

"It really isn't. You can go out with whoever you want." I manage to recover a trace of my pride.

"You're such a fool," he scolds me.

"Is that how you talk to Lauren?"

"This conversation is going nowhere."

"Where did you expect it to go?" I fail my attempt to convey indifference. "If you think you love me, why are you going out with other women? Are you hoping the two of you will fall head over heals in love?"

"I don't *think* I love you," he raises his voice. Apparently my choice of words doesn't evade him. "I fell in love once, I don't expect it to happen again. I do hope I can build a good life with someone, loveless as it may be!"

"And Lauren knows?" I ask in astonishment, almost in a whisper.

"She knows what I can give, I don't lie to her."

"Lucky girl," I whisper again.

"Elizabeth," he sighs in frustration.

"Go. You don't want to be late, you don't want to keep Lauren waiting. She might think you've disappeared," I insult him with obvious intent.

"Keep your hatred to yourself," he says, turning his back and walking briskly toward his impressive jeep.

He's going out with Lauren. He'll probably take her to a nice restaurant, make her laugh and be charming, as he always was. He'll probably kiss her, too. Who wouldn't want to kiss Lauren?

He used to be mine. His lips kissed me and burned on my lips, and his mouth whispered words that were only for my ears, and now he is going out with someone else, looking for a new life, compromising just so as not to be alone. Just to build the future he promised me. The future my daughter deserves.

CHAPTER EIGHTEEN

*C*olin Young: I'm sorry I called you a fool.

Three days have passed since he left me standing in the doorway and went out on his stupid date. In the message he sent the next day he asked me to give Vivian his love and wrote that he would come over in a few days. He seemed to want to give both of us time to quell the rage.

Elizabeth Heart: Whatever.

I still can't forgive him. Maybe I never will.

Colin Young: I just want us to get along. We have a child, and that's what matters.

Elizabeth Heart: I don't care about your apology, and you can keep playing the good father till the cows come home. We both know you might disappear as quickly as you came.

Colin Young: I'm not leaving, so you can stop waiting for that moment. I heard your layoffs went into effect.

Mr. Blunt's store was closed yesterday and I have become officially unemployed. A great addition to my daily worries.

Elizabeth Heart: I'll find a new job.

Colin Young: Doing what?

Elizabeth Heart: I'll be an atomic scientist, Colin.

Colin Young: Don't blame me for you not going to school. You made that stupid decision yourself, completely.

Elizabeth Heart: If you say so.

Colin Young: You can't blame me for that.

Elizabeth Heart: What would you have done if I had gone to medical school, sat and waited? Held a grudge because I'm smarter than you and could get somewhere with my life?

Colin Young: Is this the story? That you are smarter than me?

Elizabeth Heart: Isn't that why you left? Because you thought you had nothing to give me?

I know that's not why he left.

Colin Young: I knew you hated me, but I didn't imagine you'd become a bitch.

Elizabeth Heart: A fool and a bitch. Wow. You are full of compliments. What next, Colin, fat, ugly? You sobered up and realized that you prefer the dumb cheerleaders to me? Maybe that's why you left?

Colin Young: Sure, I left 'cause you weren't pretty enough.

Elizabeth Heart: Why don't you leave again? We were good without you.

Colin Young: If it weren't for me, you wouldn't have the money to feed our child. Look at yourself, living in a one-bedroom house, solitary, judgmental. I may not be the boy I was, but you're definitely not the girl I fell in love with.

Elizabeth Heart: She's dead! And you killed her!

Colin Young: I'm done. I can't talk to you. I'll let the lawyers solve this.

Elizabeth Heart: Don't threaten me!

Colin Young: It's not a threat. Can you even afford a lawyer?

Elizabeth Heart: Don't do that.

Colin Young: You're leaving me no choice.

My mom sips her coffee as we sit together on the swing on her front porch. The two of us can't take our eyes off my father's car that has been parked across the street for half an hour. Vivian is playing at a friend's house, which leaves me time to pour my heart out to my mom and hope for the best.

"So that's what he does?" I motion my head toward my father, who is behind the wheel.

"From the moment he finishes work until I go to bed," she replies indifferently.

"Where does he live?"

"Rumor has it he rented a hotel room." I'm sure my mom knows exactly where he lives. Her gang of gossips must make sure she stays up to date.

"Are you not going to forgive him?"

"Not soon." She doesn't seem impressed by her husband's stubbornness.

"You asked him where he had the money to pay the bullies?" I'm interested.

"An old savings plan that I didn't bother to check." She shrugs. "He was the one that handled our funds. I really don't care about the money, I would pay them myself if I knew Colin was in trouble. "

"Colin's father was in trouble," I correct her.

"And his problems have become a problem for all of us. I heard he's dead."

"Four months ago," I nod, "Colin is not talking about it."

"His liver decided it was fed up." She knows more than I do, in a way that doesn't really surprise me. "Do you know they asked Colin for an organ donation?"

"I had no idea."

"He wasn't a match." She shrugs again. It seems that ever since she threw my father out the door, she's been more indifferent. Her feelings have been dulled overnight. Like me, she must feel that she doesn't know who to trust. I'm surprised that Colin agreed to be tested. I would think he would just wait for his father to parish, but he tried to save him despite everything he did to him. Maybe he didn't change after all. Maybe deep inside he is still the same man I loved?

"He's going to lawyer up," I update her with the last correspondence. "He'll try to portray me as an incompetent mom."

"He won't." She sounds much more confident than I do.

"You should have heard him, he's aggressive, he's—"

"Desperate?" She chooses the word I didn't mean. "Elizabeth, you forget who he is, what he's been through, Vivian is all he has left."

"He didn't have to leave." This mantra is beginning to wear thin.

"He's fighting, pleading for his life, for his family, and you keep pushing him away, slamming the past in his face."

"Only thing I'm slamming is the truth."

"It's not the whole truth. He knows he was wrong and he's ready to make up for it for the rest his life, but he won't be your punching bag, he's not the only culprit. He was faced with an impossible situation, and both of you will have to learn to live with what happened. He's changed and you know it."

"What I know is that he took a break from his life, made tons of money and came back here as if he were some knight in shining armor come to save me."

"He was willing to die in Afghanistan to be worthy of you." Once again her words make me think of the desert and the boy I loved, lying on some field bed or imprisoned in some bunker under bombardment.

"Don't side with him," I lower my voice and struggle with my imagination.

"Don't be blind. He risked his life to become the man he is today." She leans forward and sets the coffee cup on the table. She strokes my forearm with her fingers and adds in a soft, compassionate voice, "He didn't have to leave, but that child suffered loss after loss, and now you want to take away the only thing he has left. You do not have to love him, but you have to let him be a father."

I don't have to love him. Since when do we choose whom to love, who to hate? Where is the line, where does hatred end and make room for something else, for forgiveness? And what if the one we once loved, wasn't really forgotten, wasn't really out of our hearts and is still there, hiding and waiting for the right moment to emerge? The thought frightens me. I pull my hand from under her fingers and get up quickly from the swing.

"I have to move."

"You're running away," she sighs as I gather my bag urgently, "and you'll find yourself facing a pack of lawyers instead of solving the matter between the two of you."

I don't stay to listen to her anymore. I go down the stairs to the driveway, take a last look at my father, who hasn't moved, get into my car and get out of the driveway.

Never.

Is he going to fight me with everything he has? And for what? The right to be part of Viv's life, mine? He would forever be an inseparable part of them. He's a part of my heart, and I can't do anything to change it. No one took his place, no one filled the space he left. Everything was waiting for him.

His leaving wasn't his fault, he ran away because of the man who sits in front of my mom's house in his car and watches life continuing without him. He left because the thought of someone chasing me was too frightening, threatening. He never stopped loving me.

The line is blurring, fading, and I'm not able to notice it anymore. I don't know if I hate or love him, want him to leave or stay forever and in another moment he could hold me hostage again, captivated by his charm.

"PLEASE DON'T TAKE me to court," I sob on the phone, standing on the balcony praying that Vivian will stay in front of the TV and not go looking for me.

"Where's Viv?"

"Inside." I sniff. "She'll see that I cried, and I don't want to explain to her, I don't know what to say."

"Let me get her out of the house," I hear a door slam, "I can be at yours in a few minutes, I'm not far away."

"I don't want lawyers," I whimper.

"Elizabeth, please, I plead, declare a cease-fire, I don't want to fight anymore, I can't fight you."

"I'm terrified, can you understand that at all?" I confess in a burst of emotion that washes over me in a surge.

"Yes, I can understand."

"You broke me to pieces, there was nothing left of me. I gave up my dreams for you."

"Let me help, dammit."

"I don't know what I need." I need stability, confidence and a new job. I need someone to lean on when my world crumbles. Could he give it to me, the guy who made me like that?

"I'll take Vivian to the movies and bring her back at eight," he goes on, "and I'll come back tomorrow morning, and we'll talk about it. Okay?"

I don't know what to say and I can't even say a word through the tears anyway.

"Elizabeth, I'll come over tomorrow morning, we'll have some coffee and talk."

"Okay," I give in and hang up the phone.

A FEW MINUTES LATER, his jeep stops in front of the house with a screech of tires. He leaps out of the car and advances quickly toward the house. One look at him, and I fall to my knees, dropping my head in defeat.

"Lizzie," he kneels in front of me, "look at me."

I shake my head. He called me Lizzie. Probably without paying any attention, probably without meaning to. He called me Lizzie and closed his fingers on my heart.

"Raise your head."

"Why?" I whisper in frustration, hating the fact he sees me in my despair. "So you can see how miserable I am, how weak?"

"Don't be silly," he puts his hand on my knee, which only makes me cry harder, "we both know you're the strongest of the two of us."

"I'm so angry!"

"I know." His hand climbs to my hair and he caresses my head, reminding me of things that have long been forgotten. Reminding me of other days and nights, good and happy and full of laughter. "I'll fix this without lawyers, okay? I'll fix it, I promise."

"Don't let her see me like this," I cry softly.

"Don't worry, go for a walk and come back in five minutes, we'll be gone."

"Thank you."

"Go." He stands up slowly and holds out his hand. I hesitate for a moment and then put my hand in his and use it to rise, and in a second I'm too close. His breathing accelerates, his huge chest rises and falls in front of me, and I want to put my head on it and close my eyes and delude myself that he is protecting me. I feel his fingers caressing my palm, refusing to leave. I don't raise my eyes, dare not meet his for fear that I will discover that there are no more lies. Only exposed truth, worry and love that haven't been forgotten.

"Go," he whispers breathlessly. I don't linger any longer, running away from him into the driveway, into the empty street that gives me a hiding place for a few moments of grace.

CHAPTER NINETEEN

"*What's happening?*" *I scream and seize my mom's hand tightly. She runs alongside the doctors who rush me out of the delivery room. "Where are you taking me? Mom!"*

"They know what they're doing," she can hardly keep up, "breathe. Just breateh."

"Don't let her die!" I cry hysterically, which makes it hard for the air to enter my lungs, only contributing to the situation.

"We're almost there, Elizabeth," the doctor in the white robe tries to calm me down without success.

"Get her out!" I can't control myself.

"You have to relax."

I feel something, fluid between my legs, reach out my hand and touch the wetness. When I pick it up, it's red.

"Colin!" I scream without thinking, without remembering that I can scream until tomorrow. He's not here, and I'm going to lose the only thing left of him. "Colin! I need you!"

"YOUR EYES ARE RED." Colin doesn't take his eyes off me as we sit at the small dining table in my miniature kitchen and drink coffee quietly. We both find it difficult to find the right words. Through the accusations and the insults that we have gone through in recent weeks, I wonder what remains of us.

"I cried all night," I admit. After seeing how I looked yesterday, I don't think anything will surprise him, and I have nothing more to hide.

"I make you so sad." He looks down at the cup of boiling coffee. "You used to be happy, you smiled, lit my day. You're not happy anymore, you're off, and it's my fault."

"I feel like I have nothing. I don't have a job, I have a child to support, and I don't know how to do it. How many years can she sleep in my room?" I look up. I know his look and the honesty that comes from him. "She needs a space of her own, and I can't give her what she needs. What kind of mom am I?"

"I repeat my offer. Do you want me to help you find a house that will suit your needs?"

"If you leave, I'll be left with a house I can't afford." That will get me into bigger trouble.

"I'm not leaving." His safe voice repeats the words he has said from the moment he returned.

"I want to believe you." I lower my head and close my eyes, the thoughts rushing through at a dizzying pace, from present to past and back to here and now. Only, the future is foggy, and I can't predict what tomorrow will bring.

"Elizabeth, I'm not leaving," he insists. "Look at me."

Don't! Don't you dare raise your head and sink into dreams that may fade like smoke in the air.

I can't resist. It's the pleading in his voice, or maybe his honesty, but like the seventeen-year-old girl I was, I yield to his request and look up into his familiar blue eyes.

"I won't leave," he emphasizes every word.

"I have to find a job." I swallow and pray that I won't say the wrong thing. That I won't give in completely and go after the words I have been waiting to hear for years.

"Why do you insist on not returning to the store?" He tries to hide the frustration in his voice without success.

"I don't want to be a saleswoman anymore," I sigh.

"And you don't want to work for me."

"Not really, but my options are limited. I have a high school education and the hours I can work are very restrictive."

"You should learn something, Liz." Again he is pragmatic, solving problems. If only he hadn't caused them in the first place.

"And how will I pay for it?" I laugh bitterly, and in response he raises an eyebrow as if the question was stupid. "Forget it, I don't need handouts."

"Would you rather be a cashier or a cleaner?" He touches a sensitive spot, hitting on exactly the work I was looking for.

"I'm a single mom, I don't have time to study," I dismiss the idea.

"I'm not saying you'll enroll in medical school," he doesn't give up, "but there must be something else, evening classes you can try. You're good with numbers, maybe accounting?"

"Really, Colin?" I roll my eyes.

"I, personally, hate accounting and pay someone to do it for me."

"You've always hated numbers." I smile a little.

"All the reports that need to be submitted, and keeping invoices." He laughs loudly. Don't you keep invoices? Is it just me who thinks it's not funny?

"Colin!"

"I'm bad at it, balance sheets, statistics."

"You can always start a modeling career if you have no other choice." I regret deeply my words one second too late. He doesn't have to know what I'm thinking about his new, compact look.

"Do you think?" He smiles smugly, not trying to hide that he is very pleased.

"Look at you." I gesture with my hand at his body.

"Do I have a new fan?" he raises an eyebrow again. Oh, shut up.

"You're photogenic, I'll admit that." Only that, and nothing else. A second later he puts his hand to my cheek, and the touch of his fingers on my skin is burning. I blush and my lip begins to tremble. Fuck.

"You're so beautiful." He strokes with his words as much as his fingers. "I didn't leave to find someone else, I always knew I would come back."

"I wish you never left." I don't stop him, I don't want him to move his hand, hugging the forgotten feeling. "I wish you'd stayed."

"I know."

"I'm trying to imagine it." My head sinks into his big palm. "You, in the desert."

"Don't." His voice turns cold and he pulls his hand gently away from my head, and the touch is gone, gone as if it were never there. "Don't try to imagine it."

"Was it as terrible as it is on the news?" I can't let it go.

"Sometimes." All I get from him is a short and laconic answer.

"You lost friends?"

"Yes."

"I'm sorry."

My mom's words echo.

That child suffered loss after loss, and now you want to take away the only thing he has left.

"That's the price of war." He refrains from elaborating, doesn't want to let me know. He doesn't want me to hear what happened.

"You didn't have to pay it."

"It was my choice," he cuts me of. "I've learned a lot about myself, I learned to take responsibility and fight for what was important to me. I love Vivian and I'd do everything for her, but she is not the only reason I came back."

"I don't know if I can forgive you." The pain in my chest

increases. "Five and a half years is a very long time, and I spent them hating you."

"Do you still hate me?"

"Sometimes," I reply sheepishly.

"And other times you don't?" I hear a glimmer of hope in his voice.

"Some nights I lie in bed," I wrap my fingers around my cup, staring at the steam rising from it, "and I'm so tired that the thoughts just creep in, and I don't fight them, and for a moment I allow myself to dream of another life. For a moment we're a happy family, but then I wake up, in this cramped and crumbling house, and get into my car that starts up only miraculously...And I hate you again."

"I don't blame you," he hastens to answer, "I hate myself. I lie in bed thinking about us, but I don't fight it. I believe that if I imagine it hard enough, it will happen."

He has to imagine it really hard, for both of us.

"What are you thinking about?" He breaks the silence.

"About Lauren," I whisper, "About you moving on."

"Tell me to wait for you."

I breathe heavily. Since his return, I have been living in two worlds that only seem to collide. Suffering from a split personality that throws me from side to side like a ship swinging on the waves. The seventeen-year-old girl begs me to forgive him and to believe him, to see again the man who promised to lay the world at her feet. But the woman and mom that I am refuses to let the walls collapse—she has too much to lose.

"I can't." The heavy responsibility on my shoulders defeats the dreamer. "It wouldn't be fair, I can't promise you anything."

"I don't need promises," his voice is quiet, "I need a chance, I just need to know we have hope, maybe . . ."

"I can't," I whisper back.

"Tell me to wait for you."

"No." I shake my head. I won't do that to him. I won't make

him wait for me as I waited for him. I know how despairing this hope, this expectation can be, and I won't drag him through the ordeal I've been through. "You need to go."

"Think about what we've been talking about," he almost pleads with his voice. "Accounting sounds like a good idea." He rises from the chair and my heart starts to pound at an uncontrollable pace. He's leaving, taking this normality of the last hour and leaving my house, and I want to scream.

"You can come again this afternoon." I raise my eyes from the coffee cup to the man towering over me. "I mean, if you have no other plans, I'm sure you're busy, but Viv will be happy."

"I'll come at five." He grabs the invitation.

"Good." My lip curls into the twinkle of a tiny, almost invisible smile. He reaches out and his thumb touches the tip of my mouth, stroking my lips gently.

"Look at that," he doesn't take his eyes off his inquiring fingers, "A smile."

"Hardly," I whisper.

"It's called a start, Elizabeth," he mutters, "one day I'll kiss those lips again."

The words he says and the way he lets them play, wake the sleeping monster and a wave of heat runs between my thighs all the way to the connection between them. For a brief moment I can feel everything throbbing, how my blood is rushing through my veins. His insolent finger teases me, taunting me. Our looks lock and knot in bonds that can't be untied, and I catch his thumb between my lips, let it slip into my mouth and meet my tongue, playing with it.

I know what he's thinking. I see the hungry look in his eyes, and after five and a half years I know that my look is the same. My body wants it.

But he'll change his mind the moment he sees how much I've changed. He doesn't know how my body looks, what remains of it after the time that has elapsed.

I incline my head sharply and pull his thumb out of my mouth.

"You need to go," I gasp in panic, getting up quickly and collecting the coffee cups to the sink, turning my back to him so that he won't see the pain in my eyes. "Come back at five."

"Lizzie," he doesn't take the hint, or deliberately ignores it.

"Don't make me feel more stupid than I already do, okay?" my voice cracks.

"Don't be mad."

"You think that's what I need now," I turn to him in an outburst of rage, "your finger in my mouth? What next, we fuck?"

"Watch your mouth," he shudders. "That's not you."

"Don't play games with me," I turn a warning finger to him, "and don't make me want you!"

We freeze at the sound of my words and then, in unison, we move, unable to stop ourselves. His body collides with mine and now it's not his finger in my mouth, it's his tongue. He wraps my hair around his fist, his hunger knowing no bounds. Neither does mine.

He presses my back against the marble and I grab the collar of his shirt. Five and a half years of longing find the place they we're looking for, falling apart into this kiss that threatens to destroy us. For a moment, during which I'm trapped between the marble and his vast body, the world has no room, and the past hasn't even a small crack to enter through. I'm protected from my thoughts, from my fears, from the next minute. I'm merely a distilled essence of yearning, no more and no less.

Our lips separate, forehead meets forehead, and our eyes remain closed, for neither of us can say what we'll discover if we open them.

Only Colin's whispered words send shivers over every inch of my skin.

"One day you'll return me my heart."

CHAPTER TWENTY

*T*his is not happening to me!

I turn the key and try to start my car, the pressure in my chest increasing. My thoughts are still vague since that kiss this morning. Since Colin left my house in silence and left me burning and confused. I can't be late. Mrs. Robbins is willing to accept many things, but delays lead to fines. She doesn't care about my car or the state of my bank account. In a mild hysterical fit I call my mom and pray with all my might that I won't have to take a taxi to the daycare.

You have money for that.

I'm not touching that money. I know what would happen. I'd take just a little, and then just a little more, and before I know it, I wouldn't have a penny left. That money is for Vivian.

"Lizzie?" My mom answers after two rings.

"Tell me you're home, that you're free." I get out of the wreck and slam the door shut.

"What do you need?"

I need a brain, and one that actually functions if possible, please, instead of kissing my ex and missing him.

"My car broke." Again. It's getting ridiculous.

"I'll pick up Viv." She saves me for the millionth time.

"Bring her home, Colin—" I blurt.

"Colin?"

"He's coming at five to spend time with her." God only knows how it will go after this morning's stupid behavior.

"I'll bring her home," she answers in a particularly pleased tone.

"Thanks, I'll call the tow truck." I'll have to find a solution for tomorrow morning or I'll have no way of taking Vivian to daycare. Dammit, it's just not fair!

"HEY," I open the door to Colin an hour later and try to keep our eyes from meeting. "Viv, Colin is here!"

"Dad!" She comes running from the back yard, leaving dusty footprints on the floor.

"Where's your car?" He lifts Vivian naturally and holds her in his arms, her legs wrapped around his waist.

"In the garage, it didn't start. Again."

"How did you get Viv back from daycare?" he frowns.

"I called my mom." As always. Welcome to my world, Colin.

"Your mom?"

"Who was I supposed to call?"

"Me," the insult in his voice is clear, "what do you not understand 'bout the sentence, 'let me help?'" He puts Viv on the floor and leans over to her. "I think we'll have dinner out today, sweetie, if that's all right with you."

"Okay." She shrugs as he gives her a hand.

"First we'll stop somewhere and help Mom and then we'll go to the playground."

"What are you doing?" I mutter in confusion.

"Buying you a decent car." He straightens up with a forced smile.

"You're not buying me a new car!" I burst out in shock. They both stand at the door holding hands and waiting for . . . something that is not going to happen!

"Elizabeth," he keeps his cool, though I'm guessing it costs him dearly. "Bring your bag and get into my car or I can choose you a ride myself. I can't promise you'll love my choice."

"Colin," I can't move, "you can't buy me a car!"

"You're not keeping your junk of a car anymore, it's not safe, and you're driving my child around."

"I don't like our car," Viv intervenes at the worst moment, "it always gets stuck, and Mom swears, but that's funny."

"It's not funny," I resent, "and I don't swear."

"She swears and then calls Granny to come save us." The little snitch…

"Colin, please don't do that."

"I'm not asking you." He waves away my resistance without blinking. "You can be as angry with me as you want, but get your bag, now."

COLIN'S CAR SMELLS GOOD. The smell of a man and of new leather and of luxury. Who knew prestige had a smell? Well it does, it smells like this jeep. Like the power and confidence it emits as it navigates the road between the tiny cars. Vivian is in the backseat, listening to our conversation with curiosity, a reminder that I have to watch my mouth at all times.

"Do you have a preference?" Colin ignores my protests.

"I love my car." I hate it, but Colin is not supposed to buy me a new one.

"Excellent, so we've decided."

Very funny.

"At least make it be black," I mutter in defeat. He's buying me a car, and I can't do anything about it.

"Your requirements need upgrading." He smiles without moving his eyes from the road.

"What do I know about cars, Colin?"

"You knew enough back when we bought our faltering beetle," he says quietly.

"I knew nothing," I correct him. "I took one look at it and knew it'd give us trouble."

"What ever happened to it?" He gives me a quick glance then looks back at the road.

"What happens to all the old cars? It went to the garage and never came back." After it got stuck in the middle of the road—when I was eighth months pregnant. I stood at the side of the road and cursed Colin for choosing it.

"It went to the garage and never came back," his mouth curls into an evil smile, "sort of like your car."

"You're funny," Vivian chirps from the backseat.

"Thanks, Viv." He glances at her in the mirror. "What car do you think we should buy?"

"Chevy," she answers to our amazement.

"Where do you know cars from?" I turn my head and stare at her in shock.

"Daryl says you should only buy American cars," she replies in the serious tone of someone quoting the most important thing she has ever heard. "He says we shouldn't give the money to others, that we should be pitriots."

My jaw drops. I don't care if she twisted the word. When the hell did she learn about patriotism? And from Daryl no less?

"Do you want to be a pitriot?" Colin immediately cooperates with her, not surprisingly.

"Yes, like you, Daddy," she answers proudly. "Daryl says all the soldiers are pitriots."

Colin's smile erases. We both know that patriotism had nothing to do with him enlisting.

"Looks like we're buying you a Chevrolet." He takes a deep breath.

"You really don't have to," I whisper, but don't get a reply. His thoughts seem to be wandering somewhere else. I should shut up and let him buy me the damn car if it would do him good, even for a moment, and make him forget what he was thinking about now.

"THANK YOU." I open the car dealership door and walk out into the warm weather after freezing under the air conditioner for the past half hour while Colin conducted tough negotiations with the owner. Vivian behaved like a sport, sat on my lap and played on my phone. Colin asked a thousand questions, which I would not have thought to ask, while I listened quietly.

My new car will arrive tomorrow, and by then I'll wait patiently. Kinda.

"Stop thanking me," Colin grumbles again. I may have thanked him once or twice in the past five minutes, but he just bought me a new Chevrolet Cruise.

"I'd love to buy you dinner." I try to think of another way to thank him without saying the words explicitly.

"Do me a favor," he pauses and gives me a look I can't decipher, "I don't want to talk about it, I just want to spend the afternoon without you thanking me every thirty seconds in any way you can, okay?"

"Okay," I nod at once.

"Thank you," he replies in an assuaged tone. "Vivian, what do you want to eat?"

"Waffle." She jumps in her place.

"Let's go eat waffle." He turns his head slowly toward me, probably waiting to hear me resist.

"Waffle sounds like a great idea," I hasten to cooperate.

"Really?"

"Great idea."

"What happened to 'real food first', and all the rules we can't deviate from or some disaster will occur?" He seems pleased with what he said.

"I think I broke some rules this morning, around nine if I'm not mistaken, and the sky didn't fall," I practically whisper.

"But you have to admit that the earth shook." He raises an eyebrow arrogantly.

"You're not serious," I open my eyes wide.

"Eight on the Richter scale, if you ask me." He picks up Viv and carries her to his car.

"Hardly four!" I call and trail after them.

"Well," he laughs,"I guess one can aspire."

"Not going to happen again, Colin!"

"Mhm." He opens the car door and sits Viv in.

"Keep dreaming." I take the passenger seat and buckle myself up, hearing Colin murmur.

"That's exactly what I'm doing."

"I WANT MAX THE GREAT," Vivian manages to say, her mouth full of whipped cream and chocolate syrup, as we sit in one of the diners not far from the car dealership. She remembers bringing up the subject of her birthday, which will take place in a week.

"Who's Max the Great?" Colin has no idea.

"The neighborhood charlatan," I bite into a potato chip. Vivian might have given up real food, but Colin and I ordered hamburgers with sides, onion rings and strawberry milkshakes.

"And what is the role of the charlatan?" Colin takes a sip of his drink.

"Blowing up balloons, and the price of course," I explain, "and he calls himself a clown."

"Oh," Colin nods, "one of those."

"He's funny," Viv interrupts, "and it's my birthday, I get to choose."

"We're not having Max the Great." I expect a loud disappoint-ment in a moment.

"Never!" She grumbles. "You never agree to anything I want!"

"Behave, please," I remind her of where we are.

"You're mean," she declares to my pale face.

"Vivian," Colin stares at her reassuringly, not threateningly but definitely determined, "there are other ways to celebrate your birthday."

"I don't want anything else," she frowns angrily. "I want Max, everyone invites Max!"

"You don't have to be like everyone else, you're special," he says in his caressing voice.

"Why don't I ever have a party?" Her lip begins to tremble and I know the tears are about to appear. "Why am I told NO all the time, and everyone gets everything?"

As I guessed, tears begin to flow, and the waffle is forgotten on the plate when her cheeks get wet. The guy sitting opposite me becomes helpless in an instant in face of the unexpected crying he is not used to.

"Viv . . ." I try to hug her, but she pushes me away, Colin panting heavily.

"You're mean!" she accuses me again.

"We'll do something else." I stare at Colin in despair.

"Viv, stop crying, you'll ruin the surprise." Colin reaches his long arm over the table and places it on weeping Viv's forearm.

"What surprise?" She looks up at him. Yes, Colin, what surprise?

"If I tell you, it won't be a surprise." He smiles. I can swear that he is pleased with himself to the roof, because his smug tone is not hidden from my ears.

"Mom never makes surprises."

"Of course she does," he says, not excited. "Finish your waffle and we'll go to the playground before it gets dark."

"Colin . . ."

"Later." He waves his hand at me as if trying to silence me.

"Okay." I go back to looking at Viv, who has gone back to eating greedily the very unreal food in front of her.

"And don't call your mom mean," Colin adds in a serious tone that makes Viv look up at him. "She loves you, don't forget that."

"I'm sorry," she nods, looking up at me for forgiveness.

"We'll do something else, I promise." I commit myself to something artful and completely incomprehensible.

"Don't tell me!" she hastens to silence me. "It's a surprise."

Yes, Viv. It definitely is a surprise. For the both of us.

VIVIAN IS WHOOSHING down the red slide. She is happy. She laughs loudly. Her blonde hair swirls in the cool afternoon breeze and her cheers echo through the playground.

Colin and I sit on a bench not far from her and look at the magical thing we've created together, romping around.

"Tell me about her birth." Colin's request makes my heart drop.

"It's a long story," I try to deflect.

"Are you in a hurry?"

"I don't like thinking about it," I sneak a quick glance at him, and my eyes meet his inquiring blue ones.

"You said she was in distress." I guess he hasn't forgotten the accusations I made when he appeared in Mr. Blunt's store by surprise.

"My water broke," I look back at the little girl I almost lost that day, "and my mom took me to the hospital in her car and I thought it would take time, you know, until the contractions arrived, like we read online."

Colin was obsessed with the birth. I remember him sitting for hours reading every article he could find. In the end, the only one who needed that information was me.

"It should take hours." He sounds troubled.

"My contractions got stronger, even before I got to the ward." I remember the unbearable pressure, the pain that followed, and the fear that I would not survive. "They put me in the delivery room and everyone was calm, until they connected me to the monitor. From there . . . everything became chaotic." Colin is silent. "She was in distress, and the monitor showed her pulse was slowing, they had to get her out as quickly as possible."

"Do they know what happened?" His voice is shaking a little.

"Placental abruption," I reply. "I started to bleed on the way to the O.R. I remember the lights on the ceiling rushing past me, my mom holding my hand, me crying. I was told to calm down and breathe, but I didn't understand what was happening, so I screamed."

"Elizabeth," he clenches his hands until his knuckles turn white, "what have I done?"

"I called for you." The feeling of suffocation makes it difficult for me to continue. "I begged God to send you, then I pleaded for Him not to let her die. He probably had to choose between my requests, and He chose right."

He also gave me something I didn't ask for—my infertility— but I'd die before I say a word to Colin. It's none of his business.

"You said she was in an incubator."

"I woke up dazed after hours. I asked to see her, but I couldn't stand on my feet, and she needed help breathing better. She was in the NICU, and I wasn't with her."

"You were there all the time, don't blame yourself."

"I didn't hug her until morning, I didn't breastfed her the way I'd dreamed, I didn't take her home the way we had planned, and from that day on, whenever she coughed or cried or even when her stomach ached because of gas, I thought she was going to die."

"I'll never forgive myself." He leans forward, resting his elbows on his knees and dropping his head.

"She still needs you, Colin." I'm trying to fix what broke long ago. "It's not too late, but you can't go away, you can't do that to her, I've barely survived your disappearance, but she's five, the damage she'll suffer . . ."

"I'll never leave her again," he murmurs in a broken voice. "She'll never be alone."

"Don't break your promise," I whisper.

"It's getting cold." He changes the subject sharply, raises his head, and the look on his face is distant. "I'll take you home."

"Vivian," I call to her, waving my hands. "It's late!"

She jumps off the slide and runs up to us, a huge smile smeared across her face.

"Ready to go?" Colin stands and picks her up.

"Ay-ay Captain!" She chirps with a rolling laugh. He carries her lightly in his arms to the car, and I follow them, praying that he will stand by his word and not break her heart.

CHAPTER TWENTY-ONE

"So, Colin bought you a new car." My mom finally comments on the car I came with. The black car is parked in front of her house, shining in the sunlight, the last rays of the afternoon caressing the metal chassis. Yes. Colin bought a new car for the unemployed, single mom, and the smell of it . . . The smell of that car, and the way it glided on the road. My driving experience has never been so enjoyable, though I'm now being extra careful and afraid any driver down the road will scratch my gift. Mostly I'm afraid of the man who is still sitting in his car across the road from my mom's, staring stupefied at the car in which I entered the driveway. I'm sure he knows who bought it, and he's probably not happy.

Vivian is watching a movie in the living room, and we drink coffee in the kitchen and try not to talk about my parents' fragile relationship. This leaves us talking about my relationship, which is certainly as fragile.

I know that now another conversation is going to happen about my ex who is trying to get back into my life in every possible way. He may have said he wouldn't woo me, at my request, but since that kiss, my body has awakened and is calling him back. The problem is that my heart is starting to cooperate, and it scares me to the bone.

"I'm surprised you let him." My mom raises her hands in front of me dramatically.

"I had no choice, he made it clear this is what was happening."

"And how does it feel to let someone else take responsibility and prevent you from having a headache?"

"Too good," I admit bitterly.

"I'm sure." She, as it seems, is very pleased with the latest development.

"He decided which car, where we would have dinner, and the feeling was like—"

"Like something you can get used to."

"I don't remember the last time someone took care of everything, and I could just breathe."

"This boy loves you so much," she says bluntly.

"I think I'm aware of that." What does it help me that Colin loves me if I can't trust him?

"Give him a chance, Liz, for you."

"I need to think about it." I stare at the coffee instead of her critical face. "I have to think really hard, because I know that once I let him in, he'll steal my heart again."

"And that's bad?" As if she doesn't know how bad it might be.

"It's dangerous, I want to be sure before I decide."

"There are no guarantees in life," she throws at me a cliché that suffers from overuse.

"I'm aware of that."

"So you have a new car."

Are we going back to that?

"New car courtesy of Colin Young." Yes, I have a new, impressive, pampering, and especially not getting stuck kind of car, and what do you know, it even starts on the first attempt.

"At least cook him dinner as a thank you."

"I'll think about it." I don't want to invite him for dinner, he may try to kiss me again or do something inappropriate. "I need to talk to him about Viv's surprise."

"What surprise?"

"Something about her birthday. He sent me a message this morning and I didn't understand anything."

"So you're not bringing that clown." My mom has heard me grumbling about him more than once.

"Max the Great," I roll my eyes. "The only thing great about him is the check he gets at the end of the evening."

"What's the plan?" She gets up and clears the coffee from the table.

"Colin said he'd bring someone," if I understood correctly, "and that I should invite Vivian's friends. I suppose I could have them in the back yard." We'll buy some snacks. It won't cost too much and won't make a mess.

"That could be nice," my mom washes the cups quickly, "Vivian will be happy."

"If he doesn't screw up." I remind her of who we are dealing with.

"Give him a chance," she grumbles quietly, but I hear very well. I'll give him a chance, and he better not mess it up.

My father is standing outside my new car. He embraces Viv, who ran straight into his arms, takes a deep breath and then slowly releases the air from his lungs, in a particularly dramatic spectacle.

"Why is a new Chevrolet parked in front of my house?" He looks away from me to the new Chevy and back to me.

"Hello, Dad," I reply harshly, not wanting to talk to him. I may be wondering if I should forgive Colin, but my father is a different story. What he did is beyond any atonement I can think of. I open the car door, take Viv and sit her in the seat.

"I asked you a question," he crosses his arms.

"Colin bought it." I enjoy turning the knife in his heart, knowing that Colin's name drives him crazy.

"Did he?" he grits his teeth.

"Yes, he certainly did." I buckle Viv and close the car door so she won't hear the rest of the conversation, in case it escalates.

"If you needed a new car, you just had to say." He moves nervously.

"From *you*," I say bluntly, "I don't need anything. We're hurrying home."

"Don't be rude!"

"You lost the right to say things like that." I open the front car door, but he grabs it and prevents me from entering.

"So now the bastard gets to spend time with you?" he rages.

"Mind your own business," I stare at him furiously. "I think you have enough trouble without interfering with my life."

"Stop fighting!" I hear Viv squeak from the backseat.

"We're not fighting," I call out to her in a futile attempt to reassure her.

"Elizabeth," he takes a deep breath, "be careful, please, this guy . . ."

"Let me go, I don't want to talk to you anymore."

He looks down and releases his hand from the car door. I seize the opportunity and sit down quickly behind the wheel, slamming the door in his face. He takes two steps back and looks at me as I start engine, pull out of the driveway and slide into the traffic on the street.

"What do you want to have for dinner?" I try to make Viv forget the argument she heard.

"Potatoes." Thank God, she doesn't ask questions. I nod at her in the mirror. We'll have dinner, I'll put her bed and I'll continue to hope I can hide the dramas of my life from her.

MY PHONE RINGS on the morning of Vivian's birthday, half an

hour after I dropped her with Mrs. Robbins, as I finish my coffee and get ready to go out and buy snacks for the party. In the bedroom closet I hid the gift I bought, the dress Vivian has been wanting for months. I hope she won't be disappointed that this is all she gets.

"Hey," I reply to Colin.

"Hey, you home?"

"I'm on my way out." I put the coffee cup in the sink.

"Wait five minutes, I need to bring something over." He sounds mysterious.

"Make it quick, I really have to go out. I planned to bake and I'm missing a few ingredients."

"Five minutes." He hangs up and leaves me time to prepare my shopping list.

A few minutes later a strange noise from outside the door makes me abandon the list and go out. It takes me thirty seconds to figure out what I'm seeing and thirty more seconds to catch my breath.

The truck parked on the road, from which porters are unloading tables, leaves no room for doubt. Colin lied. He did something and didn't tell me, and he is about to hear from me about it.

"Get out of the way, Lizzie," he shouts, "we have a lot of work to do!"

I noticed that he is slipping slowly into his old habits, and my nickname returns more frequently.

"What on earth are you talking about?" I shout with total shock. "You said you were bringing something!"

He leaves the truck and workers behind and moves toward me confidently. God, why does he look so good? In a black t-shirt and faded jeans that fall from his waist he looks . . . delicious.

"Exactly. I said I was bringing something," he says smugly as he stops in front of me, his sheer size making me feel tiny. "Well, I brought something."

"You brought a truck, and your workers are unloading tables in front of my house." I call him out on his understatement.

"And balloons." He motions his head toward the truck, just as the people unload a huge balloon bridge in shades of light blue and white.

"Colin," my pulse accelerates to maximum speed, "what did you do?"

"Welcome to Arendell." The smile on his face widens and then expands further and further until his eyes smile, too.

My hand leaps to my mouth. I'm going to cry. I look at him, and he looks at me and he is not frightened by my reaction.

"Who needs Max when we have Elsa, right?" He reaches out and gently takes my hand down. "Breathe, Elizabeth, we have a long day ahead of us."

"You didn't..." I can't get a whole sentence out.

"I didn't, we did." He reaches my cheek, stroking it. "We're a team, Lizzie, you and I. Where do you want the refreshments?"

"I haven't baked yet," I mutter in amazement. "I haven't bought anything."

"It doesn't work that way, darlin'." The word he chooses causes my cheeks to burn and memories to overwhelm me. "The refreshments will arrive at three, and by that time, a kingdom will be established in your back yard. You just have to stand aside and watch it happen."

"You didn't," my eyes gleam, "really, you didn't have to . . ."

"Elizabeth," he doesn't let go of my face, "where do you want the tables?"

"In the back." I'll surely cry before this day is over. There is a great chance that for the first time in a very long time these will be tears of joy.

"Let the good people work." He leans over slowly, his lips meeting my forehead. He lingers with his kiss and holds it another second, another moment, another breath.

"Thank you," I whisper.

"Don't you dare," he whispers back, "don't you dare thank me. You're the one who raised her, it was all you."

MY HOUSE IS A HEADQUARTERS, or so it feels, as the hours pass and my back yard turns into an ornate kingdom. If I thought the balloons were lovely, it was only because I had no idea what else was coming. The maps on the tables and snowflake shaped cartons that are hanging from the trees make the place look magical, and when the refreshments arrive at exactly three o'clock, my tear bag opens.

"Vivian will faint," I wipe my cheeks and Colin laughs at me. "You know she will."

"Did you see the cake?"

"Yes." How could anyone miss it? It's three stories high, and Viv's name is on it in curly letters. The slushy machine stirs a blue drink, and he even brought a cotton candy machine, fancy cupcakes, and tons of candies and marshmallows . . . She will faint, no doubt.

"I have to go get her," I wipe another tear.

"It's been taken care of, your mom is on her way."

"You invited my mom?" My jaw drops.

"Of course. Excuse me if your father's invitation was lost in the mail." I didn't think he'd invite him, nor do I want him here, Vivian's grandfather or not.

"Colin!" A high female voice makes my gaze turn toward the house. In the doorway stands a slim girl wearing a blonde wig and a perfect Elsa dress, waving royally at us.

She's not waving at you. She's waving at him.

"Anna!" Colin calls in a hearty voice.

"It's Elsa," I strain, my nerves pressing as she steps toward us.

"Actually, it's Anna," he laughs again. "Come and meet Liz."

No, don't come. We don't need to know each other.

"Hey, Anna Rodriguez." I shake her hand formally and smile as if I'm one of the children she needs to entertain. "Colin and I have known each other for years."

Where and when did you get to know each other, and what did you do together?

"Anna lived in LA at the time I was living there," he explains, as if his words can relieve the pressure in my chest.

"Nice," I reply laconically.

"She has a birthday party company."

"I see."

Tell me, Colin, did you sleep with her?

I shut my mouth before the question slips out. After all, he didn't abstain. He said he had other girls, so maybe she was one of them?

"Oh. My. God!" The shriek from the edge of the yard makes us all jump. "That's . . . that's . . ."

Vivian stands beside my mom and stares at Anna.

"The birthday girl," Colin gathers himself first. "Come here!"

She runs straight into his arms and he lifts her into the air. "You're so big!"

"My surprise!" She doesn't calm down. "That's my surprise, right?"

"Absolutely." He hugs her warmly. "Happy birthday sweetie."

"I love you Daddy!" Her little arms surround him with difficulty.

"Thank your Mom, it's her surprise, too," he says with confidence, even though we both know I didn't do anything.

"You're awesome!" She roars at me. At least I'm not mean anymore.

"I think your birthday gift would be perfect right about now." I hold my arms out and take her from Colin. "Your friends will be arriving soon, and we have to prepare."

We leave Colin by his Elsa's side and go into the house to put on the dress I bought, arrange Viv's hair, and wear festive shoes for the grandiose event that awaits us.

. . .

My back yard is crowded. The bustle is great but I quickly realize the magical kingdom that Colin established is a magnet for moms who refuse to leave their children and go home.

Who am I kidding? We all know that it's not due to the snowflakes hanging from the trees, but to the guy who twirls his daughter around, his chest puffed with pride and his muscular arms beautifully tattooed, spreading smiles that make us all drool.

He always looked good. I know it, he knows it and every girl who's been chasing him since we were fifteen knows it, but this body he came back with takes the hormonal state of every woman within a hundred yards to new heights.

And by God they are hormonal. Giggling, waving their hair and batting their eyelashes at him. Pathetic. So what if he looks like that? So what if he produced all of this in a few hours and brought the Elsa who's dancing with the children to karaoke? He had to make up for the last few years.

"Great party," my mom comes up behind me just as I toss another pile of blue disposable glasses from the table to the bin.

"Yes," I grumble, "nice party." This party is something that will be talked about for a very long time, and it is far from being nice. It's perfect.

"It's time you took her out of your bedroom." She stands in my way and interrupts with my cleaning and rearranging.

"And put her where exactly?" I snort.

"We'll figure that out."

"You know it's not that simple."

"Get the girl out of your bedroom and put her father back in there." Her determination makes my blood start to bubble.

"We're not having this discussion." The place is full of people and her timing is lousy. "It's not going to happen."

"So get used to seeing that happen more often." She turns my attention with a small movement of her head, and there he stands, laughter rolling from his mouth, as Lena, the newly divorced mom from daycare, puts her hand on his shoulder. She's all I'm not—well groomed, tall, thin and shapely. "How long do you think he'll wait for you, how long before someone puts her hands on him?"

He smiles at Lena. He laughs at something she said. I push the glasses into my mom's hands aggressively and move toward him with firm steps. Lena drops her hand from his shoulder, takes a few steps back and moves away. Maybe she saw me and realized she should not be there.

"Liar," I strain with clenched teeth, my eyes burning.

"Liz," he tries to reassure me softly, but I've already passed the point of no return.

"You're such a liar." The insult takes hold of my breath, of every word that comes out of my mouth. He grabs my arm and pulls me aside to the corner of the yard, allowing us a little more privacy.

"What's the story, Colin?" I put my hands together in a protective gesture, "I'm not skinny enough, not pretty enough, do you want someone who wears red nail polish, red lipstick and tight clothes?"

"I want you, woman." He stares at me hard, his words undermining my confidence. "Do you hear what I'm telling you? I want you to leave our daughter with your mother so I can show you how little I care about your nail polish. As for the tight clothes," he leans forward and puts his mouth to my ear, making my cheeks redden, "I prefer the kind I can rip off you easily." He straightens up, just to meet the bewildered look on my face. He doesn't hide his intentions and certainly doesn't want just another kiss. His whispering in my ear did the trick and caused my pulse to accelerate and my breathing to become irregular.

"So why are you going out with Lauren?" I manage to maintain some dignity.

"Why did you go out with the doctor?" He tilts his head. "Were you trying to make me jealous?"

"Are you so full of yourself you think the only reason I went out with him, is so you'd envy him?"

"Yes," he answers in a steady tone. God, he is arrogant!

"Then let me be clear, I went out with him because he asked me."

"I'm asking you, too." He doesn't stop.

"Don't be ridiculous."

"I'm ridiculous?" He narrows his eyes, much less smug and pleased with himself. "You wait more than five years, and then decided to go out with someone just when I get back?"

"Amazing coincidence," I shrug, "don't you think?"

"Stop playing games," his nostrils flare up. "We both know you're not into the doctor."

"Is that so?" I continue. If he's going to make me jealous, I can make him, too.

"You want me." He rises to his full height and joins hands on his chest.

"Jesus Christ," I laugh in his face, "do you hear yourself?"

"I'll be at your house tomorrow at eight. Arrange a babysitter and wear something comfortable."

Our eyes lock, the battle is far from over. My heart is about to burst out of my chest and bleed on the grass until it stops beating.

"I'm not going out with you," I answer decisively.

"Tomorrow, eight o'clock, babysitter, something comfortable to wear." He's delirious!

"What will Lauren think about that?" I tease.

"Jealous?"

"If I were her, I would be offended to find out that you are asking someone else out, while you and her—"

"For God's sake, Liz," he exhales, "where's your head?"

"Don't insult me!"

"Where's your head?" He gets annoyed. "Do you really think I'm going out with Lauren?"

What? You piece of shit liar. He's not dating Lauren? All this was just to annoy me? He knew it would work. He knew I'd go crazy thinking about him with someone else, and he chose Lauren, of all the women in the world. He knew that thinking about him with the captain of the cheerleading squad would drive me insane.

"Are you kidding me?" I don't know whether to rage or start jumping with joy. Both responses sound equally logical. He plays with me and my feelings and throws them from one end to the other without a drop of effort.

"What am I supposed to do with her?" He rolls his eyes.

"I can come up with a number of things you and her can do."

"None of them will include intelligent conversation." His gaze settles straight into my eyes. "I know who I want and she is standing in front of me, fighting me over a date she's dying to go out on. I know I screwed up, okay, I know I screwed you and your life and my life, too, but I love you. I've loved you for nine years now, I can't stop and I don't want to."

The world is getting smaller, closing in on me, and for a moment his words make the party and the hustle disappear, and all I hear is my wildly beating heart.

"I don't know how to stop being mad at you," I almost whisper.

"I understand that. I also know that maybe, under this hatred, you still love me, even if just a little. But you will never find out if you don't lay your anger aside for a few moments and peek in. If you don't dare, all you'll be left with is bitterness. Is that the life you want? "

"The life I want, you took away," my voice cracks.

"I'm offering it back." The light in his eyes floods me with memories. This is how he looked at me once, when we were still happy.

"It's easy to talk." I'm struggling with all my strength against the will to cry. Almost ready to scream at him and beat his chest with my fists until my power drains. I want to burst into tears and curse him for the hell I've been through, for the white dress I burned in my mom's yard, for the shame and guilt.

"I'm not talking, Liz, I'm doing," he sees the storm in my eyes, "and I'll continue to do so, because I've been taught to fight for whats important. I've been taught that failure is out of the question. Tomorrow at eight."

"No," I whisper without taking my eyes off him.

"Comfortable clothes and a babysitter."

"You never listen." What is it with him?

"Tomorrow at eight."

"Colin," I try to make my voice steady.

"I think it's time to cut the cake," he cuts me off, before I can make it clear that he is wasting his time. "I'll get a knife." He turns his back on me, ignoring my refusal and moving away toward the house, without letting me say the last word.

"WHAT WAS THAT?" Colin's conversation with me didn't go unnoticed by my nosy mom.

"He's not normal, I swear, he's lost it completely." I still stand frozen in the same place, my legs planted.

"What did he do now?" She doesn't get excited.

"He thinks we're going out."

"When?"

"Tomorrow," I exhale obnoxiously, "and he wants me to get a babysitter. I have no idea what he's up to."

"So what time should I pick up Viv?" She interrupts me with her unnecessary offer.

"Mom!" I scold her, as I've been doing for weeks.

"And do yourself a favor," she continues in spite of my

protests, "shave. God only knows what your legs look like after all this time." She's almost as insane as he is.

"He's not coming anywhere near my legs!" What does she think? How do these ideas get into this woman's head?

"Sure, sure." She responds nonchalantly. "Not coming near your legs . . . Shave!"

"Mom." My voice is shaking like a leaf barely hanging on the branch of the tree, as if any tiny breeze will tear it away.

"I know," she manages to sound a little more empathetic to my situation, "you're afraid. You don't want to take a risk, he hurt you. But I'm telling you that the moment has come, and if you don't decide now, he'll move on and you'll regret it for the rest of your life."

"You're all joined against me," I breathe in frustration.

"You're welcome to take Dad's side," she says, proving me wrong. "He'll be very happy, but you'll be miserable, and let me tell you something, your father is not very happy at the moment, at the hotel."

"Are you really not going to forgive him?" My voice trembles at the idea that my parents' marriage is over.

"It's too early to think about it," she answers in a steady tone. She's trying so hard to hide from me how painful it was to part. "He crossed the line and thought he could run your life."

"Like you do?"

"I'm just advising you, and if you're smart, you'll listen to me and my experience and you'll shave."

Maybe I shouldn't shave. If my legs remain in their unimpressive condition, there is a chance that I won't let Colin come near.

"Go out with him." She puts her hand on my forearm. "Listen to him and look him in the eyes, the truth will be there. Your past and the pain caused don't have to destroy what can be."

Our conversation is interrupted by the birthday girl's glee, and all eyes turn to her and to her father who hoists her in the air like an astronaut, like a princess, like a fairy tale with a 'happily ever after'. She is radiant, and the life she deserves is within reach. I'm the only one standing between her and the normal, perfect family she can have. I'm the one standing with her feet planted on the ground in the middle of a five-year-old's birthday party, my cheeks wet with tears.

CHAPTER TWENTY-TWO

*C*olin Young: I saw you crying.

Elizabeth Heart: Like that was a first. You've seen me cry a hundred times.

Colin Young: I love you.

Elizabeth Heart: Stop saying that. Your words mean nothing.

Colin Young: Don't lie. You can be as angry as you want, even hate me, but don't lie.

Elizabeth Heart: What do you know about love?

Colin Young: I know what it's like to lie in a tent and not know if I'll return home in one piece or in a coffin, and the only picture I have in my head is your face, your smile. I know what it's like to pray to God to let me stay alive just to see you again.

I push away the thought of Colin lying in a dusty tent and the noise of the bombs that insist on humming inside my head.

Elizabeth Heart: You always knew how to buy me with your words.

Colin Young: I'm the same guy who asked you to marry him in the park. Have I changed? Probably. But inside you know I'm still the guy you love.

Elizabeth Heart: So sure of yourself . . .

Colin Young: Why didn't you get married again?

Elizabeth Heart: Are you serious?!

Colin Young: A smart girl like you, funny, beautiful. How many suitors did you have?

Elizabeth Heart: Zero. Zero suitors in five and a half years.

Colin Young: You're lying.

I don't know if the other guys can be called suitors. I went on a date a year ago and one with the doctor. Two guys who showed interest, and none of them made any progress, mainly because of me. What if he's right? What if I haven't let my heart forget him all this time?

Elizabeth Heart: I'm not like you. I didn't jump from bed to bed for a little warmth and lust, I wanted more.

Colin Young: You wanted me. Admit it Elizabeth, you wanted me.

Elizabeth Heart: Go to hell.

Colin Young: Do you even know what hell looks like?! Because I can tell you! Broken limbs, good people who bleed to death in your arms and IED's that throw the vehicle in front of you five meters in the air. That's what it looks like, Elizabeth. Welcome to Hell!

There's no way he could get out of that the same person. I know the stories. I've heard on the news how terrible it is. I'm afraid to think how many scars he returned with.

Elizabeth Heart: You preferred this hell over me, over your daughter. Did you even ask for her forgiveness, did you apologize for abandoning her? Or do you think that if you spend your money and build a kingdom for her in the back yard for four hours, everything will be forgotten?

Colin Young: Are you done?

Elizabeth Heart: I haven't started yet.

Colin Young: Excellent. We can continue on our date tomorrow.

He's suffering from a head injury. That would explain his behavior.

Elizabeth Heart: You know what, no problem. Come tomorrow at eight and we'll continue from exactly the same spot.

Colin Young: After we kiss.

Elizabeth Heart: We are not going to kiss!

Colin Young: Look, I understand that maybe it's a little early for sex, but we'll definitely kiss. It will be good for your anger.

Elizabeth Heart: It'll be good for your ego!

Colin Young: My tongue will be in your mouth, and my hands will hold your hair and pull your head back. Your breathing will go fast, until you feel dizzy. We both know what will happen between your legs, but I will refrain from detailing at this point.

Jesus Christ, what is it with this talk? And why does it turn me on?

Elizabeth Heart: Stay away from my mouth, Colin. I'm serious.

Colin Young: We're going to kiss tomorrow, Elizabeth. Good night.

I'M SEVENTEEN AGAIN. Like the first day he came and knocked on the door. I'm seventeen with a short-circuited brain and . . . granny panties. I feel like dying! My mom picked Vivian up half an hour ago, which has left me plenty of time to stand in front of the mirror and curse every outfit I own. Our bedroom looks like it suffered a tornado. The contents of my entire closet are lying on the bed and on the floor when knocking on the door makes me jump. I let out a loud sigh, collect my hair with a hair band and remind myself that if he says one word about how I look, the night will be over. I open the door and meet Colin's smug look, as he raises an eyebrow and lets his eyes wonder down my body without a drop of shame.

245

"Comfortable enough in your opinion?" I protest, while he tilts his head to one side and makes a growling noise.

"Turn around," he instructs me authoritatively.

"Come on . . ." Stop playing.

"Turn around," he demands again, and it is clear to both of us that we won't budge from here until I cooperate. I turn around and hope he will finish with his nonsense soon.

"Your ass looks great in those jeans," he mutters, "I approve."

"Where did you get that mouth from?" I finish the round just to meet his eyes again.

"It came with my amazing muscles." He laughs and, without missing a beat, pulls his shirt up and gives me a glimpse of his crazy muscular abs. "They're really amazing, don't you think?"

"Take off your shirt," I demand, swallowing saliva awkwardly, my mouth getting wet from the sight in front of me. His muscles are not human. He fulfills my request, grabbing the hem of his shirt and pulling it forward with the obvious intention of removing it.

"No!" I almost scream, "I meant fix it!"

Not to lose it. God, if he got naked I would drool.

"Oh," he answers with false naivety, arranging his shirt instead, "my mistake."

"Those muscles got me in trouble once, it won't happen again." I take my keys out of my bag, and Colin moves aside as I close the door and lock it behind me.

I pray that we'll survive the evening. Really, I don't have great demands, I just want to get some answers to the burning questions on my mind and return home, with my heart still in one piece.

"I DROVE you crazy that day, huh?" Colin easily navigates his car to our mysterious destination.

"When?"

"The first time I came over." He gives me a knowing look. "Sat on your bed and gave you a glimpse. God, your cheeks burned!"

"Very funny," I grumble, preferring not to talk about that evening.

"It was a nice sight."

"You enjoyed every moment, didn't you?"

"Every second, and after that you couldn't resist me." He just has to continue his harassment.

"Arrogant."

"Are you not the one who begged me to do it?"

"Just 'cause I couldn't stand the thought of you finding some dumb cheerleader to replace me." We both know how many of them would have been happy to take my place in his bed.

"You wanted me, admit it." He laughs loudly.

"I'll admit nothing." I don't laugh back at his jokes.

"You wanted me, and after you got what I gave you, you wanted more."

"Big deal," I wave dismissively, "so you knew what to do in bed."

"I had no idea what I was doing in bed," he snorts with contempt in response. "I was a kid, and I thought I knew something about life."

"Do you think it's funny?" The insult overwhelms me, threatening to drown me as I stare at him murderously. "Do you think it's entertaining, that you've spent the past few years screwing and learning some new tricks?" He doesn't have the basic decency to not throw it in my face. Does he think I want to hear about his exploits? The other girls he was with, who replaced me while I raised our daughter?

"Liz," his voice is immediately apologetic.

"This was a mistake," I rush out. "Take me home."

"No." His voice is firm. "I'm sorry for what I said, it was stupid."

"Leaving me pregnant, that was stupid!" I raise my voice.

"You're trying to get out of our date, and it won't work." He looks at me quizzically.

"It's not a date," I correct him.

"No?" He raises an eyebrow mischievously. His ability to change the subject, and his mood, so quickly is an art form.

"It's your attempt to compete with Doctor Diaz," I try to annoy him, but all he does is smile. "Is something funny to you?"

"You," he doesn't take his eyes off the road. "You think his PhD threatens me?"

"He's not just a doctor," I clarify, "he's also very nice."

"I'm very nice, too."

"No you're not." I look away and stare out the window.

"I'm very nice," he mutters quietly, "and you're crazy about me."

"Where are you taking me?" I refuse to discuss it any further.

"If I tell you it'll ruin the surprise."

I think everything for him is one big amusement.

"I'm not five, and you know I don't like surprises." Unless he has forgotten. I never liked surprises, and at the moment I hate them more than ever.

"Richmond Park," he answers evenly.

I turn my head slowly toward him in a movement that goes on forever, and a little more, and give him a murderous look.

"Colin," I take a deep breath, trying to calm my guts, which insists on turning over. "You're not taking me there."

"I want to talk." He doesn't bother to look at me.

"Then find another place. Stop at a restaurant, find a cafe, a bench, you're not taking me to Richmond Park."

"There are great benches in the park."

"I know!" I shout with all my might. "I'm not stupid, not senile, and I hate this damn park because of you!"

"I just want to talk," he tries to calm me down but I cut him off again.

"You don't want to talk, you want to reminisce, but all the

park does is make me feel sad. Bad choice, Colin, a really bad choice."

"It's my date, so I decide where we're going. You can choose on your date."

"There won't be another date," I mutter angrily. "And you are dreaming if you think this will work for you."

"All I have left are the dreams!" He bursts out and hits the steering wheel with his hand. "You think I don't know I've ruined everything?" He gasps heavily, steers the car to the side of the road and stops with a screech of brakes.

"Do you think I'm an idiot?" His eyes are on me, blue and shining. I see the despair and the defeat in them.

"I'm not trying to annoy you," I murmur in a whisper.

"No, you just want me to disappear, don't you, Liz?" Our eyes lock. "Say it, you want me to leave again."

"I don't want to get hurt again, that's all."

"Let's go to court, let the lawyers run a bloody war for us. You can hate me as much as you want, and our daughter will pay the price for both our mistakes. Or you can let me take you to Richmond Park and listen to all I have to say and, perhaps, you may find a little corner in your heart to forgive me."

"I don't know where to start," I confess.

"Maybe from where you stop lying to yourself and start looking inside your broken heart. Start from the point where you realize that despite what I've done, and though you hate the thought, you still love me."

"I'm aware of the possibility, Colin," I whisper, "really. But most of all, I'm afraid to find out that's true."

"Is it easier to hate me?"

"Yes." I nod. "I'm used to that."

He runs a hand through his hair, trying to catch his breath, and seems to be calculating his steps. I don't know what to do next. I don't know what to do myself. We are trapped in his car, shackled to the past.

"I'm sorry," he breaks the silence in a cracked voice. "I'll take you home. I don't know what I was thinking."

He gives up, and I can't really blame him. He doesn't have any reason to believe that we have a chance. He's right, I'm dragging us in the mud. Vivian will pay the price, and I'll be miserable and so will he. And I still won't have any answers.

"You said you were taught to fight, that failure was out of the question." My heart brakes at the thought that we have reached the finish line, that this will end.

"I was taught to choose my battles, and I don't want to fight a lost one." His voice is distant and resigned.

"I don't want to go to court." If he turns to a lawyer, the situation will escalate, and both of us will spend a fortune on something we need to solve ourselves.

"You don't want to go to the park," he says in accusation, "you don't want to go to court, what do you want?"

"I want Vivian to have her own room, I want to keep her safe and wrap her in cotton and not let anything hurt her, and I want you to kiss me. Like you said, because I keep thinking about it, and I hate myself, Colin." I know how wretched I sound. "I hate myself for that, and for changing my clothes eight times only to end up with my jeans and t-shirt. I hate myself."

The sound of the belt buckle being released causes my gaze to rise. Colin's penetrating stare doesn't come off me. He leans toward me and his fingers find my belt. He releases it with a click and his hand climbs up to my hair. He pulls slowly at my hair band and releases my ponytail.

"That's better," he murmurs in a low voice, his fingers clasping the nape of my neck.

My skin responds to him immediately, a chill creeping down my back and a heat warming between my thighs. The temperature in the car is rising to new heights. He pulls me toward him, slowly. Builds the expectation. My mouth opens to him, wanting to meet his tongue, seeking refuge from the words, to a place where there is no speaking. He lowers his mouth and his lips flutter on mine, his warm breath dragging a desperate sigh from me.

"Kiss me," I plead.

He fulfills my wish without pausing, smashing his mouth against mine, rolling my hair around his fist and pulling it back, as he promised. With his other hand he holds my jaw, fixing it in place, so I can't move, I can't escape. He kisses me with hunger, bites my lips, pulls them and suckles them, and my head spins. I tighten my thighs together. I'm in flames. He will burn me in a fire that will reach heaven. If he puts one finger in the wrong place, if he lets them wonder . . . I won't resist. His mouth rises sharply from my mouth. We gasp, flushed and trembling.

"Elizabeth Heart," he doesn't let go of my jaw or my hair, "I love you enough for both of us."

"That's my line." I sigh and shake my head in an effort to free myself from his grasp. He will decide when, and by then I won't be able to take my eyes off him.

"I know." He fists my hair tightly, subduing me. "Let me take you to the park."

"I have a million questions to ask you." My chest rises and falls with each breath. "I don't think you'll like them all."

"I'm pretty sure I won't like them all, but I owe you answers. I'm pretty sure you won't like everything you hear."

"The ugliest truth is better than the most beautiful lie," I whisper, running my tongue over my burning lips. Colin's eyes don't come off my mouth, and he leans toward them slowly.

"I won't lie to you." He caresses my lips with his.

"I know," I sigh in response.

He closes his fingers around my heart and presses his tongue into my mouth, erasing the pain letter after letter, word by word until only fragments of sentences remain. Spaces to fill. He makes room for love.

CHAPTER TWENTY-THREE

"I can't believe the swans are gone." I fold my knees to my chest as we sit on a blanket under one of the giant trees in the park. Colin might have said something about benches, but what he really meant was a picnic on a blanket, which includes a basket he hid in the trunk, containing a bottle of wine and cheese. He even remembered to bring grapes.

"Here," he hands me a glass of white wine.

"You should have brought beers," I say, realizing that he has poured only one glass. "You've never loved wine."

"You do," he smiles. "I remember how fast it affects you."

"Look who's talking," I laugh out loud. "All I have to do is give you a can of beer and wait for you to shame yourself."

"There's only one problem," he tilts his head. "I don't drink."

"Never?" That's new. Colin was not a heavy drinker, but he downed a shot of tequila here and there.

"Alcohol pulled my father to the bottom," he shakes his head. "I can't, the thought disgusts me."

"You're not him."

"I don't want to take the risk." He shrugs his shoulders, his face remaining blank, but the pain is in his eyes, the troubled look, tone of his words.

"No risk, Colin." No matter how much we hurt each other, he must be convinced. "If you don't want to drink, it's not a bad choice, but you are not him."

"Are you sure?" He frowns, "because in the last few weeks you've been throwing accusations, implying that you're not convinced."

"It was the insult speaking in my place. I let my anger erupt, but you are not your father, and you never will be."

He nods, opens a bottle of water and sips it. We don't touch the food.

"I heard what happened to him," I say cautiously. "Did they really ask you for a donation?"

"Yes." His fingers close tightly on the water bottle.

"Would you do that?"

"Apparently." He shrugs, releasing a bitter laugh. "God, he was a shit piece of a human being and I was ready to save him. He couldn't enter the transplant list because of his drinking. I was his only option. He was a shit father, but still, my father."

"I think it's good you got checked," I whisper with great care. "But I'm glad you weren't a match, because if you had refused, you'd have beaten yourself up for it."

"When I received the negative answer, I didn't bother to come over. I didn't feel the need to part with him."

"I don't blame you." I take another sip of wine in the hope that it will dull my senses a little.

"What else do you want to ask me?" He puts the bottle beside him and straightens his legs, his face turned to me.

"I want to know what you've done all these years." I put the wineglass beside me, fold my legs and hug them. "I know you enlisted and after three years you were discharged."

"Your dad was the one who demanded I write that note to you."

Instead of answering my question, he starts from the beginning, or maybe from the beginning of the end. "But I knew he was right. I pushed my clothes into a bag and knew you would look for me. I wanted you to let go, make you angry, so you wouldn't find me."

"You wanted me to hate you." And in doing so he succeeded above expectations.

"I just wanted you not to wait for me," he clears his throat, as if the words refuse to come out and he must force them. "I know you, you would have turned over every stone looking for me. I had to leave that note for you to know that nothing had happened to me. "

"So I'd think you left by choice." .

"Yes."

"It was a shitty choice."

"It was also a shitty morning."

"Can you imagine me standing in front of our guests trying to explain why the wedding is canceled? And all the giggles coming from your friends?" My tone is edged with disgust. "I heard them whispering, 'he finally came to his senses'."

"A bunch of idiots," he grimaces with clenched teeth.

They were your friends, Colin, not mine.

"What did you expect them to think? The captain of the foot-ball team woke up and realized that it wasn't the life he wanted— a wife and a baby, responsibility. My world collapsed, and they smiled in my face. I couldn't run away from them for months. The look in their eyes made me feel like an idiot."

"I'm the idiot, not you." His harsh tone doesn't relieve my insult for even a second.

"I burned the dress." My eyes water when I think about my wedding dress, what was left of it. "That night, I went out wearing sweatpants and a tank top and threw it onto the grill, soaked it with gasoline and watched it turn into ash." The flames climbed and climbed, and the yard smelled like a campfire, until my father came running out and poured a bucket of water over it. I stood still, blurred by hours of crying, confused and helpless, and didn't utter a word.

"After that, I didn't get out of bed for weeks."

"I, on the other hand, didn't find a bed to sleep in." Again he tries to sound indifferent, and again he fails. No matter what he tries to hide from me, he won't succeed.

"You didn't have any money, did you?" The thought of him being hungry hurts me most.

"I spent a few weeks on the streets," he picks up the water bottle and sips again. "I think I was big enough not to be bothered. One day I ran into an army man who distributed flyers..."

"Recruiter," I conclude the sentence myself.

"Yes. We started talking, and from there. . ."

"You found yourself in Afghanistan." In the desert, on a field bed, with my picture in his head, I already know.

"Not immediately, but yes."

"You loved it, did you not? I hear it in your voice. You're sorry for what you did to me, but you don't regret your service."

"You have the ability to hear the subtleties in my voice no one else can," he mumbles.

"You didn't answer me." He will not evade, he will give me the answers I want.

"I loved it," he lowers his eyes, "the knowledge that I was doing something meaningful. I was no longer a construction worker who barely supported his family, or an idiot who didn't get into college, the army couldn't care less. I could prove myself."

"You didn't have to prove anything to me, I accepted you as you were from day one."

"I know."

"How did you start your business?" I pull out the next topic, which intrigues me no less. From the moment he arrived he's been writing checks as if his bank account is particularly inflated.

"I knew the right people." He remains vague.

"A business doesn't set up without starting capital."

"Smart." He smiles, but moves uncomfortably. "You should have—"

"Don't change the subject." There's no way he'll evade again. "Where did you get the money?"

Colin pauses a few moments before he answers.

"Fights." His voice falters.

"What kind of fights?" I, on the other hand, don't hesitate for a moment, my voice sharp and clear.

"The kind you don't talk about," he squirms under my penetrating stare. "My friend from LA knew I needed money. I have the right body, and it turned out I wasn't too bad."

Are you kidding me?

"I can't believe it," every nerve in my body tenses in response to his answer. "Illegal fights?"

"It's all consensual, no one is thrown into the ring against his will. Sometimes you win, sometimes you lose, but it's sports. Like football."

"Don't be an idiot, it's nothing like football." What was he thinking? Where was his head when he entered an illegal boxing ring to earn a few dollars?

"Sports, Elizabeth, no less and no more."

"Illegal gambling, Colin," I emphasize the words.

"It was a quick way to get cash, I was good and got out in time." He refuses to get back down.

"What's *on time*, before your broke your nose?"

"I broke it more than once," he chuckles.

"You think it's funny?" I'm losing it completely.

"The plastic surgeon did a good job. Looks natural, don't you think?" He turns his profile to me.

"Your business is illegal." His nose doesn't interest me for a moment.

"My business is legal." He turns his face toward me in a quick motion, and the look in his eyes is clear, he didn't like what I said.

"From the first contract I signed to the last one, it's all legal, you can ask my accountant."

I doubt his accountant will tell me anything, if I ever bother to approach him.

"Why did it take you two years to come back?"

"I needed time to deal with my mistake." His gaze penetrates. His truth resonates between us. "I had to get to the point where I had nothing to lose anymore. Your father's threat became irrelevant and I didn't care what he'd do, nothing was worth the distance from you two anymore." The distance not only from Vivian, but from me, too, I heard it well.

"So now you're rich?"

"I'm not rich," he laughs again. "I have enough. I've made the right investments, and life here is much cheaper than in Los Angeles."

"Life here is expensive," I reply coolly. "You have a child to support."

"I want to kiss you again."

His answer causes my body to stretch. I squeeze my hands around my legs, trying to soothe the struggle in my head with every nerve that wants his lips on mine. That's the power he has over me. This is the attraction that has been holding me for nine years and refuses to release. It's his fist that closes on my heart.

"Colin . . ." My voice shakes in a futile attempt to keep him away.

"Lizzie," he leans forward, forcing me to lie back, which turns out to be a terrible mistake. This is not the position I wanted to find myself in. He climbs towards me with a catlike grace that draws the air from me. My body temperature rises and my cheeks redden. My pulse insists on running wild under his enormous body.

He strokes my face with his fingers, pulls back my hair and spreads it on the blanket.

"You're squeezing your thighs." He puts his mouth close to

mine and I'm captivated, stretching my neck and giving him direct access to it.

"So you won't get any ideas," I moan, "and send your hands to forbidden places."

"My hands know every inch, remember?" his fingers smoothing over my collarbone.

"Your hands touched others," I mutter in disgust.

"My hands love only one body." He sucks my earlobe and his breath tickles my skin, making it harder to resist.

"You're all talk," I feel how every millimeter in my body responds to him. "You're full of shit."

"When was the last time you came?" he whispers, walking his fingers along my forearm, making me shiver. "You never liked touching yourself, you said you couldn't, you needed me."

Ass. He knows too much, and he hasn't forgotten. Of all things, he remembers that. Me needing him, begging him to touch me.

"When, Elizabeth?" he asks again, in an authoritative tone.

"Guess," I mutter in frustration. How miserable am I? Can't even touch myself. His name is signed on all my orgasms, from the first to the last. Pathetic.

"Are you serious?" I hear his smug tone. He scattered his orgasms across the country and forgot me. Now he's back, and he wants more?

"Your ego must be exploding now." I close my eyes and become addicted to his tongue climbing up my jaw, all the way to my mouth. His lips know the way, he doesn't need a map. He's been there a thousand times, but then my shirt rises up, just an inch, and a big hand rests on my stomach, waking me wildly from the dream.

I push his hand away, pushing hard, my head shaking from side to side. He rises, leaning on his hands at the sides of my head, as I shake under him like a wounded animal.

"Get off me." I push his body.

"Liz?"

"Get off me, now!" I pull my shirt down to cover my bare skin, hide what he hasn't seen, the memory of that night.

"What's going on?" He tilts his body to the side and gives me an escape. I jump to my feet, panting. He reaches out to grab my arm, but I shake it off.

"Don't touch me."

"Liz, what happened?" He stands up urgently, but raises his hands in submission to indicate that he has no intention of coming closer.

"Don't touch me, I want to go home." My eyes are burning and I hold my stomach tightly.

"I'll take you." He looks worried.

"No." I can't stop the tears. "I don't believe you, you'll probably try . . . I don't believe you!"

"Liz, breathe."

"Don't tell me to breathe. God, what was I thinking? I'm a joke, I'm such a miserable joke."

"I don't understand, I don't want to hurt you, I swear."

"You swear?" I roar. "You swore you'd be there for me, and now you've come back to fuck me? You're something special, you know that?"

My body can't bear the burden. The nausea in my stomach is climbing up, too many tears and feelings that have to find a way out. I lean forward, my hands on my knees, and throw up on the grass.

"Elizabeth . . ."

All I can do is raise my hand to warn him not to come near.

"Oh, hell..." he falters, but the despair in his voice doesn't bother me anymore.

You can go there—to hell and back. I wonder how many girls will wait for him there, in perfect bodies that life didn't scar?

I focus on my breathing. If only I could get air into my lungs and soothe the crying. If I could just breathe, all this would pass.

I close my eyes.

I'm not throwing up anymore. The aftertaste is bitter and salty from my tears.

You are fine.

You are fine.

You're out of your mind.

"TAKE THIS." I hear Colin's voice behind me. From the corner of my eye I discover the bottle of water he is holding out for me. Without thinking I take it, slowly straightening up and unscrewing the cap.

"What the hell was that?" His rough voice reverberates as I close my eyes again and fill my mouth with water, turning my head aside and spitting into the grass.

"It was a reminder, for me," I mutter and close the bottle. "If you knew me, you wouldn't go near my stomach."

"Why didn't you stop me then?" he asks accusingly.

"Because I'm an idiot." I try to catch my breath.

"Do you really think all I wanted was to sleep with you?" His becomes more somber and troubled by the minute.

"I have no idea what you want." I throw the water bottle at his feet.

"I want my family back!" His answer freezes the air around me. "I want you and Vivian, I want to fix what I broke. I want to take her to daycare, bring her home and teach her how to ride a bike. I want her to have brothers and sisters."

"Well you'd better find a new woman!" A sharp pain constricts my heart. "Go find a new wife, because this girl won't be able to give you what you want. Not you or anyone else."

"What are you talking about?" He takes a step toward me, but I run back.

"Stay away." I push my hand toward him, and he stops. "While you enlisted and went to fight for the country, I was fighting for myself and my child. I saved her, but I lost my womb. I was bleeding on the operating table and the doctors had no choice. So you'd better find someone else to make you kids, Colin, because the only child I will ever bring to the world I already gave you."

Even in the light of the headlamps, I can see the shock on his face, his body taut at my words, the understanding that seeps through.

"Let me guess," I say venomously, "you can't fix that."

His eyes dart, his gaze dropping to my stomach and rising back to my eyes, but it's his silence I feel the most. "Don't you have something smart to say?"

"I love you," he answers in a trembling voice.

"Don't make me laugh," I sneer at him. "You don't love me, you want the dream, the house with the white fence and the children playing in the back yard."

"We have a girl playing in the back yard."

"You want more. You probably want a little football team, or at least one son to carry your name, correct me if I'm wrong."

"You're wrong." His voice is steady, full of confidence.

"I'm not." I shake my head. "Maybe it's better for you to chase Lauren, she must—"

"Don't do that," he points his finger at me. "You know she doesn't interest me."

"I don't know anything." I burst into uncontrollable laughter. "I'm so stupid that I deluded myself that we had a future."

"You think you're stupid, because you lost your womb?" The shock in his voice is evident.

"I can't have more children." I can barely get the sentence out of my mouth.

"I heard the first time you said that."

"And you went silent."

His silence was the loudest thing I've ever heard.

"What was I supposed to say?" His blue eyes are burning at me. "That I'm sorry? Would it give you back your womb?"

"It would make you human and not an unfeeling robot."

"You think I'm a robot?" For a moment it's like you could cut the tension between us. "Do you think I don't care you were lying in the operating room alone because I wasn't there? That I don't want to scream and break something?"

"You broke enough things already." I wave my hand at him.

"Marry me."

I stare at him wide-eyed, and he doesn't take his eyes off me. We are in the midst of a giants' battle, but the giant in front of me has lost his mind.

"Jesus Christ!" Laughter bursts out of me, rolling from my belly out until my eyes begin to tear. "You're disturbed, you know that?"

I have to stop laughing, but how can I? It's so ridiculous!

"Marry me." He doesn't move, his feet remain frozen and firm. The only thing that gives him away is his chest going up and down.

"I'm going home." I giggle another little laugh as the effort to stay serious fails. "You can tidy up the romantic picnic you've organized, and return from la-la-land. You've proposed to me in this place before, and we both know how that ended, so forgive me if I refuse your seductive offer."

His silence takes its place between us when we exchange glances once more. Colin's eyes flash as I shake my head and lock my jaw so as not to laugh again at his delusional offer. I turn my back on him and walk across the grass toward the path that will take me far from the man who, without a doubt, has gone mad.

Marry him? In what parallel universe does he think it's going to happen? In what parallel universe does he think I will make that mistake again?

I don't think so, mister. You can go back to your business, to the gym, to the stupid cheerleaders who fall in your trap, but you can't come back to me.

CHAPTER TWENTY-FOUR

arry me.

    I wake up in panic from a dream, sit up panting and hurry to look at Vivian's empty bed, forgetting for a moment she is staying at my mom's.

My fingers travel to my stomach, to the hidden scar along my bikini line, no longer a secret. Now Colin knows what I've been hiding. He knows what was taken from me, and his guilt probably caused him to stop thinking logically. I'm sure that's the whole story. He doesn't really want to marry me, he simply doesn't know how to atone for his actions, and marriage seems to him like an easy solution.

Why don't the men in my life apologize? Why is it so hard for them? I'm not sure I'd forgive them, but I think I deserve a sincere apology, mostly from my father. I can understand Colin. I may not agree with the way he behaved, but it's hard for me to imagine what I would do if I were in his shoes. If anyone had threatened to hurt Colin, there is a fair chance that I would have run away just to protect him. I close my eyes tightly and the thoughts travel through my head. I picture Colin in uniform, his weapon drawn, walking in the alleys of a strange, ruined city. He could have died more than once. He could have come back in a coffin, and my father knew it while it was happening. Colin himself said he sent me money every month—money I didn't know existed, instead reaching for my father, who betrayed me.

I lie down, pull the thin blanket up to my shoulders and turn on my side. My father threatened Colin that he would end up like Brock. My mom thinks it was a futile threat and that the scumbag died in a car accident. I want to believe it, but what do I know? A month ago, if someone told me that Colin had left because of my father, I would have laughed at them. But maybe he could kill someone to take revenge... God knows he has behaved like a caveman more than once and, today, I know he is not the good man I thought he was. He's the villain in the story, and Colin the victim, but it's still not a good enough reason to marry Colin. It is not a good enough reason for anything. Now I can only hope that my heart will agree with my head's conclusion and I can stop imagining myself standing in a bridal gown beside him and becoming his wife.

MY MORNING IS SLUGGISH. It turns out that when you have no job to rush to or a girl to take to daycare, time becomes a fluid concept. Preparing breakfast takes me half an hour, and when I'm done, I find myself standing in front of my wardrobe, staring at it, aware that this is probably the most boring wardrobe in the world. My jeans are neatly folded and arranged in a pile of colors from dark to bright. My pile of shirts is all shades of gray and black. Here and there a white shirt shimmers. As a mom of a little girl, I learned that the white color is superfluous and its sole purpose is to make me mournful of trying to remove stains of ketchup, juice, or mud. I choose black jeans, a gray t-shirt I don't remember buying,, and my sneakers. My green eyes stare at me from the mirror and show fatigue, and my hair refuses to take shape, which requires me to pick it up with a rubber band. I grab my bag, leave the bedroom, lock the house and get into my new car, ready to shop for groceries.

I can't go on like this for much longer. At some point I will have to find a job, a stage I reject in frustration. It won't be simple, and if I don't turn myself to the task, the money in my bank account will run out, and I won't allow that.

My shopping cart fills up as I walk through the aisles of the huge Tesco branch and wonder what to eat for lunch. On the one hand, there is the possibility of returning home and cooking, and on the other hand, to sit in a restaurant and order some pampering portion. Indeed, the choice is impossible. A choice I didn't have until a few weeks ago. I would eat my lunches on the bench in the parking lot of the shopping center opposite the furniture store, almost always a sandwich I brought from home.

I can't ignore the change in my life since Colin's been back, since he put money into my bank account. Even Viv's birthday party was something I couldn't organize myself. He did everything.

Something stops my shopping cart and I look straight up, paling as Jimmy the bully grabs the cart and his body blocks the aisle.

"Looki here, it's Young's lady." He stares at me menacingly before smiling wickedly at Craig, standing beside him.

"I don't think he'll be happy if we bother her," Craig mutters to his partner.

"Are we bothering her?" Jimmy chuckles and moves the cart toward me with a little push that make me jumps back in panic. "Are we bothering you?"

"You better listen to your friend," I mutter in a trembling voice. "Colin won't be happy."

"Colin won't be happy," Jimmy mimics my voice.

"What do you want?" I tighten my grip on the bar. "Didn't you get everything you were owed?"

"We can always ask for more." He raises an eyebrow and my guts turn, sending a tremor to my feet. "We were sorry to hear Colin's old man died, we enjoyed doing business with him."

You've enjoyed doing business with him? You took advantage of him and blackmailed him and Colin, ruined my life, and you're still smiling?

"I don't think the police will be happy to hear about the business you've done," the words roll out of my mouth without me thinking about the consequences, without stopping to figure out how dumb it is to threaten them.

"The police?" Jimmy pauses for a moment, the smile on his face growing as if he has received a gift he's been waiting for. The next second, he pushes the cart aside, and now there's nothing between us, nothing to stop him from jumping me.

"If I were you, I'd be careful." My heart is racing. "Colin is waiting for me outside, and in a minute he'll come to see what's keeping me."

"Colin is waiting outside?" He's getting too close, not believing the lie I just invented. He clutches my arm tightly and pulls me to him, pinning me to his chest. I barely breathe, barely standing on my feet, his mouth pressed close to my ear. "I'm not the right man to lie to, little bird." The words are laced with venom.

"I'm not lying . . ."

"The next time we meet we might be in a much darker place than this." The air he breathes in my ear chills me.

I wonder whether to scream, but it might put me in a bigger problem—they might run away, but they'd find me later.

Damn you, Colin! You told me the matter with them was closed!

"What do you want from me?" I pray that he'll let me go.

"I don't know yet," he whispers, "but I'm sure I'll be able to think of something. I've never had a redhead."

"Jimmy," Craig interferes nervously, "enough playing, we have work to do." At least one of them understands that it's better to let me go.

"I hope we'll see each other again, Birdy." He releases my arm and I run towards the door, haunted by his wicked laugh.

"It was fun!" I hear from a distance. I don't stop for a moment, bursting out the door and running all the way to my car.

Just wait for the police to find you. We'll see how much fun you have then!

What am I going to do now? My heart goes wild, my hands hold the steering wheel, and I press hard on the accelerator and hurry. I'll file a complaint with the police. The store must have security cameras, and the cops will see how those two bothered me. They probably know them. Maybe they're waiting for someone to dare to complain.

My thoughts don't stop there, and the understanding seeps through me like a ton of bricks. If the police interrogate them, God only knows what they'll find out, and the thugs won't be too glad. Perhaps they're only the executive arm of a much larger and dangerous organization? Do I really want someone like that haunting me and my daughter now?

I turn right at the first intersection. I don't know anything about them. There's only one person who knows them better than I do, and he'll have to give me answers. He will have to solve the problem he created, and his solution should be satisfactory to me.

THE BIG SHINY sign above the front door of Mr. Blunt's old furniture store catches my eye as I get out of the car.

The Right Place

I open the door with a strong shove and the smell of fresh paint hits my nose at once. I don't know how many years they didn't renovate the place, but now it doesn't resemble the furniture store. It doesn't look like a place I wouldn't bother to enter, but like a place I'd come to happily. My eyes dart from the cream and brown painted walls to the new pictures, to the black signs in every corner. Danielle Cole, the last person I want to see, giggles with a client in his fifties studying a huge sitting area at the end of the store. Henry is nowhere to be seen, and I lose my patience and raise my voice.

"Colin!"

Danielle looks up, turns her eyes slowly to me, and stares at me disapprovingly.

"Elizabeth," my name sings from her red and shiny lips, "can I help you?"

"Where's your boss?" I rush out.

"In the back office, you don't have to make a fuss."

I haven't even begun to make a fuss. With quick strides, I make my way to the back office, pull open the door and stop as I try to understand the scene in front of me. Henry is sitting behind a large wooden desk, a stack of papers arranged in front of him, next to the computer screen. Behind him stands my ex, and they both look up at me with noticeable surprise on their faces.

"Elizabeth?" Colin straightens, looming over Henry, who looks like a rat in a trap.

So he works here. Why am I surprised?

"You told me your stuff with the thugs was over!" I shout at my ex.

"It is."

"So why did they stop me at the supermarket in the middle of my shopping and try to meddle with me?"

"They what?" He is obviously losing his temper. His enormous body stretches, and the muscles in his arms look as if they will burst out of his shirt any second.

"Asshole number one tried to stop asshole number two," I inform him, watching the vein in his temple swell up, his nostrils flaring and his jaw closing. "The first one pinned me to him, called me a little bird and said he's never had a redhead. What did you get me involved in, Colin?"

At the end of the sentence, my voice brakes to pieces, and I'm no longer a heroine. I'm angry and frightened, and my eyes shine. Colin looks as if someone is about to end his life in a particularly cruel way.

"Stay here with Henry," he orders as he grabs his phone and the keys lying next to the stack of papers.

"I'm going to the police," I state an empty threat, the sole purpose of which is to show him that I'm serious.

"No police." He stops to stare at me sternly. "Let me handle it."

"You've already handled it," I wave at him, "and the problem hasn't been solved!"

"No police, Elizabeth." He grits his teeth. "Promise me you'll stay here until I come back."

"I promise nothing," I inform him.

"Promise me!" I don't think I've ever seen him so angry. Seeing him now, he's not someone I want to mess around with.

"Okay, I won't go to the police until you come back."

"Henry, keep an eye on her," he throws at Henry, who seems helpless. He can't stop me, and we all know that.

"Stay here and don't move." He turns a finger at me, agitated, he walks past me and slams the office door behind him, leaving me and my friend equally stunned.

"I'LL KILL HIM!" I drop to the chair in front of Henry.

"Did they really chase you?" He moves the pile of papers to the side clearing the table.

"I think they bumped into me by chance, but what do I know?" Fear again starts to seep in. "Maybe they followed me, nothing can surprise me anymore. Are you really working for him?"

"His offer was good," he looks down. "Are you mad at me?"

"I'm angry you didn't go to school." Working here is a waste of time. Henry didn't have to stay just because of the blonde.

"I can still learn, in the evenings."

"It's not the same and you know that. I'm just saying you might have enjoyed university."

"Maybe," he shrugs, "and maybe I would suffer every moment. What's sure is I'm happy here, Colin is pleased with the work I'm doing, and Danielle . . ."

"What about Danielle?" I want to hear that.

"She's not as terrible as she wants you to believe. She's actually pretty nice."

"Really?"

"You should see her library."

My jaw drops. Is he serious?

"Henry," I ask inquiringly, "when did you see her library?"

"When we had dinner at her house."

"Danielle and you?"

"Yes, she looks quite different in leggings and a t-shirt, and she knows how to cook."

"You had dinner." I find it difficult to believe.

"And we talked about books and business, it was pretty nice."

I let out air, my head dropping. The world has gone mad, I have no other explanation.

Danielle and Henry went on a date and the bullies stopped me at the grocery store. What happened to my nice, calm life?

CHAPTER TWENTY-FIVE

Forty-two minutes. That's the amount of time I stare at the office wall clock of The Right Place and curse in every way I know how. First Colin, then my father, and finally, Jimmy and Craig, the scums that forced me to be locked in here in the first place. If I hadn't promised Colin, I would have left long ago. I also abandoned my shopping cart at the supermarket and I still need groceries, and to pick up Viv from daycare. Although there are a few more hours, at this rate who knows how long it will take?

Just as I'm about to break my promise, the door opens, and I jump out of the chair to Colin, who is toddling inside. My instincts come into play, and before I know what I'm doing, I'm supporting him with all his weight, getting under his armpit and letting him lean against me, letting out a juicy curse.

Henry gets up from the chair quickly and grabs Colin's other side. I manage to pull the chair I was sitting on over with my foot to sit the badly bruised faced idiot, and Henry runs out of the office.

"What the hell is this supposed to be?"

"I've dealt with the problem, but the room is spinning," he

mutters with a sigh. I can't stop him from gliding to the floor where he chooses to lie down. I lean over beside him and Henry appears in the doorway with a wet cloth in his hand.

"I think you'll need this." He reaches his hand to me and gives a weary look to the man who groans loudly.

"I'm calling an ambulance." I take the cloth and turn to my bag to pull out my phone, but Colin closes his fingers on my forearm.

"No police." He closes his eyes.

"Colin . . ."

"No police, Liz." I decide to postpone the argument, put the bag down and lean over to his bloody face. Gently, I put the cloth on his forehead and wipe the running blood out of the corner of his puffy eye.

"I can do it on my own."

"I know." I move his hair to the side and wipe the cloth over his cheek. "You're such a fool."

"I had to let 'em feel good about themselves, before I took 'em out." I swear that a small smile rises at the corner of his mouth, but the movement brings him pain that erases the smile immediately.

"Do you think it's funny?" I shake my head in frustration. "We'll see how much you laugh when you can't see your daughter until your face heals."

"I'll talk to her on the phone," he whispers, his eyes still closed. "And I'll tell her what happens to people who threaten my girls."

"You won't tell her a thing, Superman." With one hand I gently stroke his untouched cheek, and with the other I remove blood from the tip of his mouth and his injured lip.

"I love that name." He tries to smile again. Didn't he learn that it wasn't a good idea?

"I think you have a concussion." All I can do is stroke his hair and curse his recklessness.

"Just a few blows," he seems to be in control of the situation, "I've been through worse."

"You should go home," I whisper to the idiot, "I don't think you'll be of any use to your business."

"Can't drive." He doesn't bother getting up, instead remains lying beside me, his body limp.

"I'll drive you," I suggest without thinking. "But you have to stand by yourself."

"I'm cozy." He smiles for a third time. Seriously?

"I'm happy to hear that." I just can't get my hands off him. They're attracted to him like a magnet, insisting on stroking his face, calming him down, comforting him every second.

"Let's stay here."

"Not going to happen," I say with half a smile. The two of us are probably just as crazy. I'm supposed to be hysterical, Colin is supposed to go to the hospital, and we're smiling like two idiots.

"We'll take your car." He accepts the fact that he won't be staying on the floor. "Danielle will bring the jeep later."

"Can you stand?" I sit up to make room for him to straighten.

"No problem." He takes a deep breath and sits much more easily than I thought he would. Is he really used to this? Because every other person in his condition would lose consciousness.

"First stage executed successfully." I pick up my bag, stand up and give Colin my hand.

"Mrs. Young, you don't give me enough credit." He chuckles and makes my heart flutter in my chest. A slip of the tongue I'm not sure he meant, but I heard it as if he shouted it out loud. *Mrs. Young.* I keep silent, watching him rise to tower above me, and in one moment he is too close, too swaying, and I go under his armpit again.

"I won't fall," he grumbles.

"I'm not taking the risk." I walk him slowly to the door, leaving the cloth on the floor behind us.

"You're supposed to lean on me." His frustration is evident.

"Save your machismo for another day, stud." I open the office door and help him through the shop and out into the blinding sun, leaving Danielle and her unhappy face in the store. Colin cautiously hobbles over to my car and gets in. I close the door behind him and hurry to sit behind the wheel.

"You know I'm just putting on a show, right?" He leans his head back on the seat and closes his eyes again.

"Sure," I chuckle, "a good show. Now give me your address, and don't faint, or you'll find yourself in the hospital."

"Take me home, Liz." He slowly turns his head toward me, "I'm fine."

"The address, Colin." I remind him I'm waiting. He mumbles the address quietly, I start the car and back out of the parking lot, thinking about the chances of getting to his house before I turn and lead us straight to the emergency room. In his condition? There is no telling. Fifty fifty. If he manages not to faint, we'll be fine. More or less.

"You live here?" I stare out the window, wide-eyed, at the huge stone house opposite of which I stopped.

"Get closer to the door." He points to the double driveway and unfastens the seat belt.

"Is this really your house?" My eyes scan the impressive facade. The wooden door is carved, the glass windows are huge and shiny, and on either side of the driveway is a wide lawn. If that's what it looks like from the outside, how amazing is the inside?

"This is my house." He tries to straighten his hair back as I slide the car into the parking spot near the door.

"I'm afraid to ask how much rent you're paying."

"I'm not." He waits for me to turn off the engine and open the door. "Renting is a waste of money."

"You bought it?" I blurt out.

"I took a mortgage, Elizabeth." He leans over and manages to crawl out slowly. "One hell of a mortgage, but the house is worth every cent."

I'm sure. I hurry after him, lock the car and wait for him to open the door with the keys he takes out of his pocket awkwardly.

"Need help?"

"No." He manages to put the key in the keyhole. "Just let me handle the alarm."

He has an alarm, of course. Colin enters first, taps the code, stumbles to the massive black sofa and crashes on it.

My eyes begin to examine everything from the moment I enter. The huge kitchen in the corner of the house, the impressive dining table, the hallway that seems to lead to the bedrooms. Even my parents' house is not this big. I don't think I've ever been in a house like this.

"Do you have Tylenol?" I put my handbag on the stylized, wooden table by the door.

"In the bathroom," he raises his hand and gestures toward the hallway, "the first door on the left."

"Don't faint till I come back." I shake my head as I walk past him and find the shiny bathroom.

He must have a cleaner. There is no way he cleans the house or arranges it. Not like this, anyway. The monstrous bathtub fills most of the room, with a marble bench next to it, and the walls are beautifully covered with white and gray ceramic tiles. I try not to linger, opening the cabinet behind the mirror and finding his Tylenol. When I close the cabinet, I decide that even the sink is big. Everything in this house is too big. Everything seems expensive.

I go back to the kitchen and find the glasses in one of the cupboards. From the refrigerator I take out a bottle of mineral water and pour it into a tall glass. When I finish, I return to the living room, where Colin lies, awake and smiling.

"Hey," he looks up at me as I hand him the pill.

"Be a good boy, and don't make a fuss." I slide the pill into his palm.

"Don't call me a boy," he throws it into his mouth, turns to his side and holds out his free hand to the glass of water. "It's not sexy."

"Do you think your face is sexy right now?"

"Evidence of my undisputed heroism." He sips and puts the glass on the floor.

"Your stupid heroism, Sir Young." The adrenalin begins to fade from my body. Colin seems less out of it than I thought he would be.

"I had to establish my rule," he lays back on his back, "and now everyone in all the seven kingdoms knows who controls King's Landing."

"What are you talking about?" I twist my face.

"The Iron Throne is mine," he mumbles as his eyes close.

"I'm calling the ambulance," I say again, but he grabs my hand and stops me.

"Games of Thrones, Lizzie," he whispers, "it was a joke."

"I don't watch that series."

"Don't say that!" He laughs loudly, and a second later he sighs in pain. I hasten to sit on the soft carpet near his head and, without thinking, I gently brush my hand into his hair.

"You're such a fool," I whisper, my eyes examining his wounded face. His eye socket is purple, his cheek swollen and his lip cut.

"Craig begged like a child," he mumbles to me, "swore that he didn't lay a finger on you, so I spared him, more or less. Can't say the same for Jimmy."

"He'll look for revenge," I mutter anxiously.

"It'll take him at least six weeks to get out of the wheelchair," he says in a voice filled with disgust, "and he should be grateful I left his hands intact so he can wipe his own ass."

"It's not funny, Colin."

"No, Elizabeth, it's not funny at all."

"You shouldn't beat people up." I'm really not happy with his solution.

"They don't know any other language. They're not afraid of the police, so they have to be afraid of me. I have to instill fear in them so that the next time they see you, they will flee to the other side of the road." He doesn't apologize.

"You're so sure of yourself." I lean my head beside him.

"I know who they work for, and their boss won't be happy to hear about the supermarket incident." He turns his head toward me and opens his blue eyes. "In their world there is little respect, but once I paid the debt, the order was to let me be. Jimmy broke the order. He should be glad I'm the one who took care of him and not someone else."

"Don't do it again." I reach for his face, my fingers finding the corner of his mouth, the one that wasn't hurt, and I let them wander about it without restraint.

"If I could, I'd kiss you," he whispers. "I'm still debating how much it'll hurt."

"Quite a bit," I swallow, running my tongue over my lips at the thought of his kiss.

"Don't do that," he sighs with a smile. "It kind of turns me on, and I'm kind of miserable in my situation."

"You brought it upon yourself," I smile at him.

"It was worth it," he lets his head sink close to mine, "so worth it."

"Just so I'll take care of you?"

He raises his hand with a sigh, finds my hand and pulls it to his chest, placing it with my fingers spread over his heart.

"So I'll feel alive again," he whispers almost without a sound. "I still love you."

"I know." I'm addicted to the sensation of his heart beating under my touch.

"You should pick up Viv."

"Not yet." I put my forehead against his, our lips a quarter inch apart, and his familiar smell clouds my senses.

"Stay with me." He closes his eyes, his breath and my breath almost becoming one.

"I'm here." I lean over and close the tiny distance between us, my lips fluttering over his, barely touching.

"Promise?" He mutters, as I pull away again.

"Don't fall asleep." I close my eyes, unable to promise him anything. Unable to absorb the emotions that take hold of me, tying me back to him.

"I'll just nap."

"You have to stay awake." If he has a concussion, the last thing he needs is to fall asleep.

"Talk to me."

"What about?"

"Anything." We both open our eyes and they lock. Closer than we'd been for years, more connected than we ever were. Neither of us makes a move, dares not move harm the delicate texture of the energy that envelops us like an aura.

"How many bedrooms do you have in your house?" I softly throw out the first question that comes to mind.

"Three," he replies immediately.

"When did you buy it?"

"Elizabeth," he smiles, a motion that seems to cost him a lot of effort. "We're not talking about my house."

"Do you want to talk about the other women you had?" I mumble as I feel the pang of jealousy climbing up my stomach to my chest.

"Do you want to talk about them?" He's not afraid of the hot topic I raised.

"Was Anna one of them?" I decide to know whom I'm dealing with, and the one he brought to our daughter's birthday party is a good place to start.

"We are just friends." His tone is indifferent.

"With benefits?" I don't spare the investigation.

"No, Liz, not with benefits." He sighs, and I breathe in relief.

"What about Danielle?" I pray with all my might that the blonde didn't spend time in his bed.

"Danielle is dating your friend," he chuckles in response to my question.

"I've heard." What I didn't hear was a clear answer, if before she trapped my friend she celebrated with the man lying on the sofa in front of me.

"I didn't sleep with her."

"She's probably not your taste." Where did that come from? What do I know about Colin's taste in women?

"She's not who you think she is." He closes his fingers on my hand, which still rests on his heart.

"Are you trying to say that she *is* your taste?" I try to gently pull my hand away from him, but he doesn't let me.

"I'm just saying you never gave her a chance."

"You know something," I close my eyes to hide my pain, "you're right, I don't want to talk about it."

"There was no one serious." He releases my hand, turns on his side with a loud sigh and sends his fingers trailing down my face, my cheek, my lips.

"I don't want to talk about them, Colin." I refuse to open my eyes.

"No one serious," he insists. "I love you, I've always loved you. It was hell, and no one else could have changed the fact that I only wanted you. Please believe me. You do not know what I went through to come back."

"I hate crying in front of you," I feel the suffocation closing on my throat, "I hate being weak."

"I wanted to die." His words freeze my blood, and my eyes open by themselves to the most tormented look I have ever seen.

"Don't talk like that," I whisper in horror. No matter what he did, he mustn't say it.

"When I was in the army," he keeps stroking my cheek, creating an incomprehensible contrast between his delicate touch and the harsh words that come out of his mouth, "there were times when I wanted to die. It seemed like the perfect solution. You would get money, our daughter would get a heroic father, and you'd never find out what your father did."

"Do you think that would have solved the problem?" I ask in shock. "Do you think your daughter would want a folded flag instead of a father?"

"Some nights it seemed like the simplest way to deal with the problem."

"Leaving me to live a lie for the rest of my life?" The tears choke my throat.

"It was easier than dealing with the fact that you wouldn't love me again."

"So you prefer to die?" I can't internalize the thought, the words and the meaning they bring with them.

"I'm fighting a losing battle" his eyes sparkle, "a war I lost years ago, we both know that, Lizzie."

My heart breaks into a thousand pieces and more, and I can't stop the soft tears from beginning to trickle down my cheeks. War, and another war, struggle and then another, lies on lies, and for a moment nothing is clear and nothing matters, because we are both defeated. We both lost the life we could have had, the life Colin wants to give me now, the life he had to leave behind.

"I would give anything for you to have come to me," I murmur through my tears. "I would have run away with you to the end of the world if you had asked."

"I know," he wipes the tears from my cheek, "but I don't need you to run away with me, I don't need you to hide, I just need you to love me."

"I love you." I sob, when the truth escapes me, and I can't take it back. "I'm just not sure it's enough."

"Of course it's enough." He leans forward and puts his lips to my forehead. I know he's in pain, but he doesn't seem to care. "It's more than enough, Mrs. Young."

Now I'm sure it's not a slip of the tongue. Now I feel it in my stomach, my bones and my veins, that he meant every syllable.

"I'm not your wife," I whisper to make it clear I haven't missed his statement.

"Yet," he whispers back, putting another kiss on my forehead.

"You have a concussion," I mutter as a smile creeps up the corner of my mouth.

"For nine good years," he replies with a smile. "I believe the first symptoms appeared in the high school cafeteria, and ever since . . ."

"You're a real moron." I close my eyes and let my head sink into the corner of the couch.

"I thought I shouldn't fall asleep," he laughs quietly.

"You're fine."

"Sure?"

"Go to sleep. I guarantee that when you wake up you'll feel like shit." The blows he took will hurt and, if I have to guess, they'll hurt like hell.

"When I wake," he puts his head to my side, "I'll feel just fine because you'll be here."

Sleep engulfs him, his breaths slow down on their own. I listen to them, breathe them with him, bringing him back to life.

CHAPTER TWENTY-SIX

"*Get the fuck away from her!*" *Colin's voice reverberates in the hallway and all eyes turn to him. He moves among the students, who step aside and make room for the infuriated guy who cuts between them threateningly.*

I cringe in front of Carson Tillerman, who spent the last five minutes trying to pin me to my locker and with a fake smile asked me to help him with his algebra homework—"the way you help Colin."

"Young," Carson doesn't seem intimidated by the angry bull rushing toward us like a derailed train.

"What do you think you're doing?" Colin's face turns red, looking from Carson to me, and then back to his football teammate.

"Just asking for help," Carson says innocently. "Your grades have improved, and we all wondered what magic the redhead pulled on you."

Colin looks like he'll lose it completely in two and a half seconds.

"I didn't say anything to anyone," I hasten to defend myself. I didn't tell anyone about the tutoring, and I certainly didn't tell them that Colin and I had been a couple for a month. Maybe just Henry, and I'm pretty sure he didn't open his mouth.

"I'm warning you, Till." Colin takes a deep breath, as if trying to inject oxygen into his brain, which is currently suffering from some sort

of incomprehensible failure. Maybe he doesn't want people to know? Maybe he's ashamed of me?

Before I can take offense, the situation escalates.

"Come on," Carson moves another step toward me, "tell us what her method is. Sucking you're dick every time you don't fail?"

Colin raises his fist and hits the face of his opponent, whose head flies backward and hits the locker behind him. He drops to the floor without a single blow back.

"No one comes near her!" Colin screams at the mass of man lying at his feet, then raises his head and directs his words to anyone who can hear and to anyone who might have thought to act stupid. "No one talks to her, about her, no one breathes in her direction!"

"Relax, man . . ." Carson stammers in confusion at the aggressiveness Colin shows.

"And you . . ." He takes a big step over Tillerman, who grabs his head in his hands. I cling to my locker and hug my books tightly.

"I didn't say a word." I shake my head. My heart is about to leap out of my chest.

"I know," he snorts, grinning, leaning his hands by the sides of my head on the locker door behind me.

"How long has he been bothering you?"

"He didn't . . . I didn't . . . it was the first time."

"Glad to hear." He leans forward slowly, and the silence in the hallway is like a roar in my ears. Everyone is waiting to see what Colin will do to me. Everyone is trying to figure out what the hell the story is.

"Drop your books," he whispers with an amused smile. I obey immediately, and the books fall to the floor. Colin pulls me to his chest and smashes his mouth against mine in front of all the stunned bystanders who have just won tickets for the hottest show in town. I don't quite breathe, but my body gets a life of its own, and my hands are free to enter Colin's hair and hold his mouth to me again.

"Young is fucking the geek," someone shouts, causing Colin to break the kiss wildly.

"Who's the hero who said that?" He doesn't bother to turn his head to

the audience, and no one dares admit he has done something completely idiotic. "The next time you bother me while I'm kissing my girlfriend, I won't be forgiving." He stares at me hard, his eyes burning.

He called me his girlfriend.

In front of everyone.

His girlfriend.

"Where were we?" He raises an eyebrow mischievously and doesn't wait another moment before demanding ownership of my mouth, my heart, and my life, all together.

The voices in the hallway can jump up and call me whatever they want. Colin Young is mine, and even if no one else understands why, I know, and he knows, and that's the only thing that matters.

"ELIZABETH," Colin whispers beside me. "You have to wake up, love."

I refuse to open my eyes. It's much more fun staying in the hallway and kissing him.

"Lizzie, baby, you have to pick up Viv."

Reality forces me to get up. I open my eyes, clutching Colin's arms on the couch. A few minutes after he fell asleep I got up off the floor, lay down next to him, and covered us with a blanket I saw lying on the edge of the sofa. I'm warm and pleasant, and after all these years without him, I'm willing to allow myself a few minutes of stupidity.

"Hey." His face still looks terrible.

"Hey," I answer in the voice of a seventeen-year-old girl hovering on a cloud.

"You smiled in your sleep. I guess you dreamed of me." He smiles a tiny smile.

"I didn't dream of you."

"So you call someone else Colin?" He raises an eyebrow, "Was he as good as me?"

"You're a fool." I refuse to disengage from his embrace.

284

"You have to move."

"Five minutes." I curl up into his chest. Absolutely stupid, there is no doubt about it.

"Kiss me." His request makes my head rise to him.

"You'll want more than a kiss." A shudder passes through me when I think of the moment when he'll want more. More than I can give him.

"Not today," he answers in a sure voice.

"Don't put your hands in my shirt, okay?" We're so close, and I know that if we kiss, his hands will wonder out of habit, and they may get to the wrong places.

I can kiss him, I want to kiss him, but I don't want his hands wandering.

"Because of the scar?" He doesn't move an inch, watching every movement in my face.

"I don't like what's hidden under my clothes," I exhale. "I hate the scar, hate my body. You knew me differently."

"You're the woman I love." He seems to enjoy saying it after all the years he couldn't. "Nothing's going to change that."

"And the scar?"

"That you got when you gave birth to my daughter, the most precious thing in my life?"

His answer is meant to calm me, warm my heart, but the fears, they refuse to release, refuse to let me embrace the moment.

"I'm afraid you'll disappear," I let them straighten their heads and roll off my tongue. "Get what you want, reach your goal and loose interest in me."

"I asked you to marry me, and you refused."

"You didn't mean it. You panicked when you heard that I couldn't have children. You might want to protect me and shelter me, but there's no chance you want to get married."

"Lift up your shirt," he asks in a quiet but steady voice. All I do is shake my head. Colin doesn't seem impressed by my refusal, but he keeps his hands to himself and asks again. "Lift up your shirt."

I move the blanket with trembling hands. Colin moves back to the end of the sofa and gives me room to expose myself to him. His eyes slide to my stomach, and when I lift my shirt up a few inches his voice becomes soft.

"Pull your pants under the scar line."

I grab the tip of my pants with my fingers and roll them down until the incision is visible. I hold my breath and let him look at what I wanted most of all to hide from him.

"Is that the whole story, love?" he whispers, as if expecting some monstrous discovery that has not materialized. "That's what scares you, that should deter me?"

"My body changed." my voice cracks. "You pumped up, and I .. ."

"You've become a woman," he interrupts me, before I have an opportunity to describe exactly what I think of myself. "Do you know how attractive you are?" He looks up from the scar until our eyes cross and lock.

"You're just happy that my boobs have grown." I let go of my pants and put my shirt back in place.

"They sure did." He seems very pleased with the matter. Not that I thought otherwise.

"Horny." I roll my eyes.

"Elizabeth," his voice rattles in a second, "you have to pick up our daughter. Do you really want to open my hormone levels for discussion now?"

I didn't think about that, and I should have. This day is making me a complete idiot. First I took him home instead of taking him to the hospital, and then I sat on the carpet, stroked him and told him I loved him, and now we're talking about my boobs. Where did I think it would lead?

"I haven't been with anyone since you left, Colin." I look down, my cheeks beginning to burn. "I'm not ready."

"So we make out like teenagers," he chuckles. "It'll be fun."

"Really." I don't believe him for a moment, he's not going to want to make out with me until I'm ready.

"Lizzie," he picks up the doubt in my eyes. He reaches for my cheek and strokes it. "You need time, I understand that. You have to trust me again, and I have to prove myself."

"Are you sure?"

"I'm sure." He nods and smiles again. "And anyway, we are not going to do anything for as long as I look and feel like this."

"Afraid you'll disappoint me?" I tease him joyfully after all the times he teased me.

"My lip is bruised, baby," he replies with a grin. "I might be able to ignore that when I kiss you, but we both know where I want to put my mouth."

"Horny." I'd rather not think about his mouth right now. I know what his mouth can do, and what his fingers can do, and the burning between my legs makes it clear to me that every cell in my body knows it, too.

"Go and pick up Viv." He leans over me and kisses my forehead. "I'll call her tonight."

"What about the kiss you asked for?"

"You have to want to give it to me."

He changes the rules of the game, transfers the power to me, making me the one to act, to initiate. He knows what he's doing —he doesn't want to give me excuses. If I'm the one who kisses him, I'll have no one to blame but myself. And when his face is so close, I really don't care. Damn the consequences. My stomach flutters and my heart pounds like a racing horse on the finish line. Damn it all.

I kiss him, taste him, stroke his tongue with my tongue. Without hesitation I put my hands in his shirt, my fingers burning against his smooth, muscular skin. He leaves his hands above my shoulders, holding my face, stroking my cheeks and pressing his tongue back and forth into my mouth. Dazed by the kiss, dizzy with the heat that envelops us, we refuse to take air. Refuse to remove our lips, which speak the language we both know so well. A language forgotten and resurrected. A language that can't be silenced anymore, because it screams the word we both understand: love.

CHAPTER TWENTY-SEVEN

*D*amn my fried brain!

I try to concentrate on the story Vivian is telling me from the backseat, with my thoughts running like honey bees in a hive. I kissed her dad. I put my hands in his shirt, and God, I'll never forget that feeling. If I thought he looked good with clothes on, now I'm pretty sure I'll faint when he takes them off.

Who knew touching his muscles would feel . . . like that. Who knew his smooth skin would be so pleasant to the point that all I can think of is the next time I do it again?

I need to concentrate!

"Mama, where's Dad?" Vivian throws me into reality with one question that makes my heart skip a beat.

Your dad is in his enormous new house, and he spent the morning fighting and the afternoon with his mouth stuck to mine.

That's probably not the answer I should give her.

"He left town." I put on a fake smile, the sole purpose of which is to hide from Viv how much I hate lying to her. "He'll call tonight."

"Daryl doesn't believe he's back," she informs me, and my

blood starts to boil. That child is very fortunate to be five and a half years old.

"Daryl is not your friend if he thinks you're lying." The smile is erased from my face at once.

"When will Dad come back?" she continues to investigate.

"In a few days." I can't be sure how many days it will take Colin's face to recover, and I really don't want to think about all the times I've seen him bruised.

It never looked that bad, but his father knew how to throw a punch and leave a shiner or a blown up nose, which everybody linked to my friend's favorite sport and not to the cruel man who really caused them.

"Are you sure?" Viv's worried voice is forcing me to push aside the bitter memories.

"Yes, sweetheart, I'm sure." I calm her with another smile in the mirror.

"Where are we going?" She puts her nose to the window and looks out.

"Granny's, she misses us." She'll also cook dinner because your mom didn't shop.

"I miss Dad."

"I know he misses you, too."

"Can I call him?" her voice fills with hope.

"Yes. Now?" I got to spend the morning with him, she can certainly have a phone call.

"Yes, please." She smiles a huge smile that reveals her teeth. I dial from the speakerphone and take a deep breath in preparation for the voice of the man who turns my insides into lava.

One ring. Two.

"Couldn't stand the wait?" Colin is not using his head, which seems to have been hit more seriously than I thought.

"Hello, Colin," I interrupt, "you're on speakerphone, your daughter wanted to call you."

I swear I hear an 'oops' from the other side, as Viv intervenes in the conversation.

"Dad!" she shrieks in an unusually high voice.

"Vivian, how are you?"

"Daryl thinks I'm lying," she informs him immediately. "He said you don't exist."

"I guess we'll have to prove him wrong." I hear the determination in his voice climbing quickly.

"Mom said you went away for a few days." She jumps from one topic to another lightly, much to Daryl's luck.

"I'll be back this weekend. Maybe we'll do something together?" He doesn't check with me before throwing that out there.

"I want to ride the pony again," Viv squeals enthusiastically.

"I thought we'd do something new, maybe go to the beach, if Mom agrees."

Mom does not agree! Why is he suggesting that we go to the beach?

"It'll be awesome!" She refuses to stop screaming, and if she continues at this rate, I may go deaf.

"Do you think?" Colin partners with her enthusiasm.

"Best thing in the world! Mama, please say yes, please, please." She gives me all the weight of her sweetness, begging in a tiny voice.

"I'll have to think about it." I pour an imaginary bucket of water over her and her father's enthusiasm. He is about to get a serious lecture from me.

"Elizabeth," he keeps his cool, "you have nothing to fear, it's just a ride to the beach, everybody does it."

"I know." Sure, it's just a trip to the beach. Four hours drive, staying in the sun, and we haven't mentioned the sea yet. Do you know how many things might go wrong on the way, Mr. 'I just became a father, and I'm cool and carefree'?

"Excellent. So I'll pick you up on Saturday, we'll go together, and we'll have fun," he goes on.

"Can we talk about it later?" My voice is sharp, "in private?"

"Sure." He doesn't sound worried about my anxiety.

"Please don't say no, Mama."

"I'm not saying no," I try to untangle the mess Colin has created, "I just want to talk to your dad about the details, okay?" I signal and turn right onto my mom's street.

"Okay."

"We have to go," I blurt out as we approach my mom's house, my father's car parked in front of me.

"Bye, Viv," Colin says his good-bye.

"Bye, Dad," she answers back.

I hang up just as my father gets out of his car and starts walking toward the house.

"Grandpa's here," Viv jumps in her seat.

"Granny's waiting inside." I drive past him and into the driveway, as close as I can to the front door.

"Grandpa!" she calls through the closed window, waving at him. What am I supposed to do now? Tell her they shouldn't talk?

"Grandpa is in a hurry, say hello to him quickly and come inside, okay?" I choose the only option I see. I can't explain to her what he did.

As soon as I turn off the engine, she unfastens her seat belt, opens the door, and leaps out.

"Grandpa!"

I see him reaching down, lifting her in his arms and hugging her, kissing her head again and again. I get out of the car, lock it and wait another second, until he puts Viv back on the grass.

"Vivian, Granny's waiting for you," I call to her.

"Elizabeth—" my father starts to say something, but I interrupt his sentence with a threatening look.

"Viv, Grandpa has to go, run inside."

She puts her arms around my father one last time and runs toward the door. I turn my back on him, but he runs and grabs my arm. I shake him off with a rough movement.

"Stay away from me," I strain with clenched teeth.

"Don't turn your back on me." He walk past me and blocks my way. I stare at his wrinkled face and my heart breaks.

God, he's grown old.

His eyes sunken, his hair more gray, he looks as if he hasn't eaten or slept for days. My head and my heart are fighting hard, between wanting to ask him how he is and the urge to push him away.

"You need to go." My head wins the first round.

"You know why I did it," he insists, staying in my way. "I'd do anything for you."

"I don't want to fight with you." I walk to the right, but he moves with me.

"I wanted to protect you!"

"You stole from me the opportunity to decide for myself," I tell him. "You didn't do it for me, only for yourself. You hated Colin so you chased him away. Do you really expect me to forgive you?"

"You still love him." His face stiffens.

"Of course I love him," I reply scornfully, "he's a good man who made a mistake and has apologized for it. Something that can't be said about you."

"I can't explain," he seems much less sure of himself now, "I don't know what to say."

"How could you do this to me? How could you tell him he'd end up like Brock?"

"He told you." It's not clear to me why it surprises him.

"He told me everything, and you . . ."

"It was just a threat, I didn't touch Brock, though not because I didn't want to." His voice becomes hoarse. I'm in no hurry to believe him.

"Why did you rob us of our future?"

"You deserved more, I thought he was dangerous, that you would get hurt if he stayed."

"You don't know what he went through." My gaze is burning.

"You don't know what he was dealing with, has been dealing with for years. You have no idea what kind of house he grew up in, and what a miracle it was he got out of there in one piece."

"He was the captain of the football team." His mantra gets on my nerves, and finally derails me.

"He *was* captain of the football team!" I scream uncontrollably. "And no one knew his father had turned him into a punching bag. You and his father were equally bad, you both betrayed us, but at least his father could blame the bottle. What's your excuse, Dad?"

"I thought I was doing the right thing," he whispers in a weakening voice.

"You're full of clichés," the anger rolls from my tongue, "I almost lost everything because of you. Lucky for me Colin had the courage to come back and fight for me and Vivian and win us over, but I will never forgive you for what you did to me and Mom"

"Don't involve her in this." He clenches his fists.

"You involved her," I point an accusing finger at him, "you hid the truth from her, and now she's paying the price, now she's unhappy because of you."

"She'll forgive me."

"You're dreaming." My mom's voice alarms us both. Our eyes lock on the woman who stands at the door with a blank look, her hair sloppy, and the makeup on her face not as meticulous as it usually is. She looks terrible, almost like the man standing in front of me trying to explain himself, without any luck.

"You better leave, before I call the police."

"You can't keep me out of my own house, Darlene." He turns slowly, his body facing her, but he shows no intention of moving from the lawn.

"Your clothes are in there," she points to the garage. "You can take them tomorrow, when I'm at work."

"Mom!" I shout in shock. It's one thing to send him to sleep in the hotel for a few nights, and another thing to throw him out for good.

"Elizabeth," her voice is cold, as if she isn't really here. As if only her body remains, while she left, and it's unclear when she'll return. "Your daughter is waiting for you inside."

"Till death do us part, Darlene!" My father raises his voice, but my mom doesn't stay silent.

"Don't talk to me about death, I gave death enough!" She goes down the stairs slowly, one foot in front of the other. She walks unsteadily, holding the railing for support until she stops in front of my father. He stares at her with tormented eyes, hearing every word that comes out of her mouth in unmistakable pain. "I clung to the belief that there was some great plan I didn't understand, that God knew what he was doing. I have survived for my daughter, not for you, of all people in the world, to hurt her!"

"I love you." He takes a step toward her, but her hand raises and lands with a slap on his cheek, which turns red immediately.

"Don't talk to me about love," she flushes with burning eyes. "Take your things, and never come back."

"I won't divorce you!"

"I don't need a piece of paper to tell me I'm not your wife anymore." She reaches his chest and pushes him hard until he stumbles backward. "You gave up on our marriage when you lied to me and betrayed your family." She turns away from him, ignoring the words he is shouting at her.

"It's not over, Darlene!"

"Mom," I call out to the woman who is walking past me on her way in.

"Not a word, Elizabeth." She goes into the house, goes straight to her bedroom and slams the door.

OUR DINNER IS CANCELED. I doubt my mom will leave the room in the next few hours. Viv is watching television. I let her know of the unexpected change of plans—we'll eat outside, then we'll go shopping together and go home.

With a heavy heart I put her in the car, my thoughts staying at home with my mom locked in the bedroom, with my father who lost her, and with the notion that nothing, ever, will be all right.

CHAPTER TWENTY-EIGHT

"My family is falling apart," I cry into my cell ten minutes before midnight, after I couldn't sleep, and the only voice I wanted to hear was Colin's. I took the risk of waking him up, which I did. He answered sleepily, but as soon as he heard my trembling voice, he awoke completely.

"Now you see why I had such a hard time coming back?"

"It's not because of you." I sob on the sofa and pray that Viv doesn't wake up. "I'm just . . . My mom is perishing before my eyes, my father is a shadow of himself, and I can't do anything, I can't turn back the clock and cancel what was done. Why didn't he think about the price we were all going to pay?"

"I'm sure he just wanted the best for you." Colin is defending the man for whom he left, and my crying is getting louder.

"Don't defend him."

"I'm not," his voice is soft, "I'm protecting you, and you love him."

"I hate him, he ruined my life."

"Then fix it," he won't give up. "We'll fix them together, but they won't be whole if you keep hating him."

"Do you expect me to forgive him?"

"Yes, but for you, not for him. If I could forgive my father . . ." he stops abruptly.

"You really forgave him?" How could he?

"I forgave him enough to be willing to give him a part of my body, so I guess the answer is yes. I forgave as much as I could, so he wouldn't die because of me."

"My father is not dying."

"His heart is dying, and your mom's soul is dying, and she won't get over it if you don't take the first step." He seems to understand my mom well. "She's showing solidarity, and she won't do anything that might hurt you, but I'm guessing she is not in good shape."

"She locked herself in her bedroom." She must have cried and looked like a very unhappy version of herself.

"I love you, and you're strong." His words are a breath of fresh air. "You are stronger than all of us, Lizzie. Find a way to forgive him, as I think you forgave me."

"It's really not the same. You were thrown into the situation he created." I wipe my nose and curl up on the couch, my knees to my chest. I didn't think I could forgive Colin, but as soon as I understood the sequence of events, something fundamental changed in the way I saw him and everything that had happened. Something essential changed in my feelings for him. They woke up, and from that moment they refused to sleep.

"I was thrown into the situation *my* father created," he corrects me. "Your father saw two thugs beating me and threatening my family, and he had already lost one child, he didn't think clearly."

"Stop justifying his actions!" I release another burst of uncontrollable crying.

"I'm not justifying what he did," his quiet voice tries to calm the storm that has a hold on me. "I'm trying to understand the circumstances that led him to this, because this hatred will eat us all alive, it will hurt us and Vivian, who loves both her grandfather and her grandmother. I'm trying to find a solution to a bad situation, and that is not at all simple in the middle of the night."

We won't solve it tonight, and probably not even tomorrow. I don't think the situation will ever be resolved. All I have to do is stop trying to fix the past and look forward to the future, to what might be waiting for me and the guy on the other side of the phone.

"I miss you," I release my love for him. "I haven't missed you like this in five and a half years. You are so close, and I can feel you, I can touch you, you are not a hallucination. My head is urging me to move slowly, but my heart, Colin, wants to jump and fall right into your arms."

"Elizabeth," his voice goes rough, "I might call every night if those are the words that come out of your mouth."

"My mouth misses your lips." I blame the late hour for the confessions he hears from me today. "I'm so pathetic."

"Your mouth should rejoice that you are unemployed," he clears his throat, "because if you come tomorrow after you put our daughter in daycare, I'll give you a substantial dose of my lips."

"There's a chance that's what I'll do." There's a really good chance that's exactly what I'll do. I will lock myself in his house and kiss him for hours. It's something I can look forward to.

"I'll make us breakfast."

"*I'll* make breakfast." He makes me smile for the first time in hours. "You'll just rest on the couch. Between the two of us, Colin, if you're the one in charge of the food, we'll have to make do with toast with jam."

"Oh..." he yawns, "how little you know me."

"I need to go to sleep." I close my eyes, suddenly tired. They burn and will look terrible tomorrow.

"I have to go back to sleep."

"Sorry I woke you up."

"You can wake me up any time," he answers in his quiet voice.

"You know that, Elizabeth, you know I'll come whenever you ask."

"Not tonight." There's no point in him coming, I'm on my way to bed and I'll probably fall asleep in thirty seconds. "Go back to sleep, I'll see you in the morning."

"Good night, love."

"Good night, Colin." I let the word reverberate. I let him love me, let him save me from the loneliness that awaited his return, waited for him to defy it as no one else could. I let him be the only one I'll ever want, because he's always been and surely will always be the one I love.

FACING THE CARVED WOODEN DOOR, I stand and try to soothe my rapid breathing. It's just breakfast with Colin, but I'm still suffering from a serious lack of oxygen to the brain when it comes to him. I don't even know what ingredients he has at home. Why didn't I stop for groceries?

Vivian wrinkled her pretty face not understanding what the big deal was, as I stood in front of the mirror in our bedroom and studied my appearance. That's how it is when you're seventeen again, I thought. You stand in front of the mirror in jeans and a shirt, that long ago should have been thrown in the trash, and wonder if you're showing too much cleavage. Oh, it's quite exaggerated.

My thoughts are threatening to get a life of their own and have a conversation with the guy I'm about to see. I let my breath stop in frustration and ring the bell. Moments later, the door opens, and I experience a total malfunction between my brain, which turns into a useless tool, and my body, which feels struck by lightning.

Oh. Mighty. God. Oh mighty God of all gyms, protein shakes, and utterly illegal muscles. He is not human. I stare at his bare chest, unable to say a word. His hair is wet, and he smells like no man has ever smelled. His skin shines and the tattoos on his arms are a sight for my sore eyes.

"Good morning." An amused male voice comes to my ears. I manage to look up at his smile, with supreme effort. His face is still bruised, but I just absorbed the sight of the muscles he has hidden under his shirt.

"Good morning," I mutter, engaged in a relentless war with the fire taking place between my thighs.

Don't let him get dressed! Ever!

"Hungry?" He raises an eyebrow as I swallow. Yes, I'm hungry, but not for any breakfast he might have prepared.

"Elizabeth?" He laughs aloud at my catatonic state.

"No," I shake my head, "you're not . . . real."

"Love what you see?" He bounces his chest.

"Hate it," I manage to complete one sentence without stammering.

"Toast with jam?" He laughs again and opens the door. I stagger through the threshold and go inside, the smell of pastries hitting my nose at once.

"Eating in the living room," he gestures toward the sofa. I put my handbag on the wooden table at the entrance and head toward Colin. What is revealed behind the sofa, on the carpet, makes my heart flutter.

"Please don't tell me you made it yourself." I stare at the tray at our feet, the jug of orange juice, the plates laden with granola yogurt.

"Sit." He laughs once more and doesn't wait, his enormous body sliding down to the rug. He straightens his long legs to the side of the tray.

"Don't you think you should wear a shirt?" I send a silent prayer to God to dress the man before I lose my mind.

"Should I wear one?" he teases me and pours the juice into glasses.

"Well, if you're comfortable like this . . ." I lean slowly and sit down opposite him, fully aware of the fact that I'm in trouble, and the morning has just begun.

"So, you wanna know what's on the menu?" He hands me the orange juice, from which I take a quick sip, and nod.

"We have cheese danishes," he picks up the basket, and the smell of the pastries makes my belly growl, "Spanish omelette, and yogurt with granola."

"Where did you get everything?" I examine the danishes, which look as though they have come straight out of the bakery.

"I told you, lady, I know how to bake." He seems unconcerned with my skepticism.

"It's nine in the morning, sir," I reply with a smile. "You can tell the truth."

"I am telling you the truth."

"You woke up at seven in the morning and worked in the kitchen to make breakfast?" I stare at him closely.

"I woke up at five-thirty," he smiles, "trained, and then I went into the kitchen and made breakfast."

"And you took a shower," I blurt out.

"You noticed that did you?" He lifts a glass of orange juice to his mouth, and when it approaches his lips, I want to push it away and replace the glass with my lips.

"Did you really bake by yourself?"

"You havn't tasted anything yet," he hands me the basket of pastries. Fuck the pastries and the granola and yogurt and the whole breakfast. I put my glass on the tray, lean forward, and with slow motion make my way, on my knees, towards Colin and his bare chest.

"I see," he snarls and puts his glass on the table beside us.

When I reach him, he leans back until he is lying on the rug. I lean my weight against my hands on the sides of his head and look into his eyes. He reaches for my hair band and pulls it until my mane is free to fall on either side of my face.

He holds my nape and pulls my head down toward his lips. I

close the distance slowly, his eyes burn and my skin shivers. I smash my mouth over his with a demanding kiss that keeps me spinning until I forget how to breathe. Until it seems we both need this kiss as much as the other. Colin's lips match mine, as no other lips will ever fit, and his taste is the most wonderful thing that will ever meet my tongue. The air becomes superfluous, neither of us is willing to stop, unwilling to give our thoughts an opportunity to sneak in and disturb the thin balance. I lift my hands off the floor and flutter around his neck, all the way to his chest, with a touch that caresses his smooth skin. His breathing turns strenuous, and I feel his heart beating wildly. I gently pull my lips from his, raise my head and open my eyes, looking into his gaze, his blue eyes storming.

"Maybe I should have worn a shirt after all," he murmurs between quick breaths.

"Maybe."

"You have to move back." His trembling voice makes me regret my initiative.

"Sorry," I sit up, my cheeks turning red, "I didn't mean to force myself on you."

He grabs my arm and stops me.

"We had an understanding," he clears his throat. "Something about making out like teenagers, it's just harder than I thought. We're lying on the rug, and I remember how amazing your body feels."

"Oh." I look down.

"You're not ready, and I respect that, but I'm a twenty-six-year-old man with a pretty brutal erection right now." He ends the sentence with a weak laugh that reveals a rather serious distress.

"Oh." My vocabulary is lacking again.

"So... breakfast?" he raises an eyebrow with amusement.

"Yeah, sure." I feel stupid, just as I felt the first evening we met.

"My pastries are waiting to hear your opinion."

"You really baked them, didn't you?" I slide back and sit cross-legged at a safe distance from him, though I doubt any distance will be safe enough. As long as we're both in the same house, and he's not fully dressed, I can't say what I will do.

"Yes, Elizabeth, I really baked them." He laughs again and sits up. I pick one of the danishes up with trembling fingers and bite. He didn't lie, he did learn to cook, to bake, whatever you call it.

"Tasty?" His look is curious.

"Yes," I nod modestly, in an attempt not to inflate his ego anymore. I have a feeling that if I tell him exactly what I think, he will never let it go.

"Can we talk about going to the beach?" He takes another sip of orange juice.

"Yes," I take a deep breath, before getting into the explosive subject, "let's talk about it."

"I didn't think my proposal was excessive." His voice is steady.

"It's not the trip to the beach," I walk around the subject gently, "please don't be offended by what I'm about to say."

"I won't be offended." He leans back on his hands.

"You're learning to become a parent for the first time in your life," I put the pastry on my plate, fold my knees and embrace them defensively, "and I'm learning to share my responsibilities and parent with someone else for the first time in my life. We have to talk about things between us before we offer Viv ideas that excite her."

"Again, I didn't think it was a big deal." He doesn't seem to understand what I mean.

"You've just come back," my voice cracks, "and you're worry-free, cool, and taking everything lightly. If Vivian thinks she can get whatever she wants from you, and I'm the one who always refuses, I'll be—"

"The bad mom," he completes my sentence in a quiet voice.

"Talk to me, before you talk to her, that's all I ask."

"Definitely," he nods, "I'm sorry I put you in that position."

"It's okay, we're adjusting." I manage to smile at him.

"You're so beautiful," he whispers, his chest rising and falling.

"You're not ugly yourself," I reply awkwardly, "when your face is not puffed up with blows."

"It'll be fine in a few days," he laughs quietly.

His phone rings from the dining table. He stands up slowly, walks toward it, peers at the screen and looks at me as if asking permission to answer. I nod, and he answers in a confident voice.

"Good morning, Bryson," he keeps his eyes on me. "I'm not used to hearing from you before noon."

I try not to stare in lust at his body, but fail miserably. His sculpted muscles tease me, calling for my fingers to feel them.

"You know I won't pay you that," Colin laughs. "I'll send someone in a few minutes." He hangs up the phone and hurries to dial, turning to me. "It'll take a second, okay?"

I nod again. He may be hiding at home, but he has a business to run, and I don't want to stand in his way.

"Dammit," he hangs up and dials again. "Where is she?"

"Danielle?"

"Yes," his jaw locks. "Where the hell is she?"

"Do you want to share?"

"Furniture," he hangs up and dials a third time. "If she doesn't get in her car now, I don't know what I'll do."

"Colin, talk to me." I stand up slowly, move over to him and put a hand on his arm. His troubled eyes lock on mine as he sets the phone down on the table.

"Bryson is a vendor." He raises his hand to his hair and pulls it back abruptly. "He is clearing a huge warehouse and I know him, I want his merchandise, but I can't appear in my condition."

"And Danielle isn't answering." I wander my fingers gently along his arm.

"He won't wait. If I don't send someone, he'll call someone else, and it's a great deal. The warehouse needs to be empty in two days and Bryson doesn't care who does it." His frustration is evident.

"She'll probably get back to you in a few minutes." I really don't know what to say.

"I don't have a few minutes," he shakes his head. "Bryson's stuff is hot, and he knows it. I can make twenty thousand on it, maybe thirty." The look in his eyes changes, as if he's had an idea, something that makes me step back.

"No," I shake my head, understanding what he's going to ask. "Colin, no."

"He's a good guy. I'll wait in the car, you just have to go in and take the price down a notch."

"I said no!" I raise my voice in alarm. The last thing I need is to mess up Colin's deal. Where is Danielle when she's needed?

"Lizzie, you can do it." He takes a step in my direction, but I raise my hand in refusal.

"I don't know how to bargain."

"It's not as hard as you think, Bryson expects that, it's how it works."

"I don't understand the business!" I feel the anxiety climbing, clinging to my throat, making my breathing difficult. "Don't ask me."

He closes the distance between us in one second, puts his hand in my hair and gently pulls it back so that my head rises to him.

"You've raised our child for five years, Liz," he doesn't let me move my head in order to escape his piercing eyes. "Bryson is child's play. Do you trust me?"

"No." I try to shake my head, without success.

"It's just a show."

"I didn't take drama classes," I insist.

"You just have to pretend." He doesn't seem willing to accept my refusal, but what do I know about pretending? What do I know about dealing with tens of thousands of dollars? What do I understand about the warehouses that need to be cleared?

"I can't do it," I mutter.

"You can, and I believe in you even if you don't."

"I'll fuck up the deal for sure," my voice shakes.

"The deal will disappear anyway if we don't go."

I know I'm screwed, there is a limit to how much I can resist. He's in trouble and I can help, or at least try to help, and hope that I won't ruin everything.

"Please don't blame me if it doesn't work," I whisper in surrender. "Promise me you won't blame me."

He presses his mouth against mine, pushing me back with his enormous body until my back hits the wall behind me. His huge chest covers mine and he kisses me. He doesn't stop kissing me with lust, which in a second will make me forget the desire to move slow. I sigh into his mouth. This is definitely an answer I didn't expect.

I'll close the damn deal for him, and he'll be grateful. So help me God, he'll be grateful, and he'll show me how much. The thought dissolves when his mouth breaks away from mine.

"We have to move."

"You better get dressed." I swallow, hold my hips and pray that the sweet feeling will disappear for a few minutes so I can concentrate.

"Get your bag, I'll explain everything in the car." He steps back and stops, looking at me with his burning eyes.

"Hurry up," I mutter, "we don't want to be late."

He gives me a last, passionate look, turns his back on me and hustles into one of the rooms, putting on something that might help my brain return to partial function. Screw this. I'll nail it, and everything will be perfect.

CHAPTER TWENTY-NINE

*C*olin's jeep speeds down the road. He cuts through the traffic easily and navigates between the streets outside the city center.

"Be indifferent," he tries to reassure me in a calm voice, as if it were the lightest thing in the world and not the impossible task he has imposed on me. "We buy all the goods, not part of it, not half."

"*You* buy the goods," I emphasize.

"*You* buy the goods." He looks up at me and raises an eyebrow. "Bryson is expecting Danielle, he's used to dealing with her, you have to be just as tough."

"I'm not tough." Who is he kidding? I'm used to selling coffee tables to people in Mr. Blunt's shop. I can't remember when I last bargained.

"You have to be indifferent. He will try to show you the goods and convince you that they are excellent—don't let him. He doesn't know you, and that's an advantage, pretend you've done it a thousand times before."

"You have to tell me exactly what to do," I beg for a little bit of information to help me through the next hour.

"Don't pay more than twenty thousand." His words raise my pulse to a dangerous level. Twenty thousand dollars? Does he really expect me to deal with such amounts? It's not normal!

"Colin," I protest loudly, but he turns sharply to the right and brakes the car with a screech.

"We're here." He turns off the engine and loosens my seat belt.

"You didn't explain a thing!" My legs are shaking.

"No more than twenty thousand." He stares at me hard, which makes me shrink. I'm going to screw it up. If I don't get a grip in the next thirty seconds the deal is lost.

"Remember, you promised not to blame me." I turn a threatening finger at him.

"Go buy me some goods." He leans forward and, with a fluttering kiss, strokes my lips.

"You will owe me big time." I puff out a breath of air as I open the car door in front of the monstrous warehouse.

"I'll make it up to you. When you're ready." He blurs my thoughts for a few more moments. I slam the car door behind me so I won't hear another word come out of his mouth and remind myself to be indifferent. Bryson is expecting Danielle, and I'm not her. I'd better find within myself the bravery and arrogance of a blonde woman and prove to her, and the guy sitting in the car, that I can do it without heels and red nail polish.

"MAY I HELP YOU?" The big black haired man stands wide-eyed as I walk in the doorway. He moves toward me, scanning me from head to toe.

"Colin sent me," I reply in a sure tone, keeping eye contact and not letting my eyes wander to the vast amount of furniture packed in plastic sheets in every corner.

"Nice to meet you. I'm Bryson." He holds out his hand to me. "Danielle is busy?"

"Disappointed?" I shake his hand confidently.

"Not at all."

I'm sure he's disappointed that he didn't get another glimpse of the blonde's assets. I let go of his hand, walk past him with my back straight, sit on the first chair I find, cross legs, and put my hands around my knees.

I have to breathe and soothe my trembling legs, which makes it hard for me to stand. Colin believes in me, and I don't want to disappoint him. I want the goods to come into his hands, especially when I know how much profit he can make on them.

"Don't you want to look around?" Bryson purses his brows.

"There's no need," I shrug. Even if I look I won't know what I'm looking at and what the furniture is really worth.

"Really?" his dark eyes narrow.

"I know what I want and I won't pay more than ten thousand." Perhaps it was not the wisest thing to say? Damn you, Colin, what is the right thing? How am I supposed to look indifferent with my heart fluttering like this?

"Let's go around for a bit." Bryson makes another attempt to get me up from the chair, but I refuse to budge.

"I told you," I lean back, "the goods don't interest me. If Colin wants them, Colin will get them, and I won't pay more than ten thousand. Do we have a deal?"

The man in front of me shifts his weight from one foot to another. My impatience seems contagious.

"Listen, ma'am," he starts to say, but I cut him off.

"Elizabeth Heart, but don't let my name fool you—I don't have a heart. What I have is money, do you want it?" I tilt my head at the guy, who looks like he doesn't understand where the hell I came from.

"I don't do business like that," he shakes his head and waves his hand, but I don't move.

"How long do you have to vacate the place, two days?"

"I'm calling Colin." He takes the phone out of his pocket as if threatening to call my boss and complain about me.

"Call him," I gesture to his cell, "and tell him I said the goods smell bad. How fast do you think the word will spread and no one else will want it?"

"This furniture is new!" He holds the phone, but doesn't dial. "They're still in nylon."

"And I don't think they smell good." I'm talking nonsense, but I really don't know what to say.

"I want twenty-five thousand dollars," he doesn't shift his belligerent stance, "and don't tell me they're not worth it."

"They're not worth it," I wave dismissively. "Maybe you'll find another sucker."

"Your boss will hear from me," he clenches his fists.

"Yeah, yeah, he'll hear from you. Ten thousand dollars or I'm leaving. Did you hear that Blunt closed his furniture store?"

"I don't know him," Bryson replies with a little more curiosity.

"He had a place in the shopping center. I'm on my way to his warehouse. Do you think you're the only one with goods in town?"

The ease with which I lie makes me angry. I do it just to close the deal, but I hate it to the core.

"How much does he want for it?" Bryson can't resist.

"You don't expect me to tell you?" I laugh, a smile full of arrogance spreading over my face. Maybe it's going better than I thought. Maybe Colin knew it wouldn't be hard, and Bryson would agree to the amount he wanted to pay.

"Twenty-three thousand," he says, dropping the price without preparation, throwing his number into the air. Here it comes.

"Twelve." I stand up, straighten my back, and hold out my hand to shake his.

"Twenty one." He makes another attempt.

"Fifteen."

"Twenty thousand, and that's my last number, Miss 'I don't have a heart'." He reaches out.

"Colin will kill me," I lie again, "I don't have permission to give more than eighteen."

"Nineteen thousand," he squeezes out his offer once more.

"Eighteen, Bryson, and that's more than the merchandise is worth." I wait for his handshake.

"I really hope that next time he sends Danielle," Bryson grumbles, and then shakes my hand hard. "Eighteen thousand, make sure your boss comes by and brings the money."

"I'll tell him." I pull my hand back. "He'll send the trucks."

I have no idea where Colin is going to store all this furniture, and right now I don't care. I just want to get out of here and get rid of the terrible nausea that is climbing up my stomach.

"Have a good day." I nod my head at the man, who seems more satisfied than I expected him to be. I turn away from him and hurry away, stepping out the door and walking toward the bruised guy who's leaning against his jeep and staring at me with curious eyes. Ignoring his existence, I walk past him and over to the other side of the car.

"Elizabeth," he calls as he pushes his body off the jeep, as if trying to stop me.

"I bought the goods," I reply nervously. "It cost you eighteen thousand dollars."

"Elizabeth, stop!" He grabs my arm just before I can open the door. I turn sharply and stare at him , but he doesn't let go of my arm.

"Don't do it again," I snarl angrily. "Don't ask me to lie for you, I don't care if I can bargain, it's not me. God, I hate myself right now."

"You didn't take food from a starving child," he rolls his eyes, as if I'm making a fuss over nothing. "You successfully negotiated, Bryson is not poor."

"It doesn't matter." I don't care about Bryson, I care about me. I don't like to pretend and play the game. "I'm glad you're doing well, really, and if Danielle likes it, I'm happy for her, too, but I don't. My body aches, my muscles ache, that's not what I want to do in my life."

His fingers climb up my arm and when he takes a step, my back presses against the car door, his chest pressing into mine, and I have to raise my head to meet his face.

"Do you know what I want to do in my life?" He leans over, his words becoming a stirring whisper as his lips travel from my ears and along my jaw. "I want to kiss you all the time. I want to move my hands over your body. I don't care who's looking, I don't care what others have to say." He lets his hands do just that, walking them from my collarbone to my throat, my nape, into my hair. "I want to kiss you." His body becomes aroused and the bulge in his pants grows. I thank God we're standing in the middle of the street and not alone in his house, because I wouldn't be able to resist him otherwise. I would do anything to feel him move inside me. "I want to feel your heart go wild and know that I'm the reason. I want to know that I've survived everything to be able to return to you, that not all was in vain."

"Colin . . ." I close my eyes and sigh, pleading him to place his lips somewhere. It doesn't matter where, whether to the hollow of my neck or my earlobe. I just want them to find a place on my skin that is burning with anticipation.

"The war," his lips seem to hear my prayer, fluttering on my jaw not far from my lips, "the blood... you make me forget all the shit. I love you so much, Elizabeth, so much . . . I will never ask you to do it again..."

"I love you," I whisper.

"You're my family." He gently pulls my lower lip between his teeth, which begins to vibrate. His words bring tears to my eyes and close on my heart with a powerful pain that I can't remove, and as if to tease me the tears come and wash my cheeks. I bury my face in his chest and let them wet his shirt.

"Why are you crying?" Colin whispers.

Somehow I find the strength and I manage to answer, "I came

to terms with the fact that you were not coming back and that I'd be left alone to raise Viv. It was all right, but now . . ." Everything has changed, everything is new and confusing, and my feelings are racing through my body, making me cry uncontrollably. "You're here, and I'm not alone. My dream came true, but I can't fulfill your dream, I can't give you the big family we always talked about, and it's killing me."

"You and our daughter are all I need." His arms hug my shoulders tight and I feel his heart racing through his chest.

"You say that now, but in a few months, in a few years . . ." I want to scream, curse God for the inconceivable price I paid. "I had time to accept the situation, but you . . ."

"I just got back," he kisses my head, "and I got my family back. We're just getting started, just getting to know each other again, trusting. You don't have to think about it, we have time."

"In the end you'll wake up and want more, but I can't have more children. It will be the end of us."

"Why are you doing this?" He sighs, his voice full of pain. "Elizabeth, we're just getting started."

"I know where it's leading!" I cry out. "I can see the end in front of my eyes."

"Because you lost your uterus? You're not supposed to be dealing with that now."

"But I am." I raise my red and teary eyes to look into his tormented gaze. "I'm dealing with it, thinking about it. Even though you've just come back, I'm thinking about it, because I'm afraid you'll have a reason to leave again."

He presses against my body, pushing my back to the car door, and puts his hands in my hair and pulls it back. The look in his eyes turns from sordid to full with lust, and he doesn't bother hiding it.

"You talk nonsense, but I forgive you," he wiggles his thumb at my lip. "I'm not going anywhere. I'll propose to you again and again until you say yes. I'll stand in the church all night if that's what I have to do to make you realize I'm not running away anymore."

"My ovaries are still—" I continue.

"We're not talking about it now." He doesn't seem to understand what I meant. "Slow down, love."

"We can . . ." I insist on talking about the future, even though our present isn't clear.

"We can what?" He lowers his head slowly and finds my salty lips. He gathers my tears on his tongue and sends shivers down my spine. "I have everything I need right here. I could have come home in a coffin but I didn't. I just want you to forgive me, I just want to be a father to my daughter. Let me be her father. My dream came true. I don't need anything more."

"I'm just saying," I sigh and try to cling to him again, to stick to him until nothing can separate us.

"Lizzie," he whispers my name in a rough voice, "I'm not leaving again, and if in a few years we want more kids, I'm sure there are quite a few kids who need a home and we can give them one. But slow down, you're pushing me away for all the wrong reasons. "

"I love you," my lips grope for his, "I want you to be happy."

"I'm in the clouds, darlin'." He laughs quietly, as if his laughter can remove the cloud of worry hovering above me.

"Swear?" I kiss him. God help me I'll kiss him for hours.

"I swear," he moans into my mouth. "I'm in the clouds. So, when are we going to the beach?"

ivian is frantically hopping around our bedroom as I zip up my bag with swimsuits, towels, and a change of clothes. She is happy, while I face a murky mood. If I'm lucky, Colin will let me stay dressed in the shorts I have chosen and the too-tight white undershirt and won't force me to cram myself into the bathing suit I bought especially for the ride. Viv picked herself a pink bikini, which didn't surprise me at all. For me, I bought a black one piece and fought my tears as I stood in front of the mirror. I haven't seen Colin in the past three days, since he dropped me off at home and refused the invitation to come in.

We both knew what would have happened if he had gotten out of the car.

I fought the thoughts of him for hours. Lying in bed, imagining how it would feel when I slept beside him again, when he'd take off my clothes and kiss every inch of my skin.

"Mama, someone is honking!" Viv jumps up and runs to the door.

"Wait for me," I call after her, putting the bag on my shoulder and hurrying after her. She doesn't wait, opens the door and runs with her arms stretched to her father, who waves at her in the air and kisses her cheek.

"I've missed you." He kisses her again.

"Are we really going to the beach?" She stares at him pleadingly.

"We're going to the beach. Do you want to fasten your seat belt?"

He takes her to the curb and opens the back door for her. Viv climbs into her seat, and Colin closes the door. A moment passes before he turns to me, his eyes burning.

"Hey," I greet him quietly, but his gaze wanders to my bare feet and climbs slowly up to my chest, peeking out of the white undershirt.

"It's going to be a long day," he says in a low voice.

"Behave," I turn to him.

"If you wanted me to behave, you should have worn something else."

"Colin," I warn in a sure voice.

"I can smell your perfume," he fills his lungs up with air, "it really is going to be a long day."

"Stop acting like a teenager," I roll my eyes, "and throw my bag in the back."

I take my bag off my shoulder and give it to Colin.

"Four hours in the car with my girls." The smile on his face expands to monstrous proportions.

"I hope you remembered to bring the disc Viv asked for." I walk past him, trying to ignore the smell of his aftershave, open the car door and climb into the passenger seat.

"The girl needs new musical education, Lizzie." He's holding the door. It seems he's still dealing with the fact that his daughter is sure she'll marry Justin Bieber.

"It could have been worse," I shake my head.

"I'm not sure I agree with you." He leans forward to take in the scent of my perfume. "But I will make great efforts to behave and not say anything about our future son in law."

"That would be nice of you." I put my hand on his chest and push him out of the car. "No nonsense."

"Let's go to the sea, girls!" he calls out loud and slams the car door, walking quickly in front of the windshield and, in a second, sitting behind the wheel and starting the car.

"Ready to sing?" he glances at Viv in the mirror.

"Bieber!" she shrieks enthusiastically as the first sounds fill the car.

"Four hours," I mutter to myself. As long as he doesn't say anything about my legs or my tits, and keeps his big mouth shut, everything will be all right.

"I THOUGHT she'd never stop singing." Colin takes another look in the mirror at Viv, who has fallen asleep in her seat two hours after we left the house. Her eyes are closed, and at last we can turn down the music and talk, without our daughter's squeaky voice filling the car. Though, we both agree that her smiles are worth everything.

"I want to make it clear that she developed her Bieber affection all by herself." I lift my legs and straighten them to the windshield.

"You're lucky I know you, darlin'. There's no way it was your idea." He laughs and glances at my legs.

"If it were up to me, she'd listen to something else."

"Like what?" He raises an eyebrow, as if trying to remind me that music was never really my interest. He's right, I've never been into it.

"I don't know," I shrug, "jazz?"

"She's five years old." He laughs loudly.

"It's never too early to start."

"Start what?" he chuckles. "Playing boring music to the girl?"

"At least she won't ask to go to a concert that I'll have to refuse her," I grumble, recalling all the times that Viv wanted to go to Bieber's concerts, despite her young age.

"She wanted to see Bieber?" His mouth falls open.

"More than once, Colin. He performed in Dallas a few months ago and there were a lot of tears streaming down the house. I wasn't going to take her, and not just because of the money. I had no intention of standing in line among thousands of people and risking losing her."

This is the main reason why my daughter didn't see her Bieber, because I'm anxious and cowardly.

"Maybe she'll see him the next time he comes to the area." He shrugs his shoulders indifferently, as if this is another minor matter.

"We'll talk about it when the moment comes." If Colin wants to sit in the stadium and listen to Bieber for a few hours, good luck to him.

"Did you talk to your mom?" He changes the subject quickly, and the temperature in the car drops by a few degrees.

"I saw her yesterday. I don't know how to help her." My mom is withering away in front of my eyes day by day. "My father is still sitting in the car in front of her house."

"You know how to help her," he answers calmly.

"I can't forgive him," I shake my head.

"Lizzie, are you sure you can't do it for her?"

"You don't even know if that's what she wants," I defend myself. "You didn't see her."

"Actually . . ."

The muscles in my body are immediately on alert..

"Colin," my voice is sharp, "when did you meet my mom?"

There is no chance that they met at the grocery store or on the street. Unless . . .

"I worry about her, too." He doesn't take his eyes off the road.

Luckily. If he sneaks a look at me, he will encounter my very unhappy face. "So I went to visit her."

"Great," I say loudly. "You had to get involved?"

"I've been involved from the start, and the situation has to be resolved."

"You don't have to solve anything, it's not your problem."

"Your mom was always good to me, I won't sit aside and watch her suffer."

"Do you think that's what I'm doing?" I'm offended.

"Do you know how I felt when I got the phone call from the hospital?" His voice goes harsh. "The doctor told me that my father didn't want them to call. I didn't even know he was hospitalized."

"You were in L.A?" I carefully inquire.

"Yes, at work," he nods. "The doctor didn't beat around the bush. She told me that my father couldn't get onto the transplant list because of his drinking and that, in fact, she didn't think he had the time to wait. She said she knew her request was great, but the bottom line was that my father was going to die and that his life was more or less in my hands."

"Did you hesitate?" I whisper.

"Not for a moment," he answers steadily. "I'm willing to live with a lot of things but I didn't want his death on my conscience. I wasn't tested for him, I was tested for me."

"My father isn't going to die, Colin, nor is my mom." The gap between the situations is great.

"Can you tell me your conscience is clear?" He glances at me before returning his eyes to the road.

"Why wouldn't it be?"

"He made a mistake trying to protect you. What would you do if Viv was in danger?"

His question freezes my blood. Why would anyone want to hurt my daughter?

"You're crossing the line, don't involve Vivian."

"Your father thought he was protecting you, don't you see that?"

"No," I cross my arms, "I don't see it that way."

"In his mind, if he didn't pay, they would chase me and come after you and maybe after Viv, too, once she was born." His loathing of the two scums that threatened him is evident in his voice, "you were an easy way to blackmail me."

"He should have payed them without forcing you to leave," I raise my voice and immediately regret it, not wanting to wake Viv.

"I can't argue with that," his voice falters, as if trying to calm the storm in the car a little. "But you know his past, and I can't put myself in his shoes."

"Do me a favor," I blow out hard, "understand that it was not because of his past, it was all because he couldn't see you were a good man."

"Elizabeth," he reaches toward me and strokes my forearm, "I can't put myself in his shoes. I wasn't in your garage the day your father had to cut the rope and get Morgan off the beam."

"You weren't to blame for what happened, and he wouldn't see it." Tears well up in my eyes.

"Jesus Christ," he puts his hand back to the wheel. "Give the man a break. Do you know what I would do if someone put a finger on Viv?"

"You'll wake her up," I immediately dismiss him.

"Do you understand what he's been through?" He shakes his head in frustration, "Can you imagine it, to find out that a bunch of boys abused his child for months behind his back, drowned him in the toilet, tied him naked to a stand, do I have to go on? He didn't think clearly because he couldn't."

"You and your infinite compassion," I reply scornfully. "Is that what you told my mom, that my father didn't think clearly?"

"I told her that both of them repressed something that had to be talked about for too long. The fact that they moved to another city and hid Morgan's pictures didn't hide his existence or his death."

"And how did it work for you?" I clasp my hands. "Did she forgive him?"

"She won't forgive him until you do. Do you think she wants to be alone?"

"He should of thought about it, before he removed you from my life."

"I'm asking you to do something before it's too late." He pauses.

"What are you hiding?" I sit up in my chair.

"Show a little compassion." He dodges, but it won't work for him. He'll talk, and he'll talk now.

"Colin Young, open your mouth before you get into serious trouble." I lock my jaw and notice the deliberation on his face, aware of his deep breathing.

"Do you remember being seven and your father being sick?" He gives me another look, his eyes dark.

"Did I tell you about that?" I scrunch my forehead. I don't think I ever mentioned it. People are sick sometimes, it's not a big deal.

"Your mom told me," he looks back at the road.

"That my father was sick?"

"That's what they told you." He hesitates a bit. "He didn't lay in a hospital with pneumonia, love, he tried to commit suicide." His hand reaches my thigh, as if to keep me from collapsing.

"My father didn't . . ." The words don't crystallize into a sentence. The blood is running out of my face, and I can't take my eyes off Colin. He wouldn't lie to me.

"He blamed himself for Morgan and couldn't live with it. I beg you, for your mom's sake and for our family, don't let him go through that again, don't let him carry more guilt on his back."

"My father was a happy man," I whisper in confusion. "He always supported us, it's a mistake . . . he's didn't . . ."

322

"He was a broken man. I couldn't understand him before, but now I know," his voice cracks. "If something happened to you or Vivian…"

"Stop the car." The words spill out of me.

"Lizzie."

"Stop the car!" I have to throw up. I need to talk to my mom. What if my father tries again?

"There's a gas station a few miles ahead, we'll stop there." He presses his fingers against my thigh.

"You should have told me," I turn my head from him to the window. "My mom should have told me. You're all treating me like a little girl."

"I love you," he whispers apologetically.

"I'm sure," I reply scornfully, "you all love me, and your love is suffocating, your love is causing me so much pain."

Their constant attempts to protect me are becoming unbearable, and it's time for them to stop and treat me with respect.

I GET out of the car while Colin fills the gas tank, pacing nervously with the phone at my ear and listening to my mom, trying unsuccessfully to explain herself.

"I'm supposed to be on my way to the beach," I shout, "to lie in the sun and not think about anything, and instead I have to worry about my father trying to commit suicide again?"

"I don't think he'll try."

"You don't think?" I roar, and Colin freezes and stares at me. "What is the matter with you?"

"Your father needs to think before he acts," she repeats her mantra, but I've already crossed the threshold of patience.

"He needs to do a lot of things. You all need to talk to me and not hide the truth. I'm furious at you and him, but that doesn't mean I want him to die."

"He hurt you, do you expect me to forgive him for that?" Her tone is incredulous.

"I expect you to open the door and let him sleep on the sofa before he does something we will all regret."

"When you're married for more than thirty years, you can give me advice. And when you find out that your husband lied to you, I will listen to what you have to say. Until then..."

"Do you think Colin didn't lie?" I clench my free fist. "I'm not stupid, I know he could have called over the years, he could have come back and confronted Dad and me, but he didn't. I had to decide whether to throw him off the stairs or forgive him and embrace the life he offers me and our daughter. Isn't that what you told me to do? To forgive? Are you really ready to throw away a marriage of over thirty years?"

"Your father threw it away." She is entrenched in her position.

"If something happens to him, I'll hold you responsible."

"Nothing will happen to him."

"You don't know that. Don't you love him anymore?"

"Elizabeth," she sighs, "of course I love him."

"Then you can be angry with him all you want, but at the same time keep him safe," I insist.

"If I let him back, he will think what he did is forgiven, that it is all right."

"I'm sure he knows he was wrong."

I'm sure my father learned his lesson. My mom threw him out of the house, I'm not letting him get close to Vivian. He understands, I have no doubt about it.

"Your boy is trying to solve the situation," she accuses.

"Colin hasn't been a boy for a long time," I roll my eyes, "in case you haven't noticed."

"At my age," she defies, "you don't think from between your legs anymore, Elizabeth."

"Do you think that's what I'm doing?" I laugh with scorn. "Do you think that's how Colin won his way back into our lives?"

"Your father should internalize that there's a price for his actions."

"You better look in the mirror and find out who's paying the price." One good look in the mirror, and my mom will let him come home.

"Thanks for the advice," she replies cynically, "have fun at the beach."

"I love you," I try to end the conversation in a conciliatory tone. "Please find a way to be happy again, because I'm worried about you and I'm worried about Dad."

"I love you back."

"Bye, Mom." I hang up the phone and put it back in my bag.

"Ready to move?" Colin comes from behind me and puts his hand on my shoulder, his touch on my bare skin sending shivers down my back.

"Yes," I sigh softly.

"Viv woke up." He gestures to Viv, who is smiling at us from the window. "I hope you can survive another hour of Bieber."

"I've been living with him for a year," I chuckle. "What's another hour?"

"I guess I have more to learn," he whispers.

"You learn fast," I whisper back. "Let's go to the beach."

CHAPTER THIRTY-ONE

*V*ivian is probably the happiest person on the planet. Colin surprised us both when he pulled a blanket out of the trunk to lay on the sand, a picnic basket, toys for Viv and a parasol. Our girl is building a sand castle, after I insisted on covering her with sunscreen, twice, and I made Colin swear not to take his eyes off her. We sit in the sun, it's rays caressing Colin's tattoos, who is in a swimsuit and bare chested, drawing looks from every girl passing by.

"Mama?" Vivian raises her eyes for a moment. "Why don't you wear a swimsuit?"

"Yes, Mama," Colin mimics her, "why don't you wear a swimsuit?"

"I am." I lift up my shirt, only for a moment.

"Why don't you take off your clothes?" she insists.

"Yes, Mama, why don't you take off your clothes?" Colin raises an eyebrow and gives me a lascivious look.

"Don't you have a castle to build?" I wave my hand at the pile of sand.

"Viv," Colin tilts his head at our daughter, "should we help Mom?"

"Oh no," I warn him, "don't even think about."

"Yes!" the collaborator screams immediately. "You have to help Mom!"

"Colin, I'm warning you."

"She's warning me, Viv," he smiles at the girl whose blonde hair shines in the sun. "Do you think she means it?"

"Noooo," Vivian laughs.

"I mean it, I swear." I don't know whether to laugh at how these two communicate or cry from Colin's malicious plan to leave me in a swimsuit.

"Give me your clothes." Colin reaches out his hand to me.

"I'll burn in the sun," I try to dodge again.

"I'll cover you in sunscreen." His sentence is the last thing I need to hear. Why on earth does sunscreen sound like the sexiest thing I can think of?

His hands on my skin, every inch of it. That's why.

"I can do it myself."

"Give me your clothes and I'll let you do it yourself, if you want to so much." He tilts his head with a smile.

I don't want to do it by myself. I want to be all over him, but that's not going to happen with our five-year-old girl around.

"Not a word." I turn a finger at him to keep his mouth shut.

He gives up his hands in surrender, but doesn't take his eyes off me when I open the button of my jeans and slowly drag them down my legs, setting them aside. With trembling fingers I hold the hem of my shirt and pull it over my head, in front of the lingering gaze of my horny ex, who looks like he will jump me any minute.

"We're buying you a bikini," he snarls, completely ignoring the company beside him.

"Not in this life time." I narrow my eyes and fold the shirt, placing it on my jeans. "Are you two satisfied?"

"Bikini," he snarls again.

"Pink bikini," Viv shrieks. "You'll look so good in a pink bikini, Mama!"

"Red." Colin decides to be my new fashion consultant.

"Pink." Viv bends her head back to the sand castle.

"And I thought the trip here would be a long one . . ." Colin takes a deep breath and arranges his swim trunks.

"I told you I should have stayed in my clothes." I smile in light of his distress.

"Like that would make a difference." He bends his head reproachfully.

It's going to happen soon. Maybe not today, but we both know it's going to happen. And when it does, we'll probably lose our heads, drown, and there will be no going back. He's got my heart and is about to get my body after more than five years. My pulse is rippling in my veins, what if he is disappointed?

What if he had so many girls who knew what they were doing? What if I have no idea, and he's going to find out?

"Stop thinking what you're thinking." Colin's voice resonates sharply.

"You don't know what I'm thinking about," I defend myself from his attempt to read my thoughts.

"Are you sure?"

"You have no idea." Our eyes lock and I sees the gleam in his.

"I have three hypotheses, and if I have to guess, all three are correct."

"And none of them are things we are going to talk to about now." I point to Vivian.

"Vivian," he asks quietly without taking his hungry look away from me. "Isn't your mom the most beautiful woman in the world?"

My heart skips a beat.

"Uh-huh," she answers, dipping her hands in the wet sand.

"Don't go on," I whisper to him with a strangled throat.

"Stop occupying your beautiful head with nonsense." He locks his jaw, which makes his cheekbones stand out.

"It's not nonsense to me."

"I can't erase the past." The frustration in his voice hurts me.

"I'm not asking you to." He can't erase the past, nor can I. I wish he didn't have all those girls. I wish I didn't know about them, but I do, and their existence hurts me, jealousy burns in me. The fear of not being good enough...

"Apply your sunscreen," he says evenly, "I don't want you to burn."

"Colin . . ."

"Vivian," he ignores me and leaps to his feet, "let's go into the water."

She stands up quickly and begins to jump around, neither of them inviting me to join. Colin holds Viv's excited hand, and the only thing I can think of is every girl on the beach eyes awash with his amazing body, which moves with mesmerizing grace. I think of all the girls on the beach who allow themselves to wear bikinis and are not ashamed.

He could have any of them.

To pleasure.

To satisfy.

And he wants me.

I pull my body under the umbrella, lie back and close my eyes. I won't buy a bikini, neither pink nor red. If he wants me, he'll accept me like this. With my fears, with the extra weight and the baggage that accompanies me. If he wants me, he won't try to change the situation. He will hold me to his chest and appreciate the long time I spent without him, which brought me to where I am.

My thoughts are weary. The heat affects me, the sun and the constant concern for Vivian and my parents. The worry nibbles at me, and my brain pleads for a few minutes of silence. My body obeys, and I fall asleep on the warm sand to the sounds of the water hitting the shore.

WHAT'S TIME IS IT?

I open my eyes slowly, adjusting to the bright light. It takes me a moment to remember where I am, and another moment to sit up in panic, panting.

"Vivian?" My eyes dart around in search of my girl and her father. I don't know how long I slept.

"We're here." Colin's voice comes from behind me. I turn quickly and notice him and Viv, who's holding an ice cream cone bigger than her.

"Is this her lunch?" I open my shocked eyes wider.

"Dinner," he mumbles in apology.

"What?" I look between the two of them. "What are you talking about?"

"You fell asleep and we didn't want to wake you up, you were so peaceful."

"Peaceful?" I bark. "I look peaceful to you? What time is it?"

"Four-thirty," he mumbles again. "Maybe five."

"Maybe five?"

Okay, I have to stop yelling and pulling gazes from other people.

"How long did I sleep?"

"Four hours, I think." He puts Viv's toys on the sand. "I made sure you stayed in the shade and applied Vivian with sunscreen after we finished lunch. I think she's tired."

"I don't want to go home," Vivian howls.

"We'll come again," he strokes her head in a gentle, protective gesture.

"Tomorrow." The stubborn girl doesn't give up.

"Not tomorrow," he explains quietly. "It's a long drive."

"You shouldn't have let me sleep that long." I stand, light-headed. I didn't eat or drink, and now I don't feel well.

"Elizabeth?" His voice sounds startled. "You're pale."

"I'm fine." I stumble forward and manage to put one foot in front of the other without falling.

"You're dehydrated," he grabs me tightly and lets me lean on him, "sit down again."

"I'm fine." I try to stay on my feet but fail to steady myself. My body slides back onto the blanket and I feel safer near the ground.

"Viv, stay with your mom." Colin helps her sit beside me and hands me a bottle of water. "I'm going to buy you juice, the sugar will help."

"I'm really fine." I take the bottle from his hand and open the cap.

"Drink slowly and don't try to get up."

"Okay. I'd really like juice, actually," I whisper, hoping he'll leave us and go and buy me something cold to drink.

"Five minutes, I'll be back soon," he informs us in a worried voice.

"Thank you," I mumble and sip from the bottle. Vivian looks less troubled, licking her ice cream with pleasure and making sweet noises. At least it will occupy her for the next few minutes until Colin comes back.

"Five minutes," he repeats, turning his back and walking away with extra-quick strides. I take a sip of water, lie back beside Viv's legs, and take a deep breath. That's better. My nausea calms down, and my pulse, too. Colin will take care of me. Colin will take care of me and Vivian, and everything will be all right.

Everything will be wonderful if I can get on my feet and reach the car without falling.

HE DIDN'T LIE when he said he would do it quickly. Colin comes back in record time, holding three bottles of grape juice, containing a generous amount of sugar, to help me. He sits down next to me, opens one of the bottles and offers it to me, watching my every move.

"I'm sorry I let you sleep and didn't make sure you drank." His voice is remorseful.

"It's not your fault." I take a sip of the juice, and the coolness spreads through my body.

"I didn't think it would be right to go home in your condition," he hesitates again, "so I did something. Please don't be angry."

"Why do I have the feeling that I won't like what you say?" I mutter and sip again.

"You should lie down, not sit in the car for four hours. It's only for one night."

"We can't stay on the beach all night." I don't understand where his head is. "Viv is five years old."

"We won't stay here," he says. "I called a small hotel in the area, they only have one bedroom suite with a double bed, but I'm sure you two can sleep together. I'll crash on the sofa."

"Colin," I sigh without strength, "I can survive the ride home."

"We won't be testing that tonight," he says with a nod of his head. "We'll have dinner in the room, take a shower and go to bed. In the morning we'll get up, fresh."

"Are you sure?" I stare at him.

"That's the plan, that's what we're doing. What do you say, Viv, want to go sleep at a hotel?" He looks up at Viv.

"I never slept in a hotel." She smiles brightly.

"Excellent," he smiles back at her, "tonight will be your first time. You want to finish the ice cream and help me collect our things?"

"Yes," she nods positively.

"Don't stop drinking." He gives me another look.

"I'm drinking." I bring the bottle closer to me.

"And don't stand before I tell you to." He gets up from the blanket and starts putting the toys into the bag.

"Thank you," I whisper to him.

"You're welcome."

"It was my mistake." I don't want to make things difficult for him. It really isn't his fault. I was the one who fell asleep, he didn't want to disturb me. He stops for a moment, looks up from the blanket, his stormy eyes locked on mine.

"I'm supposed to take care of you," he says sharply. "I don't care if you like it or think I'm a chauvinist pig, you're my responsibility, and that's my screw up."

"I'm twenty-six," I remind him in a whisper.

"And you will be my responsibility when you are eighty, for better or for worse." He pauses for another moment, letting me drown in his blue eyes.

"Dad," Viv's voice surprises both of us and shatters the bubble around us. "What's chau . . . chau . . . chaumini?"

"Chauvinist?" He laughs when he realizes that the child understands everything, God help both of us.

"Yes, that."

"That's," he leans toward her, pressing his lips to her forehead with a broad, rather amused, grin, "a conversation for another day."

THE SMALL HOTEL Colin found is a ten minute drive from the beach, a trip during which I discovered Colin was right, I wouldn't have survived four hours in the car. Colin parked and helped Vivian and me out, took the keys from the receptionist and led us to the isolated suite at the end of the compound. I was particularly pleased with the clean clothes I packed for Viv. She rushed to the shower and bathed briskly with the little help I could give her, while Colin ordered dinner. After eating in the living room, Colin carried her to bed and I lay down next to her. She fell asleep immediately.

I lie beside her in silence, unable to quiet my thoughts again. What's happening with my mom, my dad, with the guy in the living room just a reach away from me? Our fun day ended differently than I imagined. I certainly didn't think I would find myself in a small hotel with Colin.

I didn't know it would be so hard to stop thinking about him taking off his clothes and lying down on the sofa. I didn't suppose the memories would flood me and deprive me of my sleep.

The bottle of juice he left on the dresser is empty and my bladder presses uncomfortably. I manage to lower my legs to the floor carefully and stabilize myself, without any major dizziness. The food helped, and I drank quite a bit in the last few hours. My situation seems to be improving.

I walk out of the bedroom and into the living room, where Colin is walking with the phone to his ear. He is still dressed and seems to have taken the time to work.

"Just a second," he interrupts the conversation and turns all his attention to me. "Everything okay?"

"I need to go to the bathroom," I motion to the toilet. He nods and returns to the conversation, pursing his forehead in concentration. I try not to eavesdrop, but I hear half sentences when I walk past him.

"I told you it was a good deal, you don't have to argue about everything. Eight hundred is a perfectly reasonable price."

He must be talking to Danielle. I open the bathroom door and close it behind me.

What was she arguing about now? Or rather, I should ask, why is she arguing? He's the boss. He brings the money, she doesn't have to make it difficult for him.

When I finish in the bathroom, I go back into the quiet living room. Colin's cell is set aside on a small wooden chest and he is sitting on the rug with his back to the couch, looking at me with tired eyes.

"You should go to sleep," I say quietly. "We have a long trip tomorrow."

"You, too." He motions to the bedroom with his head.

"I don't know if I'll fall sleep, I slept so much on the beach." I hope he won't blame himself again.

"Your body needs to rest." His eyes wander over my body, examining me carefully.

Did he really mean what he said, that he'll always take care of me? For better or for worse? The sincerity of his words didn't escape me. He will propose to me again and again until I agree.

"You're so good to me," I whisper, hoping Viv won't wake up and hear our conversation. She'll have to know one day, but her world is changing rapidly, and I don't want to shake it anymore. Not now, when everything isn't clear.

"I love you," Colin replies quietly, "why shouldn't I be good to you?"

"I can't stop thinking about the others." I look down.

"I know."

"I'm jealous, and I'm afraid to disappoint you."

"Come here." He slips his body sideways and slaps his hand over the place he vacated. With trembling legs, I approach him and slide over to sit beside him, my bare thigh rubbing against his. He puts his hand on my skin, a few inches above my knee, and gently caresses my leg. "You won't disappoint me. They were meaningless, Lizzie, I never promised them anything."

"Still, you have experience." I turn my body toward him and our eyes meet.

"I had experience from the start, or at least that's what I told myself it was. You didn't disappoint me even back then, remember?"

"Yes." The lump forming in my throat forces me to push it back down, my cheeks reddening rapidly.

"You blush," he smiles. "It's so cute."

What isn't cute are my thoughts, and my pulse going wild.

"I'm not used to talking about it."

"About sex?" He laughs quietly. Apparently, my embarrassment amuses him.

"It hasn't been an issue." At least not until a few months ago. "I didn't really have anyone to exchange experiences with and I didn't really have experiences to exchange."

"What do you think will happen when we have sex?" He walks his hand a few millimeters up and messes with my senses.

"I don't know, Colin." I pray that he doesn't notice my breathing accelerating. "It's been more than five years, I'm afraid of the idea. I feel like I'm starting from scratch."

"You're not starting from scratch, and even if you were, I don't care." He raises his hand from my leg and moves it behind my shoulder, tilts his body and closes the small distance between us. "Are you afraid it will hurt?"

"I don't know what I'm going to feel." I dread the thought. "I gave birth, what if something changed, and it won't be the same?"

"Will it reassure you that I'm nervous, too?" His face is close to mine. I'm aware of every whisper, every breath that gently passes over my cheek.

"What are you nervous about, you're the only guy I've been with. I have no one to compare you to, I don't know anything else." My voice trembles in front of the smile that comes to his lips.

"I'm afraid I'm so excited by the idea of being together again, that the whole thing will be over in a flash."

"That was never a problem." My cheeks burn again.

"I've never had you, and then waited for you for so many years before." His fear is far from justified, and right now I don't care how quickly it will end. The expectation is beginning to gnaw at both of us, and as we postpone the moment, we fill our heads with anxiety instead of thinking of how amazing it will be.

"What if the others knew how to do things I don't?" I find it difficult to let go of the fear.

"For example?" He puts his other hand, which until now was far away, between my knees, gently spreading my legs a few inches apart.

"I don't know . . ." My mouth gets wet as he draws his fingers on my skin. "They must have been more experienced than me."

"They were meaningless, do you hear what I'm telling you?" He puts his mouth to my ear and whispers, his fingers matching themselves to the words. "It's not the same, being with someone you love. It's not just your body there, you're not just chasing your physical satisfaction or your partner's."

A soft sigh escapes my mouth and Colin continues whispering, and caressing.

"I remember the first time we did it... your toes shrinking, your skin growing bright, your breathing accelerating. I remember how afraid I was to hurt you."

"It hurt less than I thought." I tilt my head back, exposing my neck to his lips.

"I know," he kisses the sensitive part behind my earlobe, "you told me. I remember hugging you for hours, and we couldn't fall asleep."

"You kissed me all night."

I would give anything to have him kiss me all night long. But we are risking it tonight, like two sixteen-year-olds who don't want to get caught but can't stop. Thank God our daughter knows how to sleep through the night, and thank God he doesn't stop, because I need him. His words and his lips, which slide into the hollow of my neck.

"I think you're afraid of being ready, moving on to the next stage, because you remember how much I hurt you in the last few years. You don't want to get hurt again, and your head always reminds you of the risk, and reminds you not to trust me."

"My head and my heart are fighting, and it's exhausting."

"Maybe it's time to pick a winner." He climbs his hand further up my thigh.

"I'm afraid you won't like what you find under my clothes." I don't think my fears deter him, nor are they stopping his warm breath or his desire.

"I want to be inside you," he presses his body against me, "I want to bury my face in your hair and smell it, to hear you panting in my ears." His fingers tease me, moving closer and then gliding away from the connection between my legs. If he doesn't stop, I'll have to beg, even though I would explode if I allowed him to touch me higher than the place he's already touching.

"We can't," I sigh, "Viv might wake up."

"There's no way in the world we'll do it for the first time when she's in the other room," he sucks my earlobe, "because I can assure you I won't be quiet."

"You were never quiet." Blood rushes through my veins.

"I know. You said I was talker."

"I said you were a babbler, and your mouth was as dirty as your thoughts."

"As far as can I remember, you liked it, and I'm happy to tell you it hasn't changed."

I cling to Colin, close my thighs on his hand and with my body I beg him not to stop touching me.

"Elizabeth," he whispers, running his thumb over my clitoris, an unsatisfied sigh slipping from my mouth, "we have to stop now."

"I'm ready," I whisper back.

"Not tonight," he moves his thumb once more, "soon, I promise."

"Please . . ." I just want him to touch me at that exact point, to give me what only he can.

"My love," he says, burying his head in the hollow of my neck. "We can't, not like that."

He slowly pulls his hand away from the warm place it found

between my legs, and it's gone, not on my skin and not inside me. My guts turn upside down, because he took me where he wanted and played my body, and I let him. I begged like someone without a backbone and a will, like someone who depended on him.

I push myself away from him, gather my thoughts, move my back from the sofa and, without looking at him, stand up. He tries to grab my arm, but I pull it away wildly.

"Good night, Colin." The impact of my voice resonates sharply.

"Lizzie, you know I want you."

"I'll see you in the morning," I straighten my shirt with teary eyes. "Go to bed, we have a long drive tomorrow."

"Don't do that."

I refuse to answer him. Turning my back on him, I go into the bedroom and close the door.

What humiliation. How miserable can I be, begging him to satisfy me only to hear him refuse. His ego must be exploding. I get into bed, close my eyes and listen to Viv's breathing.

He knew we couldn't do anything, so why did he start at all? Why did he put his hand between my legs? Just to prove what power he had over me? Turn me into a marionette dancing to his notes?

The insult lashes me like a whip, leaving red marks on me.

That's what he wanted, to prove that he can always get what he wanted from me. To show me that eventually I won't be able to resist him, and he succeeded.

CHAPTER THIRTY-TWO

*T*hunderous silence reverberates in the living room of the suite as I step out of the bedroom and notice Vivian is eating breakfast. She is sitting on the carpet in front of the television, and next to her is Colin, who is quick to look up at me.

"Good morning," he greets me quietly, and is completely ignored. I walk past them and close myself in the bathroom, brushing my teeth with a toothbrush left at the side of the sink, courtesy of the hotel.

He wants me to be nice. How convenient, he just forgot what happened or didn't happen last night. I have to pretend that everything is all right, for my daughter's sake, and I curse the day that awaits me. I curse Colin's fingers, which made me not sleep half the night, and his lying lips. I curse the universe. I take a deep breath and walk out of the bathroom as Colin stands up and takes a quick look at Viv.

"Sweetie, Mom and I need to talk. We'll be in the bedroom, okay?"

"Uh-huh." She nods without losing interest in the program.

"Elizabeth," he gestures to the bedroom door.

"I'm fine here," I firmly refuse to move.

"Get in there, please." He doesn't drop his hand.

"I don't think so."

"Don't be stubbon," his sentence takes me out of my imagined calm immediately.

"Don't use her presence to get me to do what you want," I grind my teeth. "The good days are over, sir."

"To the bedroom," he insists. I think he's holding back raising his voice as much as he can. "Now."

"I'm not your soldier and I'm not taking orders." I cross my arms.

"I didn't order you, I asked nicely." His eyes narrow. "Would you please go into the bedroom so we can talk before we shut ourselves in the car for the next four hours?" He shifts weight from one foot to the other.

I smile at him falsely, let out a breath and walk into the bedroom. Colin comes in behind me and closes the door.

"What's the story, Liz?" We stand opposite each other and exchange dissatisfied glances.

"You tortured me!" I shout at him, though not so loud that Viv will hear. "You played with me. Why did you start something you knew we couldn't finish?"

"I didn't plan to get so carried away," he replies. "God, the drama."

The drama? Who does he think he is?

"Until you came, I was independent," I accuse. "I had a job, I supported myself and our daughter, I didn't let anyone play with my head."

"Is that what I did?" He snorts with contempt. "I've been playing you for my pleasure, is that what you think of me?"

"No one has touched me in more than five years, Mr. 'I don't know how many girls you've been with'," I give him another nickname. "So maybe you didn't play, but you woke up body parts that were practically dead."

"I understand," he tilts his head to one side. I swear that if he continues like this, I will lose it. "You're suffering from sexual frustration, and I'm guilty."

"You're guilty," my finger turns to him. "It's your fault that I'm so . . . pathetic. A few whispers in my ear and I do what you want."

"You're far from doing what I want, but that I will handle when we're alone." His sentence resounds in my head like a wild roar. "You're not the only one suffering certain effects, the only difference is I know how to take care of myself. Maybe that's the first thing we need to solve, maybe it's time you didn't depend on me to satisfy you."

"That's why you're so relaxed? 'Cause you took care of yourself?" He thinks that's what I needed to hear, now? That I should imagine him, touching himself?

The situation is only getting worse. If I was in distress before, that picture, stuck in my mind now, is going to send me over the edge. This is another one of his tricks to make sure I don't stop wanting him.

"I don't think any of us wanted me to stay up all night because of an erection that refused to come down. Do you think it's easy for me? I've waited for this moment for years."

"I don't want to change," I try explaining to him the depth of the problem. "I don't want to be dependent on you or anybody else. I want to stay independent, to find work and support myself. I want to make my own decisions without my brain going on a forced vacation just because you're around."

"No one is stopping you," his brow shrinks. "Did anyone tell you not to find a job?"

"I don't know what I want to do."

"So you're not doing enough to find out, Lizzie. Start imagining your dreams."

"I don't have dreams," I interrupt his motivational lecture with hostility. "I didn't dare have them, because they were not within my reach. I'm like a girl who just graduated from high school and doesn't know what to do next."

"You're not a high school graduate," he waves his hand at me, "start making plans, for God's sake. I'm here, I can help. I want to help. You can work at any job or study, you can stay home if that's what you choose, stop worrying about bullshit like when are we going to have sex and think about the big picture."

"It's not bullshit to me." I'm deeply hurt.

"It's bullshit," he continues, ignoring the shudder in my voice. "It'll happen when it happens. What you want to do with your life, that's the question you need to be asking yourself."

"I want to go home." What's the point of staying here and fighting more? What's the point of being in this hotel if we can't be in the same room?

"I'm taking you there." He pulls his hair back. "I'd appreciate it if you didn't accuse me because *we both* got carried away. We have enough drama in life without adding to it, don't make up stories in your head."

"Don't touch me if you have no intention of going all the way," I explain in case he didn't understand until now. "I'm on the edge."

"Noted," his voice falters. "Please pack your things."

"We're packed, you can start the car as soon as you finish eating."

"What about your breakfast?" Mr. 'I'm in charge of you' is taking care of my health.

"Not hungry." There's no chance that anything will enter my stomach while it is making impressive flips like it is.

"As you wish." His shoulders drop, and he goes to open the door.

"Drop us at my mom's, I want to see how she is," I ask in disappointment. Our first vacation was completely destroyed. At least Viv is not aware of that, at least she will have a good memory.

"How will you get home?" He glances at me over his shoulder.

"She'll take us home in the evening." He nods, as if I need his consent.

"Let's go." He gestures toward the living room with his head, crossing the threshold, leaving me for a few moments in the bedroom, gathering myself and my unhappy thoughts. Four hours. It's my test, to survive four hours with him and his smell and my imagination, which insists on drawing a clear picture of Colin taking care of himself. Damn it. He'd better take care of me, and he'd better do it soon or an atom bomb would fall on our town and leave ruins behind.

COLIN STOPS his jeep in the driveway in front of my parents' house, after we barely survived the trip. Vivian didn't fall asleep, and we spent the last four hours listening to singers named Justin. I have an overdose of Bieber and Timberlake, and Colin seems to be in a similar situation. I get out of the car and open Viv's door, Colin taking my bag out of the trunk.

"I'll talk to you tomorrow," he mumbles as he hands me my bag by the strap, which I hang on my shoulder.

"Okay." I give Viv a hand.

"Don't be mad."

"I'm not mad." I struggle with a suffocation that threatens to take over every good part of my life. "Just trying to deal with your return, Colin, is not simple."

"I know." He crouches down, his face in front of Vivian.

"Take care of your mom, okay?" He strokes her hair.

"Okay, Dad," she nods seriously.

"Love you," he kisses her forehead.

"I love you back," she chirps in a sweet voice. He straightens up again and looks at me with bright eyes.

"I'll call you or something," he says with a shrug.

"Or something," I mutter.

It would be best if your 'something' solved the problem, Colin!

"I want to see Granny." Viv pulls my hand toward the house. "We have to go."

"Tomorrow," he nods, and I follow Viv. She opens the door and runs inside to look for her beloved grandma. The next thing I hear is her scream, which resonates loudly.

"Grandpa!"

My heart leaps, then lands back inside my chest. She took him in? She listened?

"Hello, Elizabeth," my father says in a hesitant voice as Vivian climbs into his arms.

"Dad . . ." I'm not sure what to say.

"Your mom is in the kitchen. I'm sorry for the mess." His head points toward the sofa, beside it lays his backpack.

"I understand." She has you sleeping on the couch, well done!

"It's temporary, you know, just until . . ." Until when, until you've flattered her enough for her to forgive you? Oh, I'm predicting a lot of flattery.

"Viv," he says, lowering my child back to the floor, "go say hey to Granny, she's baking cookies." Vivian doesn't need another invitation and runs to the kitchen, leaving my father and me alone.

"I can't talk right now." I raise my hands in surrender.

"Can you listen?" He sits on the couch and slides into the corner to make room for me.

"Dad," I sigh.

"Please, you just have to listen."

"Okay, but do it quick, I don't want Viv to hear." I walk to the couch with a heavy heart and sit down next to the man whom I never thought would hurt me the way he did.

"I don't expect you to forgive me," he begins, his voice hoarse.

"I don't expect Colin to forgive me, or for your mom, who has shown great compassion by letting me back in, even if I sleep on the sofa."

"That was my idea," I inform him. "After I found out the truth about your pneumonia. Are there any other lies I need to know about?"

"Lizzie," his voice restricts further, "you were seven."

"I'm not seven anymore, in case you haven't noticed."

"It's not something I talk about."

"This is not a house where people talk, period," I declare. "My life is based on lie after lie, betrayal and treachery, pictures hidden in a closet. That's what I've learned, to lie to my child telling her she doesn't have a father, hiding his pictures in the closet and pretending everything is okay, but it's not okay."

"You're right." He doesn't argue. "Nothing's okay and it's been like that for a long time, mostly because of me."

"Morgan was my brother," I whisper in pain, "and I don't know him. I don't know anything about him, as if he never existed. The only thing left of him is the accusation against the man I love, who had nothing to do with it."

"I can't talk about him," he shakes his head. "Please, Elizabeth."

"You will talk about him and what happened to him, and we won't pretend that you are fine or that Mom is fine. We won't wait for the next time you find a scapegoat to blame for what's eating inside."

"Do you think I'll ever be fine?" He stares at me with a look that breaks my heart, his eyes shining with tears. He looks down and laces his trembling fingers. "Do you think that if I talk about him, it will change something? Will the smell of the garage disappear from my head, or the image that appeared before my eyes or the sound of my screaming?"

"Dad . . ." I put my fingers on his fingers, close them tightly to make it clear that I'm here and that I'm not moving from him.

"My son," his voice brakes, a tear streaming down his cheek, "my son suffered. I wanted to protect you, and when I went into your house and saw Colin and those thugs, I thought they would chase you. I thought they'd use you to blackmail him. I had already lost one child. You were pregnant, and Colin couldn't keep you from them. His father would get in trouble again, and they would come back."

Colin's dad really did get into trouble again, and they really did come back, but I shouldn't say anything. My dad will panic, and God knows what he'll do this time.

"You could have said something and not let me live with the thought that he stopped loving me."

"You would look for him. You would go to the end of the world for that boy." He protests the tears. "Look at you, you raised a beautiful daughter on your own. You were protected, you were both protected, that's all I wanted."

"I love Colin," I whisper in fear, lest he deny it. "Still, in spite of everything, I love him. He's a wonderful dad and he's a good man."

"You're going to marry him, aren't you?" My father gives me another look.

"It's still open for discussion," I lie to myself, most of all. "He asked, but I refused. If he asks again, I don't know what I'll answer."

"Don't make him sleep on the sofa," he laughs bitterly. "We don't like it."

"You have to think before you do stupid things."

"Stupid," my father breathes in a broken voice, "that's the last thing your brother called me that morning. He wanted to stay at home, but I refused, threatened him with consequences. He went to school, slamming the door on his way out, and I sent him straight into the hands of the scum. Only the previous evening they had ... "

He doesn't continue the sentence, we all know what happened. We all know how Brock tied him naked to a stand, and how all the football players took turns with the eggs, and how no one was punished. 'Boys will be boys, it's a shame to ruin their future,' they told my parents after Morgan hanged himself. Morgan's future didn't matter, just the boys, the football team, and the university scholarships. My father couldn't live with the knowledge that his son had ended his life without anyone paying a price.

"Morgan knew you loved him. Sorry for the cliché," I whisper, "but you know it, the way I know you love me."

"You're not my little girl anymore," he puts his fingers together. "I wish you'd have stayed five."

"I'm sure Colin feels the same about Viv."

"If he knows what's good for him, he'll take care of you and his child, and I don't mean the new car he bought you, Chevrolet or not."

"He'll take care of us or he'll have me to deal with," I press his fingers. "Please stay away until things calm down."

"I can do that." He nods in agreement.

"Now I'm going to check on my daughter, and then you can take us home." I stand. The weekend took all my strength out of me. I just want to get to bed early, close my eyes and sleep.

"Wait," he quickly stands up, "I have something for you."

Without pausing he goes to the bookcase, moves a couple of volumes, and pulls out a picture. "He would have liked for you to have it."

He presents me with the picture, in which I'm about four years old hanging on Morgan's back, who's carrying me piggyback.

"I don't remember that day." I feel the picture with trembling fingers. The only picture I have of Morgan is resting in my palm, and I don't remember when it was taken. I barely remember him.

"In our old house, on his birthday, not long before he . . ." The sentence is cut short. "I'll tell you sometime, it was a good day."

"I'd be happy to hear it." I look up at him.

"I love you, Elizabeth, and I'm really sorry."

"I know. Don't betray my trust again."

"Agreed." He holds out his arms to me, I guess he needs a hug more than I do. I let him wrap me in his arms. I set aside the drama to make room for a better future. For the future I deserve.

CHAPTER THIRTY-THREE

The steam from the cup in front of me fills the house with the smell of coffee. I stare at it dissolving in the air and disappearing into the kitchen. At least I managed to sleep. I woke up early, made Viv's lunchbox, took her to daycare, and now . . . nothing. Now I'm not doing anything, not looking for a job, not knowing what I want to do next. Are my options really unlimited, like Colin said? Is it time I go and study something or keep looking for a job that will allow me to be home early, as I had gotten used to? I sigh in frustration. How many mornings will I spend arranging and cleaning the house until I make a decision?

A knock on the door interrupts my thoughts. I get up from my chair and go to see who's lost in the neighborhood and in need of guidance.

"Who is it?" I call through the closed door.

"Your future husband." The answer that comes is meant to amuse me, but does the exact opposite.

It accelerates my pulse and forces me to take a look at my clothes—a pale pair of jeans and a dull black t-shirt.

Pathetic.

What does it matter what you're wearing?

I open the door with the obvious intention of putting Colin in his place, but as soon as he steps in, the door slams behind him and he turns me and presses my back to it, holding my hands above my head.

"Tell me she's not home," he grumbles.

What? Oh, God help me. The pennies drop one after the other with loud clangs in my mind, when my body realizes what is going on.

He's done waiting.

"She's . . . no . . ." My eyes shine.

"Not at home?" His chest crushes against mine.

"Not home," I repeat his words, like a parrot.

"Glad to hear." His lips lean slowly toward my lips.

Now? We're doing it . . . now?

"I made peace with my father," I blurt out the most stupid thing I can. Colin freezes.

"Babe," he breathes deeply.

"I ate with my parents yesterday. My mom . . ." I can't finish the sentence, as Colin cuts me off with a growl.

"Please don't talk about your parents when we're about to have sex."

"Sorry," I whisper in embarrassment, sending hot waves to my reddish cheeks.

"Where were we?" He leans back toward my lips. My breath turns short, my head tilts back as I lean against the door and prepare my lips to meet his mouth.

"Ready?" he whispers, a second before our lips meet. I nod without being able to answer. I'm a stupid seventeen-year-old in a brutal hormonal attack, that's what I am. A mass of hormones going wild. "Good, because we're done talking."

The next moment he smashes his mouth against mine with a sweeping kiss that demands my thoughts. My head spins and my tongue plays with his. He releases my hands and they go straight into his hair. His hands come under me and he lifts me to him. I wrap my legs around his waist, our kiss becoming more demanding. He carries me lightly to the bedroom, opens the door with his foot and puts me on the edge of the bed. I bite his lip, trying to keep him close, but he straightens up, grabs at the end of his shirt and wildly pulls it off, flinging it into the corner of the room. My mouth waters. Standing in front of me is a sculptured mountain, making my breathing difficult. A mountain of a man who wants to take my body to places I haven't visited in a long time.

"I'm going to spoil the party for thirty seconds, during which time you can be upset, jealous, and make a scene." He gives me a penetrating look, confusing me. "This will be the last time we talk about it, so be prepared to throw everything you have at me."

"What are you talking about?" I'm still panting from our kiss.

"I guess you don't have condoms." He reaches into his back pocket, takes out some silver covers and holds them in front of my eyes.

"Wow," I lean back on my hands, aware of the fact that the party has indeed been dealt a blow. "Someone came ready."

"Someone had to think about it." He doesn't move, the condoms still in his hand.

"Someone slept with others," I mutter in disgust.

"Twenty seconds," he interrupts my time.

"I hate you." I take advantage of my last chance. "I hate them and I don't even know who they are. I want you to myself. I hate that they all stare at you and your inhuman muscles. I hate the idea that we need condoms because you left me."

"Ten seconds." He waves the silver bundles to tease me.

"If you leave me again, after you get what you want, I will haunt you to the end of the world, and you can be sure that I will find you and avenge myself."

"Five seconds," he answers in a steady tone.

"Have you slept with someone without protection?" My voice shakes with indignation.

"Yes." He doesn't take his eyes off me when he chooses not to lie.

Son of a bitch. Couldn't you beautify the truth?

"Recently?" I pray to God that I'll receive the answer I want.

"Not recently." He doesn't dare come near me, not even a single inch.

"Are you clean?" The tears come to me from the very thought that I should even ask, that I don't know. I was supposed to know everything about him, and here stands the man who was supposed to be my husband in the room that was supposed to be our bedroom, and he is a stranger.

"I'm clean. I'll still wear a condom, and your time is over." He throws the covers on the bed and they land beside me. He pushes me back, his body lying on top of me, covering me, his bare chest calling for my fingers to caress it.

"You ruined the party," my voice brakes.

"It starts now," he leans over my lips again. "The matter is closed, now kiss me."

Now or never. Now or forever I will regret the moment when I didn't kiss him, and I don't want to regret it. I don't want to wait another minute and miss my second chance. I kiss him like I never have before, with my lips and tongue, with sighs released from my mouth and my quick breathing. I kiss him and bite his lip and pull at his hair, holding him against me. He runs his hand between us into my shirt, pulling my bra down and clenching my breast, playing my nipple with his fingers until I moan with pleasure. I lift my hips, but he pushes them back to the bed, his erection pressing me to the mattress.

"Time to undress you," he mumbles as I feel his erection between my legs again.

"Help me."

He slides off the bed with a light movement, unbuttoning my

jeans and releasing the zipper. He puts his hands in the space between my pants and my waist and peels them away slowly, torturing me, making sure I feel every hungry inch of my skin.

"Sit." He throws my pants to the floor and holds out his hands to me.

I use him to sit up, raise my hands and let him take off my t-shirt, leaving me in my bra and panties.

My gaze wanders over his body as he dislodges his shoes and socks, unbuttons his jeans and pulls them off his muscular thighs, his calves, until they disappear into the pile of clothes, and all that remains are his boxers.

My trembling fingers barely manage to release my bra. I take off one shoulder strap, then a second, feeling a strong desire to cover my chest with my hands.

"Don't hide," he climbs back to the bed.

"I'm shaking," I mumble and lie down again.

"I can see that." His mouth meets my collarbone. "Breathe, Elizabeth."

He walks slowly with his lips toward my breast. I spread my legs, and Colin lays between them, placing himself above me, flipping his mouth over my nipple. His teeth tease it, command it to stand up. He doesn't pause. His kisses slide down to my navel, toward my scar. His tongue inquires, chilling, not missing a millimeter. He rolls down my panties, pulling them down my thighs and knees until they cross my ankles and are thrown to the floor. I remain completely naked beneath him. Under his mouth, blowing at the knot between my thighs.

"I'm going to kiss you, Lizzie." His head dives again, his lips clinging to the hill hidden between my legs and he sucks with lust, until I shout, and my head is thrown back wildly. He's not done, he's not even started. He doesn't take mercy on me, and before I can catch my breath, his fingers are inside me. I drizzle, I feel them slide in effortlessly, my body urging him to continue. My back arches, Colin reaches for my pelvis, holding me in place, his tongue everywhere. The tension is building, begging to break free with every sigh I release. He increases the rhythm with his fingers, inside me, on my clitoris, with a force that sends lightning up my spine.

"I . . ." I can't breathe or finish the sentence or tell him I'm close. So close he must not stop!

He bites and pulls, strokes, and I scream like I have never screamed. My body swings on the bed, a wave of pleasure exploding between my thighs and misting my senses. It doesn't stop him, he squeezes my orgasm more and more, and in the next moment he rises and stands beside the bed to remove his boxers.

I gasp when his erection springs out. He reaches for one of the silver packages, opens it skillfully, and rolls the condom on the throbbing organ. Then he climbs toward me briskly, puts his hands to the sides of my head, his erection wanting to go where his fingers were.

I spread my legs more, grasping his shoulder blades and not taking my eyes off his as he penetrates me, slowly pushing himself into me. His forehead drops to mine as he hisses a juicy curse. My heart goes wild, my lips searching for his, finding them and kissing, my tongue squeezing into his mouth.

He moves inside me. He comes out, then in, refusing to increase the slow pace. Savoring every second, every breath, my fingers scratching his skin.

"You're killing me," he claims. "I'm sixteen again."

"Sorry." I sigh and lift my pelvis to meet his next move.

"Do that again, and I won't be responsible for what I do." He growls like an animal.

"This?" I groan as my pelvis rises to him uncontrollably.

"I warned you." He slams himself to the hilt.

Oh God!

"Again?" He slips out slowly.

"Yes," I answer, and he fulfils my wish, increasing the pace abruptly, the slowness disappears. Now we are one body moving in perfect synchronization, in and out. He captures me, I groan and wrap my legs around his waist as his penetration deepens.

"Jesus Christ!" His skin shines with sweat, our eyes locked. "Elizabeth . . ."

He slams into me again and again, breathing rapidly, until his body shudders and he curses, pushing himself deep inside me, his head thrown back with a loud sigh.

"Lizzie!"

He falls into my arms, his head in the hollow of my neck, his chest rising and falling.

I kiss his hair.

I run my fingers on his back.

I love him, and I'll kill whoever tries to come between us again.

If it was possible to stop time, this is the moment I would choose, the moment before the words. The seconds where the eyes speak, the breath and the fingers travel on the skin. The silence in my bedroom and Colin's lips on mine. When the world is locked out and is not permitted entry into our temple.

This is the moment I would choose to frame, the picture I would bury under my pillow and look at every night.

His look says it all.

"Are you okay?" he whispers almost without a sound, without disturbing the perfection.

"Yes. Are you?" We lie so close, face to face. The air comes out of one and enters the other, like a circle without beginning or end.

"No," he softly presses his lips against mine, "I'm not okay."

"Why?" I frown.

"You're not my wife. Yet." He raises his eyebrow mischievously.

"Oh," I swallow, "that."

"Marry me," he asks, again. A moment after he met my body and my heart, a moment after he got what he wanted, he wants more.

"You won't stop asking, will you?" My voice cracks in a whisper.

"No." He smiles.

"What will we tell Vivian?"

"The truth. We'll tell her Mom and Dad love each other and want to be a family."

"I'm afraid of confusing her."

"She's five. If we're clear, she'll understand."

"Don't you think it's unnecessary?" I lie down on my back and stare at the ceiling, but Colin won't accept the distance, his body clinging to my side. "We don't have anyone to invite, just my parents, and Henry and Danielle."

"Since when are we getting married for them?" he asks with a smile.

"Since when are we getting married?" I remind him that I haven't said yes yet.

"I thought it's what you wanted."

"I thought so, too, but now it seems unnecessary."

"What's changed?" He strokes my forearm, chilling me. I don't want to hurt him, but things have to be said. The dream of the white dress suddenly seems so childish, almost unreal.

"A wedding won't change anything," I reply hesitantly. "If someone wants to leave, nothing will stop them. Not a signed document, not even a pregnancy."

"Are you still waiting for me to leave again?" he murmurs in frustration.

"No."

"Good."

"I'm just saying that a wedding is not what will stop you." It didn't stop him before, and it won't stop him in the future. He will stay because he'll choose to, not for any other reason.

"So a wedding in your eyes was a safety measure?" He seems to have trouble understanding. "Is that what you thought before, that this is the way to tie two people together so that they can't part?"

"Yes," I realize how naive I was, "and I was wrong. Now I don't think it's something I need."

"And what if it's something I want?"

"You'll have to convince me." It won't be easy.

"Okay." His voice is confidant.

"Okay?" Is that all he has to say? Is he not going to present me with an argument and prove his righteousness?

"You don't want to get married, I do. We have to talk about it more, but right now we have five and a half hours for ourselves, and I won't waste them talking."

Ah. That explains a lot.

"What do you have in mind?" I turn my head to him.

"Your orgasms." His answer causes my cheeks to burn. "You need a few more, and I haven't been inside you for a long time."

"It's been fifteen minutes since you were inside me."

"Like I said," he kisses my lips, "long ago."

"You're going to exhaust me, aren't you?"

"Hell yeah." He has a mischievous spark in his eyes. God only knows what he's thinking, what ways he has to leave me breathless.

"Why did you bring condoms?" I insist on destroying the moment at the worst possible time. Why can't I shut up for once?

"What do you mean?" He purses his brow.

"You said you were clean."

"I didn't say I expected you to believe me."

"Did you think I'd ask to see your blood tests?"

"Yes, and I wouldn't blame you." He knows me. He knows I won't accept his explanations easily, certainly not when it comes to my health.

"I want to see your blood tests," I whisper in the hope that he won't be offended.

"I'll email them to you. Will that satisfy you?"

"No." I smile mischievously, and with slow motion I climb on top of him, straddling him, his body under me, moving my pelvis on the erection growing between my thighs, as Colin reaches for the nearest condom. "You will satisfy me, and you have five and a half hours to do so."

CHAPTER THIRTY-FOUR

*M*y legs are shaking. I'm sitting in the passenger seat of Colin's jeep, on our way to pick up Vivian from daycare. Bieber's disc plays in the background, but neither of us jokes about it. We haven't said too much since we barely crawled out of bed. We even gave up our lunch. We had every intention of eating, and we wondered whether to warm something up or go to a restaurant. But then we found ourselves on the carpet in the living room, and then . . . well, on the rickety table in the dining room, which only by divine grace didn't break under us. We are teens again, unable to take our hands off each other. Even now, I'm stroking Colin's arm resting on my thigh.

"Her daycare teacher is named Mrs. Robbins." I don't find anything smart to say.

"I know," he nods. "Viv told me about her, she loves her."

"She doesn't like anybody being late. You have to come on time, always."

"I'll always come on time."

"Even before time. I don't like Viv to be last."

"Before time."

"She knows where her bag is," I start to say, but he interrupts my sentence.

"Lizzie, I'm sure I'll learn where to hang her bag," he gives me a reassuring smile. "I'm sure I'll learn everything over time, but maybe I'm not the only one who has to learn something new?"

"I told you," I know where he's going with this, "I don't know what I want to do."

"You just have to think about it."

"Turn right," I sign with my head.

"It won't go away if we don't talk about it." He doesn't let my obvious avoidance pass.

"I don't have anything smart to say on the matter," I take a deep breath. "I didn't come to any conclusions."

"If you want to stay home—"

"Why would I want to stay home?" The contempt in my voice echoes through the car.

"I'm just saying you can."

"What you're saying is that you'll fund me like a Sugar Daddy. You know me well enough to know it won't happen." I raise my hand obnoxiously, losing the urge to touch or caress him, or to explain to him how insulting his idea is.

"Do I look like a Sugar Daddy?" He laughs and grabs my hand before I can get away from him. He puts my hand on his thigh and strokes my fingers gently. "All options are open to you, that's all I'm saying."

"Sitting at home is not one of them," I say confidently.

"Excellent." He signals to the right to enter the parking lot. "I think we're here."

"Let's go pick up our daughter. Maybe now Daryl will believe her father is back."

"Yes, let's go and get to know the young man." He laughs again.

"He's five, Colin."

"Let's hope Viv is like you," he gives me another smile. "I'd love not to deal with young men until she's old enough."

"And when do you think that will be?"

"When she's about thirty, give or take a few months."

"You're optimistic." I roll my eyes at him.

"That's me, baby." His laugh bursts out. "let's go pick her up, we don't want to come in last."

MRS. ROBBINS IS STARING INQUISITIVELY at the mountain of a man next to me. Her gaze shifts from me to him and comes back to me, watching every movement we make.

"Nice to meet you, Mr . . ."

"Young," he fills in the missing detail.

"Daddy!" The cry of our daughter comes a few seconds later, as she runs straight into Colin's arms, who flaunts her in the air.

"You grow too fast." He rubs the tip of his nose with her nose, "Ready to go home?"

"Yes!"

"I'll bring her bag." I smile mockingly at Mrs. Robbins' curious eyes.

"I think your mom is tired." Colin sits Viv on his arm. "How about we drop her home, let her rest while we go out together?"

"I'm fine," I try to resist, even though he's right. I'm exhausted and it's his fault. The thought of the many reasons my muscles hurt make my cheeks burn. How many times did we do it? Enough times to make any movement between my legs notice-able. Maybe that's what he wanted, to leave his mark on my body, to make sure I couldn't think of anything else. I pick up Viv's bag and follow them to the jeep. Colin puts Viv in her seat and gets behind the wheel, me at his side.

"You have to sleep," he throws at me as he starts the car. "Vivian and I'll be all right."

"Are you sure?" I yawn uncontrollably.

"Yes. We'll drop you off. You can join us for dinner at my house."

362

"Are you taking her to your house?" I'm not sure why it surprises me. She'll get there sooner or later.

"I'm taking her to my house, join us at seven." He's letting me know how it's going to be, and I don't have the strength to argue.

"I'll be happy to rest," I look back at Viv, who is following the conversation. "Are you all right?"

"I want ice cream," she informs me of her priorities.

"I think I have some in the freezer, Viv," Colin smiles at her in the mirror as he glides out of the parking lot. "Why don't we go check?"

"Don't give her too much," I whisper anxiously, and he gives me a quick look that makes me shrink. Okay, I have to relax and not make a fuss over everything. I get it.

"I love this song," Viv interrupts us, with Bieber's voice breaking in the background.

"I think we all know that," Colin turns up the volume. "Let's go home, girls."

He presses the accelerator, as if hoping to get out of the car as soon as possible and away from the music our daughter has been forcing upon us for days.

"My mom is waiting for me." I try to pull my lips from Colin's, but he refuses to release me or take his fingers out of my hair. "I'll see you in a few hours."

He's funny, really. Sometimes I think he's more excited than I am. From the moment he proposed, he was bringing up silly ideas that, if I had agreed, would make our wedding look like an average Mardi Gras. Among the suggestions I rejected outright was a tropical reception (coconut trees, Colin, really?), a dress code (No, I won't ask all the guests to wear hats) and I can't forget the highlight – a fairy tale wedding (you're not hiring a carriage and horses!).

I just wanted a white dress and to get married in the church with the pastor I've known all my life. I don't even have a bridesmaid, not that I need one. My mom is too much to deal with, and if this day goes as she plans, I'll get to my wedding not looking like myself.

"Let's elope in Vegas," he whispers under pressure, "give Elvis the honor."

"I'll see you in a few hours," I take a step back, trying to get his body off mine. "Be a good boy and don't do anything foolish in my absence."

"Elizabeth Heart," he seems to be using the last chance to call me by my maiden name, to which I will say goodbye today, "I wish I could make you as happy as you do me."

His words take my breath away.

He doesn't believe me when I tell him how happy I am.

He doesn't believe it when I tell him I'll never love another.

He needs me to prove it to him, and that's exactly what I'm going to do.

So I kiss him. I kiss him and hold him close to me, sighing as his tongue pursues mine hungrily, in pure need.

I'll show you, Colin Young, that you're the only one.

I ROLL OVER IN BED, surrounded by his smell, curled up in sheets I didn't change when I got home. I had trouble falling asleep. I wanted to feel close to him. I wanted a few more hours to sniff my pillow and feel everything waking up inside me again.

My phone rings, I pull it from the dresser, and answer my mom wearily.

"Hey, what's going on?"

"My car won't start." Her sentence is the last thing I want to hear. My father is still at work, she needs my help, and there's no way I'll refuse her after all the times she's been there for me. How the wheel turns.

"You need me to come over?" I sit up in bed and stretch, waving goodbye to my afternoon nap.

"Yes, please. I need groceries, the house is empty."

"I'll be over soon." I take my feet off the bed and go to search for my clothes.

"Thank you, see you soon." She hangs up the call. All I can hope is that our shopping won't last long, and I will have plenty of time for myself before dinner at Colin's house.

AN HOUR LATER, I'm dragged around the store by my mom, who came equipped with a list that would not shame a cook in a banquet. Her cart is loaded, and we find it difficult to have a conversation, as she is running from shelf to shelf.

"Mom," I sigh loudly, "I don't want to be late."

"You won't be late," she walks past me on her way to the pastry department, "just a few more minutes."

She said that fifteen minutes ago, so I don't think we're going to be finished soon. I drop my head and grumble to myself. This wasn't my plan. I was supposed to be in bed, with his smell. Maybe it won't fade until night and will linger for a few more hours, long enough for me to dive into the bed and be surrounded again.

"What are you dreaming about?" My mom's voice makes me jump. I don't think she wants to hear exactly what I'm dreaming about.

"I'm worried about Viv," I lie, I'm not really worried about her. She's with her dad, eating ice cream and having fun in his perfect house.

"You always worry," Mom puts a bag of rolls in the cart. "You'll learn to let go."

"You sound so sure," I mutter. "What if it doesn't happen, what if I got used to being like that?"

"Are you enjoying yourself?" She stops her running around. "Is it good for you, when every little thing frightens you?"

"You know the answer," I reply indignantly.

"Why don't you trust yourself?" Her gaze penetrates.

365

"I'm trying, really."

"You should be proud of yourself. You've raised Viv to be a loving and confident girl, smart and funny. You've put her first on your priority list, and now you're allowed to think of yourself, your future."

"I'm really scared, Mom," I confess in a whisper in the middle of the giant store. We couldn't choose a more strange place to conduct this conversation.

"You deserve to be happy."

"I know."

"Do you really believe that?"

"When I manage to deal with the doubts that constantly arise, yeah, I do. After all, I didn't think I would love only one man, I didn't think he would leave, and I certainly didn't believe he would come back. "

"You got a second chance, don't throw it away."

"We have to finish," I interrupt sharply, "Vivian and Colin are expecting me at seven."

"Trust your judgment," she puts a hand on my shoulder, "trust your heart, you'll know what's right."

I nod without words and push the shopping cart toward the cash registers. I'm not sure where we're going from here. I try to lock my fears away and not confront them. They've been running me long enough, and I won't let them ruin my second chance.

At six-thirty I burst into my house panting, rushing toward the bedroom, flinging my clothes on the floor. I turn on the hot water in the shower and walk through my wardrobe in my head while my hair is getting wet.

What should I wear?

I know he doesn't care, and if it was up to him, he'd prefer me wearing nothing. I understand him, because I personally would like to undress him and stroke his bare skin.

Five and a half hours were not enough. They were just the appetizer, a taste of what awaits us. A reminder of the mystical connection that has been there from the first second we exchanged glances.

I wash my hair and the soap from my body and turn off the water. I must have a dress in my closet I can throw on. Something sexy.

My God, what do I know about sexy? What the hell is going on in my poor mind?

I wrap myself in a towel and move to the bedroom. One normal dress to feel good about, that's all I need.

You'll feel good only when he peels it off you.

What did you do, Colin? You've made a monster out of me, it's so ridiculous. A hormonal monster who wants more of what he gave me this morning. God, please help me. Help me survive one evening with him without smearing all over him or looking at him with longing. One evening without imagining how we can slip away from Vivian for three minutes and shut ourselves in the bathroom.

The situation is lost. I'm lost. And I'm late for dinner, too. It's time to hurry up.

I pull at my closet door and freeze. My eyes stare at the shelves, but my head takes a moment to understand.

Where are my clothes?

A forgotten memory hits me, of Colin's empty closet and the empty shelves waiting for me on our wedding day. The house is the same house, the bed the same bed, but this time my clothes are the ones that are missing.

My eyes catch the note on the middle shelf. I pick it up and read the words, my heart about to explode.

I love you. Still and forever.

I read it again, just to let the words seep in.

He exchanged one note with another. His words, that shattered my life in the past, now offer me the future I dreamed of.

The seventeen-year-old boy who sat in my room and studied for hours, enlisted and saw horrors I might never understand, is unveiling in front of my eyes, revealing the man he has become, his heart.

When I pull the door to Vivian's closet open, tears rise in my eyes. My wedding day was a nightmare that lasted too long, and Colin is ending it. I know where my clothes are and where our girl's clothes are and, if I have to guess, my mom's car is fine.

She cooperated with the plan.

I fold the note he left for me, wipe away the tears and go to pick up my clothes from the floor.

COLIN'S HOUSE looks bigger than I remembered as I park my Chevy and get out with trembling legs, stopping in front at the door and ringing the bell. Colin opens it with a look that I hardly recognize.

"I wanted to wear a dress," I stare at him, eyes glistening, "but what do you know, my clothes are lost."

"They're exactly where they're supposed to be." No muscle moves in his face. "Welcome home."

"Colin," I begin to say, but he interrupts me.

"Welcome home, Lizzie."

"What will we tell Vivian?" How can we explain to her the hasty move her father planned behind my back?

"I think you'll find she doesn't need any explanation." His voice is steady.

"Are you sure?" He'd better be sure, because my legs are going to crash.

"You are my family, your place is here." He takes a step toward me and holds my head in his hands, staring straight into my eyes, his chest rising and falling. "Elizabeth Heart, I'm sorry for all the suffering I've caused you. I want to live with you and make you happy, make sure you and our daughter are safe and loved. So loved."

"Don't leave us again," I whisper, and his answer is all I need.

He pulls me to him and demands ownership of my mouth, of my lips. He kisses me greedily until we both break the kiss, panting. My eyes are shining and his are, too, and I'm protected, safe and beloved.

"You made plans with my mom," I whisper.

"With your mom and Vivian, she helped," a mischievous smile peeps out at the corner of his mouth.

"Where is she?" My eyes peek through the gap between his waist and the door in search of her.

"In her room." He finally opens the door for me.

"She has a room?" I walk into the house where my clothes are, and the life I want.

"Of course." He closes the door, walks past me, crossing the large living room, and down the hallway to the open door.

"Viv," he goes into the room, "your mom is here."

"Mama," her excited cry makes me jump just as I get to the doorway. "You have to see!"

I see.

And I can't completely believe it.

Viv's room is huge by any standard. The walls are painted pink, and when I look up at the ceiling I see the stars painted on it. If I have to guess, they glow in the dark.

"I have a palace bed!" Viv climbs into what she calls a bed, her mattress hiding in a palace decorated with diamonds and lace curtains.

"Please don't be angry," Colin whispers apprehensively. "I couldn't help myself."

"I'm not angry." I'm thrilled.

"Viv, ready to go out?" Colin turns to the girl who is hiding inside the palace.

"Yes," she jumps out enthusiastically. "Wait till you to see the back yard, Mama."

"Come on," Colin motions with his head, giving Vivian a hand and leading us out of the room, through the living room, opening the french doors set in the wall. I'm speechless at the sight before me. I stand on the wooden deck and to my right are cushioned sofas, all surrounded by the smell of flowers. The wide yard in front of me is lit by little lanterns that hide in every corner, but it's the gazebo I can't take my eyes off of.

It's decorated with lamps, hanging from the wooden beams, and fabrics, hanging around the poles that support the structure. In the middle is a set dining table with candlesticks and lit candles.

"Like?" Colin whispers.

"It's perfect." Just perfect.

"Our house, our yard," he gestures around, "and later I'll show you our bedroom." He finishes the sentence with a growl.

Mr. Colin Young can't wait. I look up at him and he stares at my lips with obvious intent.

"Colin . . ." I'm startled by the idea of kissing in front of Viv.

"She's going to see a lot of kissing and a lot of love, Mrs. Young."

He doesn't slow down, lowering his lips to mine gently, tenderly, in perfect contrast to his enormous body.

He's kissing me and fixing everything that was broken, giving me back everything I thought I lost long ago.

He finds the key, and sets my heart free.

EPILOGUE

COLIN

Two years later

IF THAT DAMN dog doesn't stop barking . . . Goddammit, Lizzie, you said you'd handle him! I open the door carefully and prepare myself for the coming attack. After only a second, a large, black, furry creature tries to leap on me, his tongue ready to lick me, my clothes, and everything else that he can reach. I slam the door, leaving him inside and me outside my house. I'm hungry and I've been on my feet since five-thirty in the morning.

"Lizzie!" I roar helplessly, "I'd really love to come inside!"

"Sorry," my favorite voice in the whole world yells from the other side. Okay, one of my three favorite voices. "I was sure I locked him in Viv's room."

The door opens and in front of me stands my beloved wife, who couldn't refuse our daughter and adopted a dog from the animal shelter.

Yes, our girl gave up the dream of becoming an astronaut.

Now she wants to be a veterinarian, and any future veterinarian needs a pet, or that's what her mom told me.

"Remind me why we didn't get a hamster?" I stick a wet kiss to her lips, counting the seconds until she shoves me and tells me there are things left for the bedroom.

"You're hungry," she mumbles into the kiss.

"Where's Viv?" Since she hasn't stopped me, the girl is not around.

"With my parents, they wanted to spoil her."

They always want to spoil her, but I suppose tonight more than usual. After all, tomorrow morning she goes to second grade, and the excitement is in full swing.

"Does that mean we have time?" I lower my head in a silent prayer for the answer I want. Dinner can wait if it means I'll get a chance to drag my wife to bed for a few minutes.

As if a few minutes would satisfy us.

If either of us thought the situation would calm down after a few months, we were wrong. When it comes to our sex life, we are still in our honeymoon period and it doesn't seem to be changing any time soon. Thank God for Vivian, she's the main reason we get dressed and leave the bedroom.

"They're on their way home," my darlin' wife smashes my hope for some sex.

"Wonderful," I growl as I take my wallet, phone and keys out of my pocket and put them on the table at the entrance.

"Mr. Young," she grabs the collar of my shirt and pulls me in her direction, "do you want to file a complaint with management?"

"I want to have sex with my wife. What are the chances management will agree to that?" I don't have high hopes on the matter.

"When your children fall asleep, you'll get what you want." She pulls at my shirt and kisses me again. I'm about to push my tongue into her mouth, when a cry from our bedroom shatters my plans to pieces.

"Someone's hungry." I get on the job right away, walking down the hallway with Elizabeth following me.

"He wasn't himself today," her voice is filled with worry. "I hope he doesn't develop anything, because my mom doesn't like watching him when he's sick, and if I miss another lesson, I'll be in trouble."

"I'll stay home if it comes to that," I reassure her, approaching the cradle and picking up my two-month-old black haired baby. We didn't think it would happen so soon. When we applied for adoption, we thought it would take months or years before we got the call. We even went to Vegas and got married officially, just to show the adoption agency our marriage certificate in the hopes of avoiding problems in the future. We never dreamed the phone would ring so fast.

"Elliott Young," I turn to the baby in a serious voice, "are you misbehaving?"

"You'll scare him," she laughs as the baby stops crying and stares at me for a second.

"He knows I'm kidding."

Elliott starts crying again. He doesn't seem to be in the mood for joking. He probably wants to eat, and he won't wait patiently for his bottle. Lizzie goes to the kitchen to prepare food for him while I sit down on the sofa and cradle him.

"I have something to show you," she says as she hands me the bottle a minute later, "on my phone."

I lean back and let the little one eat, while Liz uploads the pictures on her phone.

"Look," she turns the screen over to me.

"You made this?" My eyes jump from the picture to Elizabeth and back to the small screen, on which is a two-story cake shaped in sugar dough.

"In class. Nice, right?"

"Nice?" I snort, "A chocolate cake with candy on top is nice. Babe, this cake is crazy."

"It's okay." My wife shrugs her shoulder and puts the phone back in her pocket.

"Did you hear from that pastry shop on Drum Street?"

"They liked what I showed them and asked me to come back next week for a trial run." She blushes.

"You're sure you want to work for them, 'cause my offer is still valid."

"Yes, Colin," she gives me the same answer she has been giving me for a month, "I'm sure I don't want to start my own business. I'd rather be their employee and learn more."

"As long as you're happy, I'm happy." I look down at the baby in my arms. "And you're pleased, too, aren't you?"

The doorbell rings and Elizabeth gets up to open it for Viv and her parents, with whom I have an… interesting relationship. Liz's mom is pretty much crazy about me, which make Liz's father grumble more, but he keeps his mouth shut and says nothing, 'cause after what he did, no one wants to hear it.

Vivian comes running into the living room waving a twinkling pencil case that almost blinds me.

"What did you get?" I pretend I have no idea

"A pencil case with pictures of dogs on it," she climbs up on the couch beside me, "look how cute they are."

"Your dog almost ate me when I got home." I raise an eyebrow with amusement.

"Bobby doesn't eat people, Dad." She rolls her eyes, just like her mom.

"He was 'bout to eat me, I tell you." I take the empty bottle out of Elliott's mouth and turn him over my shoulder to burp him.

"Can I?" Viv asks permission to help in a particularly sweet voice.

"Gently." I nod and let her pat gently on Elliot's back until we both hear clearly a belch over my shoulder.

"That was a huge one!" she bursts out laughing.

"Definitely," I agree with her. "Have you had dinner?"

"Yes, with Granny and Grandpa." She slides off the sofa onto the rug and leaps to her feet.

"Don't let Bobby out," I call after her as she runs into her room.

"Hello, Colin." My mom-in-law's hearty voice comes from behind me. I stand slowly and smile at her and the man standing beside her, his face blank. At least we are no longer enemies.

"Colin," he greets me formally.

"Frank," I shake my head, "how are you?"

"We're well," Darlene updates me. "How's my grandson?"

"Liz says he wasn't well today. I hope the night will be easier." I really hope he'll sleep well, as he knows how to do. Elizabeth told me that Vivian was a particularly alert baby, and the nights with her were hard. After overcoming another wave of guilt, I was glad Elliott is completely different.

"We're going home, call if you need anything." Darlene smiles at me warmly.

"Sure will." I turn to the crib in the living room and place a sleepy Elliott into it.

"Dinner is ready," Lizzie calls from the kitchen. "You're invited to the table."

My parents in law exit our house, leaving me and my beautiful wife alone in the kitchen. I approach her as she's standing with her back to me, wrapping my arms around her waist.

"Hey," she whispers, I swear I can hear her smile.

"Hey." I kiss the back of her neck.

"Aren't you hungry?"

"I love you," I whisper in her ear, "do you know that?"

"I think you told me a few times this morning," she giggles. I told her, and if I'm not mistaken, I also wrote that in a message this afternoon.

"Who knew life could be so good?" I kiss her neck again.

"You work too hard." She takes the opportunity to protest again about the long hours I spend outside the house.

"I know, but I come home on time every evening, do I not?"

I know how much she hates me being late, so I make an effort to get home as early as I can. Especially now that our family has grown. I take Viv to school every morning, Elizabeth is the one who picks her up, and we make our dreams come true, one after the other.

"It's pretty crazy, don't you think?" she sighs, my lips chilling her skin. "Do you remember where we were two years ago?"

"In the back yard," I whisper, "at our pretend wedding."

Elizabeth thought I had gone crazy when she came home to the wedding I arranged for us, to which only Vivian was invited. Well, maybe it wasn't a real wedding, because there was no pastor, just us and the rings I kept for years. Either way, I put the ring on her finger and made her cry.

"It was the most perfect wedding in the world." She pushes her back into me.

"I agree," I embrace her further, "when the bride is perfect, the wedding can't be anything else."

"The groom was okay, too," she teases.

"That groom will do anything for you."

"I know." She leans her head back on my chest where she can feel my heart going wild. "I love you, Colin."

"I love you, too, Elizabeth Young." I kiss her red hair, close my eyes and thank God for the wonderful forgiveness he graced her with, and for the family I got back. "I love you, and I'm here. For good.

The End

Thank you so much for reading Heart in a Box!

If you are ready for more, I have Ben Storm waiting just for you in Lace and Paint, I don't think you will be disappointed!

LACE AND PAINT

Talia Blum should have known better.

Escaping to London and moving in with her older brother, she finds a way to manage the urges and whims of her never-too-controlled bipolar disorder. She has it all worked out: stick to her routine and everything will be okay. **Ben Storm** is not part of that plan. **Arrogant, seductive, and her brother's best friend, he's a sure recipe for addiction.** He is the wrong guy to fall in love with. He is the wrong guy to chase. There is too much at stake, too many lies to tell. She shouldn't risk her carefully balanced lifestyle, not with the guy who could bring her down... *But what if her heart has a mind of its own?*

LACE & PAINT is the first instalment in the explosive True Colors series, that will take you on a roller-coaster of emotions and leave you breathless as you're swept by Talia and Ben's tornado.

ACKNOWLEDGMENTS

I would like to take a moment and thank the many people who saw me through this book; to all those who provided support, talked things over, read, offered comments, stood by me and encouraged me when I felt like I was getting lost.

To my husband and children- I know this is not what you guys signed up for. Never in a million years did any of us think this will turn out to be my career. I was merely a woman who sat by her computer at night, typing words, and nine books later- here we are. Thank you for always being there, through my exhaustion and sleepless nights, my tears and laughter, you are my rock and safe haven. I love you more than I could ever express.

To my editors in Hebrew and English- Ariela Barmecher and Shannon Eversoll- thank you for your amazing work, advices and support.

To my PA Lainey Da Silva- thank you for saving me day in and day out and for your friendship, knowing you are there allows me to actually sleep at night!

To my very own Nina who loves her anonymity (hence- Nina is NOT her real name LOL), thank you for running all the office stuff I truly suck at! You know who you are and you know I couldn't do this without you.

And last but most important- to my readers. You guys have been with me for the last four years, ever since I self-published my first book. Thank you for your messages, hugs, jokes, ideas and endless support and love. Thank you for accepting me for the crazy person I am, and daily reminding me of what this is all about- our common love for books.

I couldn't ask for a more amazing group of people beside me.

You are the best.

40265922R00228

Printed in Poland
by Amazon Fulfillment
Poland Sp. z o.o., Wrocław